"THE HAND THAT MOCKED THEM, AND
THE HEART THAT FED."

PERCY BYSSHE SHELLEY

OZYMANDIAS

THE FORBIDDEN PARALLEL

KEVIN CARVER

Provender

PRESS

Published in the United States of America by Provender Press
309 NE 3rd Street Ste 5, McMinnville, OR 97128
www.provenderpress.com

This is a work of fiction. The story, all names, characters, and incidents portrayed in this production are fictitious. No identification with actual persons (living or deceased), places, buildings, and products is intended or should be inferred.

ISBN 979-8-89431-013-8 (Hardcover Edition)
ISBN 979-8-89431-014-5 (Paperback Edition)
ISBN 979-8-89431-015-2 (eBook Edition)

First Paperback Edition: May 2025

Cover Design by Juan Padrón
Interior Design by Angela Grace

for Tim

____

THE CAST AND THEIR STATIONS

THE KINGDOM OF KULLOH-SOR

The 38th Parallel (Mt. Eccoulous)
King Kulloh-Sor and his Swords

The Holster of the 38th Parallel (The Treelands)
Jah'ri, *Hammer*

Sindhi, *Hammer*

Saz, *Hammer*

Felton, *Hammer*

Vaera, *Hammer*

Commander Prime, *Machinarch*

The 35th Parallel (Mt. Eccoulous)
Dffai, *Wizard*

Rfael, *Wizard*

The Court / The 30th Parallel (Mt. Eccoulous)
Naor, *Child of the Court*

Lady Eyrilia, *Chairwoman of the 18th Parallel*

Ricard, *Citizen of the Court*

Shaeron, *Philosopher*

Z'rai, *Philosopher*

Jonn, *Elder Hammer*

The 5th Parallel (Mt. Eccoulous)
Mother, *Nail*

Jowe, *Priest*

Atan, *Hammer*

The First Parallel (Mt. Eccoulous)
Layala, *Nail*
Daelan, *Hammer*
Pon, *Hammer*
Holo, *Elder Hammer*
Salamohan, *Priestess*

THE BATTLELANDS OF THE WILD FEW

Prir (Trisrca)
Eda, *Viceroy of Prir*
Mourad, *Listener of the People*
Haasher, *Former Viceroy of Prir*

Einn (Trisrca)
The Chieftain
Cavl, *Viceroy of Einn*
Akhil, *Listener of the People*

Veir (Trisrca)
Merl, *Viceroy of Veir*
Saim, *Listener of the People*

The Rho (Ornvia)
Faziah, *Leader*

THE SEA OF CASHMU

The Denan Fleet
The Captain

Brecca
Shyloc

THE FORBIDDEN PARALLEL

THE SPEAKER OF THE SPIRIT-SHARE

Come closer. Sit, sit. You want to know? About Sor's Parallels and Hammer Jah'ri. About Naor the Brave, Layala of Wavelo, Viceroy Eda, and still the others: the Nails, the Wizards, and the line of Denan. About the weight of blood. About an unjust world breaking and rebuilding, shattering and stitching, bleeding power that quenches dry bones, rising. About that formless cloud, the one we call Meaning, violent in its carelessness. Swinging like the fang of Shyloc.

We will spirit-share and you can decide for yourself. Here. Drop your coin.

AROU IS A lonely but large planet, a blue and orange lantern in an otherwise dark system. It is known for its mountains, which are both monstrous and magnificent, the size of other worlds' moons. Survey the passing peaks and clutch one. Breathe deeply.

Swirling, thin wisps of minerals from atop the world fill your lungs. Place your hand upon the unsullied surface. Grasp some scree. Squeeze your hand and feel neither smooth nor callus rock, for they were not designed for mortal touch and at this height, simply refuse your hold.

Arou's mountains are ancient beings, or thought of as such, with an enormity that breeds reverence and engenders religions. Their environments range as they rise with ecosystems that are diverse in beauty and bounty, as well as the life that thrives within them.

They do not all take the shape of cones.

Mount Maeihlah bows in the middle. Mount Sabmousli, also called Racjz, evolved with strange angles and shapes, millennia after millennia, twisting and turning, unlivable with no order or reason, like a child's toy tower. Some say its shadowed peaks are haunted with the souls of swallowed adventurers. Mount Grav is hollow; whatever archaic, prodigious creatures it once housed are now gone. The historians of Arou—and every kingdom had them—returned to their courts and taught of what they learned, what they saw at Grav: the fossils they found, the long, scratch-like indents in the stone, the hardened empty eggs ossified by time but devoured by memory. For their bravery the historians were cheered, given medals and mead, but never again did they sleep soundly. Such was the price of nameless knowledge.

Never mind the howls behind you. Inside the cave mouth you are safe. Here, throw this in the fire. It will warm you. This world you found me on, squally and dark, its mountains are separated by oceans and land, territories that either expose or protect their inhabitants with flora that provides and fauna that depletes. Arou is no different. Between the mountains, there is ocean, there is land. It is similar to your world, I assume. Where are you from? In time, in time.

Arou's mountains exist because they simply do, and the planet is spoiled with them.

Cultures, kingdoms, and wars. On Arou, these are what makes a mountain great.

Arou's proudest mountain is not the largest nor is it the most beautiful, but it has wrought many wars over many millennia, for it is the prize of Arou, a protected fortress overlooking the Sea of Cashmu that rises from the shore and presses against unscalable cliffs on either side. Inland, natural resources, both clean and abundant, surround it. The Ancients called it Eccoulous. Hammer Jah'ri's kingdom proclaimed it Sor's Crown.

HAMMER JAH'RI. ALL champions are pushed forward by voices that are heard not by the ear, but by the heart. Jah'ri, if he indeed was a champion, heard such a voice. It did not push him as much as it pulled him, raising him through the Kingdom of Kulloh-Sor and its many Parallels.

In time you will understand Sor's Parallels. From the mountain's base to the peak's plateau and even higher, stretching into the castle tower, Parallels created society, taught Nails to worship the worlds above them, the ones they could see but never reach, not until they were plucked and taken to Sor's Staircase, where they stepped into the sky and . . .

Listen. You hear it now. Don't you? The bitter wind from the Sea of Cashmu, pelagic and arcane, cacophonic with the gulls who caw and the Nails who scream as they fall every day to their doom. Turn a corner and the wind is beat. If you know the way. Follow, follow.

And that voice that speaks to Hammer Jah'ri?

Wait a little longer, and you will hear it as I do.

PART ONE

ASLEEP IN THE HOLSTER

You are no longer a Nail. You are a Hammer. Say it again. You are a Hammer. You are a tool that builds up and tears down. No reason. Only order. You are not just any Hammer. You are a Hammer in the 38th Parallel, the King's Hammers. Your purpose is a mystery to the Kingdom of Kulloh-Sor. You spent your life getting here. Asking, searching, rising. You learned the 38th does not serve the King directly. The 38th is but another test and for this test, you endlessly train. Congratulations. Strengthen the grip. Sharpen the claw. Reinforce the neck. Brace the cheek. Harden the head. The 38th has its mantra. Terror. Rage. Hammer. Pain. Speak it. When Commander Prime begins the mantra, the 38th finishes it. Those who fail to match its volume are cancerous with treason. No half measures. The Hammers are as one. The Holster, where you sleep, is your home.

Say it again. You are a Hammer. Believe the lie and it will become true.

1

JAH'RI

Hammer Jah'ri dreamed of the ocean. It was all they were allowed to dream. The lapping was as endless as it was pointless. Waves surrendered to the shore only to pull back at the precipice of death for another charge at glory. His brain was confused. Why did the waves crash into the sky? Suddenly, Jah'ri was a drowning fish. He was flopping on flat sand, tail thrashing, each push harder and heavier than its last. He rested, just for a minute. Just for eternity. Something tickled. Did you feel that? The water. The tide had come! Jah'ri was loved and cherished, for the ocean did not forget its child. He was lifted and carried back to peace and purpose. But then, a shadow! Wings, a beak. Once again Jah'ri the Fish was lifted, but salvation had turned to terror. This was no rescue. This was death and he was awake for every stab and chomp and dig. The bird had its meal. What was left of the fish emptied onto drying sand and Jah'ri waited and waited and waited but death never came. Death was a sleepless night.

Jah'ri opened his eyes. Five pocks in the stone ceiling above him formed a quincunx, and Jah'ri's brain trusted what it saw. He had returned from the dream.

The 38th lived together as one collective consciousness and dreamed as one collective mind, but as the test drew nearer, each Hammer's dream had begun to splinter to unique finality. They were more vivid now. No longer just theater of the mind, the dreams were an extension of their training; whatever magic summoning their dreams was purposeful in this way. What was there to fear after tasting your own blood and living your own death night after night?

Jah'ri rose, ran hopeless fingers through his shoulder-length brown hair. His muscles ached, his body a chorus loudly singing. Was it from his training or the dream? He could not yet tell. His frame had lost weight here at the Holster, preparing for the test, new strength emerging from a more slender figure, the result of swimming, always swimming, and defeating whichever aquatic creatures ambushed him in the Holster's instruction pond.

Deeply, he breathed until his heart slowed.

A Hammer cannot fear. A Hammer is only a tool.

"Sure," he mumbled to himself. "The King's hungry tool."

Jah'ri felt the blinking weight of eyes coming from the weary face of Hammer Felton lying in a nearby cot. Thirty-eight Hammers slept there, filling cots in uniform rows. The spacing was generous in Cot Hall. The ceiling was low, but the room was wide and deep.

To Jah'ri, it looked like Felton woke with less color in his face. Jah'ri wondered if the same was true of him and instinctively raised a hand to his cheeks, feeling cold stubble. A phantom lizard scattered through his mind. He abandoned the memory and shrugged his shoulders at Felton, whose troubled eyes remained fixed on Jah'ri as if puzzled and stuck.

Another day in the Holster.

And yet, this was not true, was it? This was the day before the test. The Hammers of the 38th Parallel had never had a day quite like this one.

Jah'ri pissed. He yawned. He dressed. He pulled the blade from his boots, sharpened it on a stone, and shaved with it. His unsteady hands worked through tremors, but he survived with only minor cuts, exhaling relief when the task was done. There was no formal edict on a Hammer's face or hair. Most of the Holster's Hammers quit shaving entirely as the nightmares loosened their once steadfast hands. But if Jah'ri could get through shaving, he could get through the rest.

Little lies we tell ourselves.

Washed and finished, Jah'ri stared into the opaque looking glass that reflected a clean-shaven traitor. He breathed through his doubt.

"Stare all you want, but he won't speak until you do."

In the glass, Jah'ri lifted his eyes and found, once again, Hammer Felton staring at him.

"I venture, what kind of name is Jah'ri anyway? I thought Nails didn't have names."

"So today it's me. I'm the game?" Jah'ri spoke of distraction, the game they all play every day, the avoidance of their doom.

Felton didn't reply. Jah'ri crossed his arms and stood with a slight tremor. "You have known me for an age, Hammer Felton. Surely you have a guess."

"So, you admit it. A Sharpened Nail. Whose hammer did you claim?"

Jah'ri turned from the glass and returned Felton's glare. "As is written, a Hammer has no past." Jah'ri turned to leave, but against his better judgment, in a low and solemn tone, added, "Even those of us unfortunate enough to have a past."

Felton sighed. "Pray tell. Whose hammer did you win?" Jah'ri pretended not to hear as he walked away, returning to his cot. Only a minute passed before the training facility's automated lights changed from sanitary white to forest green, signaling the morning meal. The Hammers of the Holster followed the smell of slop to Feed Hall, where, between slurps, they discussed and deciphered their dreams.

How far did you make it? What did you see? How did you die?

Upon listening to today's frantic chatter, Jah'ri had learned that Dream Jah'ri was the only Hammer who failed to reach Shyloc, the ancient sea serpent they would soon confront. He was the only Hammer who died on the shore. He was the only fish.

Early in his training, Jah'ri dreamed he was merely a man, neither Nail nor Hammer, clean like a citizen of the Court, lost and sitting alone on the shore, watching Hammers march into the cold water. He could not move or speak. Eventually his dreams changed and in them he joined his fellow Hammers, swimming endlessly through dark choppy waves. Nights and nights of this. Then he started dying. Painless and quick. Swimming, suddenly, into nothing. But last night the dream changed again.

No Hammers, no Jah'ri. Just a bird and a fish.

Hammer Saz listened to Jah'ri's recall. Saz sat like a beast half transformed, his immense arms wider than his legs, broader than his chest. His short, thinning red hair stood on end as if it were shocked. When Jah'ri spoke of the fish, he heard chuckles from the benches closest to him. They're all listening to him, he realized, and Jah'ri felt weak from the attention, naked and dragged under the penalty of nonconformity.

"Not good," Saz said. "Not good at all."

Jah'ri asked him, changing the subject, "Tell me your dream, Saz. You never say."

"You sure we're not still sleeping?"

Jah'ri smiled. Saz was a miracle of a Hammer whose talented tongue undercut every serious moment with a simple taunt or twist of words. The Hammers were a collective tool, but they were not clones, and Saz was a good reminder of that small and powerful truth. They had brains as well as bones, hearts as well as hands.

"Yeah, well," Jah'ri began, searching for levity, "at least my fish death serves a higher purpose."

"Tell me your great purpose, oh Fish Tail," Saz cajoled before slurping.

"Feed the bird so it will shit upon your head as you swim." Jah'ri goaded Saz whose wit he could never match, though the attempt had become something of a sport.

"Tell it to squawk first, so I know when to open my mouth." He grimaced, squeezing slop through his missing front tooth.

"Saz, tell me. Do you see the beast in your dreams? Its shape?

Its color? Its eyes?" Jah'ri wanted to know, for the unknowing of what shape awaited him was a burden he was eager to unchain.

"Ah, Jah'ri, it's a curse. Is better you don't see it, no?" Saz paused, seemingly recalling his dream, chewing mindlessly on the brown rubbery bits in the morning slop, a favored source of cursing for most of the Hammers in the 38th. For Jah'ri, the slop was a rare solace. The citizens of Court fed their dogs with it, though when Jah'ri was stationed there, he snuck steaming cups back to his quarters. The Hammer had never tasted anything so divine, a carryover from his isolated and hungry childhood as a Nail scraping crumbs and chasing reptiles.

"A curse?"

"Death in the water," Saz explained solemnly. "Without shape or color."

"I saw color," Jah'ri heard another voice say. He turned to find Hammer Rannold sitting on a nearby bench. "Something like lightning."

The lights in the Feed Hall changed to a deep red and every Hammer stood at attention, awaiting Commander Prime's imminent entrance.

"Psst, hey Fish Guts." Jah'ri heard Hammer Vaera whisper from his left. "You know what I see in my dream?" Jah'ri did not break attention, nor did he give his to her. "Victory," she said.

"Speaking of gull shit," Saz said then blew his lips.

Vaera scowled. "I saw you too. You die very quickly, Saz. Your spirit is weak and you drown an hour into the swim. I take a brief rest on your floating corpse before finishing the mission."

"Funny," Saz said, "in my dreams you are also on top."

"TERROR!" they heard Commander Prime yell.

"RAGE!" the 38th responded.

"HAMMER!"

"PAIN!"

"Settle."

The lights in the Holster returned to their default stasis, a sanitary bone hue.

Commander Prime walked the line with a prickly gait. Its silicone skin sagged from its frame, exposing the metal underneath. A "machinarch," the Holster's Commanders were called, built by the castle's wizards and programmed for this function alone. They reshaped the Hammers, forged them into test-ready tools. Break them if needed.

"My King's Hammers," it said. "Congratulations. You are near the culmination of your life's utility."

Blocky eyes pulsated white in the unpredictable cadence of its speech, which modulated as if at random. Exposed gears swirled where its mouth should have been. The machinarch stood a head shorter than most of the Hammers, including Jah'ri, a sign that the parts required to upgrade these modular machines were costly and in short supply.

"Your instructions are clear. Today is a day of rest. Tomorrow evening you swim in earnest. However, I speak to you offering an adjustment of schedule. I received notice the 38th will have a visitor tomorrow. The King will wish you well as you embark upon your journey. React."

The Hammers of the 38th broke attention. They cheered and clapped, thumped fists, slapped backs, and hugged. Others simply laughed from the shock of it, the surprise. Jah'ri felt the tingling awareness of Commander Prime's gaze and raised his head to find glowing eyes.

"React, Hammer Jah'ri."

"There's no word for it, like I've been stunned, sir."

Commander Prime processed. "Good." The machinarch stepped away and allowed this boisterous scene to continue for a little while longer before again yelling, "TERROR!"

"RAGE!"

"HAMMER!"

"PAIN!"

"Settle."

They reformed, thirty-eight Hammers standing at attention. Commander Prime walked the line again. Hammer Stroom's right foot excitedly tapped from adrenaline. Stroom did not notice until Commander Prime halted in front of him and glared. Stroom's foot stopped.

"Our kingdom was granted to us by Sor. The Hammers hold the Parallels, but the Swords serve the King himself. Only a few of you, if any, will return to join their ranks within the holy throne room of His Parallel. The King will speak to you tomorrow aftermorning before your test begins in the evening. Rest now. That is your only mission for today. Continue."

Brusquely, Commander Prime turned away from the line and proceeded back towards the door no Hammers would dare enter. The machinarch clinked as it walked. The faint smell of burnt oil and lubricant filled the Holster's still air and would remain there for many hours afterwards.

Jah'ri refused to look away until the commander was gone, but his mind was elsewhere.

The Forbidden Parallel. The holy throne room. The Swords.

The machinarch spoke as if these were all within reach, and Jah'ri understood they finally were. Anxiously, Jah'ri yearned to touch the wall and feel it real. Hammer Jah'ri was on the cusp of becoming a Sword of the King.

All he had to do was survive the swim.

The Hammers broke from the line and re-engaged their morning meals, some still red faced and in awe. Those that were finished filed out. Jah'ri remained standing, less rigid than at attention, but nonetheless still, paralyzed from his pondering.

"Never thought I'd see the day," he heard behind him. Jah'ri turned to face the gruff Saz, who again was seated with his large arms spread wide against the wall behind him. "Hammer Jah'ri letting his slop go cold."

"You ate it," Jah'ri accused.

"A few of us are playing Scraps." It was Felton. He approached Jah'ri. "Do you play?"

Saz stood, slop streaking through his long goatee, and smiled.

KILLING TIME, THE King's Hammers spread languidly throughout the well-worn passageways, chambers, and corners of the Holster, like ghosts in an attic, trapped, searching for new discoveries yet knowing they would find none. Five Hammers gathered around a table for a simple game of Scraps. Played throughout the Kingdom of Kulloh-Sor by Hammers and Nails alike, by citizens of the Court, even philosophers and priests, its rules differed depending on which Parallel it was played in and which resources were available for tokens. The Nails in the lowest Parallel, that ocean crusted heap at the mountain's base they called

Shit's Bottom, were rumored to play with stones, sticks, dried kelp, and whatever trinkets had fallen from the Parallels above. In the Court and Capital Castle, atop the mountain's peak plateau, resources were richer. There, players traded with proper tokens and gems, or occasionally even detailed scroll cards designed by the Court's philosophers.

However it was played and whatever pieces were used, the goal was always the same: collect thirty-eight scraps and win the game.

"Recall that only the gems can be wild," Felton said.

"What do you mean 'wild'?" Sindhi asked. "The Wild Few?"

"I imagine they play Scraps with earlobes and eyeballs," Hammer Rannold offered with a wink. His voice was deep as his shoulders were broad. There was a low boom to his voice that subtly reminded Jah'ri (though he could not identify it without meditation and contemplation) of the portcullis that formally separated every Parallel path, vibrating through the ground as it settled. By skin and stature, Sindhi and Rannold could have been mistaken for siblings, but they arrived as strangers. They both stood short for Hammers with darker skin and thick black hair. There were differences, of course. Rannold's smile was magnetic. Jah'ri assumed Rannold imagined it warmed even the coldest bolts of Commander Prime. Sindhi often stood aloof with a proud, thoughtful scowl.

"Wild. Only the gems can be a wild token," Felton clarified, annoyed from the effort.

Jah'ri studied his tokens. It was his move to make, and he made it. Out of the black silky pouch he pulled a smooth river rock painted into the likeness of a caterpillar. A Grub token.

"I see," Sindhi said. "We call them lucky. You turn one token into a Lucky Scrap by trading it for a grub, or gem, or rock, whichever you need, really."

"Lucky?" Felton said, sounding offended. As Jah'ri listened, he wondered if, like everything here, his offense was an act. Felton often overcompensated. He always had something to prove.

"Yep," Saz said. "Lucky Scrap, that's how everyone plays it. Never heard it called Wild."

"We used Lucky Scraps, but it was discouraged," Rannold offered. "Skill and patience were rewarded in my home Parallel. And the winner ate first."

"Sounds like a recipe for blood," Sindhi said, meaning the game likely ended in violence.

Rannold paused at his turn, then said, "Well, if we're using Lucky Scraps, then I'll trade this rock for a grub."

"That's your one for the game," Sindhi reminded.

"Wait, hold your piss," Saz began, in between burps, "it's not one per game. One Lucky Scrap per hand. You just can't have more than one at a time. Trust me. I've played this way in multiple Parallels. Sor himself would—"

"Wild," Felton said.

"No one's calling it Wild," Saz replied, meeting Felton's narrowing eyes with a wink.

"This is getting confusing," Sindhi said.

Rannold offered, "Once per game then. Winner goes into the water first."

"Or last," Sindhi replied.

The chatter quieted, the game progressed. Jah'ri knew it was his turn to talk and offer something of value to the conversation, but these types of situations challenged his solitary shield. The Hammers of the 38th were unusually bonded. The other Parallels he'd served in had offered little opportunity to connect with other Hammers, and to Jah'ri that was fine. Here, discourse was freer, and he feared revealing too much of himself. That he would accidentally project the dissonance within and ruin a traitorous, decades-long plan just as it approached completion.

But a Hammer was ready for any challenge, including the grating task of small talk and fellowship. Jah'ri never would admit it, nor would it be wise, but he did enjoy this table's company. Did it matter? In the 38th, fellowship was a foolish and fruitless quest. They were cattle approaching slaughter, and tomorrow the blade would swing.

"I never played," Jah'ri said artlessly, adding, "I saw children play it in the Court. They had everything. Hand-drawn cards with rules and silk pouches with shiny, polished gems."

"Funny way to play Scraps," Rannold said.

Felton cleared his throat. He looked at Jah'ri with a reminding glance. The Hammers were not permitted to share specific, personal history. It was widely assumed, by those brave enough to assume anything, that Felton was sourced from a high family of the Court, but Jah'ri knew it couldn't be true. The Court never called anything Wild. Wherever he came from, Jah'ri suspected strong family ties helped Felton skip ahead. He possibly never served anywhere.

"Nine grubs, five gems, and one rock," Sindhi announced, pushing all her pieces into the center of the table. She waved her hands like a street magician. "Scraps!" she yelled. The group groaned. Rannold dropped his tokens. Saz slapped the table.

Jah'ri nodded.

Felton, red faced, said, "I thought grubs were worth four points. Are you sure?"

Saz laughed. "Uh huh."

Though the game finished, the Hammers did not leave.

"Have any of you ever seen the King?" Moods were brightened and a proud posture returned. Jah'ri had asked the right question. "Up close?" he clarified.

"Never," Rannold answered.

"Once," Felton began, "I have seen his flying disk. Passing just below a cloud blanket. When I served in the Shield."

"Lies," Saz said carelessly, without looking, and chuckled. "You were never there."

Felton promptly stood, his metal chair flipping behind him, banging and echoing along the Holster's halls of stone and concrete. "I speak no lies, Hammer. Twist your tongue again and it will be your—"

"You never served anywhere," Jah'ri announced, loudly enough to halt the argument. An eager pause hovered. Felton seemed to understand Jah'ri's gesture, a favor returned. He sat, a look of surprise lifting his eyebrows.

Saz looked directly at Felton and kissed the air. "That's right, only the 38th, like all of us."

"Of course, a Hammer has no past," Felton said slowly. "Forgive my blunder. It was a mistake."

Jah'ri nodded. "And mine. I shouldn't have mentioned the Court earlier. May Sor wipe away our transgressions and refill our vessels with purpose."

"Long may His line reign," they all collectively repeated.

Felton admitted, "I just want to get this wretched task over with."

After a pause in the conversation, a voice said, "Ah, the very thing Saz's mother said as he suckled from her tit."

Surprised, the group turned to Sindhi before erupting into laughter. Fists were pounded on the table. A few tears shed. Saz stomped his feet. Despite himself, Jah'ri laughed too. It felt good to laugh, he realized, like breathing cleaner air, but after some time, their joy faded and the silence returned.

"The King, a living descendant of Sor. Shaking our hands. Patting our backs. Can you imagine?" Rannold asked no one in particular, his eyes clear and hopeful.

Realizing the group was nodding in agreement, Jah'ri conformed.

Sindhi concluded, "Whatever happens, we can rest knowing we have served our King and that he has gifted us, us, with his presence." The group nodded again, Jah'ri, this time, in harmony.

They departed to various ends of the Holster, pacing without purpose or seeking for new distractions. Jah'ri found his cot but avoided sleep. There was no rest to be found in dreams, and the day was still too young and long. Again, he lied and studied the ceiling. The quincunx dots looked like swimmers surrounding an isle. He wondered, as he has so many times, about the Hammer before him who carved those marks into the ceiling. Perhaps that Hammer slept under the stars as he once did and looked back on the same constellations.

From those dots, fine cracks splintered throughout the subterranean stone, a reminder of the weight of the world above him, above the Holster. Jah'ri had been here an age, yet still found it strange how the Hammers of the highest, most revered Parallel were stationed off-mountain and underground. Hidden in the Treelands. Nowhere near the 38th.

There were more lies in the kingdom than there were mosquitoes.

"Hammer Jah'ri," he heard. He rushed to stand at attention.

"Settle," Commander Prime said.

"Sir."

No light change, no warning.

Command Prime and his subordinates regularly patrolled the Holster to the detriment of any Hammer flirting with insubordination, a friendly reminder of their attentive surveillance. Normally, echoing footfalls upon stone passageways revealed their presence, but Jah'ri was lost in the maze of his mind, wrestling the fool. He should have been properly meditating. In that act he had perfected the practice of split presence.

The mound of his mistakes became clear.

Many careless words had slipped today, he knew. Jah'ri himself spoke of his time in the Court during Scraps. He readied his abdomen. He had yet to be punished by Commander Prime or its subjugated machinarchs. A result of Jah'ri's infinite caution, but today he was careless. Jah'ri would not swim tomorrow if his bones were broken.

Commander Prime trundled closer to him, its cloud-white eyes pulsating.

"You had a winning set."

Jah'ri thought. "Scraps? I did not know you were watching, sir." He quickly added, "Nor did I know you knew how to play.

Perhaps next time—"

"Why did you not claim your victory, Hammer Jah'ri?"

Jah'ri paused under the increasing pressure of punishment. Every second was a risk. The machinarch could spring like a trap and strike fast. It was obvious, however, that Commander Prime had been weakening. Whatever parts it was made from were failing. Jah'ri learned from Hammers like Rannold, who have served near the wizards of the castle, that machinarchs do not last forever and were ultimately pulled apart, boiled, and remade.

Jah'ri did not have an answer for Commander Prime. The simple truth was that he did not need to win the game. Sindhi did. Not because she was weak-willed or even needed the favor, but because these fracturing Hammers were all fragile. There had been enough loss in this whole damn kingdom, he believed, and especially here, night after night in this corrosive facility. Enough death to fill every Parallel.

The rationale sounded like mercy, and Jah'ri thought better of speaking it. To his great relief Jah'ri found his answer, like a gripped tail just before the burrow.

He told the machine, "A Hammer must know when to strike and when to hold. I did not come here for games."

Commander Prime processed.

Jah'ri waited, the machine only inches from him.

It was not enough.

Jah'ri felt the machinarch's hand grip his throat before he understood. Silicone and metal squeezed. Jah'ri kicked as he was slowly lifted. Glowing, Commander Prime's eyes glared as the gears in its mouth spun.

Finally, the machinarch spoke. "You did not come here

for games? You play a king's game, Hammer Jah'ri. You are his token. React."

Jah'ri's arms involuntarily swung, searching, clawing out, finding only squishy skin that ripped. Commander Prime's arm remained steady despite Jah'ri's panicked clutching. Its hand squeezed tighter. Air, suddenly precious, retracted from Jah'ri like a fleeing tide, and the fish fought to breathe.

Even in the throes of this waking nightmare, floating on the precipice of unconsciousness, Jah'ri was aware of the other Hammers who watched the scene unfold. They ran into the room. They stood. They paced. They covered their mouths. They did not aid, for that was the lesson.

"When you reach Shyloc, you take any opening you can find. Even if it means feeding the beast your nearest ally." Commander Prime lifted Jah'ri higher, its arm extending. Now it spoke louder, to all the Hammers in the 38th, though Jah'ri didn't hear the rest of the speech. Nor did he feel his head hit the ground.

Jah'ri was back on the shore, muttering grave prayers into the drying sand.

2

SINDHI

Dream and memory are unfaithful lovers, prone to mischief and indulgence. Neither advocate for the truth. What the eyes see, what the hands hold. What bleeds. These are what mattered to a Hammer, the hardened enforcers of Sor's Just Society.

The philosophers taught it as this: Sor created Arou and formed the great mountain with his own hands. He granted it to mortals who turned evil and forsook His blessings. The Battle of the Soulless Kings ended in triumph with their defeated rulers in exile. The accursed Wild Few now roamed those barren Battlelands and occasionally still attacked the borders of Sor's kingdom in perpetual retribution for the righteous punishment of their wickedness. Before Sor left Arou, he established his Parallels upon the mountain and promised to return at the completion of his temple, Sor's Staircase, where the Hammers brought the

Nails to die.

Jah'ri groaned.

Sindhi glanced, tucking silky black hair behind a scarred ear.

To Sindhi, Jah'ri was a doomed Hammer forever trapped between dream and memory. All Hammers were haunted by nightmares in the Holster, but it was their duty to conquer the weary mists of doubt and resurface, to find their strength in the shadows of the Swords and overcome the traps of the mind. Jah'ri, she finally decided, was weak.

From across Cot Hall, Sindhi watched the weary Hammer wobble. Jah'ri crawled, climbed, and collapsed onto his cot. Like the others who witnessed Commander Prime strangle him in the air and discard him to the floor, Sindhi assumed the Hammer had died. It wasn't until she heard mumbles followed by frantic shouts that she knew not only had Jah'ri lived, but that he had returned to the dream state. Sindhi had no sorrow for the Hammer. Not here. Not in the Holster. This was their apotheosis. The cost of their ambitions, and the price of their admission. Soon she would be a Sword, standing atop Arou in the Forbidden Parallel at the right hand of the King. The world under her feet.

"He lives," Hammer Stroom muttered, his cot next to hers. Stroom, a lanky Hammer, twirled his long, braided beard with his tattooed fingers. "Perhaps better he didn't."

"Is never better to die, Stroom," Sindhi argued, her voice more annoyed than she felt.

"You have read the logs, yes?"

"You've seen me with the logs. You know I can read them."

"Holding parchment does not mean one can read. You could be looking for gulls in the scribbles, all I know. We all have hours to fill. Moments to pass. Another and another and another. Drops of time, drops of time." Stroom smiled as he talked, his eyes bouncing.

"You're nervous," she accused.

"And you're a woman."

She hadn't yet looked at him but now decided to. "You just noticed?"

"You claim to have read the logs," Stroom continued. "You must know the odds."

"No need to read them. Commander Prime informed me on my first day in the Holster. 'Only three women have ever become Swords.'" That first day, which now seemed so long ago, Commander Prime also shared how none of those women were petite like Sindhi was. How they had been stout and tall with bovine frames that could break ramparts and pin forest beasts. "It is better that you know." Commander Prime's toxic tellings both weakened and nourished the Hammer, for motivation is a strange, mysterious thing.

Sindhi rolled her eyes at the memory. She had never looked the part.

In every Parallel she served, indifferent superiors assigned her undemanding tasks. Smirks curved the lips of her fellow Hammers whilst ambitious Nails, predicting easy wins, challenged her for her weapon. Not once did Sindhi ever drop her combat hammer in the ring of the Sharpening. She leaned into those trials. Learned to enjoy them. Taunted her challengers even. Kinetic and crazed, the hot stinging splatter of blood on Sindhi's brown skin unlocked a fierceness she couldn't fully explain nor willfully recreate on command.

"I fear I almost thirst for their blood during combat," she once wrote to her father, an Elder Hammer stationed in the Northern Arm. His reply was swift but brief, hastily scribbled on a ripped scroll: "Eyes upon the enemy. Hand upon the hilt. Feet upon the wind." The Northern Arm's battle cry. "And darling," he jotted in postscript, "keep drinking."

Stroom's anxious voice returned Sindhi to her thin, worn cot. She felt again the pulse of unbound time pressing upon her shoulders like the cracked stone slabs of the Holster itself. She stared again at Jah'ri. "It's not always better to live, and there are better ways to die."

"To die is to die," Sindhi offered, shrugging.

"To live is to live."

She glared. "If I didn't know better, I'd say you sounded like a Hammer regretting his assignment. The mission is tomorrow. The swim a matter of hours. Shall I call the Commander to choke you?"

His eyebrows furrowed. "I only suggest Hammer Jah'ri breaking early could have been a sort of . . . a sort of mercy. We all know what awaits us. For most, the swim itself will be a crusade, but what follows . . . Well, you saw. Jah'ri handed you that victory during the Scraps game. There's no fight left. The Hammer dreams of fishes."

"Perhaps," she said, growing tired of Stroom.

Stroom's anxious gaze deepened into his slowly weaving fingers. "The Nails we plucked, huh? Sor's Staircase took them all. All of them. The Holster is like this for us Hammers. They climb, we swim. No difference."

"Our mission is not a death sentence. We swim to Brecca,

not Sor's Staircase."

Stroom corrected, "We swim to Shyloc."

"Returning a Sword is my only concern." With finality she turned away from him. He spoke more, but she did not care to hear it.

The Swords.

Her brain echoed.

Few had actually seen them. Some Hammers claimed to have glimpsed the Swords entering the sacred skyship accompanying his greatness King Kulloh-Sor towards the heavens to trade from the sky. Others spoke of more heroic records, of blade-banded warriors rescuing captured Hammers, returning with collections of heads from the Wild Few dragging behind them on strings; of dragons and bearmen, goblins and sea breathers. Sindhi knew those stories likely originated from the Court's committee on Proper and Just Tales.

One legend proved true.

The Swords carried a stout battle-blade sharp enough to reshape the core of Arou itself, its steel forged with breccel, an obscure and ancient mineral. Sindhi could see it in her mind's eye. The scoop of black breccel dust in her palm. Her Victory Vial filled.

Reach the isle, collect its breccel, and return home a champion to forge your battle blade.

The mission Sindhi ached to start.

It was torture, the waiting. The seconds dripped like blood.

PER THE LAWS of Sor, a Hammer's past was prohibited, but that did not stop Sindhi from guessing. Most were easy.

Stroom, anxious, bitter, the fastest swimmer and the grayest skin. Raised in the subterranean pools of the 25th Parallel.

Felton, refined speech and high taste, all too easily annoyed by courser cadences. From a low-ranking family of the Court.

Saz, murderous eyes and slack tongue, skin permanently burned red. Born and raised in the barren pits of the Shield.

Vaera, forever irritable and desperate for control. Born a Nail, possibly in the 29th, watching privileged children of the Court pass and scowl on their pilgrimage.

Rannold, charming eyes hiding sinister impulses. A rare castle-born Hammer.

Sindhi could continue down the line. To Petyr and Nima, to those whose names she never bothered to learn, to the boiled bolts of Commander Prime if she dared, but what, what, what did she know of Jah'ri?

The Hammer had proven the most difficult to read.

Jah'ri had no accent. No quips or turns of phrase. He was a Hammer from everywhere and nowhere with a disposition designed to blend and disappear. She suspected it was purposeful. Blade to her head, Sindhi would guess Jah'ri was once a Nail, for he ate like someone who intimately knew hunger, his only tell. Confusingly, Jah'ri was the first Hammer she had ever seen meditate, a common practice of priests, but unusual outside the profession and certainly unexpected outside of temple walls. Whatever burdensome, inescapable weight lay below his skin stuck to him like a curse and haunted his breathing.

True, Jah'ri had let her win at Scraps, and Sindhi hated him for the dishonor of unearned triumph. What was worse was that Jah'ri didn't seem to care about winning at all. It was deviant logic, the kind that could only occur in the humid, echoing chambers of the Holster, but it made Sindhi feel like Jah'ri had somehow still won the game, that her own victory was now devalued and stolen.

Perhaps Jah'ri was brilliant.

Movement. Shuffling.

Jah'ri again, the final mystery of the Holster. With what looked like great effort he stood from his cot and languidly limped to the wall-sized painting of the great mountain and, true to his nature, stared at it, looking much like an exhibition himself.

Stroom asked, "What's he looking for, you think? When he stares at it?"

Motivation.

She answered, "Fuck if I know."

Sindhi stood, fixed her eyes again on Jah'ri, and approached the mystery.

3

JAH'RI

"The neck will ne'er sprout from the foot,
Or an ear from the heart.
Life demands it.
My Parallels are my Body.
Equal but separate."

—*The Scrolls of Sor (rumored)*

The enormous, gaudy painting in Cot Hall was one of the few flourishes found throughout the Holster. The only other decor Jah'ri had seen came from the kingdom's sigil: a battle blade through a hammer over a peak. The sigil was found at least once in every room, impetuously slathered directly onto the compound's gray walls, often in red. The painting of the great mountain of Kulloh-Sor, however, was lavish as it was out of place. Framed and attached to the wall, the painting took the length of it, hanging low enough for Hammers' hands to touch, though none dare would.

Jah'ri never saw such a rich depiction of the mountain before coming to the Holster, nor had he seen its entire shape, the Parallels clear.

The painter's perspective was angled from the sky, facing towards the mountain from the sea. In the painting, the great mountain, Sor's Crown, was backed against ocean-facing cliffs and appeared to grow out of the sea itself. Jah'ri had often debated this interpretation. Was it bursting from the waves or plunging into them? Perhaps the mountain was a weapon crashing into Arou like a celestial hammer striking the ground. Jah'ri could not help the comparison. It was all he knew. At its bottom, the mountain was wide but irregular. The middle jutted deep and wide into the Sea of Cashmu. To the south, land retreated quickly and steeply, whereas to the north, three tall craggy claws, each one Parallel high, competed against one another to dominate the view. The First Parallel was depicted on the northernmost curve. The painting was not overly concerned with the Parallels themselves; few brushstrokes were given for these isolated communities. Jah'ri's mind filled in the missing elements: groups of Nails, forever burdened and hungry; their carts and store houses, their caves leading to corridor systems that burrowed and splintered like tendons.

Many Parallels, such as the First, provided both interior and exterior shelter, often called districts. Most outer districts Jah'ri had seen were carved from the mountain's rock, though some used natural ledges and mesas. The 5th Parallel, Jah'ri's long abandoned home, was like this. He did not realize until later that he was privileged to have slept outside, to have traced the stars, as cold and lonely of a child as he was.

Other Parallels were not as kind.

The 7th, 8th, 9th, and 12th Parallels were entirely cavern communities, rich only in torchlight, whose Nails mined the very metals that later equipped the Hammers' weapons that enforced them. Those Nails lived without daylight. Eventually, those who were plucked for Sor's Staircase stood atop the mountain and felt the warmth of the sun, the salty breeze of the evening, and the blessing of the moonlight. It was a brief reward before the clutch of death pulled them over their precipice. Indeed Jah'ri was lucky, if luck was a word that could be used in this wretched kingdom, for at least he had never had to serve in those dark and hopeless cradles.

His eyes next scanned the rolling hills along the larger mass. Steep slopes over mesas. Ridges carving valleys. Mountains within a mountain. Jagged peaks commanded the local climate, the temperature. Regional rain could be precise and deadly, like in the soaked and miserable 25th, a hidden village of boats, rafts, rope bridges, and hammocks. No two Parallels were alike, not really. Most community settlements were founded near the northern facing edge of the mountain where the kingdom's pulley carriages transported plucked Nails, but not all settlements could be. Natural peaks over the 6th, 18th, and 28th Parallels cast imposing shadows over unforgiving lands; those communities spread wider across the mountain's face. Jah'ri had escorted Nails along those perilous cliff-edged trails to the cable carriage. He recalled steep, deteriorating stone bridges between wind-howling peaks and shivered at the memory.

Next, Jah'ri's eyes settled on the plateau of Sor's Crown. A bluish gray half-dome, the Court, rested on its surface. Towering above it, the spires of Capital Castle appeared to grow right out of its center. Beside both begin the twisted, spiraling stairs, spiraling up and around the towers of the castle and into the clouds above. The tallest structure on all of Arou.

Sor's Staircase stretched to the top edge of the painting's canvas.

"Entrancing, isn't it?" a voice asked. Jah'ri turned to see Hammer Sindhi. Cautiously, he wondered how long she had stood beside him. Before today's game of Scraps, he had no memory of ever speaking to her directly. Saz, in comparison, never really gave him a choice to speak. But Sindhi contained herself much like Jah'ri did, as most of them should, rarely volunteering words. But today was different. The day before the mission. Everyone's lips were bending.

"Usually," he replied. "But today it feels so . . ." sad, he wanted to say but abandoned the thought, leaving the phrase unfinished.

Sindhi pointed. "Look at all those greens. Who knew there were so many shades of green? And browns there, and grays and blues. This color, right here. I have no name for it."

"Purple," Jah'ri replied. "Wild reed, knee-high. Grows in the slopes outside the 15th."

Jah'ri immediately regretted sharing history. Breaking the silence between them, Jah'ri recited, "A Hammer has no past. All that matters is the hand gripping us now."

"Praise Sor and his exalted son, King Kulloh-Sor," Sindhi instinctively muttered.

"About Scraps." Jah'ri began another sentence he didn't

know how to finish, so he didn't.

"Forget it," Sindhi asserted. "A Hammer has no past."

Jah'ri, suddenly unsure if she held a weapon, nodded. As if she sensed his unease, she raised her empty hands and pointed again at a spread of wild reeds. In truth, Jah'ri had never noticed the colors. The entirety of Sor's Crown in clear view, the mountain overwhelmed him, more today than it ever had before. Its lines, its faults. Within them he found the shape of his duty-bound life, revenge-trodden, every twist and turn a command. Even the shrouded voice in his head, the one telling him he would find his purpose in the murder of the crown, had become something of a burden. Staring, Jah'ri had never felt more wasteful and empty than he did now.

"You disappear in here, don't you?" she asked him. "I can never tell if you're worshiping the painting or frightened of it."

"Perhaps a little of both," he admitted.

A moment of silence passed between them. Sindhi sighed. Then she seemed to find the words to continue. "Striking, the view of Sor's Crown from the sight of a skyship."

"No. I . . . I believe it's through the eyes of a falling Nail."

Sindhi turned toward the Hammer. "Strange, that interpretation."

Jah'ri declared the conversation over by leaving Sindhi alone at the painting, parting without another word. He disliked whatever game she was playing. Jah'ri felt like a loose token in a game of Scraps. When he returned to his cot he closed his eyes. It was time to give into the act of meditation. He breathed.

Settle his nerves and strengthen his spirit.

He breathed.

Settle his nerves and strengthen his spirit.

He breathed.

Earlier, Commander Prime caught Jah'ri lazily drifting, but now he would approach seclusion and extract a scar with precision. Cradle it like a lost child. Taste the reverie and spit. Jah'ri picked at it like a scab upon his brain. For in him the Swords carved a memory.

4

JAH'RI

A false wall pushed open, as if in a dream, and behind it, nervous visitors silently argued.

The boy touched the wall, but his mother would take his hand and lead him away. "With wings, my darling Jah'ri." Dirty brunette hair tangled atop hazel eyes, she fed him stories. She bathed him in hope. She hid parchment underneath rocks or deep inside dusty crates and from those she could read. Nails were not allowed names but she gave her son one anyway.

Mother Nail, did she too have a name? And was she really his mother? Where did she learn to read? The boy did not have the foresight to ever ask these questions before her death, and by the time he was a man, the past was but a stinging mist. Much later, grown, Hammer Jah'ri would visit whores in every Parallel he served and search for moving, hidden walls. He never found what he was looking for, nor did he ever find a harlot who could read the scribbled parchment he handed them. He paid the pretty Nails with food and thanked them for their confused kindness, hurriedly leaving before his wits left him. Frustrated, the form-less shape of his memory continued to taunt him like a shadow swallowed by a cave mouth. What exactly had his mother been?

Fathers of Nails did not stay with their children. Jah'ri re-membered him only as a Nail with a builder's frame, a spotty, stubby beard, and a headful of thick and twisty auburn hair. Oc-casionally he would visit. One voice among many in those frantic secret meetings. Jah'ri plunged his ear against the false wall but could never hear above the dull consonants and pointed vowels. His father, a word he wouldn't know until he later served in the Court, once emerged from behind the wall with the spirit of progress on his brow. Upon his exit, he paused when he saw the young Jah'ri. It was the first and only time their eyes met.

"Boy," he said. His gruff voice lacked the lilt of a question, nor did it speak with much finality. Perhaps the Nail wasn't sure if there was more to be said to his son. Then, hastening to leave, the boy raised his shaky voice to stop the man's exit.

"Jah'ri," he told his father.

The Nail rolled his eyes, shook his head. He blew air. "She shouldn't be naming you."

"There's power in names. Mother Nail says so."

His father's beard opened to reveal a weak smile. He ruffled Jah'ri's own thick hair. "Things will change," he told the boy. "Soon we will—" The sentence never finished. Near them, on the shanty's floor, the hatch began to pound like a heart. His father slowly stepped backwards as the pounding increased, growing into something like an insistent fury.

They heard a shouting voice below the floor.

"By order of King Kulloh-Sor, his Greatness, anointed by the gods, who is himself a god in the form of a king, requires fourteen Nails for Sor's Staircase, our immortal founder's glorious temple, that He may find it well and good and complete . . ."

The hatch burst open and chaos consumed the shanty. Hammers poured in like fire ants and grabbed every Nail both behind and in front of the false wall, knocking through it as they pursued. There were more Nails than Jah'ri realized. Frozen, he watched as the man he would later call father be clumsily pulled down through the shanty floor, screaming as he went.

A large body approached the boy. Neck crooked, the shanty ceiling was too low for his towering frame. He wore golden vambraces upon his forearms and a matching gorget on his neck; otherwise, the man was clothed in white with a short cape trailing behind him and a large, sheathed blade on his side. Mother Nail confronted the Sword with protest.

No, no. The Swords do not come for Nails. That is a Hammer's duty, to collect the Nails.

Hammer Jah'ri would later pluck them himself. He could not trust the memory.

Yet he knew it was true.

The vision of a powerful stranger wielding a stout battle-blade. His hand holding her throat, squeezing and breaking it. The blade through the mouth. A shattered skull. Pointless death delivered by a careless creature. Jah'ri's mother was alive and spirited and frustrated by the day's heat. Then she was overwhelmingly lifeless, a wasted and spent corpse left to rot. The remaining Nails were plucked and the Sword ordered it over and done with, only half-heartedly glancing at the weeping boy before he left. The shanty was still. Jah'ri slept next to his mother's broken body for unknown days until they were both found by a faceless Cleanser who shared some sour water and hard bread. Coarsely, the Cleanser dragged Jah'ri into the floor, through the maze of stacked shanties and eventually outside, forcing him to live.

A DIFFERENT TIME, another memory. Broken teeth spit onto the ground.

One bone in the middle.

Surrounded by four.

JAH'RI PASSED FOUR ages surviving alone in the 5th Parallel. He was an orphan, lonely and scared and excluded from the Nails' stacked shanties, sleeping instead in the shadows of the mountain's corridors or outside on the flattest rocks, waking to vultures nipping at his toes. He struggled to understand why the Nails did not help him after his mother's death, for they had closed their hearts, their hands. Even the friendliest, most familiar faces had turned sour. They pushed Jah'ri out of the temple's daily mash line and blocked him from reentering. The boy was forced to source his own food and eventually became exceptional at the task. He mastered catching rats and lizards, even wayward gulls that landed for rest and later the snapping vultures that prodded his sleeping toes. It was there Jah'ri learned the difference between stalking and striking.

Scouting for food consumed him. Not unlike Arou's scrawniest animals, Jah'ri's eyes roved at the shadows and leered toward creatures, large and small, feathered or scaled, no matter how many legs squirmed as he swallowed. Sustenance became his only purpose.

One day, when a temple priest called Jowe incautiously stepped on a beetle Jah'ri had been anxiously following, the nearly feral Jah'ri screamed and jumped towards the priest. He was quickly swatted away by an accompanying Hammer the boy had not cared to notice. The priest swiped the beetle's guts from the bottom of his sandal but otherwise continued pacing through the 5th Parallel's outer district without a hint of impedance. Jah'ri absently rubbed the bump on his head as he followed the holy procession, for Jowe was followed by three Hammers total, one holding a box. The boy watched the scene unfold. The Hammer presented the box and placed it in the middle of the market square; the priest stepped atop it.

"Quiet!" Jowe roared into the crowd.

The priest was short in stature, but his voice boomed. Thick, dark gray robes outstretched past his feet and covered the box making him look disorientingly tall, almost floating. Across his chest, Sor's sigil was stitched in red. Sweat covered his plump, pale face. Soon, a ring of Nails slowly formed. Satisfied with the attention, the priest spoke: "Once every age, a Nail from every Parallel may challenge a Hammer for their weapon. For it is written in the Scrolls of Sor, 'Test the strength of my tools, both the Hammer and the Nail, my instruments shall be sharpened, lest I ne'er return.'"

The Nails chittered. Knowing his place was outside the

crowd, Jah'ri watched with great interest from afar on top of a boulder. The priest continued. "But only one can survive in Sor's Just Society. If the Nail falls, then it was never worthy of Sor's glory, nor His Staircase. If the Hammer falls, then the Nail will be sharpened into a Hammer, ascending into the halls of Sor's greatest Parallels. Bring forth the unsharpened Nail."

The circle split. One Nail entered the ring. Jah'ri had noticed this Nail before, many had. They watched him as a pastime. He rolled the Parallel's largest boulders to build his strength, including the one Jah'ri sat on now. Now he understood why. The Nail had been preparing. Now, the man stood empty-handed in the crowd's circle. He tore off his tunic and let it fall below him onto the stone slabs of the market square. He grunted and pounded his chest. He was not burly, for there was not enough food for that, but the man was shaped for strength and larger than most.

Jowe told him, "A Nail cannot hold a hammer. Take her weapon and you will become something greater. Fail, and the line of Sor will laugh as we leave your corpse for the ants."

Jowe yelled once more, "Bring forth the unsharpened Hammer!"

The Hammer they called Atan pushed through the quieting circle. She entered the ring adorned in her standard uniform: light gray trousers, an armored burgundy tunic, a black belt with a holster for a combat hammer, and a small blade sheathed in her boots. She was neither small nor large, though her shoulders were broad enough and her arms strong enough to withstand a charge. The Nail was larger.

"Death decides it," the priest announced. "May you both battle honorably in Sor's worship. Praise Sor and his exalted son,

King Kulloh-Sor!" The crowd repeated the last line in unison as Jowe carefully stepped off the box and shuffled to the edge of the circle where he crossed his arms after swatting a passing fly.

Most younger Nails did not know the Sharpening existed, including Jah'ri, whose mouth grew dry from hanging. According to the voices that spread throughout the ring of bodies, no Nail from the 5th Parallel had ever ascended through the Sharpening. It was all over swiftly. Atan pulled her boot blade and threw it into the challenger's muscular throat. He fell to his knees, clawing and gasping. The Hammer approached the Nail's convulsing body, pulled her combat hammer from its holster, and repeatedly crushed the Nail's skull until it cracked and squished onto the stone slab. The crowd was silent. Jah'ri watched it all with great interest.

"Alas, the Nail was blunt. The Hammer has been sharpened." Jowe declared the ceremony's end with the conviction of a man ready to return to the cool shade of his Temple.

LATER THAT NIGHT, Jah'ri returned to the market square. The Nail's body was gone, likely shoveled into the Parallel's drainage pipe before it could grow rotten in the sun. The boy Jah'ri lay next to the stone where the blood had dried and already mixed with dust from the evening's bluster. Jah'ri returned every night for an entire age, sleeping there.

In daylight hours, he found a new purpose in studying Atan. She was a proud and effective Hammer, certainly domineering. On patrols, her presence was quickly noted. The Nails, hauling their daily loads, straightened their spines upon seeing her shadow. Even child Nails quieted in fear of punishment. The elderly, if there were any left who hadn't yet been sent to Sor's Staircase, held their phlegmy coughs. Atan, however, kept the closest eye on her own uniform. Frequently, Jah'ri would find her patting the dust away or straightening the buckle of her belt, which had naturally gone askew.

Atan was plagued by power, as all Hammers were, but dirt, grime, germs, these unleashed her temper.

Jah'ri was not yet striking, only stalking, but he needed to test his theory, and one day he found his nerve. Purposefully, he tripped into her and knocked her down into the muddy ground, a rare rainy morning in the dusty, dry climate of the 5th Parallel.

"I slipped!" he yelled.

Atan punished the boy. Jah'ri absorbed the hits but took from them many lessons, like how quickly she lost her temper and how hard she swung when she was enraged.

During his fourteenth age, as best as he could remember and count time, Jah'ri had fully healed. He had lost weight and therefore lost muscle. There was nothing to be done about it. The young man, scrawny as he was dirty, approached Jowe as if out of the ground itself and declared for the Sharpening.

"This is not a game, Nail. You are too young. There are better ways to die."

"I challenge Atan for her hammer." Jah'ri did not leave.

The priest shook his head. "Why the Sword didn't also snuff you out is beyond me."

"You know me? Did . . . you know Mother Nail?"

"The trouble is in the blood. That's what is known."

The comments he didn't understand, but in that moment

Jah'ri felt different, briefly, like something connected to something else. He had forgotten the feeling.

The room was quiet before the priest abruptly announced, "Tomorrow then," and he waved the Nail away. The boy ran from the temple and though his body trembled, he did his work for the day, suppressing the squeamish throes that plagued his belly.

That night, Jah'ri laid for what he knew would be his final time on the stone slabs of the market square, tracing a subtly wobbly stone that was now surrounded by loosened dirt. He watched a seed snake pass through rocks in the silvery moonlight and decided to let it live, succumbing, finally, to sleep.

The priest declared the Sharpening the next day and a crowd gathered, as it did the age before, forming a circle in the market square. Jah'ri stood empty handed. The midday sun warmed his naked back as he listened to the priest's pedantic speech and waited for his opponent. Atan did finally come, but this time when she pushed through the crowd she laughed when she saw her challenger: the small scrawny boy in front of her. "What madness?" she said. The priest shrugged his shoulders. The Hammer folded her arms and said, "Let's get it over with."

"Death decides it," Jowe announced.

Young Jah'ri trembled. Urine flowed into his trousers and puddled onto the lithic ground of the Sharpening ring, which was sandstone and mostly flattened. Generations of Nails' weary feet had stumbled through here. They hauled minerals mined from their Parallel's exterior mesa, hard labor for unknown purposes. Hammers followed their Nails closely as they delivered the minerals to the Parallel's pulley carriage station, kicking them along for good measure.

Now, the work had stopped. The entertainment had begun.

When Jah'ri looked down at his shaking, urine-soaked legs, the surrounding crowd of Nails laughed.

"The son of the bitch," he heard.

"A fitting end," he heard.

"Give 'em what he deserves," he heard.

Jah'ri fell to his knees and put his hands in the air. "No, no, no! Please!" he yelled.

Atan approached from the other side of the ring.

"Too late," she said with a shrug, sounding rather bothered by the whole affair. Next, Atan pulled her boot blade and quickly threw it. Dodging it easily, Jah'ri leaped away. He knew it was coming. The blade landed near him, but he rebuked his temptation to reach for it. The blade was not part of the plan. Jah'ri crouched into a squat.

Hammer Atan shook her head before approaching him again.

Only steps away, she next pulled her combat hammer from her waist and raised it. He spit on her boots. It did nothing but momentarily stalled her as she looked down. Jah'ri spit again. The Hammer reddened.

Over the last age, all of Jah'ri's watching, all of his waiting engendered a simple, stupid strategy. But then a snarl curled her bitter lip, and the first fruits of Jah'ri's plan were revealed.

The boy knew he'd have to move out of the way of the Hammer's strike, but he couldn't move too soon or Atan would catch him on the backswing. Hastily, she surprised him by swinging a second sooner than he thought possible. The combat hammer struck stone as Jah'ri rolled away. He felt the ground jolt from her hit.

Jah'ri recovered once more into a squatting position, facing Atan. From the crowd behind him, he felt something warm and viscous hit his head and shoulders, then his back, realizing it was spit. He ignored the hecklers.

Atan swiped the boot blade off the ground without losing sight of her opponent. Jah'ri heard the scratchy sound of her blade sharpening on sandstone as she regained her advantage. His stomach dropped. He swallowed. It was a risk he shouldn't have taken, leaving the weapon there; later, Jah'ri would reflect on that moment many times over. That scratchy sound.

She held the dagger again for only a quick moment before whipping it through the air. Jah'ri's eyes popped as he fell backwards. The blade pierced his trousers near his left shin, pinning him into the ground.

The crowd gasped, then cheered.

This time, there was nothing casual about Atan's approach as she ran at him with her combat hammer swinging in the air. Jah'ri rolled again. Because of his plan, which now seemed foolish in the sobering daylight of the Sharpening ring, Jah'ri had to roll into the direction of the blade—not away from it—giving himself a scar on his shin he would carry for the rest of his life.

Screaming as his skin ripped over the blade, Jah'ri freed himself and moved with only a half a second to spare, merely escaping Atan's attempted strike. Jah'ri heard the stone crack near his head, for she had swung at the same chunk of stone earlier, the one marked by dried urine.

The crowd cheered for its oppressor.

Once more, Jah'ri spat on her boots. Little liquid escaped his dry mouth, so Jah'ri quickly scooped blood from his leg and popped a goopy blob onto his tongue. He swished and spat a foul blend of saliva, blood, and stone dust, covering her tunic, pushing her backwards as if she were punched in the stomach. Atan growled out of exasperation, her snarl turning rageful.

On his feet, Jah'ri circled the Sharpening ring, leaving behind a trail of bloody footprints. He shook off a wave of dizziness. How much blood had he already lost? He couldn't afford to look, nor did he want to. He didn't think he was limping. Not yet. But he wasn't sure—

Atan charged him.

Jah'ri saw his own feet in the air before he understood what had happened. In only a second, or perhaps more, in the midst of blood loss, panic, and adrenaline, he couldn't say for sure, Atan had lunged toward him and swept her leg. Landing hard on his back, Jah'ri felt the air crush out of his lungs.

He gasped but couldn't breathe.

If Atan had swung her weapon, that would have been it. Instead, the Hammer backed away. Jah'ri's flying legs had flung blood into her open eyes. She wasn't screaming, for no Hammer was squeamish at the sight of blood, even one as particular and unfond of grime as Atan, but she was blinded all the same. Quickly, she worked the blood out of her eyes with her fists.

By the time Jah'ri had caught his breath, Atan's combat hammer had swung again. Jah'ri could only move his head, but it was enough to clear the weapon's path. Steel crashed into sandstone. The clanging nearly burst his ear drums.

Atan yelled and raised her weapon again, yearning for the final strike.

Jah'ri rolled. He tried to stand but tripped over his own bloody feet.

The Hammer followed him.

Jah'ri crawled.

Atan grabbed his bloody shin, her thumb fingering the wound, and dragged Jah'ri back towards the center of the ring in the direction of her boot blade. The boy screamed.

The Hammer released Jah'ri's leg when she scooped up the weapon.

"Hammer!"

"Look!"

The Nails tried to warn the Hammer.

Jah'ri had found his moment.

She spun back around.

Atan's knee popped when Jah'ri kicked it, and that was enough to free the combat hammer from her hand. Jah'ri seized her weapon and slammed it back into the stone slab, already loosened from Atan's previous strikes. He freed a small, sharp chunk, a little larger than his palm. Jah'ri approached Atan with the combat hammer in one hand, holding it high. Though she was unable to stand, Hammer Atan easily blocked Jah'ri's swing with her forearm.

She did not see his other hand.

Tears rolling as he screamed, Jah'ri dropped onto Atan's chest and crushed the chunk of rock in his hand into her mouth, shattering its brittle guardians. His palm bleeding, he shoved the rock again, lodging it deep in her mouth where it couldn't be retrieved. Stunned, Atan clawed at her mouth and twisted her body to unpin herself from under Jah'ri's knees.

Jah'ri, his body heavy and unmoving, regained his grip on Atan's combat hammer.

With a shaky, sweaty grasp, he raised it high once more to finish the task, but from behind a hand clutched his wrist. Another pulled his arm. The Nails, furious and spiteful, his own kind, pulled Jah'ri back into the crowd. They tripped the boy and pushed him down. Kicks landed into him from every angle, hateful legs stretching from familiar faces. Jah'ri covered his head and his body as best he could.

"Enough!" Jowe yelled.

Hammers broke up the mob.

Bloodied and shaking, Jah'ri braved to look. He found the priest shaking his head over the lifeless Atan. The Hammer had choked on her blood, her own teeth.

"Death decides it," Jowe said again, forlorn. "Pick up your weapon, Hammer."

On the sullied ground, the weapon laid near cracked stone, head down and handle up.

"BIRD GUTS. PSST, hey Bird Guts," A voice pulled him back. It was Hammer Vaera's scratchy warm tone. She leaned her waist against a small corner post of Jah'ri's cot and waited patiently for his eyes. He yielded them. "You live to swim, I see."

"What is it, Vaera?"

"It is strange, isn't it? Your dream."

It took him a moment, for he had just been swimming in reverie, another place, another time, but now he grasped her meaning. "Yes," Jah'ri said plainly. "I admit interpreting the dream is difficult. Do you know what it means?"

Vaera laughed. "That's not the right question."

Jah'ri paused and thought through her comment. "I should want to know why the dream is different. Not what it means?"

"You don't remember me, do you?" She sat next to him on his cot. "I wasn't sure at first, but I believe we served together in the 22nd. Briefly. I was going out as you were coming in."

Jah'ri did not spring her trap. "Hammers do not have a past," he recited. "We are tools of the King."

She snickered and rolled her eyes. "You know, you are more obvious than you realize. This whole . . . act. A real patriot does not want to fall in line. It needs to. And you so desperately want to." She was close enough to kiss or kill. Jah'ri was not sure which. The Hammers were allowed to mingle and even mate in the dark of the night in the Holster. Two Hammers had suggested this to Vaera throughout her age of training. She wounded one and mated the other. Jah'ri took her advice and relaxed.

He would not kill or kiss the Hammer, though he was not immune to the desires of his flesh. He had fantasized for Vaera as well as for Rannold during his time in the Holster: waking visions of taking each Hammer alone or occasionally together, groping and grinding until exhaustion broke them. Nothing had come from these desires, of course. To Jah'ri, mating was another tactic he had mastered; desire had never overwhelmed him to the point of mating without purpose. But now Jah'ri saw the shape of her neck, evocative and ensnaring; he wanted to taste it and follow his tongue where it led him. He was hungrier for her than he was comfortable with. He felt weak and stupid. But it was tomorrow's promise of death that made him low and desperate.

Nothing more.

"You consider me. And I you," Vaera said.

"Hammer Vaera," Jah'ri took her hands in his. "Please kindly piss off."

She chuckled and stood. "You never asked me the question."

Jah'ri sighed. He thought, becoming surprisingly thankful for the challenge. He looked into her eyes. "What is it you see, Vaera? It's your dream, isn't it? What are you not telling me?"

Vaera was tough and stubborn. She had, perhaps, the strongest will in the 38th, but he found in her a sudden weakness. He saw hints of, possibly, a young, scared Nail who hid somewhere within her. "Lately I have seen Shyloc every night. Every single night. The ugly bastard always kills me. Brutally. Sometimes before I even understand what's happened."

She sat again and lowered her voice. "But last night, in truth, damn it. Jah'ri, if you tell anyone this I will pluck your eyes and force them into your ears. Understand? I was nowhere near the isle. I was a Nail. A filthy fucking Nail. Building the steps of Sor's Staircase. Can you believe it? And I fall. I fall forever. Guess what passes me?"

"A bird," Jah'ri answered quickly, surprising himself. She nodded, and Jah'ri figured out the rest. The bird had recently feasted. She saw blood on its beak. It did not save her, nor did it eat her. It flew by, careless and unconcerned of the screams from a falling Nail.

What she said next Jah'ri could not have guessed. "Before I perished, I saw . . . I saw it fly into fire. Inextinguishable smoke and flame, hungry, furious . . . and Jah'ri," she added, swallowing to breathe, "the bird had your eyes."

5

NAOR

Naor listened. Right ear pressed against the floor, the line of light violent upon his eye. His left hand absently massaged his bedroom door, his thumb faithfully following the grain's concentric circles like somber priests prayerfully pacing a courtyard.

There was a normal pattern to things, and Naor trusted the pattern. Lessons, playtime, dinner, sleep. Every evening Naor was sent to bed at a proper time for a boy of eleven ages. After, Father would dim the lights in the family's lounge room. Naor would sneak out of bed, lay upon his floorboards, and listen to the opening of bottles, the clinking of glasses. A pattern.

Father and Mother frequently spoke in their important, protected murmurs, as if they knew their son was prying. Other nights, they spoke openly and clearly, as if they forgot they had a son altogether. What he did hear, when he could hear, particularly when his name was not mentioned, was often so boring (Elder Hammers, Court politics, committee chairs and their haughty dissenters) that Naor would fall asleep on the floorboards, leaving Wiglaf the dog alone on the bed.

There were evenings with anger. Mother and Father, against one another, scolding, demanding, shrinking. Father delirious. Mother steady. And occasionally there were joyful sounds he didn't quite understand, a rousing and a rustling, and Naor would return to bed confused and yet not confused, aware of everything and nothing, for that is the power of childhood, a consequenceless ignorance.

Tonight, the light coming from his family's lounge room was unusually bright. Some voice, a visitor. This late? The woman spoke with the cadence of a temple priestess.

Then he heard his name. Naor. It over-seasoned their conversation like Muloh-Sor salt, and he knew immediately what it was all about. Nauseous, Naor rolled away from the door. Climbed into bed. Little Wiglaf stood, yawned, and circled a few times as Naor's bony, growing legs found their way into the smooth linen.

The voices grew with intention and malice.

Naor, Naor, Naor...

He pulled the blanket over his face. Only his messy, thick black hair poked through like a frightened marmot in courtyard grass. The boy would not cry. Not again. He promised himself. He promised Mother. His panicked lungs ramped rapidly as if trying to outrun tears, yet it didn't matter. He scrunched his face and wiped blurry eyes.

The slamming of a door. The stomping and pacing of feet. Cursing.

Mother declared, "You're embarrassing yourself, Ricard."

"The gall! That sniveling pawn!"

"Lower your voice."

They did, and Naor could hear little else. He didn't dare escape his bed again. Predictably, fatigue followed tears. His cheeks dried, and his lungs slowed. Sleep took him. Naor immediately slipped into a gray dream. An awful dream. Mother said such terrible things to him. Her voice was so close, so real. Her form shimmered and whispered like smoke.

"Naor will embark soon," her voice said.

The ground opened. His eyes spun, his stomach twisted. Below him hideous flames grew. "If not, we must push him out of the Court ourselves, and that will be that."

. . . and that will be that.

Mother and Father's rigid forms shrunk as Naor plummeted. He couldn't stop or speak or scream. His weightless arms stretched as he reached. The fire swallowed his plunging body.

"THAT WILL BE that," Naor recalled, faintly remembering shapes of the dissipating dream the following morning. He still felt the heat and wondered if he had caught a sickness. He would have to remember to ask Mother for wizard's spice.

Wiglaf pushed his bowl along the tiled kitchen floor as he ate, his industrious snout entranced and dedicated. Naor smiled. Instead of laughing, he merely remembered laughing, the exercise of a bouncing belly. After eleven ages, Naor's once boyish, jubilant laughter was becoming a foreign and taxing affair. Wiglaf still made a show of it: plunging his white ugly face into the bowl, slurping the slop, and raising a wet dripping head, now turned brown. He shook off the slop and loyally returned to his dish to lick the few remaining bits of intestine and gizzards, scooting the bowl across the room as he did it.

Naor grabbed a cleaning cloth and stooped to rub the slop from Wiglaf's ears and snout. "Your highness," he said, a joke he learned from Father but did not understand. He finished the task and scratched the dog's neck.

A distant thud.

Wiglaf moved his head and whimpered.

"Oh, you are a baby. Nothing to fear," he told the dog. Another thud settled in the distance. Boy and dog looked into nothingness together. "The wind must've shifted," Naor said, a line he lifted from Mother.

The children of the Court did not visit Sor's Staircase before their pilgrimage. Up until then, the larger world, and the privileged truth of Sor's Just Society, was hidden from them. Of course they were aware of the spiraling temple's existence, unfinished and ongoing, forever beckoning Sor to return from the Realm of the Gods, for the staircase's foundation stood next to the dome of the Court, sharing the great mountain's plateau, the 30th Parallel.

All the children knew was the pounding. Whenever the Sea of Cashmu blew its angry air or whenever Sor blessed the Court with fresh rain that funneled through the dome's catching tunnels and refilled the courtyard's many ponds the pounding increased. Children were told those slams were the sounds of progress. Noises safe to ignore.

Citizens of the Court called them Nails.

Cheap and endless in supply. Tools of the King.

Naor's pilgrimage would unveil the world to him and upon his return home, the path his life would take. The yawning detritus of citizenry, Father had once called it.

Naor stumbled back to his room, removed his sleeping clothes. He pushed into trousers. He found his favorite tunic, green with gold shimmers, and added upon it a brown vest that he could now proudly tie himself. His stockings were next and then loafers. A boy who dressed himself was ready for anything. Even a pilgrimage. He stared at the wall for a while, knowing he could not stay in his room all day and certainly not forever.

He picked up the letter from his desk, read it again. Nine words.

Hey Chumbum-
See you soon. Hurry, won't ya?
-Piers

It hurt seeing his friend's name, Naor admitted to himself, but he thought of him fondly nonetheless. He remembered Piers' smile that came with a proud new pair of boots, the type given to children just before they embarked on their pilgrimage.

"They look heavy," Naor told him.

"Nah. Not too bad."

"You lie! You tripped all over your room today. Your cat is flat."

Piers punched Naor on the shoulder. "Shut it, Chumbum. I'll be a citizen soon. All the way."

"You sure you wanna go?"

"It ain't really a choice, Naor."

"I'll go, I will."

"You should've gone already."

"Mother told me to wait."

Piers looked at Naor as if he could see through him. Naor's insecure eyes landed on his own loafers. They looked soft and fragile next to Piers' boots.

"Well, see ya." Naor hugged his friend and ran away to a quiet corner of the courtyard where he cried until dinner. There was sadness in Piers that day too, Naor thought, but maybe Naor only invented that in memory. Piers was simply carried away that day. He was made of the wind and always had been. Naor was a stupid tree.

MEANDERING THROUGH THE courtyard on his way to lessons, Naor recalled the Battle of the Soulless Kings. Legend told of how Sor triumphantly recaptured the great mountain from the clutches of the evil men who briefly stole and defiled the mountain. Sor returned it to the rightful rule of the gods, establishing his Kingdom and his Just Society. It was a tale of war and warriors. Of Swords. Of valiant bravery. The type of tale that made men out of boys.

Naor next imagined he was summoned to the castle where he ascended to the King's Parallel. "Tell me what you saw, my young warrior of the Court," the King would ask him. Naor would bow and say, "None greater than you, my King." King Kulloh-Sor would nod. "You are worthy to join my Swords. I am in need of bravery such as yours!"

Naor quickened his pace through the courtyard, which surrounded the Temple Complex and splintered throughout the dome. Many lost their way in this tree-scaped labyrinth. Occasionally, Naor did venture onto new trails and stepped into unexplored paths, but the boy knew his limits, especially without his friends to guide him, to push him. Home was never beyond five turns. That was his rule. Perhaps this was why Naor delayed his pilgrimage. Too many turns and no clear path home.

His feet slowed, but they did not stop as he approached his lessons chamber on the outskirts of the industrious, sprawling Temple Complex—the center of the dome. Reverently, he entered an open-air corridor and felt his feet grow heavy. He slowed even more. He swallowed. He knew if he stopped he would stay there forever, so he blinked through the urge and continued. Naor followed the path to the private chamber where Philosopher Shaeron prepared for her lessons. She sat studying scrolls. Her beige philosopher gown looked darker today. Naor noticed the sleeves stretched to her fingers. Her neckline was covered just under her chin making her head look like a proud trophy. She looked both saintly and dreary. The boy had loved the wise old woman since he was three. Now, he would seek for the valiant words just under his tongue. She turned when she noticed his presence.

"I'm . . . I'm ready for . . . the . . . You-Know-What."

Shaeron had always been kind to Naor. She had held him. Consoled him. She chided the other children who teased him. She shared little truths about the larger world, only giving Naor what she knew he could handle. Now, she gave him nothing.

Naor did not know what response he expected in return. Her ancient face was neither happy nor sad. Naor began to wonder if their unbreakable bond had been entirely imagined. She was an old cranky, miserable philosopher, after all. The other children said so. Most of the children from his lessons preferred Z'rai, her younger, friendlier assistant. Now a new thought occurred to Naor. Was it really a temple priestess who had visited his home last night? Could it have been Shaeron?

She let go of his hands, rising, and said, "I need to hear you say the words."

Naor could only breathe. He looked at nothing.

"The words, Naor."

Just north of a whisper he uttered, "I declare for Sor's Pilgrimage and seek the blessings He will bestow upon my return, for I am no longer a child, but a citizen of Sor's Just Society."

Her tired, wrinkly face produced a smile. "Then we have accomplished a great many things, Naor. Praise Sor and his exalted son, King Kulloh-Sor."

"Praise Sor and his exalted son, King Kulloh-Sor," Naor repeated mindlessly.

"I will tell the others."

Later, when lessons began, ten children of various ages—Naor the largest of all—sat on the ground in front of Shaeron and Z'rai. Upon a chair with rolled scrolls atop her beige linen lap, Shaeron began. "Today we seek the holy blessing of Sor upon our lessons."

The children spoke in unison: "Praise Sor and his exalted son, King Kulloh-Sor."

"May He build our hearts such as He built his own Kingdom."

"The Great Mountain Builder, our hearts are open," the children recited mechanically.

"Arou is his soul," Shaeron continued.

"The Parallels are his body."

"And what connects them all?"

"The spine of Sor's mountain: the faith and its temple."

Shaeron nodded to her assistant Z'rai, who took over, saying, "Let's begin with the most wonderful, urgent news. Philosopher Shaeron has informed me that Naor, the blessed son of Lady Eyrillia, Chairwoman of the 18th Parallel, has declared for Sor's Pilgrimage."

A pudgy, confident little boy named Frenklin laughed the loudest. "Him?" The other children giggled.

Shaeron stomped and the children quieted.

Z'rai looked down at Naor with a bittersweet glance. Naor couldn't interpret it, as he hadn't known Z'rai long. But now he grieved anew. Unfair, not to get to know her better. The children would get her all to themselves. Couldn't Naor stay for at least another week? Z'rai, as if reading his thoughts, answered as she continued: "Naor will depart in two days at the rising of the Swelling Moon. As you all know, he is no longer a child. We will pause the lessons for you to say your farewells."

Shaeron added, without emotion or even a sideways glance, "You will not see him again until your own pilgrimage is completed." She walked to the corner of the room, guiding Z'rai with a soft push of her elbow, as the children surrounded Naor.

"Took you long enough, Quiver Lip."

"Frenklin!" Shaeron scolded from across the room.

"It's okay," Naor spoke for himself. After all, he was eleven and on the precipice of his pilgrimage. Naor had a quiet strength within him now that he hoped Shaeron would see. That they all saw. Mother would be so proud. Naor would never cry again. He was done with all that.

"When it's my turn, I will leave right away," Frenklin promised to the group. "What took you so long?"

"Mother has been busy with her committee. I was asked to wait," Naor lied.

"Ha!" Frenklin laughed again and pointed at the liar.

"Future Chair of the Committee of Crying Children," goaded another child, Lillen.

Philosopher Shaeron watched the children tease Naor, but must have decided she could no longer protect him; it no longer did the boy any good. Maybe it never did. She smoothed her brown robe with her hands and silently left the room. Naor watched her go and suddenly felt very alone, despite the children surrounding him. He knew he would never see her again.

Z'rai stayed in the room but remained out of reach and off to the side. Her eyes darted to the ground when Naor looked to her for help

"You're not ready," another child of the Court teased. "Uh uh."

"I am! I swear it!"

"Suuuuuuure."

And there it was.

Naor felt the familiar welling in his face.

His fingers began to wiggle as his right foot twitched.

"I am!"

"Here it comes!" Lillen cried. "Wait for it!"

Naor heard them laughing as he fled the room. He ran through the open air corridors connecting the Temple Complex and back out into the courtyard where he disappeared far off the path and into a cover of thick trees where he halted and collapsed to the ground. He breathed hard and fast. Father once taught him to control his emotions by first sensing his own breath and next by focusing on an anchor from his surroundings. He tried it. He smelled the minerals under the grass. He listened to the trees rustle. He heard a loud bang on the dome, shortly followed by another.

The nails are falling fast today but the steps will prevail, Praise Sor.

He never did cry, Naor realized, and he let out a noise, like a laugh.

"I didn't cry . . . I didn't cry! Suck a slug, Frenklin."

The trees rustled louder. Or were those footsteps he heard?

A man, a thing, rushed towards Naor. Its ripped skin revealed muscle and bone, its torn clothes stained with dirt, blood and other bits. It had a face, or something like a face, but its teeth poked out from the wrong places. Naor's eyes grew wide as the creature's wretched hand shakily stretched towards him. Naor could not scream, for his voice no longer worked. It mattered little. He saw something in the creature's battered skull that unexpectedly steadied him. One eye was proper, the other was dead and dangling like a clobbered pond-fish on a string. But in the eye that worked, Naor found tears. The creature was crying.

Naor stood and stared at the thing.

6

LADY EYRILIA

Naor's mother, who was called Lady Eyrilia by citizens of the Court, watched her son leave for lessons through the kitchen window that stole so much of her time.

The trees of the courtyard comforted her. She could count the greens of every branch that differed, as if Sor himself painted each leaf with dashes of brown and red and blue. Together, their long, skinny leaves blended into a mosaic that slightly swayed from the predictable, controlled wind of the dome, funneled in from the Sea of Cashmu's wild breeze.

Eyrilia was lucky, she knew, to have a view of the courtyard at all. As chair of the committee overseeing the 18th Parallel, she was grateful for what she had. Other chairs had much worse views and smaller homes, particularly those overseeing the Parallels below the 18th, lower down the mountain and further out of reach from Sor's holy number of thirty-eight.

Every townehome in the dome of the Court was measured according to the residing family's rank and title: priests and priestesses, chairs, committee members, philosophers, and citizens. The chairs representing the higher-mountain Parallels enjoyed larger, more lavish spaces, fresher meals, and more visibility to the watchful eyes from the castle looming over the Court. These families often lived closer to the edge of the dome, and from it they could see the ocean and the endless horizon beyond it.

I would hate that. Too much wind, too many squawking, shitting gulls.

The ocean was wild and untamed, like an unbreakable Nail.

The courtyard was quiet and controlled.

The courtyard was also where the youngest citizens learned to run and explore and, later, upon maturing, learned to flirt and kiss and whisper. When the children grew into proper citizens after returning from their pilgrimages and getting ranked and assigned to committees, the courtyard's darkest trails and passages were used for rendezvous in the night once again, often for devious and political ends, though occasionally still for passion.

She closed her eyes and sipped her tea, which smelled of lavender and honey.

Eyrilia did not stare out the window and pine for the Hammer she once knew.

No, he would not steal her thoughts today.

More than a decade ago, they had used each other and the transaction was fair. She took his seed, he took her information. Eyrilia saw him many times after patrolling the courtyard or in the hallways of Temple Complex. She would nod and smile and continue. He would neither smile nor look, and she wondered if he even remembered their passionate purchase. The Hammer's seed took root, but he left the Court before she was showing. It was for the best, she knew. Nothing to cover up. No one to disappear.

Naor's failure to mature was odd and unexpected from a seed so strong. The boy was weak and small for his age. Prone to crying and tantrums.

Only a week prior she had given Naor a dictum, during their morning meal.

"My son, you shall not cry. Not for one week." Eyrilia spoke simply and coldly, as if it were but a routine order to pluck Nails, handed down to one of her feckless committee members.

"That's my boy," Ricard said, placing a reassuring hand on Naor's. "You can do that, can't you?"

Eyrilia rolled her eyes at her partner's approach, which stunk of weakness and coddling. Eyrilia's father would never have encouraged such frailty. She added it to her list of things to speak about with Ricard later.

Naor had nodded his head, which increasingly looked like a wobbly boulder. "Yeah, sure." His eyes immediately watered as he tried to sniff the tears away.

Eyrilia's patience failed her, and she yelled, "Naor, you shall not cry!" She slammed her hand on the table, jarring Ricard and sending Wiglaf the dog into hiding. The boy also ran away, to his room where he thumped into his bed and sobbed louder and harder than she had ever heard him cry. Naor yelled at himself. He called for his friends, for Piers, for Cedric, for Sai. For every child of the Court who left him behind.

"That's one method," her milquetoast husband had remarked, softly childing her.

She took her partner's plate and dumped his unfinished breakfast into the waste bin.

As the week passed, Eyrilia's dictum proved fruitless. Naor cried every day and worse, he still failed to declare for his pilgrimage, despite his late age. Soon he would be a foot taller than every other child who hadn't yet embarked, an unfortunate and embarrassing affair from the child of such a respected and important chairwoman.

An unusual boy,

She sipped her tea, her eyes still following the curve of the tickling leaves through her kitchen window.

And that Hammer who gave his seed to Eyrilia. Perhaps he was not as strong as she remembered being. He was unusual too, was he not?

Jah'ri. Jah'ri. Jah'ri.

A foreign sounding name. Possibly from the Southern Arm. He was solemn and strange, rough but comely, desperate and distant even in the act of love. There was a simple sadness in the Hammer, she remembered clearly now. She saw that sadness in Naor though perhaps that was just madness of the mind, the searching for answers where there were none.

No, if anyone was to blame, it was her bumbling, barren husband. Ricard whimpered more than the dog, and he should have been beaten the same.

Eryilia turned away from the window.

That is enough for today.

Suddenly, like a sprouting leaf, she knew that today Naor would announce his intent to embark on his pilgrimage. Naor had not told her, but mothers always knew their sons' secrets, often before they did. The children were their own little Parallels, she thought, not for the first time. Children were so close to their parents and yet so entirely separate, never fully one with the Parallel above them.

As if waking from a dream, she heard the temple's bells and dumped the rest of her tea down the drain, smirking at the thought of Naor becoming a respectable citizen, at the burden she would no longer need to carry.

WHEN EYRILIA ARRIVED at Committee Hall of Temple Complex she wasn't surprised to see Alcon, her deputy member, impatiently pacing outside the large, burgundy door labeled "Committee for the 18th Parallel."

"Lady Eyrilia," he said, nervously whispering and bowing.

Alcon's white robe looked sweat-stained from his fleshy, flabby arms, but she didn't mention it. Eyrilia suspected Alcon would never know nor care that she intentionally installed a bumbling idiot as her second in command. Job security meant distancing yourself from the ambitious and the shrewd, something her predecessor hadn't known anything about. That disgraced fart now stamped scrolls for the 7th Parallel's committee.

"The, the, the . . ." Alcon looked around as he spoke. "May we go inside the committee chamber?"

Eyrilia saw the hallway empty, but nodded nonetheless. Whispers carried here, and there were always willing ears to hear.

Alcon opened the door, and she pushed by him. Though the rest of the committee would not arrive for some time, she walked up the steps to her rostrum and took her position at the desk just behind it, the uppermost seat in the room.

"My Lady, our Elder Hammer of the Court summoned me early this morning."

"Jonn? What, he actually rose from his mattress?"

"Good jest, my Lady. Yes, Elder Hammer Jonn rose and has requested his favor."

Eyrilia set down the stack of scrolls she was mindlessly shuffling and turned to look at Alcon, pursing her lips. Alcon's eyes looked desperate, exasperated. Why was she continually surrounded by weak men? Then she remembered it was by choice, on all accounts.

"Alcon, my loyal friend, it will be okay. So, he's calling in his favor, no big concern."

"Your son, Naor. I'm sure it was worth it, letting him stay an extra age and all. Please, don't take my grief as anything else. He's a special child, of course."

"Slow your tongue and speak no more of it. Delaying Naor's pilgrimage was only one of many deals I struck with Jonn. You know of only what I trusted you to know. So, Jonn wants his favor returned?"

Indeed, Elder Hammer Jonn had helped her buy time with the Court's high priest. Eyrilia knew she had used too much capital delaying Naor's pilgrimage, but she could simply not have dragged the boy out of the Court screaming and crying, which is what would have happened had she forced him. The damage to her chair would have been too severe, her power threatened.

Alcon nodded quickly like a jabbering jay, one of the few birds who nested in the Court. "There is a troublesome new Hammer, recently assigned here. Goes by the name Daelan."

"I've heard his name."

"Young, ambitious . . ." Alcon gave her a scroll, and she unrolled it.

"And a pain in the ass wherever he goes, looks like."

"Yes."

She read through all of his reassignments, all the postings. This Hammer had seen more of Sor's Kingdom in just a few ages than most saw in their lifetime. Looking at the logs, she saw the problem. Jonn could not reassign Hammer Daelan without a willing Parallel to take him, and Daelan's reputation had likely already spread.

"Jonn wants us to send him to the 18th?"

Alcon shrugged his shoulders. "I do not know if Jonn really cares. He just wants him gone."

Eyrilia nodded. She thought through it. The easiest thing to do would be to force the Elder Hammer of the 18th Parallel to take the troublesome young Hammer. Not every chair held such power and sway over their corresponding Elder Hammers as Eyrilia. But Eyrilia didn't want to insert problems into her own Parallel. She had plenty already.

Eryilia closed her eyes. As if falling down the mountain, she envisioned every Parallel, every committee, every favor. It didn't make sense until she reached the very bottom.

"Summon Reli."

Alcon gasped. "Shit's Bottom?"

Eyrilia rolled her eyes, annoyed at having to explain it. "The

First Parallel is always in need of Hammers, Alcon. And they are the most out of touch. The First will take this Daelan. The trick will be convincing Daelan to stay there. To stay patient and not wear out his welcome. If he's reassigned again then the favor will come back to us. But the best type of favors are those that are beneficial to all and eventually forgotten."

"I see," Alcon said, nodding and waiting.

Eyrilia found the answer. "We will offer this Daelan the rank of Elder Hammer, after Elder Hammer Holo's reign ends. Give him that sea-soaked stench of a Parallel. Never see him again. Everyone's happy, and we all move on with our lives. I'll meet Daelan tonight. We'll send him first thing tomorrow."

"My Lady, that is Reli's prerogative, is it not? As Chair of the First Parallel?"

Eyrilia laughed. "Reli owes me a favor. Not to mention, a fresh batch of blue spotted crab."

7

———————

LAYALA

Layala retrieved the rope. Feet perched on sea rock and planted at jagged angles, her legs withstood the ornery tide, whichever way it swung. She wrapped the rope around her elbow, her hand, her elbow again, taut and steady as she was taught. The weight she felt told her there were four, maybe five crabs in the trap. Gulls passed overhead. Their flock flew low over the tempered morning water. Layala watched them for an excuse to rest. Beyond those gulls, the sun awakened after its brief pause, for the nights were short during the long months of Arou, the Swelling Moon brilliant but brief.

Behind her laid the enormity of the great mountain. At this distance, at this angle, you could choose to forget about it. No Parallels or ports. No Hammers. Not even Holo. Out there, eighty-three swim strokes from the beach port, the horizon was home.

The rope jolted and Layala returned from her reverie.

Faithfully, she resumed pulling.

When the trap broke the surface, she pulled the heavy cage onto the small islet and proudly counted. There were only three crabs, but they were heavy and mature. None less than three hands wide, all blue and spotted. "Good," she said, followed by a cheer, long and loud, her voice echoing off the waves, seemingly skipping forever into the endless sea like a smooth stone. She squatted and stared into the trap. "Beautiful."

The crabber had now seen seventeen ages. She was taller by a head than most of the men in the First Parallel, which was unfortunate: it was males who carved the Parallel's cavehomes and corridors; men who built the storehouses and market square. Every time she hit her head she cursed the builders who were long dead and wondered why she must be made to suffer in a Parallel made for short men.

"You can learn to bow your head, Layala." Her father, Thomas, taught her many lessons at which she rolled her eyes. Thomas was a practical man and could afford to be. He was short. Instead of learning to bow, she once wore a battle helmet she found along the shoreline. She wore it for many days and evenings at home until her shoulders and neck protested. She eventually traded it for another makeshift crab trap, the one she was holding now with three crabs, claws open, ready for their final fight.

There was only one way to collect a blue spotted crab without getting pinched or losing fingers. The crabber had to find a way to flip it. The task was not easy, but Layala was patient and committed. She shook and swerved the trap, careful not to rip or break it, till the crab she wanted flipped and landed upside down. She picked up the feisty, squirming creature and stuffed it into her gear sack, repeating the process twice. She tied the gear sack to a rock and let it float in the water while she retrieved and checked her other traps. One by one, she collected each cage, refilled the bait bags, and finished her task by returning all of her traps to the sea. Layala had caught ten today of differing species, more than expected. The Swelling Moon was known to alter tides and change creatures' behaviors. Lazily, Layala wondered if this was true for humans as well.

Tethering the gear sack across her torso, she jumped into the water for the return voyage.

OUT THIS FAR, before the path grew deadly, a swimmer could safely wade and measure the momentum of the tide. It had a wild pulse that could never fully be tamed. Now, the rising sun warmed her back. Layala gazed upon the base of the mountain, her ugly world, during the only hour of the day it looked beautiful. The smuggler relished her quiet, lonely view.

Central to all life Layala knew, both aquatic and land-based, the great mountain was a world in itself. Her brain could never fully comprehend its enormity. Much of it was clouded by weather, of course, elemental garments that both concealed and enticed, suggesting all the secrets Layala's shadowed feet had stumbled into over the last three ages of her wandering smuggling: hidden passageways to clandestine chambers, proscribed temple crypts for the worship of forgotten gods, or abandoned hoards of peculiar spices and stolen, spoiled fruits.

The kingdom's sewage pipe could not be seen from here.

Visitors complained of the smell in the First Parallel, and they had the right to. The stench was strong. The locals, however, cared little. Layala learned to call her home Wavelo, but most others knew it as Shit's Bottom, because the great mountain's sewage pipe finished near there. All the waste of the kingdom—shit, piss, bodies, blood, scraps, everything—emptied into a small cove on the southern side, pooling there. But the nose depreciated, forgetting what it smelled, and with that benefit, locals lived their lives without threat of the kingdom's more aggressive and present rule, which plagued all other Parallels. Even the more obvious smugglers like Layala were known but unbothered.

Facing south, her right, Layala couldn't see the pipe, which was blocked by the Fingers, three long shore platforms that angled off the mountain's base and reached far into the water, stretching like demented docks. Like docks, the first two Fingers were where most of the Parallel's official crabbing and fishing occurred.

Looking north, her left, towering cliffs shimmered blue and gray; philosophers claimed it was a fortress wall installed by Sor Himself. The cliffs also stretched southward. The mountain backed into the middle of these cliffs, splitting them, dwarfing them.

All of Arou's coldness and warmth, the mysteries of the rising world, reflected back onto the water's surface, scarred only by scattered skerries and rock stacks. Layala's long arms swayed through it, cracking the mirror.

"You ready?" she asked, looking back to her floating gear

sack. The smuggler stretched through the surface, breathing, holding, pulling, releasing, holding, pulling, the scent of salty mist, early and rising, the taste of telluric minerals, chipped and bleeding from tide-beaten rocks. Layala felt the crabs dragging behind her. Never pack more than you can pull, her father also taught her, and that was a good lesson.

Swimmers reentered the First Parallel through the northern swim port, which was a beach, but if the swim was long enough, or if the situation was dire enough, they could also re-enter through the mountain's southern muck pool and find a neglected entrance back into the Parallel. Swimmers would have no sense to swim towards the Fingers, where violent and turbulent seas crashed against unforgiving rock.

The route to the northern shore was no simple swim either; surviving it meant avoiding and embracing the tide's traps.

"Name them," her father once asked her, when she was still a child and still learning.

"I know them and can do it."

"Tell me," Thomas demanded.

The girl rolled her eyes. "Swim between FishTail and Crab-Claw and you avoid SwirlBait." She pointed at the sea marks as she spoke.

"Good," he said, nodding. "Shorter, with some danger, but you don't tire out. What about full tide?"

"Dad? Really?"

"What about full tide?"

"You don't swim out at full tide."

"Layala."

She folded her arms. "Swimming back, you mean."

He blinked. She knew he would stand out here all day until she recited it.

"Guhhh, wait for the push and let it carry you through SwirlBait."

"That's right. Very good. Tail and Claw are covered, and there's death just below the surface."

"Dad, I know."

"I know you know. But it's easy to forget when you're out there by yourself. The wind can change any moment. You might see threats you didn't plan for. Respect the tide. Watch it work."

She remembered now as she swam the route alone. Layala had felt the tide getting stronger as of late. The Swelling Moon approached with its full face and would soon lean into Arou for a nice close look. Layala and Thomas had never known why the moon affected the tide, but the knowing of a thing does not require its understanding.

Look and feel its pull. See it push and flood the beach stronger than any other season. The beach itself is never dangerous, until it floods, swirls, and vanishes.

She reached the beach without incident and laid on its warm sand. Her gear sack still strapped to her torso, she watched it bob around aimlessly as the shallow water tickled the shore. She looked at the cove and the sea beyond it. Her view was now reversed. It was neither stunning nor bland to her, it was just what Layala had always known.

Even staring out to sea, it was difficult to ignore the mountain above and behind her.

The kingdom's politics and royalty meant very little to Layala, let alone Wavelo. She knew the mountain was ruled by a king. This king claimed to be a descendant of the Great Mountain Builder, who many called Sor. Wavelo was known to others as a Parallel. There were many other Parallels, perhaps as many as fifty, as few as twenty. Frequently loot washed up, and occasionally unlucky bodies fell from the sky. Perhaps they were trying to fly. Hammers arrived every so often, but they did not last long, except for Holo, the Elder Hammer she had known since birth, and Pon, the guardian Hammer posted at the Parallel's beach entrance.

Whatever Layala collected, a portion went to her family and a portion went to the market for trading. Most she smuggled out. But not before Holo and Pon got their portion.

Smugglers' tax.

Everyone ate. Everyone was happy.

WHEN RETURNING TO the Parallel, all crabbers, fishers, and collectors would submit their haul to Hammer Pon. She decided first how much of the haul went to the kingdom and how much stayed with the Nail. Pon was a tired, careless woman who thrived in her role as the First Parallel's entrance inspector, for she gave it minimum effort. Never once had she asked for more than half, and she frequently asked for less. The more Pon claimed, the more she had to haul. Urgency came only when the Court or castle requested fresh sea fare, and today there was no bulletin.

Layala dropped two crabs from her gear sack onto Pon's table, upside down.

"Keep one," Pon said without looking.

Layala returned a squirming crab to her gear sack, already

twistingly full.

Pon added, "New Hammer. Tonight, maybe tomorrow."

"Oh, thanks," Layala said, nodding, glad she had crabbed today instead of tomorrow. New Hammers could be challenging, but most settled in over time.

Pon pulled her combat hammer and smashed the remaining crab on the table. Layala jumped from the scare that she should have seen coming. The crab's legs wiggled wildly as the Hammer kept pounding. Pon ripped a leg from the fading creature and lustfully sucked its juice.

"Hammer, sir," Layala said and left. Pon grunted as she sucked.

Layala entered the Parallel's passage threshold. Here, a rocky cave with a low ceiling quickly emptied into a wide, flat outdoor marketplace of barterers, community fire pits, and playgrounds. To the marketplace's immediate left, cavern entrances led into the corridors of the mountain's interior district. To its right, the ocean churned just below the rocky edge. Layala's familiar community space was still waking for the day, not unusual, since she often woke early to swim and crab.

Layala ventured inward into the mountain. Quickly, she turned left into a new corridor, then right, then left again. Again and again. The endless sound of dripping filled the candle-lit cavern corridor. Nothing else came. From here her task changed into a fight against boredom. She had walked these steps more times than she could count (though admittedly, most Nails cannot count very high). She did not know how long it would take to walk across the mountain's base. Thankfully, she travelled only to the third Finger, less than halfway across. The passage she was on now would still take many hours. The interior's twists and turns took her deeper into the mountain where it was coldest. Some candles remained but most were gone. The darkness could overwhelm, and the echoes of footsteps had been known to elicit madness, but long ago Layala mastered these fears.

The smuggler continued through the mountain's core.

THE SCENT HAD been growing stronger with each step. It mattered not how numb the sense of smell got in the First Parallel. Nearing the pool of muck was a fresh challenge for even the oldest, most steadfast Wavelos. Layala stalled near the corridor's exit that led toward the sewage pipe. She took little steps here and there, but leaned most on patience and instinct, as always, allowing her mind to build its defense against insanity and regurgitation.

When Layala was ready she moved forward, exiting the mountain. She walked a narrow cliffside trail far above the surface. Her footsteps fell on shaky scree. The mountain pebbles were flattened and stamped long ago but the hazards of slipping remained. She followed the path steady and true to the west on the opposite side of the third Finger to where the sewage pooled in the muck cove, and turned a corner.

She saw it, the kingdom's massive sewage pipe: a temple of waste and privilege and ingenuity. It was white and corroded from generations of ocean air. The pipe blended into the rocky mountainside that held it as if it were leaching its color; in fact, it would have been easy to mistake the pipe for colossal rockfall if it hadn't protruded off the cliffside at such an engineered angle.

A constant stream of waste fell out its end and emptied into the muck pool below.

Further inward to the cove, Layala drew nearer to the pipe. The trail she walked included an ancient archway that briefly fed underneath its shaft. She examined the construction and the craftsmanship as she passed. Many Nails doubtless died for it.

On the opposite side of this archway, Layala's journey ended. There, a lone rope dangled from above, from some unknown Parallel. Another world. All smugglers had their spot and this was Layala's. She pulled the rope hard three times and waited.

No answer.

"Typical," she said.

Layala sat on the ground of the trail, her feet over the edge. Time moved slowly at the bottom of the world. There was nothing to do but throw pebbles into the muck pool below. She could see vague shapes of creatures swimming, small and large, though it was never clear what they were. Some told stories of cove octopus, Layala called them mucktopus, scooting atop of the surface like slippery spiders. Layala had never seen one. If they were real, perhaps they were shy. Maybe the mucktopus were more like kingdom cats, free wanderers who scavenged between Parallels and did their best work without an audience.

When sleep took her, she dreamed she followed a mucktopus to its home out beyond the cove in a bubble underneath some rock stacks. It had a family to feed and care for. She tried to tell the mucktopus she meant it no harm, but in her hand she found a trap cage. The mucktopus younglings were terrified and held onto each other. Layala's hand would not release the cage. "I'm sorry," she told the mucktopus family. "I'm so sorry."

She awoke. It was the middle of the night, the moon bright, but not yet swelling. She cursed herself for sleeping so long and shook the slowness from her waking mind. In her gear sack the crabs still moved, though slower. She stood and pulled the rope again. This time the answer was swift. She heard the faint clang of a bell.

Layala pulled the rope nine times, one for each crab. She waited.

A bell clanged five times.

She pulled the rope once, accepting the offer.

More time passed, but the rope-tied basket eventually lowered. It held five goods: a small pouch of wine, a bottle of mead (likely watered down), a bag of mixed grain, boots, and a combat blade adorned with a creature on the hilt she did not know. Layala took everything but the boots, which were cheap in Wavelo's market.

Layala emptied the crabs into the basket, keeping one for her family. The crabs were lifeless but still living and would be good to eat for some time, as long as they didn't spoil on the way back up to wherever the basket was going. She pulled the rope once more, knowing the basket would ascend and return. Layala watched it go.

She didn't need to sleep, but Layala knew it would do her no good to travel back in the middle of the night. She would only annoy her mom, getting in late and waking her brothers.

She laid on the trail, the back of her head in her hands, and watched the basket disappear entirely. This time, Layaya slept deeply without dreams and woke with the first chilled rays of sunlight.

She promptly rose, rubbed the rocks out of her skin, and strapped her gear sack, which now felt heavier than before she came. A good haul.

Layala's return trip always felt faster, though she suspected that was just a trick of the mind. The accomplished smuggler was still tired and aching. She was hungry. She allowed, to her own muting objections, mindlessness. She walked for hours, twisting and turning through the mountain's interior corridors, the alleys and shortcuts, the long stretches of black and brown and stone, the brief stenches of humidity pulsing from acrid ore and slivers of crystal.

Finally, Layala's journey ended. When she re-emerged into the light, arriving back at the northern end of her Parallel, her home, it wasn't long before cruel fate brought her directly into the path of an unfamiliar face, the newest Hammer patrolling the outer district.

8

DAELAN

A base of stone and a plank of wood, the feast table was vast. Hammers and Nails sat together. Even the First Parallel's lone philosopher and priest joined the indulgent, midday meal. An ancient fish large enough to feed a smaller Parallel covered the plank. Its tail spilled over the side and reached the sandy floor. It was an enormous catch that managed to dwarf the table, even with fifteen or so gathered around it. The fish was roasted whole except for the guts. These were purged and saved for bait and, for those who asked, other esoteric uses. Pretty Nails, nearly nude, fed each other in the darkest corner of Holo's Hall, lounging near cracked canisters of Rho Dust, casually stacked and predominantly empty. Other Nails within the Elder Hammer's entourage plucked and blew into smuggled instruments, some likely recovered from the shoreline, others from the muck.

Laughter overtook much of the music, however, as did Holo's voice. It projected from his mustachioed, chubby face like a drunken otter.

"Haha! The Nail boy says, he says, 'Holo, sir, Elder Hammer, sir, there's not enough room. The boat's too small! We will sink!'" Holo laughed again, the loudest and the longest before playfully lowering his voice, saying, "I says, I says, 'Don't worry, boy. Just swim faster than the cove sharks!' Haha! Haha!"

The group erupted with laughter. Most had heard the story before, many times, but to Holo's credit, his proud, mammoth voice infused his tales with the gravitas needed to satisfy repeat listens. Even Hammer Daelan, who watched this treasonous scene of Hammers and Nails eating together from the doorway with disgust, allowed himself a small dry laugh.

Holo was everything Daelan had heard and more. He was inexplicably large. Not just fat, which was unusual outside of castle walls, but corpulent, like the bears that roamed the Tree-lands. But unlike those bears, Holo had many friends. He was loquacious and charming. He was lazy. He was a fool. He was no Hammer.

"Daelan, Hammer Daelan! Welcome! Join us! Don't be shy, son. Plenty of fish here."

Daelan remained standing at the door, leaning. A brief, awk-ward silence filled the room, but Holo gave it little space to linger.

"Well if you don't like fish," Holo, again, paused to lower his voice and reel in his audience before exploding with noise, "I have some bad news for you. Haha! Haha! All we have is fish! Haha! Haha! Welcome to the First Parallel. Haha!"

His laughter was loud and wet, like a crashing wave. The

group around Holo's feast table followed his lead, joining in an echoing chorus of laughter.

Daelan had seen enough. Without formal leave, he abandoned the indecorous scene and disappeared back into empty mountain corridors of the First Parallel. Daelan could hear Holo's echoes haunting him like a goofy ghost. Before Daelan was completely out of range, the last thing he heard the blustering fool say was, "Eyeballs pop like grapes if you don't overcook them."

IT WAS WORSE than Daelan imagined and more terrible than he was told.

The First Parallel was almost a free land. It was one thing for an Elder Hammer to debase himself. Unfortunately, that behavior was not unusual in the Kingdom of Kulloh-Sor. Daelan had seen similar behavior throughout the many Parallels he had served in. But to eat with the Nails, to grant them names, to let them come and go without consequence; no rule of law or fear for Sor's Justice . . . The Hammer's stomach churned the more he thought about it.

Daelan believed he was born to rule a Parallel, but with only thirty-eight postings, openings for Elder Hammers were uncommon, and the ascension line was long and filled with Hammers he had already managed to agitate. It did not help that Elder Hammers had a habit of living long, uninterrupted lives. A Nail could challenge an Elder Hammer in the Sharpening ring, but it never happened, for Elder Hammers were afforded the ability to find a champion in their stead. Worse, rarely did Elder Hammers even patrol their own districts. They primarily existed to reinforce the kingdom's power structure and, of course, to commune with the Court's committee that managed their Parallel.

Daelan envisioned himself as a much more active leader.

Someday he would show this kingdom how a true Elder Hammer would wield a Parallel in accordance with Sor's Just Society. It was no secret Daelan desired these positions. His frequent, unrequested correction resulted in quick movement throughout the kingdom, quietly and briskly, even before each Parallel's annual service requirements were fulfilled.

It was ridiculous, really. Daelan was not some problem to be handed off to yet another incompetent leader in some other sloppy Parallel. They were the problem.

And he could fix it.

Overnight, he could fix it all.

Gritting his teeth, Daelan punched the cavern wall of the First Parallel. He looked at his trembling fist before sucking the blood from his knuckles. This time would be different.

With patience, this Parallel is mine.

He remembered the note.

The stumbling through the courtyard.

The whisper in the dark.

IT HAPPENED NOT long after getting reassigned to the Court. The Society of Whispers, as it was called by those who had served there, and the epithet was correct. Not long after his assignment there, Daelan found a note in his private quarters inviting him to meet discreetly in the courtyard. He assumed it was a test from his new Elder Hammer and accommodated the command, venturing into the unfamiliar trails of the courtyard that twisted into darkness. He counted his paces and turns per the note's instructions. Feeling lost, his temper flared. His face flustered red. Then, through the maddening, controlled breeze of Court's dome, he finally heard that whisper.

"This is delicate."

The whisper jolted him. On instinct, Daelan pulled his combat hammer.

"Reveal yourself," he demanded to the shape in the darkness. Later, he would curse himself for the weak, wavering tone of his voice.

"Lower. Keep your voice down." A Lady of the Court emerged from the shadows. "You Hammers are all alike, you know. Dull to the ways of secrecy."

Daelan complied, lowering his voice, but not by much. "Speak, then. What is this all about?"

He held the note and threw it before the stranger's feet. She promptly picked it up, ripped it into small pieces, and dropped it into a nearby inlet of the courtyard's splintering pond. The papyrus dissolved.

"I hope you remember your steps back," she told him. Her face remained hidden in the shadows, but he could see the evening light reflect off her lips, which twisted into a smile. There was an air of elegance and gracefulness to her movements, to her speech.

"I'm not used to these . . . rendezvous," he told her.

"Let's proceed then. Shall we? Hammer Daelan, it is no secret you thirst for power. You were just removed from the 29th

Parallel, were you not? Ruffling old feathers again."

"A Hammer has no past. I am merely a tool of the King."

She sighed. Daelan could not interpret what it meant.

"Good," she finally said, stepping closer. For the first time, Daelan saw the seriousness of her gaze, and it moved him. This stranger grasped a form of power Daelan had always craved but had never yet seen.

She continued, "You are a rarity, are you not? A Hammer born in the pits of the Shield, nowhere near Sor's Crown. The son of a Hammer and a Nail would be a Nail anywhere else, but in the Shield children are omens. The boy was raised by his father and told he was important. The boy believed it. He became entitled. He became a problem in every Parallel he served, expecting only greatness and announcing every little flaw along the way."

"The Parallels are full of weakness. Laziness. Sin."

The woman shook her head, stepping closer. "There isn't a soul on Arou that enjoys the revelations of its own failures. You would do well to pace yourself. Earn respect first, then demand it. A leader—"

"Souls are matters for the priests and their temples. Let them bicker over who reaches the Muted Realm and who reaches Sor's Glory."

The woman smiled.

"A leader sends problematic, entitled twerps back to the Shield to die fighting the Wild Few, which is bound to be your next stop. But I can stop that. I can give you what you want. An assignment, a real assignment. A path to Elder Hammer. A favor, we'll call it."

"I regret coming," he said and turned to leave, feeling as if he was falling into a trap. Daelan was new to the Court, but he had already been warned by his new Elder Hammer the ways of its plotting people. There were no gifts in the Society of Whispers.

The woman raised her voice, silencing the chittering crickets. "Your ambitions stink like sweat. You so desperately want to lead a Parallel. Oh, it's so obvious. But, but, but... There are no openings and you are too young, among other, shall we say, personality flaws?"

"Say another word and you will regret it."

The Lady of the Court ignored his command, saying only, "The First Parallel."

He halted and turned around. This time, he approached her.

"Shit's Bottom? What of it?"

"I can move you there as soon as tomorrow. It's a journey. The pulley carriage only takes you to the 3rd Parallel, and from there you walk the rest of the way. Pack plentiful provisions. You will not see fresh fruit again for some time."

"Doubtless you want something from me in exchange? I'm sorry, Lady. You pursued the wrong Hammer. I do not trust whispers in the dark."

She stepped within a breath's distance of his own, and he saw her face in the full glow of the dome's false evening light. Striking, the line of her chin and the curve of her lips. In the false evening light her eyes shone like ice. He could smell the wine on her breath. She was not young, but not yet old either. And Daelan, still a young man, could only swallow and step backwards, crossing his arms.

The stranger replied, "You can trust there are many layers to this plot, most of which have nothing to do with you. We all crave power, Hammer Daelan. Leave it at that and do as you're told. Find truth in these whispers: you are wanted, you are needed."

The Lady of the Court left him standing alone, staring at the ripples in the pond, wondering how many secrets had been dissolved there.

SOON AFTER HOLO'S festivities finished and the feast hall was cleared of his entourage, Daelan was summoned. He found Holo still sitting at the same table, tapping a fish bone.

"You sent for me, Elder Hammer?"

"Just call me Holo, Sor-be-damned."

"You are an Elder Hammer. I will address you properly. Sir."

"And don't ever walk away from me again. If I call you to feast, you feast."

"Of course, Elder Hammer."

Holo looked Daelan up and down. He snorted and flicked away the bone. He fished for a nearby spilled tankard and refilled it from a decanter shaped like a kraken. Like the mountain itself moving, Holo grunted into standing. "Walk with me," he said slantwise.

The Hammers began their tour of the northern side of the First Parallel, the livable end, progressing through various cavern corridors, taking shortcuts through inner rooms Daelan would likely never remember. Eventually they found the market square along the outer district, which overlooked the water. Holo moved faster than Daelan expected, but he still paced himself, because the Elder Hammer was drunk and walked with a rickety rhythm.

"I imagine this is all a bit of a shock to you."

Daelan thought on Holo's words, began to respond, but was interrupted.

"It's a lot to take in, I know, I know, son. The smell of shit. The lack of kingdom presence. The freedom."

"I do admit—"

"You just stop smelling it one day, and then this Parallel smells like any other."

They turned a corner and entered the busiest section of the outer market. Daelan smelled, for the first time, something less foul. Smoky spices and bright, floral herbs. Salt. Holo waved to his Nails who smiled wide when they saw him. He shook their hands. He patted their backs. They progressed through the aisle and reached the overlook and rested upon the half-wall there.

"Look," Holo said, breathing heavily. "I give this talk to every new Hammer who joins us, not that we see many new faces. They usually send me either the youngest sprouts or the troublemakers. You seem to be both. Haha! I do wish to know your tale. Another time, another time. There are only three of us Hammers, four now, with you. Look at us! Four Hammers! Haha!" Holo hit Daelan on the arm. "We'll be stormin' the Wild Few any day now. Haha! Haha!" The Elder Hammer howled.

Daelan, feeling exhausted, waited for the laughter to die before asking, "Why are there so few Hammers? This is the largest Parallel. Certainly, you must need the help."

Holo caught his breath. "What do you see, Hammer Daelan? Really look." Holo gestured toward the market. Daelan obliged. He saw busy traders bartering food, beeswax candles, salt crystals, spice flowers, nets, tunics, boots. It was peaceful. It was pleasant. "We don't need help when we don't have problems," Holo explained. "It is important that you understand that."

"But you eat with them. Entertain them. Is that not too far? Sor would be—"

"Sor's not here, son. Look around. Sor's sleeping in the sky. And where are we?"

"Nails eating with you. Coming and going out of the Parallel. No order, no rule."

"You'll come around," Holo said. "And if you don't, you can leave in an age. Do me a favor will you?" Holo leaned in close to Daelan. He lowered his voice. "Take a bath. You smell like shit. Haha! Haha!"

Daelan's brows furrowed when he saw the joke. Holo bent over to breathe and wiped his eyes. "I love that one," he said. "You're dismissed, son." Holo hit Daelan again on the arm and left him. Daelan watched the Elder Hammer approach a trader, a young boy. He distracted the boy and stole a small rotten fruit. Holo turned back around to Daelan and winked.

Turning away from Holo, Daelan faced the open water and listened to its whispers.

"Layala," Daelan overheard a Nail say.

Layala? These Nails have names?

Daelan turned and saw her.

9

———————

LAYALA

When she approached to pass the new Hammer, he moved to block her way, extending his arm to formally halt her. He was tall, she noticed first. Layala was taller still, but not by much. The Hammer was handsome, she noticed this next, and bore no scars she could see. He looked, simply, like a boy near her age. The Hammer's expression was hard to read. His mouth reminded her, she decided, of a dark cove in unfamiliar waters.

"Sir Hammer," she said and bowed her head. Every young Nail in the kingdom, even in Wavelo, knew to tread carefully with the arrival of a new Hammer.

"Look at you," he said.

"The new Hammer. We heard you were coming," she said, adding, "Welcome."

"Where were you, just now? You're filthier than the others.

What's in your bag?"

"Bartering, sir Hammer. On my way now to submit to Holo and Pon, of course."

"Elder Hammer Holo and Hammer Pon."

Layala grimaced and privately cursed her own laziness. She should know better, but he caught her hungry and exhausted, as ill-prepared for questioning as she would ever be. "Forgive me, Elder Hammer Holo and Hammer Pon."

"And what did you trade?"

"Crabs," she replied plainly.

The Hammer's eyes widened. "Oh? I have been looking for you."

"I am a crabber," she offered. "They live in the water, and so must I." She raised her hands into claws and then pinched the air, a cute move and a risk. The Hammer ignored it.

"I am told Nails are only allowed to crab the Fingers. Doubtless you know this."

She searched for a quick response, but her mind halted when she felt the Hammer's finger slip into the strap of the bag across her torso. He slid his finger slowly down the strap from her shoulder across her chest and down to her waist. Perhaps only in Wavelo could a Nail feel violated. Layala stood as still as she could.

They come and they go.

She closed her eyes. When the Hammer reached the top of the gear sack, he yanked it open.

"Blue spotted," he said. His eyes returned to hers as they opened. "Quite the catch. You know, for a Nail swimming in shit, you don't smell too bad."

"Thank you, sir Hammer. You will learn that our cove is clean here. The water fine."

"Hammer Daelan, you can call me."

She met his eyes again and searched for kindness. She was not sure what she found.

"Layala, daughter of Thomas and Laya, swimmer and crabber," she told the Hammer, immediately regretting it.

"No," he said, shaking his head. That odd smile returned. "You are a Nail. Your name is Nail. You serve King Kulloh-Sor and his Hammers."

"Yes, Hammer Daelan. Forgive me." Layala lowered her eyes and bowed her head again. She tried to move, but he did not yet let her go, nor did he move out of her way.

"I brought with me an order for blue spotted crab. Find Hammer Pon at once."

She felt his fingers slowly release from the strap around her body. He did not move his frame, however, forcing Layala to brush her body against his as she left. Suddenly shivering, she headed back to the Parallel's port entrance to give away her last crab.

LATER, ON HER way back to her cavehome, dispirited after losing her last crab, Layala heard her name echo through the corridor. She soon reached her friend, Vann, a girl her age, who was already showing with child. Layala placed a hand upon her friend's belly as they greeted.

"Vann!" she replied. Next she stooped to Vann's belly, saying, "And my little Layala-la."

"Nice try, but I've already told you. It's a boy."

"But why."

Vann rolled her eyes. Layala felt the thrill of teasing and catching up, despite her own exhaustion. Her feet ached. Her shoulder was raw from the gear sack strap. Vann continued, "Lay, I look at you and I think, do I really want to make another one of you?"

"Funny Vanny, always so funny. You should tell Holo that one. He would repeat it for ages. I should punch you for that, but . . ." she stooped again, "I don't want to harm little Layala-la." As she cooed and tickled Vann's belly, Layala ripped her hand away. "Is she kicking?"

Vann cleared her throat. "He is kicking, yes. Doubtless asking me why I run around with the likes of you. Not that we run around all that much anymore."

A silent pause crested like a wave forged long before anyone could see. Layala stood but neither looked each other in the eye. Never the one to remain quiet, Layala didn't let it linger. "I know, I know. I've just been . . . you know, busy. Honest. Daddy's been getting older. I'm crabbing more. Momma is useless as ever."

"You see," Vann began, "this is why I don't want a daughter. I want my child to love me."

"Oh now, Vann."

"It's true. What hope do mothers have when they have a daughter?"

"That's just crazy baby belly talk."

"I am scared, Layala. I just . . ." Vann looked away, her eyes cold and tired. Layala, tall as a mountain, crashed into her friend. They held each other in the middle of the cavern corridor.

"Crazy baby belly talk. You have your boy. Ladada, we'll call him."

Vann snorted. Breath turned into giggles and suddenly there were two hugging friends laughing, howling, openly and freely. The unrestrained sounds of an unbothered Parallel. Their shoulders subsided and Vann gently pulled away, her face as red as a fish egg.

"It feels good to laugh, Vann. I'm so, so tired."

"I heard about Thomas. Is he feeling better?"

Layala's smile faded. Her heart quickened. "What happened?"

"That new Hammer. You weren't . . . where were you?" Vann's voice dropped to a whisper. "Tell me you weren't smuggling again."

Promptly and curtly, Layala interrupted her friend with a final hug and left without another word. She ran as fast as she could through the low corridor, her shoulders stooped but her head high.

That new Hammer.

Likely prospecting the port for defiant Nails. All new Hammers cooled over time, but Hammer Daelan ran warmer than most.

Upon reaching her family's cavehome, she noticed first the silence. The space felt smaller than it did even two days prior. Her family had only been in this space for a few weeks now, having rotated away from an open window towards the sea, as was common practice in Wavelo where all stood equal against the tides.

Thomas, and her mom, Laya, rested on a straw bed in the

largest room of the cave. Here, her family slept together. Her brother of nine ages, Silus, played on the floor with toys carved from fishbone, and Marin, Silus' twin brother, played a small stringed instrument no one had a name for. They did not greet her or even look her way.

"Well?" Layala asked her family.

"Daddy's sad about the new Hammer," Silus said.

"I am not sad," Thomas said.

"He is scared," Laya clarified.

"I am not scared!"

"Hammer Daelan. I just met him. What did he do?" Layala asked. She stepped closer to her parents' bed and found her father's face unfamiliar. Beaten blue and red. "Swell's mercy," she blurted. "I will kill him."

The boys stopped playing and looked to their mother.

"Of course not. To even joke about a thing like that," Laya said.

"I didn't bow to him," Thomas said. "I didn't really even see him. He had an order for blue spotted, and I didn't . . ."

Laya turned to her daughter. "Did you say something to that Hammer? Did you do something?"

Layala felt her cheeks reddening. Her mom could unlock a fury in her Layala could not explain nor control, and she was too tired to fortify her defenses. "This is my fault?" she yelled.

"Of course not, no, no." Thomas attempted to rise from the bed but instead made it only so far to rest on his elbows. "Your mother isn't saying that." He looked at his partner, and though his face was bruised and swollen, Laya must have seen his meaning plainly.

"You know what I meant, dear," Laya said. "I was just asking if you said anything . . . when he approached you."

"I am so sorry this happened. I should have been here."

Clumsily, she reached over her mother and softly placed a cool hand against Thomas' cheek. "Where did you tell him I was? So I know."

"That you were praying in the temple, of course."

Silus sniggered. Marin chuckled.

"Shut up, it's serious right now, Marin," Silus ordered his brother.

"You laughed first!"

"Boys," their mother snapped.

"He laughed first!"

"Layala in the temple," Silus repeated and scoffed.

"Hey," she said, setting down her gear sack, an ornery smile finding life upon her tired face. She slowly stepped towards Marin. "In fact, that's exactly where I was. The priestess gave me the Holy Kiss of Sor. Here, let me give it to you!"

"NO!" Marin jumped and backed away as Layala approached, her mouth open wide, tongue wildly spinning.

"Momma!" Marin yelled as she chased her brother. Silus was giddy as he watched. Layala abruptly turned and Silus' eyes popped. Now she chased both boys in the small space. As they ran, she glanced at her father and found joy showing in his puffy face. The room was alive with screaming and all at once it felt lighter, somehow brighter. It was home again.

"Okay, okay," Layala said as she slowed. She closed her mouth, puts hands on her hips.

"What a dud," Silus said, the family's favorite phrase. Layala's back found a cavehome wall, and she fell to the floor with an exhaustive sigh.

"What did you earn?" her mom asked.

Layala pulled up her gear sack and opened it. "Mead for Holo. Wine for us. Grain for our neighbors. A blade for me."

"I want the blade," Silus said with the hint of whining.

"You want your fingers more. Trust me." Thomas raised his left hand to remind his sons of the two fingers he lost as a young Nail.

"But you lost them from a crab," Silus argued. "Not a blade!"

"It was a Hammer. After he stole a toy from the market," Marin corrected.

Layala added, "Of course not, dumbos. His fingers were caught in a crab rope when the tide swiftly pulled. That's why we hold it like we do."

Laya looked at Thomas and Thomas shrugged his shoulders. Their mother said, "I'm afraid his fingers were lost to whichever lesson you children currently needed to hear."

"I was playing with a blade I found," Thomas began, but his children laughed and shouted at him. When the commotion died, Layala told her family she lost the last crab.

"I'm sorry," she added.

"Dear," Laya said. "That's not your fault. We'll find food, we always do."

The family collected itself in the strange, thoughtless pace that families do, though they moved a little slower than usual. Thomas was weak but steady. Their father had seen his share of injury, but he knew how to find his will again in the hardest and darkest of days. Laya grabbed the pot, the children their shoes.

They left their cavehome and joined the community kitchen, where the fire pit was always kept warm and the food was cooked and shared.

Wavelo, the only Parallel where no Nail went hungry.

Ripped bread with some sort of mush was followed by a sip of wine and though it was spent quickly their spirits were filled. They sat together near the fire and searched the stars far above the horizon, this warm Wavelo family, like broken pieces of the same shell.

10

JAH'RI

"Do your thoughts ever pursue the creature?" Felton wanted to know.

"Shyloc," Saz clarified, "or Pond Scum?"

"The latter. The thing that swallowed us. Ushered us here, into the Holster."

"Oh," Saz said, and he burped. "Right."

The Hammers rarely spoke of the creature who marked them.

Cot Hall of the Holster was otherwise quiet. Vaera had returned to her cot and mindlessly bit her fingernails. Rannold doodled on parchment. Stroom chewed on dried bovine. Sindhi studied the log scrolls of the Hammers of the 38th, available to any Hammer that could read. Others mindlessly wandered throughout hallways. Hammers with nervous bowels visited and revisited the latrines. Jah'ri laid alone again, returning in and out of memory, vaguely listening to Felton and Saz bicker and prod each other.

A mutual service of spirit; the day before a mission can make enemies into friends whenever discourse distracts from doom.

"Commander Prime said we owe it our proteins. That it marked us."

Saz picked his teeth with his boot blade. He nodded his head. "Yeah, well. I don't see no mark. Was all a dream, as far as I'm concerned. 'Nother Holster trick."

"Doesn't bother you then?"

Their conversation paused, briefly, before a grin captured Saz's chipped teeth. He leaned in. "How about it? You ever screw a Nail, Hammer Felton?"

"Disgusting. Can we return to—"

"That means yes."

Felton sighed, relenting. "The Kingdom does not discourage this. As long as one's Elder Hammer endorses the—"

"How many?" Saz said, pushing. No matter how Felton responded he knew Saz would twist the answer into something humiliating and deflating. There was no right answer with Saz. Perhaps this was what drove Felton crazy, but Jah'ri, overhearing, could only guess.

Contently and thankful, Jah'ri waited for their inevitable argument to bloom.

More empty hours burned in the Holster.

"One."

Saz slapped the table that buffered them. He laughed, howled. Felton shook his head.

"I knew it!"

"Drop it, Saz."

"You fell in love, didn't you? You and your little throbbing hammer."

"Cut it out."

"Fuck 'em and pluck 'em, that's what I always say. Bend 'em and send 'em."

"Sor-be-damned, Saz." Felton stood as if he would leave, but where could he go? No training mission. No laps to swim. No gatherings. All that remained was rest, and like all others, he dared not sleep. There was nothing here but anxious Hammers counting time in the sterile, cold halls of the Holster, nestled deep in the underground training facility hidden in the Treelands, awaiting the swim.

"Sure," Felton sat again, looking lost. "A Nail engendered feelings. I left myself vulnerable and put the entire kingdom at risk. For what?"

"Stick 'em and flick 'em."

"I do hate you, Saz."

"At least you've had one. Jah'ri over there fucks only fish."

Softly, Jah'ri snorted.

AFTER THE SHARPENING, where he won his combat hammer from Atan, Jah'ri was shackled and removed from the 5th Parallel, taken aboard a pulley carriage that transferred Nails and Hammers up and down the great mountain along a primitive cable transportation system that was rumored to be designed untold ages earlier by the castle's mysterious wizards.

When Jah'ri reached the mountain's windy plateau for the first time, he briefly saw the ancient architectonic temple—Sor's Staircase, its base carved out of the stone plateau itself. Beside it, a majestic domed city. The castle's towers rose high at its center, as if the whole structure had grown from the dome like a crown of stone. Sor's Staircase surrounded and occasionally leaned onto the castle for support, but eventually all of it was lost to the clouds.

Jah'ri knew it ended somewhere, somehow.

There was an entire world to see, but the Hammers didn't let him linger.

He was quickly pushed into a covered wagon and, from there, taken into the Treelands, inland and east of the mountain through a hidden trail that descended through a thick canopy of tall, twisted teryl trees, as if they too formed a dome.

The voyage was long, and he shared it with other young, soon-to-be Hammers.

None were like him.

Those privileged children were from families of the Court (he learned that was the name of the domed city beneath the castle tower). Upon returning from their pilgrimages where the truth of Sor's Just Society had been revealed to them, each child learned their destiny. Those in the carriage discovered they would become distinguished Hammers, likely fast-tracked to positions of power and convenience: secretaries and couriers, some would later become Elder Hammers if their family ties were influential enough.

The privileged children in the wagon surprised Jah'ri by speaking to him openly and thus showing him kindness. They shared their food. Jah'ri had never eaten so well, even from their scraps. They watched him consume and snickered to one another. Jah'ri did not mind. He quickly learned how to earn their laughs by leaning into the role of a desperate Nail tasting sugar for the first time. He learned there, in that moment after fourteen ages of life, that people of privilege desired attention most of all, for it was the only poverty they had ever known.

Jah'ri slept through much of the journey as the wagon traversed well beyond the Treelands and into a desolate region called the Shield. A wide land, open and flat, hazy and hot, with herds of cattle, training camps, prison camps, and deep-dug wells that turned into fire pits after drying. The Shield bordered the Battlelands. There, in a walled city, home to the kingdom's largest training camp, Jah'ri and his compatriots were fashioned and, over time, hardened into tools of the King.

Jah'ri progressed faster than the others.

Waiting only on his age and size to keep pace with his ambitions, he ate much and gained weight and muscle. Training led him into the Battlelands where he was asked to retrieve relics from the Wild Few stationed nearby along the border. Exercises increased in difficulty. Cadets often failed and some never returned, but Jah'ri was patient, knowing when to stalk and when to strike. He retrieved the fingers, toes, and teeth his quota required. They never asked him to capture scalps. Those he nicked willingly out of boredom and perhaps a desire to prove his own cruelty. That, to his surprise, completed his training.

"ASSUMING WE ALL expire tomorrow..."

"Hold on," Saz interjected. "If we're dying it won't be tomorrow. We launch late. Then we swim. It'll be two days, at least, before we reach Shyloc and die."

"Fine. Assuming we all expire in three days," Felton offered.

"That's better."

"Tell me your story, Saz. What is there to lose? There's nothing left."

"Felton, you're smarty, yes? More 'gence in the noggin than the rest of us. We all know because you tell us all the time. How smart you are."

"I have never once said anything even close to that," Felton argued.

"My brain ain't vapid."

"Do you mean vacant?"

"Do you hear yourself?"

"Speak, I urge," Felton pleaded.

"You Court-types. Always proving," Saz said with a refined accent.

"You non-Court-types. Always provoking."

Saz pulled in his chair, as if he could come any closer, his large arms bumping the table, the chair, the wall, everything. "I ain't no idiot. We both know Commander Prime listens even now. You want me to break the rules, so I get bitch-choked like Jah'ri over there. Sorry, bud."

Felton crossed his arms, looking impressed. "You are close to accurate."

A DECADE PASSED before the winds of the plateau called to Jah'ri once more.

Sometime near his twenty-fifth age, Hammer Jah'ri earned a position in the 30th Parallel, a place of prestige many called the Court. No longer did Jah'ri spend his days enforcing Sor's Just Society by plucking Nails, chasing thieves, and intimidating beggars.

The Court might as well have been on a different planet.

It was quiet and clean. He felt soft grass, plucked wild fruit from thorny vines, and, perhaps strangest of all, watched grazing animals saunter, unharmed by hungry hands. He smelled the fresh air of a sprawling lucious, tree-scaped courtyard that offered shaded and secretive paths for politics and plotting. The Court was also powered and lit by a warm glow. Maidens giggled at Jah'ri as they caught him staring at the strange bulbs of light. This was no magic. He had heard them call such things science. Jah'ri captured his cheer and eliminated it. Dutifully, he reminded himself of the mission, his true mission, quiet and lonely, and reoriented himself to its newest chapter, his latest posting.

The longer he served in the Court, he learned his station would not increase with the old methods of brutality and strength, because the Court did not celebrate such trivialities. Rumors and wit were the only currency needed in the Society of Whispers.

On patrols, he met secretly with philosophers. He studied scrolls and better grasped their words. He was told there was value to worshiping Sor with showmanship. He learned to love and bedded maidens and squires, ladies and priests, each teaching him something new about the kingdom in return for information that could only be whispered in bed.

He heard of the Court's families who filled their days seeking placement on the best committees, about the squabbles and petty betrayals that upended chair assignments and punished members by sending their children to the Shield to become Hammers. He was told of the territories outside of the kingdom, and the true numbers of the Wild Few.

Some whispers were better than others, but Jah'ri remained patient.

"What of the Swords?" he implored a temple priest, earnestly and acerbically, as his patience finally waned from the exhaustive and fruitless search. "The soldiers who guard the King directly. Where do they come from? How do I find them? They do not visit the Court."

The question was met with a disheartening sigh.

"My sweet young man," the priest replied tranquilly, kissing Jah'ri's face with lips calloused and cold, "this is a question whose answer can only be found in the Forbidden Parallel. Even the priests do not know."

"I'LL TELL YOU what does bother me," Saz said. "This place. This Holster."

"Not enough Nails, Saz?" Felton joked, trying to lighten the mood.

"We work our entire life, serve the kingdom up and down that shitty mountain. Then they send us to the Northern Arm, the Southern. The Shield. Everywhere. We shit in frozen holes and sweat in the sun. We punish. We pluck. We fight. We behead.

Our big day comes, don't it? We join the 38th Parallel, whoopee doo-dah, the sun in the sky we've all been staring at our entire lives. And what happens?"

"We don't actually go there."

"We don't actually go there!"

"You'll bring this up tomorrow, then? I'm sure King Kulloh-Sor is desperate for wisdom from Saz the Great."

"The Forbidden Parallel, supposed to be ours. Look out the window. See the whole world below. Take a piss. It's all I've ever wanted."

"Complete the mission and you will," Felton reminded him with a hint of kindness.

"Yeah," Saz said. "The mission."

The Hammers in the Cot Hall held their breath. A sort of peace filled the air before Saz thought better of it and quipped: "Will they let you go this time?"

"Hilarious," Felton replied, taking his time with the word. It was true, Felton had been in the Holster the longest. Commander Prime approved each season's team and, frequently, a few were left behind. "I will be amongst the first to enter the water."

"Pussywillows grow around the shore, I hear."

"I have trained the longest and am the most prepared. I will reach the isle first."

"Fish boy and I are going and we haven't even been here an age. Now that's funny."

Felton glowered.

THE SEARCH FOR answers took from him many ages of his life, giving Jah'ri new wounds and scars along the way, but every step took him closer towards his goal: the mysterious Forbidden Parallel, the 38th, where it was said the King ruled with his Swords, gazing down at the world Sor built from the highest point in Arou.

A long way for a head to fall.

An image Jah'ri frequently envisioned.

Would revenge change anything?

Would it bring back his mother?

Would it halt the nameless voice within him that lusted for blood?

No, of course not.

These questions haunted him, but he gave them little room in his mind, for he could not stop his own feet from climbing through the kingdom, nor his hands from reaching higher in every Parallel he served.

Though he was eventually assigned to the lower Parallels of the castle, directly above the Court, he discovered, to his dismay, the castle was mostly empty and had little need for Hammers: they shipped them to postings on the farthest territories of the kingdom, such as the Southern Arm, the Northern Arm, and back to the Shield to help train new cadets or protect against the Wild Few along the kingdom's border. He led battles against trespassers. Squashed rebellions. Supervised salt mines. He absorbed the sunlight from the Southern Arm and briefly considered dying there among the citrus groves or along its prismatic pebbled shoreline where the warm seawater pooled clear, despite occasional tar escaping from Arou's unseen fissures, collecting itself in bubbles like an offering to Sor's kingdom. The Southern Arm harvested and used that tar for buildings, for weapons, for fire.

In his thirty-fifth age, Jah'ri was ordered back to the castle to serve in the Parallel below the King. Here, seasoned Hammers were handed a peaceful and private position. Though life spans on Arou reached 150 ages, Jah'ri was already known as a seasoned warrior, respected for his discipline, and frequently promoted.

In the 37th Parallel, Hammers guarded and served members of the royal family who spent most of their days bored and bickering. Jah'ri frequently watched the youngest of Kulloh-Sor's grandchildren, Taela-Sor, aimlessly throw food out of a castle tower window, just to see what the gulls would do. He sighed and said nothing, ignoring the temptation to push the girl through the stoop, similarly wondering what the gulls would do.

The shifts were dull and long and little was learned.

But Jah'ri knew every day brought him closer.

Once the Hammers of the 37th fulfilled their service obligation, which was subjective and dependent upon available positions throughout the other Parallels, Hammers were rewarded with a rarity seen little throughout the kingdom: an open choice. They could stay in the quiet 37th and grow old, and some did, or they could move on and request any Parallel. Some returned to the 30th to live out their days enjoying the pleasantries of the Court. Others requested the lowest Parallels, for the lower the Hammers descended, the higher their status became.

When Jah'ri's obligation was fulfilled, which came sooner than he expected, he approached his Elder Hammer's quarters and kneeled. "Humbly, sir, I request assignment to the 38th Parallel. I wish to become a King's Hammer in his holy Parallel, to fulfill my utility beyond measure."

"Rise, Hammer Jah'ri. But do stand down. Anywhere else, I beg you. Go to the Southern Arm and taste the citrus. You don't want the 38th."

"It's all I've ever wanted, sir."

The Elder Hammer rubbed his hoary beard. His face looked like a dirge. Likely, the man's skin had not felt the sun's warmth free of tower walls since before Jah'ri was born. "You see, it's my job to talk Hammers like you out of it. The good ones. You're wasted there."

"Out of it, sir?"

"You won't come back. You can go anywhere else. Why would you go there?"

Jah'ri thought on the man's words. The Southern Arm. Temptation flooded the marrow of Jah'ri's bones, and he had to close his eyes. Hastily, before sense prevailed, he replied, "This is no impulse, sir. My only aim is to serve the King in the Forbidden Parallel."

The Elder Hammer had given this lecture many times, Jah'ri could now tell. He wondered how many ages lay in front of the man before him. Lately, Jah'ri often wondered the same about himself, a consequence, he suspected, of being stationed in the melancholic, penultimate Parallel.

"Very good. I'll inform Commander Prime."

"Commander Prime, sir?"

The Elder Hammer left without saying more. Jah'ri retired to his room in the castle. He leaned into a corner and looked out at the dark world. He cranked open a small rusted window, and the wind rushed him. Past it he could see nothing. He inhaled deeply, trying to steady his shaking hand. Emotion. He did not know that word, but it ambushed him. He fell to the floor and wrestled his tears, falling asleep there, his hand outstretched, as if reaching for a fallen combat hammer, a phantom from memory, as the wind continued to swirl in the room, pressing him down and covering him like a blanket.

"I HAVE ENJOYED this, Hammer Felton. Do you love me?"

"Okay, Saz."

"How much time have we killed?"

"Not enough."

Saz and Felton were in a stalemate. Felton could not leave the table first, because that would show defeat. Saz sensed Felton's predicament and fed his anxiety like Muloh-Sor salt in a battle wound. Jah'ri had grown tired of the entertainment, so he called Saz to him.

"Not now," Saz said. "I'm closing the deal on Felton here."

Felton slammed his fist on the table. "Everything's a joke to you, but I perceive the fear in your eyes, Saz. Feign all you want. You're pissing your sheets like the rest of us."

Saz nodded his head. "I knew I smelt something."

"Saz!" Jah'ri yelled again. "Over here."

Saz stood. He winked and blew a kiss to Felton while stretching. Felton shook his head as Saz walked away.

"Well, what is it?"

Jah'ri shrugged his shoulders.

"You son of a bitch," Saz said. "Interrupt me again and I'll throw you back to Pond Scum."

"Ah, so you admit the creature rattles your brain?" Felton bellowed from across the room, rather triumphantly, it seemed.

"Unbelievable," Saz moaned.

SOMETHING IN THE shape of a man approached Jah'ri. It was the first machinarch he had ever seen, though he could not say for certain what it was. Its gait stuttered. It looked to Jah'ri like a trick of the eye, as if Arou itself was skipping in and out of time. When it met him there along the muddy shoreline of a pond, Jah'ri understood this was a machine. He waited for words and one eventually came.

"Swim," the machinarch spoke in the voice of a man that was slightly altered and cold, like the echoes of a dungeon. The lone Hammer gazed upon the large pond. The body of water was dark and suspiciously serene, crowded by a dense treescape. Runoff from surrounding foothills and bergs must have sustained the pond, though he could not spy a primary source. Jah'ri did not know how to swim and said as much.

The machinarch, who he later learned to call Commander-Sergeant, seemed distracted by a waterfowl flapping just over the water's surface. "Of course," it finally replied, "a tool can only be controlled by its hand. A Hammer sinks alone."

Jah'ri remained patient. If the entrance test to the 38th Parallel involved swimming, he was in trouble, though he suspected this was merely a riddle, some puzzle to solve.

"Does this mean . . . the kingdom will teach me to swim?"

Whatever science powered the machine's body was not perfected, for Commander-Sergeant smiled with only half its face. "Walk into the pond, Hammer. You will either drown or find the way."

"I have never seen this much still water," he said to no one in particular. It mattered not, for the machinarch did not reply. Jah'ri nodded his head and kicked off his boots. His feet squished in the sludgy mud. He looked down and resisted an urge to pluck the worm that wiggled over his toes. It had been so long since he had felt that form of desperate hunger, yet it clung to him still. He came to quickly realize he was distraught as he trudged into the pond. His brain tried to outthink the steps of his feet, but to no avail. Soon, the water tickled his waist, his shoulders, his neck. He began to shuffle his arms and jump. Commander-Sergeant watched quietly from the shore, its half-smile still stuck. "Further," is all it said. Jah'ri took one last breath, a deep and harrowing inhale. Even from there, standing in the pond in the middle of the Treelands, the shadow of the great mountain covered him. Its obscured shape he could see through clouds. Perhaps it would be the last thing he'd ever see.

Then Jah'ri disappeared underwater.

The Hammer had stepped off some sort of platform and plunged. Darkness ambushed him. Coldness shocked him. Jah'ri refused to panic, because a Hammer did not panic. A Hammer was only a tool.

But where was the hand?

Quickly, hope fled him. He began to wonder if the 38th Parallel really existed at all. Perhaps this was where Hammers were punished for their ambitions, or where traitorous Hammers, unknowingly caught, were sent to die. Maybe there was no reason at all. He would die for nothing. This was the language of panic, Jah'ri recognized, so he cleared his mind.

His lungs burned, and his arms grew heavy as he fought the plunge.

Again, Jah'ri cleared his mind.

Pressure squeezed his skull. His mouth ached to open.

Jah'ri cleared his mind.

This was a test. It had to be. Something to solve, something to kill.

A tool cannot swim. A Hammer sinks alone.

Jah'ri had been fighting the descent, he realized. He opened his eyes, raised his arms, and let his body fall deeper into the abyss.

When his eyes adjusted to the stingy darkness he saw benthic flags tied to tight ropes that stretched somewhere towards the bottom. At once he knew this was the test. The mission. He would have to grab the rope and pull himself to the bottom, if only he had more time, more air, more anything.

Panic seeped in his mind again after his third grasp of the rope proved fruitless. He felt his brain shutter. Wildly swinging his arms in weightless nothingness, the tip of his finger brushed the tip of a flag. The flag, he promptly learned, was not a flag nor was it connected to a rope. The tentacle wrapped around his body. Jah'ri released whatever miserable air remained in his ailing lungs as he was pulled down into the muted depths. Out of the darkness a grotesque mouth opened wide. Jah'ri saw light behind its maw.

Death.

It is bright.

"CONGRATULATIONS," A VOICE said as Jah'ri awoke. "You are a Hammer of the 38th Parallel. The King's Hammers." Jah'ri sat up and squinted. He vomited water and coughed for longer than he was comfortable, but when he found his lungs he squinted into the light and saw a figure, similar in size and shape to Commander-Sergeant. This one wore a different robe and a tighter face.

"I am your Commander. You are joining thirty-seven other Hammers. Some have been training for ages, others for months. Some Hammers, like you, are new. When you are deemed ready, you will be selected for the mission. If you are deemed incomplete you will continue your training. On and on this will go until you are ready or until you quit, in which case your life utility will complete, and we will give you back to the creature that pulled you into this facility. You were marked by it. You owe it. When you are done with your body, the creature will feast on your proteins."

Jah'ri wiped the ooze from his face. "What is the mission?"

11

EDA OF PRIR

"The Soulless Kings bore a gracious title.
Call them them what they were: stewards, men-
dicants, parasites,
Of the Great Mountain Builder.
Dishonoring with their disbelief,
And their haughty wickedness,
Sor banished their diseased flocks to roam the
flatlands,
To gnash their teeth in an accursed and empty
realm,
Suitable only for a Wild Few."

—The Scrolls of Sor: The Ethics of Joeth-Sor,
Second Generation of the Reign of Sor
(rumored)

I f Eda heard another word about the prophecy she would shit her trousers and fling it at the Chieftain of Trisrca. His fanatical speech ramped again for what she hoped was its conclusion.

Unlikely.

The old man burned through words like a twisted stack of dry wood in a funeral pyre. Viceroy Eda, the unbeliever, considered turning to prayer in earnest for the first time.

The chieftain and his viceroys, the province saints, the battle captains, the tribal leaders—these were the keepers of Ornvia. Sor's mountain kingdom called them The Wild Few. Many donned a different title: The Wild Free.

For as long as Sor's line had reigned, his Nails, Hammers, priests, philosophers, and even courtiers of his kingdom had fled the great mountain and escaped to Ornvia's desert to join whichever community would have them. Many found Trisrca, the most civilized and developed community, east of the Treelands and the Shield. Refugees still came, but in much lower numbers. Now, almost all the Wild Free were born in this land. Most had only ever seen the outline of the great mountain in the distance; its plateaued castle and spiraled temple staircase were but unknowable, impassive thin figures often veiled by weather.

"How long must we sit here," Eda whispered to Mourad, her Listener of the People.

"Time cannot be measured by sticks," he whispered back. "Time flows." Mourad, her elder cousin by two summers, was tall and skinny. Perched from his balding head were two wide ears. Eda often wondered if they had grown larger since claiming his new, prestigious title.

"Never correct me," Eda quietly blurted.

"Of course, Viceroy."

They stared at each other until a puckish smile broke upon her stubborn lips.

"Viceroy," she repeated in whispers. "It has almost been an age and yet the word sizzles my tongue. When will that end?"

Eda supervised the province of Prir under the rule of the Chieftain of Trisrca. Having seen only forty-five ages, she was the youngest to ever hold the title. The viceroys were elected, but the chieftain ruled over all of Trisrca, also known as the Three Hearts, Einn, Veir, and Prir, until his death.

"Tsk tsk," Mourad replied and then clicked his tongue twice, a Pririan tick. "You must master the word if you are to master the title, Viceroy of Prir. Be proud and confident or you will certainly not keep the title for long. Time is already against us."

Us.

She rolled her eyes, suppressing an impulse to click her own tongue. Her cousin had comfortably settled into the ambitions of leadership. Eda, in contrast, daily wiped the beads of fraud from her brow. She asked her listener, "So now—"

An aggressive shush from the row behind reminded Eda to lower her voice.

"So now time is measured?" she whispered.

"No sticks," the listener said plainly, without looking. "The current pushes swiftly."

Their chatter faded, and Eda focused again on the chieftain, a centenarian who spoke with the thunder of an orator half his age. He would likely live another fifty summers, Eda knew.

Cruel, how Arou rewarded fanatics with long lives.

The chieftain's eyes were charged, and his square, blocky

face glistened from the sweat which also darkened the strands of his long white hair. She despised the fervent man and all he stood for but admired, at least, his grasp of the theatrical and his commitment to the stage. He spoke now in greater depth with more specificity than ever before about his momentous preparations for war, all of Trisrca's resources he had claimed, much to Eda's continual chagrin. The stockpile of weapons built, the horses bred, the carriages retrofitted. The people themselves, mostly the young, sequestered for his infantry.

For a war that will never happen.

THE SPEECH OF the Swelling Moon culled all with influence to Einn, the chieftain's province and the largest of the Three Hearts. The chieftain's greatest sycophants crowded the base of his stage and gyrated their raised hands as he spoke. Leod, the chieftain's most senior advisor, tilted back his head and planted his hands on his cheeks, an Einn gesture of reverence and surrender.

"Look," Eda nodded, smiling. Mourad followed the angle of her eyes into the crowd.

"You would be wise to align with Leod, Viceroy. He is a powerful player in Trisrca's game. You outrank him only in title, remember. Play the game, play the game."

Silently scoffing, Eda replied, "You speak of games like hunger is a card, life a gem. The Pririan people did not elect me to play. That was Viceroy Haasher's style, and Prir lost a decade under his rule."

"Haasher . . . odd he is not here," Mourad said, scanning the crowd with new realization.

"He hasn't been seen in some time, Listener. How do I know more than you?"

"Yes—" Scolding, an errant voice shushed Mourad, and he lowered his voice again. One eyebrow raised like the Flag of Prir atop of the viceroy's chamber, Mourad turned and scowled, just briefly, at the source of the shush. "Yes, the old viceroy has disappeared, that is known. But look around. Everyone has traveled here. I expected him. I was hoping you could—"

"Let me guess . . . Align? Make a show of it? A cozy, corrupt hug."

"He still has many followers in Prir, Viceroy. Not to mention important allies in the chieftain's chamber."

"That was the problem. Yet here we are, Mourad, discussing Leod as if we should host him for tea. The loogie just killed my reform order, should I remind you."

In protest, Mourad clicked his tongue twice. "Compromise does not mean defeat, Viceroy. Progress. It means progress."

Their conversation waned as Eda breathed through her vexation. Who was Mourad to tell her about compromise, defeat, and progress? Prir was tired of compromise and exhausted by inaction. Leave politics to the other viceroys. She found them in the crowd, Spineless and Brainless, Eda privately called them, with their own coalition of stooges who shouted plangent praises. The Province Saints were here, of course, many Eda knew from her own time serving in the role, some she didn't. She saw decorated Border Captains proudly wearing their arbalests draped upon their backs, more ceremonial than dangerous. Along Trisrca's border, they helped ensure Prir's brightest lives were needlessly spent on useless skirmishes with the neighboring mountain kingdom. Eda moved on quickly lest her temper grew.

She next noticed the visiting tribal leaders. Farmers, ranchers, gypsies, and hunters. They traversed across Ornvia's expansive desert lands every age to trade and strengthen alliances with Trisrca's leaders. Some came and went with no obvious purpose and in doing so provided an irksome mystery to the bureaucrats of Trisrca's nosy chambers. "Fruitless farmers playing hard to get," the chieftain was rumored to have privately said.

Her eyes settled on Faziah.

The leader of the Rho stood tall with black curly hair that was tied tight and pulled forward where it opened like a blooming flower. Her exposed torso, sweating from the heat of the Chieftain's Hall, blended with some foreign oils that shimmered on her dark skin. Large gold necklaces covered her breasts and below, a thin braided petticoat with strands of silver and lace and teal swirled as she moved.

What radiance.

She looked down at herself and found plain trousers, an overworn green tunic, a leather belt with a blunt dagger, and a necklace with the blockish black viceroy pendant. Her own tan skin was thicker than tree sap and lately felt more horse than human.

What misery.

Eda had abandoned her cape in her gondola for fear of the hall's heat and now cursed herself for leaving behind the only tasteful item in her wardrobe.

Perhaps Eda could sneak away, for she was to meet and host the Rho leader after the speech concluded, should the chieftain ever grant the kindness of a conclusion.

It had been Faziah who requested Prir's hospitality specifically.

Little was known of the Rho themselves. Whispers carried rumors. It was said they were Seers, a people who could harness visions. "Conveniently sourced by the dust of their poppies," Mourad quipped when he first heard of their intention to visit. He spoke of Rho Dust.

Far from the Three Hearts, the mysterious and controversial Rho previously sought an alliance with Prir, which Haasher, Prir's former viceroy, refused. Most of the scattered desert tribes preferred to ally with the Einn or Veir provinces where the splintering threads of their many faiths found a common needle. But Prir was the most progressive province of the Three Hearts and proactively renounced any political influence from the old gods and their many rituals for a promise of a free future that was equitable and logical. Many considered the Rho a perfect alliance for Prir, but Haasher had been dubious. Eda thought he simply wished to avoid unnecessary risks to his reputation. Eda, though nervous, had grown thrilled for their encounter in recent days. After all, Rho Dust was a safer drug than tar, the homemade smudge that currently gripped much of Prir's unhoused and orphaned citizens. Rho Dust could cause damage too, of course, but it was an aristocratic problem; its price withheld it from the reach of most peasants.

Faziah, then, would be Eda's first tribal visitor as Viceroy of Prir, and she would gladly welcome the leader, despite her own nerves. Eda knew better than to share insecurities with Mourad. The overpaid jester would only scold her for it.

"She looks our way," Mourad whispered. "The new Rho

leader."

Our way.

Eda clicked her tongue twice.

THE CHIEFTAIN'S SPEECH seemed to go on forever. Not for the first time, Eda found herself contemplating her home province of Prir and how it was so different from Einn and Veir.

Trisrca's provinces had always differed greatly from one another, but the gulfs between them widened as the chieftain grew older. The leader was desperate for his Holy War: the invasion of Sor's kingdom and the retaking of the great mountain from the false gods. It was a fruitless dream and, for Eda, a nightmare. Fortunately, the chieftain could not wage war without alignment of the Three Hearts' chambers, led by his elected viceroys.

The three provinces together made Trisrca, the Three Hearts. They shared the Lake of Life, which was fed from the Endless Range beyond Ornvia. The lake splintered into rivers that created the borders of the triangular provinces of Einn, Veir, and Prir.

Einn was a stately province with the largest and proudest temple, the cleanest streets, and the lowest crime. Province saints patrolled often and thoroughly. In truth, one could not live in Einn without the approval of the chieftain himself. Even babes were presented to the chamber and would pass under the chieftain's proper nose for his sacred blessing. Citizens' homes, built with sanded stone, raised tall by pillars, and surrounded by personal courtyards, served a shrinking population. Most homes stood empty. That was the true cost—and benefit—of the chieftain's zealotry. Einn no longer accepted refugees. Citizens of the Three Hearts could travel between each province freely, and many came to Einn each day to earn a wage or pray in the principal temple, but all who visited were watched closely until returning to the scrimpy oar barges that brought them.

Veir boasted a busier market square with streets that were often crowded morning and midday. The Lake of Life was deepest when closest to Veir, and long ago the province built a port to accommodate its fishing industry. The lake and its many rivers could be fished anywhere, but the long floating docks of Veir provided most of the Three Hearts' daily waterfare. Vier had always been the most naturally beautiful province, and for many ages that privilege provided enough pride to satisfy the ambitions of its vainglorious, solitary chamber. Streams trickled through the city and watered its vibrant vines, shrubs, and flowers, their aromas changing with the season and always in bloom. The trees stretched tall there and twisted far from their base, providing shade along Vier's warmest walkways. Vier was spacious, however, and offered plenty of escape from the crowds. East of the province, surmountable rock walls led to playable fields surrounding another hidden lake only Vier had access to. Horses were bred in the meadows there. Wild bears and boars were observed in the low hills of the Endless Range, and large spotted cats hung from trees. These animals were hunted, of course, but not easily. Under previous chieftains, and even when Eda's chieftain was a younger, earnest man, Vier was a neutral province that cared little for holy wars or political leanings. Ages passed and viceroys were planted. Veir's chamber now wholly served its desperate chieftain.

Then there was Prir. It was a scrappy but proud province,

grimy where Einn was scrubbed and churlish where Veir was civil. Prir's Garments District, with its cloth cutters and needle men, leathersmiths and furriers, shoemakers and milliners, employed most of Prir and produced clothes for all of Trisrca and even some of the scattered tribes of Ornvia. Being the westernmost and southernmost province of Trisrca, Prir was also the widest and most developed of the Three Hearts. Necessity made it so. Its population grew steadily every age and pushed against the seams of its borders. The few open spaces that remained were occupied by humble rows of crops. Every ear of corn, vine of tomato, or bloom of squash flower were needed to feed its booming populace. Difficulties persisted. Prir remained committed to the egalitarian principles of its eponymous founder, but children still slept hungry, crime grew steadily, and sickness spread, particularly in the flood season when the rivers would rise and the lowest streets disappear. Even in Prir, the poorest always suffered. Eda contended fiercely in her chamber debates that Prir had its troubles but it did not need to be saved. What it really needed was to stop funding the chieftain's endless and aimless battles along the border. Let Prir's tributes fund the reform it needed to raise its streets and reinforce its housing. Freedom, in the true egalitarian sense, could be attained, Eda often argued to yawning faces.

Little help came from Einn and Veir. And yes, it was true, Prir's chamber slowly warmed to the chieftain's rants. A religious uprising came to Prir, and Eda did not secure her election easily. The split vote was decided by chance rocks that landed in her favor. Little did the chance rocks know they were keeping all of Trisrca from war, from killing itself. That day, fate favored peace.

No, no. Leave fate to the children's tales.

"His tongue will live on long after we are all dead," Mourad moaned.

"It is too hot for this," she whispered, returning to the moment. Her pits could boil a duck egg.

"You cannot leave," he reminded her. "The province saints will revolt and your viceroyship will be threatened. This is what the chieftain wants. This is why he speaks without end. To test your resolve."

Mourad was right and she hated him for it. Eda could not leave. In Einn, every action and non-action was measured. Whispers led to rumors and rumors led to bloodshed. Leaving the hall before the chieftain finished his speech would be enough cause to incite unrest, particularly in those fragile times. The chamber would vote and the chance rocks would likely roll again.

Let the old man talk.

She steadied her resolve with a cross of her arms and an irreverent crack of her neck. When she leaned back for comfort, the chieftain glanced her way and paused mid-word. Now, it was his turn for his stubborn lips to break a smile.

"Friends, the hour is late. The True Gods have spoken. They have told me to finish with a blessing. May Zeit reach into our lungs and breathe into us." The crowd inhaled deeply and held. The chieftain waited, impossibly long, and then relented. "Exhale with the strength of Leit."

The crowd exhaled.

THE VICEROYS LEFT first, as was tradition, and Eda had never been more thankful for her privilege. She reached the chieftain, who stood at the exit and bowed to each leaving attendee. Eda put a hand to her heart, bowing slowly and low, leaving her head down for five long respectful seconds. Eda, too, could play to a crowd. When she rose, she saw the chieftain anew: wet gray curly hair, red drooping cheeks, and tired eyes. The only hints of his age. Otherwise the man stood tall, his shoulders proud.

"Stay safe, Viceroy," he said. "We can hear Prir's Swelling Moon celebration all the way up here. Doubtless you have increased your guards?"

"It is a joyous night for all, chieftain, the quiet and the loud."

"Have a blessed Moon, Viceroy." His eyes looked beyond her and with that Eda knew she was dismissed. Outside, the sun passed over the peaks of the Endless Range and she breathed in the fresh evening air deeply. The Chieftain's Hall was raised and overlooked all of Trisrca. In the distance, she saw fog settling upon the Lake of Life, which rested below her. A gentle breeze peacefully pushed the fog along the lake's surface.

Something beautiful in Einn.

Her moment of tranquility was ruined by the clicking of a tongue.

"Let us leave before the chieftain begins another prayer," Mourad begged.

"The leader of the Rho," Eda said, looking.

"It will take her some time to leave the hall. It is her first visit. The chieftain will likely steal a few minutes with her. Nothing we can do. I have sent word to her company. They will meet us at the docks in Prir."

"You are useful, after all," Eda quipped. "I wish to refresh before I meet her. I smell like a horse bathed in sweat."

They began their short return journey to the viceroy's gondola via the Nobles' Corridor, a private walkway with a stone slab that was brushed white and cut through a wide rose garden that ended at Einn's dogmatic docks. Beyond each side of the garden, province saints stood watch on tall lookout posts. They reminded Eda of the towers along the border where the daily battles raged.

It did not take long to summon her memories.

How she struck a Hammer who rushed her.

How she held him until his heart surrendered.

How her tears fell into his wound.

How she swore off the shedding of blood, innocent or otherwise, for as long as she would live.

"The garden is more beautiful in the evening, I'm afraid," Mourad said.

Eda balked. "This garden should be a row of homes. Or growing food."

"Tsk, tsk," he said, before clicking his tongue twice.

They reached the entrance of the docks and saw, to Eda's fright, a small, hooded group huddled near their gondola. It was already hard to see in the dusk, but Eda knew it was Faziah and her company of three female servants. Eda glared at Mourad before approaching Faziah with a short bow.

"I apologize, Faziah of Rho. I did not know you were waiting. I was told—"

Mourad cleared his throat. Eda interpreted the gesture. She began again in the Sacred Desert Tongue. "Leader of Rho, were you waiting long?"

"Viceroy of Prir," Faziah said, returning a quick bow. Faziah was taller up close and more stunning in the shimmering moonlight. Her eyes reflected a glint of purple. "A short wait after a long speech. We were just enjoying your Lake of Life. The fish jump as if looking for a plate."

"The fish put on a show at dusk. I must admit, Leader of Rho, they can be a nuisance and jump into the boat. They have been known to knock a man off his own ship."

"Good thing we are not men," Faziah said. She offered Mourad a friendly smile. "We have much to discuss, Viceroy of Prir." Faziah turned and scanned the land behind her, the chieftain's elite province. "And I'd rather leave Einn before we do."

"Of course," Eda said in the Trisrca tongue out of habit. She extended her hand and the gondola master opened the door. It wasn't long before the boat was pushed away from the dock, beginning its hour-long journey back to Prir.

Eda left them in peace and took Mourad to the front of the gondola, where, regrettably, she retrieved her very tasteful cape and draped it over her tired shoulders. It was too late to make a better first impression.

That's the thing about taste and culture. It's too easy to leave in the boat.

"She likes us," Mourad whispered in her ear, low enough for only Eda to hear.

"I still don't understand what she wants with Prir," Eda whispered back.

"She is a new leader, much like you."

"Meaning?"

Mourad smiled, shrugged his shoulders, and clicked his tongue. "Anything is possible in the early months of leadership. All I have heard of Faziah is her beauty. This is good. It means no one knows her yet. Her quest for an alliance might be genuine."

Eda gazed at Faziah as they whispered. She returned Eda's gaze with her own.

"Nothing comes easy," Eda reminded her listener. "Nothing comes free."

An hour passed. The closer the gondola approached Prir, the louder the province's noise echoed off the lake's surface. Drumming, chanting, cheering, fire breathing, screaming, singing, thousands of Pririans pushing and pulling in the Revelation of the Swelling Moon. Prir was well lit and would not sleep for three nights.

Eda stood and spoke loudly to her guests. "Prir is the blood that flows through me, but even I would not walk these streets tonight. In the morning, you will receive a proper tour of our great province. Until then, follow us closely until we are inside the chamber."

Their gondola was tied to the dock. The party exited the ship. Faziah said nothing but followed the viceroy and her Listener of the People to their chamber, which rested close to the water. The guests from Rho were shown their quarters and a servant informed them when and where dinner would be. The groups bowed and departed.

"Mourad," Eda said as they walked away together.

"Yes, Viceroy?"

"Leave me alone. I deserve an hour of peace."

"We should prepare. It is your first tribal visit, and I believe I have learned more."

"You prepare," she said and patted his shoulder. "I need to piss."

12

EDA OF PRIR

Lavish dinners had been a hallmark of Haasher's reign as viceroy before her. Only once, as a Province Saint, had Eda attended such a meal. Platters, decanters, rotating courses. Eda had never seen so much food. The sight of it turned her stomach and she consumed very little that night, for nothing upsets an appetite more than discovering the corrupt principles of an inspiring leader. When elected viceroy, Eda promised herself that she would eat what the commoners ate: little food with lots of spice. Eda's chamber dinners would eschew five courses and endless decanters of wine. The day she ate five courses would be the day all of Prir did.

But principles have a funny way of failing under the onslaught of busyness and the absence of planning. Eda had not once considered the menu for tonight's dinner to host the visitors from Rho. When the first course arrived, overflowing dishes of roasted beets and carrots over fishtail, Eda gulped. This was exactly the excess she had been opposed to from the beginning.

Mourad, sensing her discomfort, whispered, "Alliances are hard to secure on an empty stomach. Eat, Viceroy. Apologize to the poor later."

Eda grimaced at Mourad. She sensed her cousin hungered for more than just dinner, perhaps a luxurious life neither of them have ever known, nor should claim. It worried her.

"Compromise," she finally said.

As was the custom, the Rho company waited for the evening's host to take the first bite. Eda grabbed her forke and regretfully punctured a soft carrot. She bit and tasted the herbs, the warm sweet juices. She could not help but close her eyes, for the sharp and savory flavor overwhelmed her tongue, and when she opened her eyes anew, she found Faziah staring at her with a fond and patient smile.

"It is good," Eda said. Satisfied, the company formally began its dinner.

Light discussion accompanied the meal as each side of the table took turns sharing and querying each other. Eda and Mourad learned more about the Rho, their customs and rituals, their poppies that grow in the long months and their other crops, like garlic and onion, that sprouted in the short months. Faziah and her servants learned of Prir's Garments District and Arts Alley where Prir's entertainers performed stories on stage and painted and sang for the joy of the people.

"The chieftain hates it," Eda bemoaned. "But only because he doesn't like to share the stage." She realized she may be showing her hand too early, and the look on Mourad's face told her to be more cautious. Inching slowly, he tried to push her wine goblet away from herself, but failed.

The second course—dusted lamb and pickled eggs—arrived expeditiously, as did the wine which continued to flow freely into every goblet, mostly Eda's. The third course—buttered duck and potato mash—was eaten slowly, a sign that bellies were filling. Eda whispered to Mourad who briefly left the room and found the servants. He informed them that fourth and fifth courses would not be needed. "Dessert is welcome at this time. And you!" Mourad pointed to a young servant holding a decanter. "If I see you fill the viceroy's goblet again, I will beat you over the head with my shoe."

Mourad returned to the dining room and to his horror, heard Eda openly criticizing the chieftain's prophecy with the slightest slur of wine speech. "... children's tales, Faziah. If he were ever to look at the ground instead of the stars, he'd find—"

"I asked for dessert," Mourad interrupted. He sat and loudly scooted in his chair, aggressively smiling at his guests. The scolded servant entered the room, head lowered, and began slowly refilling guest's goblets first.

"Thank you, Listener," Faziah said. "The viceroy was just sharing her distaste of prophecies."

"Perhaps a bit rude when hosting Seers," Mourad offered. Eda met his glare.

"Not at all," Faziah returned her attention to Eda. "You honor us with your truth. There are many types of Seers. Not all deal in prophecies. Some see the future, some see the past, some see people."

"People, what does that mean? People? We all see people." Mourad asked, perhaps a bit too suddenly, and he felt hot around the collar.

Faziah searched for the words, seeming to translate between languages in her head. "See through people. Their deceits, their ambitions."

"Sounds a lot like what my listener here does. Are you looking for a job?" Eda quipped.

"I might be after this dinner," Mourad said in the Trisrca tongue.

The servant reached Eda. "Forgive me, Viceroy Eda. My decanter is empty. I will return."

"Please do!" Eda replied, sternly, her red tongue dry and thirsty.

The servant quickly looked to Mourad who cleared his throat and said, "Just bring the damned dessert, will you?"

The servant left the room in haste, replaced almost immediately by a young Pririan girl who set an ornate covered platter on the table. When uncovered, Eda saw scattered pieces of salted sweet orange candy, powdery on the outside and rocklike on the inside. When broken open, as they were now, the candies shone like crystals against the flickering candlelight.

It was an unfortunate choice.

Eda had learned early in leadership, as a province saint, many dirty secrets. Such as how Trisrca's salt was imported from Sor's mountain kingdom, while at the same time, Sor's Hammers killed endless Pririans along the border. All the useless death caused by warring neighbors, and yet, at the same time, trade partners. Trisrca's chambers claimed to use middle-traders who stood between enemies, but Eda knew that truths were often hard to find in the halls of leaders where commerce was king.

"Forgive me, I think I'm just too full. Please go ahead," Eda insisted, suddenly feeling very sober. Faziah's company studied the salted candy and they too abstained. Mourad clicked his tongue and reached for the sweets. Eda tried to stomp his foot underneath the table, but Mourad was too fast. He moved his foot and plopped a candy in his mouth.

"I'm afraid my cousin will eat until he pops," she said.

"Ah," Faziah said with a bright smile, her widest and most genuine of the night. "I also keep my family close. My servants are my sisters."

"Three sisters, wow," Eda said. "I have neither brother nor sister. Only an older cousin I can't seem to evade."

Faziah's sisters chittered. Faziah explained, "I have fifty-three sisters and twelve brothers."

Eda turned and smiled at Mourad. Her Listener of the People must have recently lost his hearing. Mourad sensed his cousin's frustration and whispered sweetly in the Trisrca tongue, "Preparation." She rolled her eyes.

A few more minutes passed, and Eda saw plainly the meal was done. She stood and announced that the evening was complete. The rest of the group followed her lead and moved away from the table. Eda said, "Faziah, Leader of Rho, may I borrow you before we all retire? I have ordered water twist and ginger to settle our stomachs."

Mourad raised his eyebrows. "Preparation," she whispered back to him, and then louder, "You are dismissed, Listener. Thank you for your service." Eda bowed with a formal good-night gesture Mourad had never seen before.

"I see," he said and clumsily returned the bow to Eda. He bowed to Faziah and her sisters before leaving the room with a faint spirit of defeat. Faziah also released her sisters, and behind them the doors closed. Eda and Faziah were alone. In a moment of sheer bravery, influenced perhaps by the barrel of wine she had consumed, Eda locked arms with Faziah and guided her to the balcony overlooking the Lake of Life. Water twist waited for them on the table near the couch where they sat, their knees touching. Eda poured her a glass. She handed the glass to Faziah, their fingers touching at the pass, and then poured her own.

"A'scoullee!" Eda said with a hint of coquetry, and they clinked glasses. "It means 'drink and live' in our tongue."

"This is the part of the evening when we say what is really on our minds," Faziah said.

"What we want, yes. You are a Seer. You must know what I want."

They both drank.

Eda, who had never been braver, placed a hand on Faziah's knee. "What do you want, leader of the Rho?" Eda considered all the customs she was breaking, the risks she was taking. Whatever happened next, Eda could only blame herself, and the fear of it all began to surface in the seconds Faziah did nothing.

Thanks be to all false gods in this realm and beyond, Faziah placed her hand on top of Eda's and massaged it with her thumb.

She reached forward with her other hand and placed it on Eda's knee. "I want, so desperately, Viceroy, to talk to you about the prophecy."

13

JAH'RI

Jah'ri soaked in the moonlight. He breathed deeply, the forest air sweet and chilled, while a breeze picked up over the nearby pond as if it too were exhaling. He stood alone in the Clearing. As alone as they'd let him. Commander Prime granted the King's Hammers thirty-eight minutes above ground, so they had run up the long subterranean ramp, kicked open the unlocked hatch door, and promptly scattered away from one another. There would be no evening training in the Clearing tonight. No laps in the pond. Only fresh air with space to stretch and no threat of retribution. No walls. No cots. No Commander.

Thirty-eight minutes of unstructured time.

Jah'ri squatted and brushed the grass with his hands. The dark teryl trees just beyond the Clearing rustled. He wondered what creatures roamed beyond them. Certainly, Hammers must have tried to escape the Holster and abandon its mission. Perhaps the threat of returning to the creature hidden deep in the pond was enough to calm the tempest in all of them, but he wasn't so sure. Would any of the Hammers from his cohort seek escape? Despite Commander Prime's best efforts, weakness persisted within all flesh, even in the King's Hammers. Jah'ri just wanted it all to be over. Soon it would be.

The breeze picked up.

Footsteps approached from behind.

Saz was the only Hammer, it appeared, without much need or understanding for companionless solace.

"That pond can blow me all night."

"Ok, Saz."

"Fuck the Holster."

"Not much time left. Just enjoy it."

"You don't get it. I'm not going back down there."

It took a few beats before Jah'ri realized Saz wasn't joking. Jah'ri wasn't sure what his role was here. If Saz wanted to break Commander Prime's protocol, what was that to him? "Fine," Jah'ri said. He left him, walking over to a new spot closer to the pond. Saz didn't follow. Jah'ri shrugged off the interaction and returned to his own thoughts, watching the water's edge. Eerie how the moonlight shone right to the shore before dying on the dirt. Unexpectedly, his dream returned to him. The fish and the bird. The sand and the shore.

Jah'ri decided to attempt meditation, a practice he learned from the priests of the Court and later refined in the Southern Arm. Meditation, for him, was a controlled dream, an exercise of the mind that built inner strength and greater understanding of the world, his mission, and his obstacles. Meditation was not a vehicle, as the priests of the kingdom claimed. Jah'ri could not transcend into other worlds or become a new person or animal or entity. He could not communicate with the gods. The priests told him he had a soul. "Oh really?" he quipped and laughed. "The priests, maybe. Not us Hammers." Forget the spiritual realm. Jah'ri found that if he slowed his heart and steadied his breathing, he could fight any fight, temper any anxiety, and overcome the haunting of any dream. Through this method, he learned to capture his feelings, as if into a bottle, and plug them with a cranial cork. You could put many things into a bottle, Jah'ri had learned. Fear, lust, sorrow, loneliness, hate. Sometimes the bottle burst and you had to find a new and bigger bottle.

Jah'ri counted his breaths. He felt the hair growing on his head. He followed the blood flowing within him and traced its journey through his body. At once he was aware of everything and nothing. Eyes wide open and shut. Arou was a ball in his hand.

Flashes.

Blood in the shore, flowing with the tide, the ocean in the clouds, something with eyes, rising through time. And teeth.

Jah'ri was floating, he realized.

"Time," Commander Prime announced, and Jah'ri returned to his body sitting along the shore of the hidden pond inside the kingdom's forest. He heard a chorus of grunts. Jah'ri stood. Whatever he just experienced did not help him and maybe nothing could. Was that the point? Tomorrow Jah'ri's journey would end. It was better to know, he decided. He walked back, passing Saz who remained steadfast in his disobedience, staring at the moon, or perhaps nothing at all. Jah'ri saw Commander Prime approach Saz, but Jah'ri didn't stick around to watch. He returned to the Holster through the hatch and descended the ramp.

All Hammers did eventually return. After one last pass to the latrines without anyone saying much of anything, the lights dimmed and the Hammers found their cots. The mist would soon come, and they would all sleep. It was the only way any of them would, especially tonight. Jah'ri heard a pattering of soft crying and anxious prayers. Soon cots began to creak as bodies lifted from them. Hammers found each other in the darkness. Jah'ri did not know who. It did not matter. Their grunting, their breathing, their straining, echoing throughout the hall. Another pair of Hammers found each other. And more. Some advances were unwelcome, leading to arguments and fights. A madness of yelling and cursing and fighting and fucking filled the Holster. Jah'ri dug his head under his pillow.

"Turn on the mist," he said to no one in particular. "Or we will all die here tonight."

A hand found his back and caressed. Was it Vaera? Rannold? Another? The hand lowered and he grew strong. The madness started to take him, too. He felt weak from desire and yearned for more, for everything, faster and harder.

The mist came. He heard a sigh.

"Some other time?" asked a whisper in the dark. The Hammers returned to their cots and sleep took them all.

As Jah'ri faded into sleep, the memory of his first day in the Holster came rushing back to him.

JAH'RI WIPED THE ooze from his face. "What is the mission?"

His question was not answered. Not right away, at least. Jah'ri was promised details of the mission, what he came to the 38th for, what he spent his whole life chasing, but he would have to wait a little longer. There were other Hammers who were new to the Parallel, too, and Commander Prime scheduled a formal briefing. Until then, he would remain in the holding cell.

Jah'ri managed to learn he was deep underground, below the pond of the creature that marked him. Another Commander-Sergeant (there were many machinarchs here, he discovered) explained that Hammers trained outside every day, but the distance was far and the ramp was long. In time, Jah'ri would learn the way to the Clearing and the schedule of his training.

"Training for what, exactly?" he asked, but received no reply.

Days passed.

He sat alone in a dark room that progressively felt more like a trap or small prison where he was visited by walking machines that left him sustenance and talked little. One day, the door opened wide and Jah'ri was led to a bright open facility that was gray and sterile. As he passed through a long hallway with various openings he caught glimpses of the Hammers there. They watched him walk by and after he passed he heard whistles and chatter.

Jah'ri then entered a briefing station with two other Hammers already waiting inside. Commander Prime, who he had not seen since he awoke for the first time in the Holster, formally began the briefing.

The 38th had only one mission, the machine explained. Swim into the Sea of Cashmu, find the volcanic Isle of Brecca, collect the breccel from its base, and return to the castle. Once they returned, the Hammers would seek the wizards in the 35th Parallel who would mix the mineral with steel and forge an unbreakable blade.

Then and only then, a Hammer became a Sword.

Swim, collect, return.

"Simple," Commander Prime concluded.

"That's it?" Jah'ri asked out of turn. He realized, embarrassingly, the foolish impulse and tone of his question before lowering his eyes.

The machinarch ignored him and continued. "Ninety-seven point three percent will fail."

"Show me your work," Saz said, a brave joke.

Commander Prime replied, "You can trust that I have correctly calculated the numbers."

"I am so relieved," Saz said. Commander Prime slammed Saz's head on the table.

Saz fell to the floor, cursing.

This was the first time Jah'ri had really looked at the other Hammers in the room. Hammer Saz had a strange form. Large arms, small neck, missing teeth. He had an accent from the Southern Arm, which meant he likely worked on the boats before joining the Hammers, or perhaps he helped scoop the natural ocean tar that pooled there. Jah'ri would never ask, of course, because Hammers did not have a past. The other Hammer, he would later learn, was Sindhi. Both he vaguely recognized from the halls of the 37th Parallel and perhaps other postings throughout his many ages of service. He had never spoken to either of them, as was proper of a Hammer in the Kingdom of Kulloh-Sor, particularly one looking to avoid unexpected revelations.

The machine calmly continued the briefing and again summarized the details of the mission: the Hammers would enter the sea through the Cove of Kullan-Sor on the eve of the Swelling Moon. They would swim to the Isle of Brecca.

"This is where your life utility will likely complete. Congratulations."

The room was quiet.

Commander Prime continued. "I see I have failed to provide adequate context. Protecting this isle is an ancient and giant sea beast. It circles the volcanic cone in what is theorized as perpetual slavery. Our philosophers call it Shyloc. Its form will be revealed to you in your dreams. We do not know whence it came. What the kingdom does know is that Shyloc is a fierce guardian who will destroy you. You will endeavor upon this quest knowing failure is dishonorable. For it is written in the Scrolls of Sor: a warrior's blood enriches the soil but spoils the sea."

Quietly, Saz returned to the table.

"From the two point three percent of you that avoid Shyloc, reach the isle, and escape with your reward, only one point eight percent on average will make it back to land. Those who return with a vial of the breccel will serve King Kulloh-Sor as his own Sword. Ask your questions."

Sindhi spoke first. "Why must we swim? We can charter a ship from the King's fleet and wage war against this beast."

"Kill it for once and for all," Saz continued the thought, cautiously, his hand held underneath his nose. "We've stomped out uglier sins in the Shield."

"Because it's a test," Jah'ri replied in realization.

"Correct, Hammer Jah'ri." Commander Prime's eyes settled upon him. Jah'ri did not yet know how to interpret its gaze, but the machinarch stalled as if stuck in contemplation.

It spoke again. "My King's Hammers: You will need this confidence when you are wading in the rising electric waters of Shyloc. But do not forget that, first, you are but tools of the King. Blunt instruments are not designed to think. Only the hand holding the tool can change its course. We are finished here."

Jah'ri, Saz, and Sindhi looked at one another. "Well, shit," Saz said.

"Could be worse," Sindhi offered.

Jah'ri said nothing, and training began shortly after.

14

JAH'RI

The water. The sky. A bird. Its beak. Stabbing into him again and again.

Jah'ri had no choice but to wait and watch the dream conclude. The bird would feed. Jah'ri the Fish would slowly fade and watch the water abandon him until death granted release. But this time, the bird never left. It stopped eating. It stared at Jah'ri the dying fish, guts hanging from its beak.

"Terror," it calmly said.

Jah'ri woke to the sound of vomiting.

It was still dark. Rannold maybe, or Felton, were on the floor in pain. They will surely die early in the swim, he thought. Perhaps that is what their dreams showed them, or maybe all they saw was nothingness, a blackness that rattled them worse.

Fear and fate hovered above their cots. The fear was in him

too, and it frustrated him. The shaking was stronger than he expected. There was no more searching or serving or training or meditation left. All he had to do now was rise from his cot without vomiting.

"Pussywillow," Saz whispered. He said it loud enough for the Hammer vomiting on the ground to hear. Jah'ri could see now that it was Felton. He heard the slight and pulled the blade from the boot next to his cot. He jumped to his feet and rushed Saz.

"Say it again," Felton yelled, his blade at Saz's throat. "I have had enough of you!"

"I said you are an honorable tool. The strongest hilt, the bluntest of objects."

Felton held steady. All Hammers in the Holster were now awake and Felton felt their eyes on him. Jah'ri calmly approached and placed a hand on Felton's shoulder. It was neither threatening nor encouraging, but an attempt to ground the Hammer. Felton released the blade from Saz's throat with a laugh. "You will fall into Sor's pit soon enough. Shyloc will ensure of that. You are a disgrace and bring shame to our Parallel."

Felton looked to the other bunks, seeking agreeable eyes and head nods, finding some, and then returned to his cot, avoiding his own vomit on the floor. Saz pulled his blade, hidden under his pillow, which parted the air and soon found skin. The blade plunged into Felton's right hand. "Saz," was all a disbelieving Felton managed to say before the lights turned red. The 38th Parallel stood at attention as Commander Prime entered.

"TERROR!"

"RAGE!"

"HAMMER!"

"PAIN!"

"Settle. Good morning. I trust—" The sound of dripping disrupted the machinarch's speech. Commander Prime scanned the room and found a small pool of blood growing next to Felton. "Hammers do not bleed. So, what am I finding, Hammer Felton?"

"Sir—"

"It is blood. That is a blade sticking through your hand. You are done."

"Sir?"

"Grab your gear and head to the chamber."

"Sir!"

Commander Prime's hand moved faster than the Hammers could see. From Felton's reaction, who was again on the floor coughing, Jah'ri concluded Felton was punched or knocked in the throat. "Take your lame hand and abandon Cot Hall. You will be debriefed in the chamber."

Felton pulled Saz's blade from his hand and again rushed him. The Hammers converged like an exploding wave. "You took this from me!" Felton screamed as he was pulled away.

This was how the day started.

THE HISTORY OF the 38th was not hidden from its own Hammers. Those who could read discovered that many Hammers never made it into the water. Some killed themselves with lunacy on the day of the mission, some killed others, some quit and begged for mercy.

They were all given back to the creature who marked them.

Instead of breakfast, the Hammers were injected with sustenance. This ensured they had enough strength to sustain the swim, there and back. Every age, the few Hammers that returned from Brecca were the few that had managed to eat before their mission. The kingdom instituted a Correction and began injecting sustenance to those Hammers (almost all) with weakened stomachs. Their compliance did not matter. Hammers were tools of the king and individual decisions were irrelevant. The Correction had resulted in a 32.4% success rate in Hammers reaching the warm waters surrounding the volcanic isle. Once there, however, in Shyloc's domain, the death rate remained the same.

After their forced consumption of sustenance, the Hammers were led to the Clearing, near the pond where they had prepared for the last age, swimming and killing the smaller lake beasts that were farmed and released for the purposes of combat training. For now, the Hammers stood at attention in the Clearing, awaiting their royal guest. Two hours passed before the King's skyship slowly approached. It was a white circular disk that spun at the height of the surrounding trees. It hovered for a while, impervious and provincial. The Hammers waited. Jah'ri plotted the climbing of a nearby tree, the leaping from a branch to the skyship, the path of his combat hammer from holster to skin. An unlocking sound, both sonorous and vivid, returned him to the present. The Hammers watched a door detach from the skyship's hull. A figure emerged on the surrounding deck: King Kulloh-Sor, his greatness, anointed by the gods, who was himself a god in the form of a king, as was taught to all since youth.

A king's visit was one of the greatest honors that can be bestowed upon a Hammer. Tears fell from many eyes, and Jah'ri was annoyed that he too found moisture in his. How strange it was, Jah'ri admitted in his heart, to feel the sting of patriotism. Conflict lived within him like an organ he could not function without. He discovered that even a traitor could feel pride for his king. But Jah'ri's tears were multiplicitous, for he knew his mission—the one buried deep in his heart—was almost complete and that, too, overwhelmed him. His life had culminated to this moment, in the Clearing of a secret facility and in the shadow of a flying ship. How did one count the ages? The postings? The toil? And here was the King, so close to Jah'ri yet just out of reach. The man he would kill and whose kingdom he would burn.

"My tools," King Kulloh-Sor said, his arms open wide. Though he had seen the skyship before, this was the closest and clearest Jah'ri has ever seen the godman himself. His robe was immaculate. His beard was long and clean and blue. He was bald and fat. He was old. His fingers were stained orange from the rare powdered salt candy that grew along the streams of the Southern Arm. He coughed and spit off the side of the skyship.

"Today you bring great honor to my kingdom. It is true that most of you will not return and will therefore disappoint me, but find solace in death, my tools, because you have been used to completion." He again cleared his throat and took a long drink from a chalice. Someone handed the King a parchment, and he clumsily unfolded it.

"What is there to say about the one who awaits you? Shyloc is a mystery. Yes, he patrols Brecca but where did he come from? To which Sor does he answer? Even these questions I will not know until I join my royal ancestors in the next realm. Shyloc is a giant and ancient shape, a serpent of the sea, a monster who fills the water with lightning and hunts those who trespass."

The King dropped the parchment. He drank again. He seemed to take in the Hammers, in depth, for the first time, and his tone dropped.

"Make no mistake. Today you are no longer a Hammer. Any Hammer who enters the water will . . . well, sink." The King laughed. He became distracted and lost his pace. He nodded his fat head. Four Swords revealed themselves from the interior of the skyship. The Hammers broke attention and started cheering. The Swords waved. Disappointed, Jah'ri recognized none of them. In memory the Sword who struck down his mother stood like a giant. These rarified men and women claimed only average height, slightly taller than their slumping King.

Retribution had taken too long.

Now only the King was left to kill. Perhaps an entire kingdom would fall by Jah'ri's hands. Would it be enough? Only blood could quench that accursed thirst. His throat felt suddenly sandy and dry, skeletal even, desperate to taste.

"Yes, yes," the King continued, waving his hands to lower the unsanctioned noise. "These are my Swords. Bring your reward home and join us. TERROR!"

"RAGE!"

"Fiiiiiiish . . ." The King smiled and moved his hand like a fish. The Hammers of the 38th Parallel abruptly silenced, seemingly embarrassed by their own confusion. "Go swim." He cleared his throat and spit one final time before retreating back into his skyship.

"Praise Sor and his exalted son, King Kulloh-Sor!" Commander Prime initiated the worship, and the 38th repeated it. "Praise Sor and his exalted son, King Kulloh-Sor!"

The door closed.

"Praise Sor and his exalted son, King Kulloh-Sor!"

The skyship spun.

"Praise Sor and his exalted son, King Kulloh-Sor!"

The skyship flew away.

Jah'ri again felt his hands shaking, but it was not from fear nor was it anger. He discovered it was hatred that now took hold of him. Jah'ri knew somewhere deep in his sour heart that his quest was doomed, but hatred revived and bonded him; it would all be enough to push him into the water, and if he died—when he died—he would loudly and lustily curse the King's name as the sea beast closed upon him. That would be his vengeance.

The weight of eyes seared into him. Jah'ri panicked. He realized he had not been worshiping. Commander Prime's spinning machinarch eyes glared. Felton's eyes were on him. Vaera's. Sindhi's. Saz. All the rest. Jah'ri joined their chanting. He began yelling louder than any other Hammer in the 38th, because tools did not hold secrets. A tool could not be treasonous. A Hammer worshiped the hand that held it.

His failure to worship was not why they stared at Jah'ri, nor was it suspicion. Something else. Some new tension. Jah'ri felt the weight of the entire 38th, the Hammers glaring at him.

The only fish in the Parallel.

Their eyes did not look away.

PART TWO

AWAKE IN THE CURRENT

*W*here do memories hide? When do memories die? Do they expire with the body or before? Or after? Perhaps only memories survive death and swirl in the salty wind that beats against you now. You walk past the shore where you died as a fish flopping until feasted, and here you stand ankle deep in the Cove of Kullan-Sor and dream no more.

You suddenly think of the Cleanser who found you, the Cleanser who forced life back into you, a lost and rusted Nail of the 5th Parallel. "Leave me," you begged, but he did not desire more bodies to cleanse. He was faceless. It was either a mask or deformity, you were unsure. Hard bread. Sour water. You swallowed more food than your throat could handle. Then he grabbed you by your hair. He pulled you down into the floor and through the maze of shanties until the two of you reached a threshold. You watched each other

157

for a moment. You ran back to him as he slammed shut the door between you. Mother's body remained inside with the Cleanser. Outside in the open air you wept. You pounded the door with your fist, but it never opened again.

This you remember. The wind makes it so. The salt in the air revives the smell of the Cleanser. Hopeless, you search for Meaning, for Purpose, for Hope, but the wind does not give you this.

The wind is done with you.

15

JAH'RI

"Capital Castle complete!
Sor's Staircase governs the clouds.
Thus, the Queen decrees:
Protect our borders from the resurfacing threat
of Evil!
The 31st and 32nd Parallels, their Nails to the
Southern Arm,
The 33rd and 34th Parallels, their Nails to the
Shield,
The 35th and 36th Parallels, their Nails to the
Northern Arm.
Blessed are the Nails who will remain in the
37th and 38th Parallels,
Serving the royal family."

—By Decree of Queen Sua-Sor, 5th Genera-
tion of the Reign of Sor (rumored)

"This you can never repeat." A finger in the dirt drew the simple shape of a mountain. "We are told this is our world, Jah'ri, that all of Arou is only a mountain, surrounded by water."

The boy's mother added squiggly lines in the dirt at the bottom of the cone.

"The truth is our planet is far too big for any one eye to see. There are other mountains, Jah'ri. Forests. Jungles. Flat-land Parallels. Sea townes."

Flickering, the dwindling flame of the candle post danced within her eyes. The boy cherished Mother Nail's tales. Soon he would sleep and dream, but now he fought to bury his yawns, desperate to convince his mother, and perhaps himself, that he was simply still too awake for sleep.

"Plan-ette?" the boy bemused, unfamiliar with the stretchy syllables. Mother Nail often spoke in riddles, words he didn't know, sounds other tongues never uttered. Bedtime myths. "Jungal?"

She smiled at the boy, perhaps seeing what all mothers saw when they gazed at their sons, the very beating of their hearts. Parallel souls sharing blood. Patiently, she tilted her head, looking. Information was dangerous, but ignorance deadly. And what of innocence?

"You will see it all, Jah'ri. Everything Arou offers will be yours. I promise."

"Are there really . . . flat-land Parallels?"

She nodded, thinking. "Cities. They call them cities. Or townes." Her finger returned to the dirt. "The ocean you can see from our Parallel does not surround the entire mountain, Jah'ri. Only half. On the other side is what they call the Treelands. In this Parallel, we have only three trees. But here," she drew tall lines around the mountain, "there are too many to count." Jah'ri's eyes grew wide. She continued. "Past the Treelands are three territories. The Northern Arm, a settlement above us. Down here lies the Southern Arm. And between both, the Shield."

"They don't look like arms." The boy studied her crude circles. "Whose arms?"

"The reach of Sor's kingdom, Jah'ri, that is all. Beyond Sor's arms, there are deserts and tribes. Other kingdoms. And rows of mountains, smaller but infinite. The Endless Range."

The boy looked away from Mother Nail, at nothing really, letting his mind wander.

In the exterior district of the 5th Parallel, Nails lived in long rows of shanties, a slum of huts interconnected and built atop one another, their doors and windows angled in the floors and ceilings. In any shanty it was common for heads to appear, like solemn weeds sprouting from the dirt, as each shanty led to another. It worked like a trail system. Some Nails would navigate twenty or thirty shanties to find their space, others climbed through just a few. The shanties were all similar in size and space, but Jah'ri's was the only one he had ever seen with a false wall, a hidden room. The boy stared at it now.

"Momma Nail, what's beyond the water? Is there anything?" he asked.

Stridently, she swiped the dirt and cleared the map. They watched two Nails climb through their floor and push onto the next shanty, their weary frames bored from the journey.

THE HAMMERS OF the 38th Parallel stood in formation on the sand of the Cove of Kullan-Sor, named after King Kullan-Sor, from the fourth generation of the reign of Sor, who established both the Swords and their quest.

The Commander's skyship was smaller than the King's. Commander Prime could fit only two, maybe three machinarchs. From the sky it would lead the Hammers to the isle of Brecca when the clouds parted long enough to allow them to see its lights. It would also monitor the Hammers' progress—and tally their losses.

Commander Prime stood on the bottom of the ship's ramp and released the Hammers in pairs. The machinarch watched them file into the water. "Swim," he said to Vaera and Perrault. Ahead of them were Sindhi and Rannold, who had entered first and officially began the mission. Six more pairs of Hammers awaited their orders behind Jah'ri and Saz, who were next. The moment was almost upon Jah'ri, he realized, but none of it felt particularly real yet. Was this another dream? He suspected he would know once he was in the water, for his dreams always abandoned him lifeless on the shore. He looked to the sky for birds and found none.

"Commander Prime, sir?" Saz began.

"Training is over, Hammer."

"Just one last question, Commander Prime, sir."

The machinarch did not reply, its metal eyes remaining towards the shore.

Stuttering to mock the failing machinarch, Saz said, "When I become a Sword, will I out rank you? Will your breaking-down ass serve me?"

"Saz, what are you doing?" Jah'ri whispered.

Commander Prime's head turned but its eyes still looked far away, as if clutched by the horizon. "I'm afraid neither of us will live long enough to find out, Hammer Saz." Commander Prime's voice dropped an octave as it spoke.

"We'll see—"

"Swim." Commander Prime raised its hand and pointed to the ocean.

Jah'ri grabbed Saz's arm and pushed the Hammer forward. They marched together, filing toward the shallow shore.

"You insane?" Jah'ri whispered.

"Don't you see the upgrade?" Saz asked him, laughing. "It's in the skyship at the top of the ramp." Jah'ri glanced back. Indeed, a new machinarch stood with its arms folded. Skin tight. Clean. Strong. The replacement Commander Prime had arrived.

"The bucket of bolts deserves to melt," Saz said, striding forward.

Their feet briefly walked on wet sand before the cove's warm shallow water covered their ankles. An unimpressive small wave concluded at their ankles.

It convinced Jah'ri: he was awake, and this was real. The test started now.

In pairs, the Hammers continued to march. Jah'ri and Saz ventured further, deeper into the sea. The temperature dropped with every step. Soon, the surface brushed their waists.

"Terror, rage, hammer, pain," Saz said. "Cold, balls, I'm, insane."

"It's not too late," Jah'ri offered.

"Sure it is. I'm not going back to Pond Scum. How 'bout

you?"

Yes, yes, they were marked. If they abandoned their mission they would return to the pond, because they owed the creature their lives. But was this another fabrication from a kingdom full of false tales? Jah'ri suspected he would never know.

He remarked, changing the subject, "So conserve your energy, Hammer. Focus. Stay on mission."

"And what is your mission, Hammer Jah'ri? It sure as hell isn't fetching a scoop of breccel and forging a battle blade." Saz halted. Jah'ri joined him, though not easily; the water was just above their waist now, and the tide was already strengthening.

"Of course it is," Jah'ri repeated with a quizzical smile. Saz laughed, and they both continued walking. Jah'ri knew what Saz was thinking, that Jah'ri would be a deserter. He had read of the Hammers who disappeared in the water under the guise of drowning only to be found ages later in the Southern Arm among the portsfolk. Of course they were found and returned to the creature who marked them. There had never been a successful deserter, so said the literature.

The water reached their chests, and that was enough. It was time to swim. Jah'ri said, "See you on the other side, Hammer Saz."

"Didn't you hear," Saz said as his large arms began to pull away and swim ahead, "we're fish now. How about that."

Saz disappeared in the waves ahead of him. Suddenly, Jah'ri felt very alone in the water. He knew Hammers swam all around him at various distances, but he could not see them nor would he look. The fellowship of the 38th Parallel had officially concluded. Swimming was his only task for the next two days. Two or three, depending on the storms ahead and how fierce the wind would rise. The horizon looked troubling but not impossible. In previous missions some swims had taken four or five days. Other cohorts swam into storms that raged early, and those Hammers all found their end on the first day. Jah'ri distracted himself with a song.

Terror, rage, hammer, pain.
Cold, balls, I'm insane.

THE OCEAN WAS forever. It was his forever. Everything connected and nothing all at once. One hour passed. Four hours. Eight. Night turned to morning. He remembered his training and stopped to take a drink through a filtered straw. A reward, he gave into his curiosity and allowed himself to turn around and gaze upon the giant mountain while treading water. This was the northwestern view. From the water, one could not see the entire mountain. Its Parallels were hidden by many layers of clouds. It disappointed him, for he wished he to see Sor's Staircase from such great a distance. He wanted to block it with his finger. Directly above, Jah'ri glimpsed a faint light blinking in the morning sky and adjusted his compass. He continued the swim. Time did not exist out here, not really. Jah'ri was no longer a Hammer. Not a Nail. Nor was he a peasant orphan. He was certainly not a fish. Oh! What a marvelous realization. Jah'ri finally understood the dream. For the water was the sky, and the sky was the water. Jah'ri was never the fish at all. He was the bird. This was why he would never wake from that terrible dream. This was why he swam in the sky. Jah'ri was the predator. Jah'ri was the Terror.

And the swords? The beak was a sword. No, no, no, no.

These were the thoughts of madness, he realized.

Empty your mind. Remember your training.

The morning retreated and surrendered to midday heat. It was both welcome and wretched but brief, for dark clouds blew in and covered the sky. An anxious storm arrived. The wind pushed against him. Waves built and passed, growing larger with each set. Jah'ri found himself trapped in the shadows of passing mountains with current that seemed to push and pull without reason. Jah'ri dove underneath and attempted to swim forward but the momentum of water twisted him to the surface where he was clobbered and disoriented. There was no fighting this beast. All he could do was salvage his direction and conserve his energy. At the demented, disorienting peak of Arou's largest wave and under the flickering brilliance of errant bolts, Jah'ri counted five Hammers, three far ahead and two behind. He would not know which way was truly forward and which was backwards before the clouds cleared. Until then, the wind and the water continued their argument. The waves would not break on him, Jah'ri knew. They had other business. But the storm would kill him if he ignored its holy wrath. Rain began to fall hard as more lightning tickled the choppy surface. Days had passed. Hadn't they? The world might have ended, for all he knew.

All at once, the clouds did clear. The wind settled. The surface flattened. The evening sky revealed itself as the early stars shone, both the true and the false. The Hammers, those that survived, found their compasses, located their skyship, and continued the swim.

Jah'ri figured the storm pushed him back further than he expected, but he swallowed his annoyance and continued. What could be done? The mission rambled on.

Evening turned into a night so bright it could only have been the Swelling Moon. He swam forward, gazing at the enormity of the celestial eye and appreciated all the nothingness it brightened. There was something in the distance, he discovered, its fin cutting through the surface like Sor's Staircase breaching the clouds. He waited and watched, but the creature never fully revealed itself. Jah'ri wondered if it had been just a vision or a waking dream. Either way, he was ready for its attack, as all Hammers were trained to be. All swimmers were fitted with the same gear: a blade on the back, a combat hammer on the waist, a smaller blade on the ankle, filtered straws on both arms, and an empty vial strapped to the shoulder for collecting the isle's mineral, Breccel.

Brecca was not yet within sight and neither was its beast.

THE SWELLING MOON remained brilliant, but during the long months of Arou, when the daylight prolonged, the moon was an unreliable and whimsical ally, leaving faster than Jah'ri preferred. Daylight returned quickly, emboldened and angry. Nonetheless, Jah'ri swam. His arms grew achingly tired, but the sustenance they had injected him with proved its worth. It must have also helped him stay awake, for he did not fear falling asleep, not yet. The skin of his arms progressively reddened from the sunlight, which also reflected off the surface and stung his eyes. There wasn't much progress to be made during the morning glare of a cloudless day, he decided, so he floated until the sun eventually rose above his shoulders. He began again. Hours passed. Days flew. Generations died. Kingdoms burned and fell. It was happening again, those strange thoughts, creeping like rats in a castle pantry. He shook his head to clear them.

The sun relented. Jah'ri watched the sky change from blue to orange to gray to black. He had swam the right distance. He had followed the right stars. He had monitored the false star, when he saw it, and adjusted course.

Yet, there was no island. No monster. No other Hammers. Jah'ri swam.

More, more, more.

His arms and legs were but levers of an instrument.

His body, a machine.

Humanity, an inconvenience.

Was this the point?

To work so hard, to climb so high, to get so close.

To lose yourself in the holy mission.

And become inhuman.

Shedding.

Shedding your skin, your power, your self.

Life inside a tomb.

The sun, the moon.

Jah'ri eased. Had he been swimming this whole time?

Realizing now that the water had been growing warmer for the last few hours, he covered his eyes and cried.

Ahead of him, its outline now clearly visible in the darkened evening sky was the fiery peak of Brecca. It was exactly as he imagined it to be, not that his dreams ever took him here, but it was what his mind's eye predicted: an island with a steep cone at its center, the size of a tower one Parallel high, brimming with a river of elder fire that spilled down its side.

Jah'ri had made it.

Shyloc's domain. He quickly dove underneath, hoping to catch a glimpse of movement or to see the lightning the beast attacked and stunned its prey with. He found nothing underneath, but as Jah'ri returned to the surface, he heard a strange and awful sound: screaming Hammers. A stern, bellowing roar followed, and then a surge of lightning spread throughout the surrounding water and reached high into the air above. The bolt revealed a treacherous and slippery shape. Shyloc loomed bigger than he had ever imagined or thought possible, and Jah'ri suddenly felt like a silly child shaking in the shadow of a monster.

The curve of a snake, the fangs of a dragon, the fury of one thousand ages.

What foolish pride, or sick lust for death, convinced souls to trespass this accursed realm?

Jah'ri forgot his training. It was of no use here.

16

THE THING

Climbing Sor's staircase, the wind pierced through the Nail's long beard like a terrible brush. He stood sopping wet from the cloud's mist. Absently, he heard a rattle in his bones and felt the faint pull of the ground calling to him like a lethal lover. The Nail found his balance and, after the deepest breath his lungs would hold, the wherewithal to continue. The railing finished hours ago and now Sor's Staircase offered no protection, just a steep drop on either edge. He had not yet risen above Capital Castle. The tower still climbed as he did.

Wide and momentous, Sor's Staircase spiraled around the castle, and, like ligaments, occasionally connected to the castle with buttresses for stolid support. The Nail could have begun his quest from the steps inside the castle, safe and warm, he now realized. There was no sane reason to begin at the bottom of the staircase exposed to Arou's riotous elements for the entire journey, but Nails were plucked for purposes of the gods, not for the rationale of men.

His climb was momentous.

The Nail was plucked from the 18th Parallel. The memory was bitter and almost felt fraudulent. Someone else's life, not his. Surely this was just a vivid dream. Hadn't he just been enjoying a cool morning breeze along the dusty footpath? No. That was hours ago. Days?

Living in the 18th Parallel had not been a miserable existence. It was just existence. The Nail's days were long and hard, but he found his pride, perhaps his purpose, in routinely avoiding seasonal plucking. Survival was like a badge that puffed his chest and raised his chin. Mother Nail, who lived still, instructed him long ago, lessons he taught his own younglings: tithe loudly so the temple priests hear you; give your food to the Hammers, leaving only what you truly needed to cramp suffering. Hunger is better than death. Her unfortunate motto, for it was known Nails were soulless instruments, and the next realm would not welcome them.

The priests announced another plucking. It was an unusual quota, the third round of that age alone. When the Hammers raked through the thinning Parallel to collect their batch, he stood on the side of the footpath, confident and unconcerned, watching the scene unfold until, to his bewilderment, a newer, younger Hammer unexpectedly darted towards him and clutched his arm. In the Nail's confusion he did not move, offering the Hammer only a disturbed and unbelieving look. The Hammer yanked, and the Nail flailed, falling to his knees. He pleaded. He cried. He slapped his own face. He did all the things he judged the others for, but, certainly, this young Hammer would understand the mistake if he could only just explain it to him. The Nail's rambling of frantic words inconsequentially fell upon the young Hammer like rain upon stone.

Flushed with annoyance, the young Hammer launched his knee into the Nail's chin. He pulled his weapon and with conviction, began beating the Nail on his arms, his shoulders, his head, each impact an injection of tremors and the haunting promise of splintering bones. Another Hammer approached for assistance. They raised the beaten Nail to his twisted feet and laughed when blood seeped from his skull and blinded his eyes. The Nail blinked through it. He felt a gag push into his mouth and soon after that lost consciousness.

Later, he awoke when liquid splashed his face. Somehow he had already been standing. A hand pushed into his and formed a mold. "Drink," the voice said, and a small cap was given.

Even in the deepest darkness the Nail knew he could only see out of one eye. He could feel other Nails pressing against his arms, smell their stench, the sweat and the blood and the piss. He could taste their hunger. Faintly, he began to see the outlines of their weary shapes. He drank the cap of water. A proud, lofty voice spoke with the cadence of a priest.

"Awaken from your slumber and celebrate! Sor, and his exalted son King Kulloh-Sor call upon you to help fulfill His promise. Build the stairs, stone by stone, and touch the gleam."

The priest explained to the plucked Nails that they were now in the 30th Parallel: the plateau of the great mountain and the base of Sor's Staircase. Despite what they had heard, the priest assured, their death was not in the kingdom's best interest. There was far too much work to be done. "Climb. Place your stone. Come back, and we will give you another, praise Sor."

The Nails were draped with thick, pocketed raiment. Sand and glue filled each pocket; the dust lingered in the air and smelled of clay. Next, a thin metal door rolled open, and Arou's effulgent light blinded what little remained of the Nail's fledgeling eyesight. He realized, rather immediately, the faint swinging sensation upon his cheek and assumed it was an eyeball. He was not brave enough to raise his hand and explore it.

The Nail was yanked from the staging room and soon pressed into the windy flats of the great mountain's plateau. His bare feet walked upon warm red dust. A cubic stone was handed to him, the size of his chest and the weight of his children. "Worry not," the priest told him. "Sor's glorious staircase is just up ahead. Its magnificence is unavoidable. Take your steps."

The Nail was to die, that was clear. All Nails would eventually be spent, and he realized he was foolish to ever think good, selfless deeds would spare him. Emotions ambushed him, enraged him, assaulted him. His languorous eyesight adjusted, and he saw it clearly for the first time: Sor's Staircase.

In front of him rested the base, a massive structure carved out of the plateau's rock that started wide and quickly raised and twisted to intoxicating heights. Arcane symbols were chipped and smoothed into the first few levels of the steps, blended with plaster and corroded verdigris, each row of steps presenting a frieze that from a distance created a mosaic, a larger image the Nail did not understand, but reminded him, vaguely, of the patterns he found within the stars. Along the first flight was an ornamental balustrade, a railing too immaculate to use. The Nail fell to his knees and, despite his disappointment, his anger, his pain, pulsating equally and paroxysmally, could only praise the ancient temple before him.

Hammers stood as sentries at each side of the staircase's base. They approached him and scooped him up, returning him to his feet. "Praise Sor as you climb, Nail," one Hammer said as the other returned to him his fallen stone. They pushed the Nail forward, and eventually he reached the first step, where he briefly paused, closed his eye as best he could, and breathed.

Slowly, the Nail climbed. Tears seeped and stung him, but, holding the stone, he could not wipe his eyes, nor would he want to for the continued fear of brushing whatever dangled on his cheek. After many steps he could see the domed city of the Court laying far to his right, but it wasn't until the stairs began to twist directly toward its townscape that the Nail understood the dome to be a Parallel. Through its lightly clouded glass he saw wide streets, trimmed trees, simple creeks, and friendly ponds. He saw spacious, ornate buildings and some strange magic that illuminated it all from hanging bulbs. He saw comfort and abundance. Peace. His stomach turned, and when the Nail left bile on those revealing steps he noticed, perhaps, the stone stained a little differently there. The Nail stood and stubbornly lifted the block.

How could one Parallel have so much while the others had so little? While he had so little? His children? The hunger he had so often justified . . . what a fool he was to ever think he had any thing at all. Poverty was a disease of the wealthy, and he was but a boil.

"Get moving, Nail" a distant Hammer yelled from below, his

order quickly disappearing into the quickening wind. Hammers were stationed on platforms along the way to supervise the Nails' early progress, but guards were no longer needed after the height became deadly and the wind turned ugly. The Nail listened to the Hammer's order and moved.

The early hours progressed with little exhaustion. After the shock of the dome relented, the expanse of the open world offered much to see, and it distracted him greatly. He beheld Capital Castle, the home of the King and the pride of the kingdom, which rested atop the dome. He climbed higher. At times, the staircase wended closer to the castle tower. He saw little fingers sticking out of windows, their curtains hurriedly closing by larger hands. Some floors of the castle looked abandoned entirely: no motion, not even shadows.

Does anyone live here?

The staircase led away from the tower for a little while and then snaked back.

NOW, COUNTLESS HOURS into his climb, he finally saw another Nail. It was only for a moment, a scream and a glimpse; the woman plunged into the forever below. He shivered anew, remembering soberly that today was the day he would die. Funny how easily the brain distracted itself from doom. Any minute, any second. He would not scream, the Nail decided, and that would be his final, selfish act.

When the Nail stepped forward he slipped and fell to his hands, banging his knee. His stone tumbled down a few steps, and, like an errant die-cube, it rolled off the side of the staircase.

The Nail cursed the stone, the stairs, the sky. He wept.

He was slow to look at what he slipped in.

The fluid was likely from another Nail who climbed ahead of him. Maybe they lost control of their stomach or their bowels. Perhaps it was a bit of battered brains from a wayward skull that slammed and bounced away. His fingers were sticky with it, the yellow bile. It was not from a Nail, he realized with relief, for he saw egg shells nearby. How strange to find eggs without a nest. In the 18th Parallel, the gulls built their nests in the trees that splintered out from the mountain's edge and hung far above the void. Many Nails fell from the hunt, others returned with eggs and gave them to the Hammers in exchange for their favor. It was a sacrifice that seemed good and true at the time.

He sucked the yoke from his fingers. Then he heard something tear through the air with a whistle. Another egg flew and this one hit his shoulder. Another immediately pelted his face. He heard cheering from the tower. His first thought was that they were wasting food. Another egg was thrown, but it missed him.

The Nail looked toward the castle and saw them all standing there. It was a group donned with pretty dresses, fine robes, and silvery silk, pressed and barely worn. Closest to the open window and leaning over a large ledge, a young woman pointed directly at him, holding an egg, instructing the children. A Hammer stood close by, holding a large basket of eggs and distributing them with a smile. They counted down together. They launched.

The Nail understood.

Upon his death, he would be given a terrible knowledge that Sor's Staircase was but a joke to the wretched, withering hearts of the castle. Arou was rotten.

The Nail heard chanting as another batch of eggs launched through the air high above the world. The eggs found him and pushed him closer to the ledge. His slimy fingers failed to grip, but it was a wild slap of wind that finally took him over. Just as he fell, he heard them cheer.

The Nail ripped through a thin layer of clouds.

He saw everything, things he didn't have words for, an entire kingdom: the Northern and Southern Arms, the Treelands, the great mountain below, the Sea of Cashmu pushing against it, a glimpse of the mysteries beyond the horizon; and far in the distance, maybe, was that an island? He was flying, floating, and falling.

Could he swim the air and fly to safety? He stretched his arms but all was for naught, and he knew it. Death was here. The Nail whispered the secret names of his children.

17

NAOR

Naor stared at the thing.

"You need help," he said. "I can get you help."

The creature stumbled backwards, afraid. Naor stepped towards it with a confidence that surprised even himself. He saw it very plainly now. This was no creature. This was a man. And this man, this stranger, had some sort of terrible accident. He should not have been alive, but Sor blew air into his lungs, praise Sor and his exalted son, King Kulloh-Sor!

The boy opened his palms to show he was friendly. The delirious, battered man did not flee. Cagey, they each looked at one another a little longer before Naor spoke again.

"I am sorry for whatever happened to you." The man was a terror to behold, but Naor could not look away. "I can take you to the Temple Complex," and he pointed.

The disfigured man nervously shook his wretched head. A sound similar to "no" came out of his mouth, and he repeated it again and again until its quivering voice became a gurgling sound, as if he was drowning. The man coughed through it and found his ugly breath.

"We can stay right here," Naor offered, feebly. He did not know if he was comforting or helping. The man was clearly frightened. Naor wondered if an animal did this to him. He had heard tales of wolves sneaking into the Parallel, stalking the courtyard. A chill ran through him.

"Did an animal do this? Was it a wolf? What is your name? Who are you?"

Naor's nerves took over, and the questions kept coming. He peered at the shadows and listened for growls. He remembered other tales, the ones told to him by the older children, the stories he stopped believing in, like the hungry shapeshifting bearmen from the Treelands who snatched children from the Court whenever the Swelling Moon approached.

The man, the stranger, the thing, this creature before him could be anything, Naor suddenly considered. He readied his feet to spring, but the man finally said something that sounded, much to Naor's surprise, like "Naor."

"How do you know my name?" he asked the man, his fear rising.

The man shook his head and tried again, desperately, his tongue lifting with great effort.

"I . . . Nail . . ."

Naor shook his head, confused and—

"Naor?"

He turned to the new voice from behind, a woman's.

"Philosopher Z'rai?"

Z'rai stood in between trees, her eyes wild and her mouth agape. Slowly, she stretched her hands out towards Naor and beckoned him.

"Come here, please."

"He needs help," Naor said, staying where he was and answering a question that wasn't asked. "I don't know. You can help him right?"

The Nail, having seemed to just now clued into Z'rai's presence, cowered and shook. He bent his knees and placed a bloody hand on the grass.

Z'rai's eyes darted back and forth from Naor to the Nail. "Are you alright?"

Naor hurriedly nodded.

Looking mortified, Z'rai said, "I followed you . . . wanted to make sure you were . . ." She never finished the sentence. Her mind wandered every time she looked upon the Nail.

"Help him!" Naor yelled. "Aren't you some sort of healer?"

"Shhh!" As if coming to her senses, Z'rai swiftly approached the Nail, falling to her knees at his side. The Nail squirmed, but he did not flee. "Naor, you must lower your voice if you wish for me to help him. This . . . he is not welcome here."

Z'rai looked through the small gear bag on her side and retrieved a mixed collection of tinctures and powder potions. "I studied apothecary and healing rituals in the Temple before being reassigned." Her hands shook. On her wrist, spilling just out of her sleeve, Naor saw the smallest, simplest tattoo of a quincunx on her wrist.

"Naor," she finally said, turning, "I cannot help him."

The Nail softly wept.

"Should I get more help? Philosopher Shaeron?"

"No!" Z'rai yelled and jumped to her feet. Naor backed away. Lowering her voice, she said. "I'm sorry. No, please. I will handle it. Run home. Speak not a word of this until after your pilgrimage. I will find you after."

The Nail coughed his terrible, grimy cough.

Naor bent down, telling the stranger, "Z'rai will help you. I will come back and check on you."

"You need to leave," Z'rai insisted, "and never come back."

Naor rose to leave, ignoring the weeping pleas.

"Philosopher Z'ari," he said, "Why does he call himself a nail?"

Z'rai lowered her head. "Naor, you must go."

"Why does he call himself a nail?"

Soberly, she turned to him. "Your questions will be answered on your pilgrimage."

A DOOR SHUT. Footsteps.

A chorus of voices yelled, "SURPRISE!"

Naor raised his eyes to find his home filled with visitors. They pointed as they laughed.

"Look at him!" someone said. "Total shock!"

Mother approached him first. He almost didn't recognize her. Earnest and emotional, Lady Eyrilia smiled wider than Naor had ever seen her smile. She looked warm and pleasant. Informal. Normal. In the crook of her arm she held a boxed gift.

"Naor, son. I'm so proud of you." She turned back to the small audience. "I thought this day would never come!"

They laughed.

Naor forced a grin, his face feeling thick and heavy.

"For your pilgrimage," Mother said, giving him the box.

He took it.

"Should I . . . ?"

Again, Mother smiled, wider than the dome itself. He couldn't believe it. Mother was happy. Naor forgot himself and returned the smile.

"Oh!"

They embraced. Ricard approached next. "Come here, son."

The visitors applauded.

One of them yelled, "Open it!"

Naor obliged, ripping away the lacey ribbon with ease. Inside he found what he expected, what he had so long dreamed for and delayed: his boots.

The same ones Piers had before he left for his pilgrimage. Piers, Naor realized he would get to see Piers again. And all the others. All his friends who had left him behind. All his friends who had left him behind. Had become men, women, citizens of the Court.

"Look here," Mother said, her voice cool and easy. She pointed to a small, natty inscription knitted just below the laces: Brave.

Naor nodded.

Much later, panic woke him in the middle of the night.

That's when he remembered the Nail.

NAOR CREPT DOWN the stairs, his new boots creaking with every step. To his utter shock, he found his mother in the living room, fully dressed and preparing to leave.

"Naor?"

"Oh."

"What are you—"

"Why are you wearing your boots?"

"Oh," Naor said, looking down. Thinking fast, surprising himself, he replied, "I just . . . Trying to break in the boots, you know. I just needed some water."

There it was. That smile again.

"I'm so proud of you."

"Are you going out, Mother?"

"Some business. I won't be long."

"Everything okay?" Naor asked, worried she was leaving for the same reasons.

"You'll see, when you become a citizen and someday, a committee chair, just like me, business never ends. It's our duty, as leaders. I'll be back soon. Get some rest."

Naor watched her leave and stood there by the door for a while, waiting. Wiglaf sleepily came to his side and sat.

"I have to check on something," he told the dog. "Keep the bed warm."

Wiglaf yawned.

Naor rushed to the courtyard, his new boots crunching the midnight grass. He turned onto the trail he took earlier, remembering the odd strange path he had found himself in when he met the stranger. Deeper he traversed into the courtyard until he recognized a group of the trees, their perfidy formation looking more sinister in the dark.

Brave.

He slowed. His hands pushed through a bush. He gasped.

On the ground, the Nail laid dead. Alone. He still wasn't sure this thing was human. How could it have been? How could the human body endure such tragedy? And where was Z'rai? Hadn't she helped him?

Naor approached the body. He kneeled. Even though one eye dangled to the far side and rested on the ground, Naor waved an uncommitted hand over the Nail's face. Naor got even closer. Slowly, he lowered his head and hovered his ear near the Nail's mouth, listening for air, for breathing, for anything.

Nothing.

Nothing but the most wretched of smells.

Naor sat back up and coughed, trying not to gag. He breathed through it. He settled. Then, while looking at the lines and shadows of the corpse, dimly lit by a false moon, the body raised. It shook. It rolled to its side. It stood. It screamed.

Naor fell backwards.

He scattered away.

The Nail stomped towards him. He no longer cried but growled.

Naor screamed.

The Nail closed the distance between them within a second. He grabbed the child and raised him, shook him. Naor pissed himself. He screamed again.

"Help! Help!"

He kicked away the monster and freed himself, running away.

"Heoooooppppp," the monster said.

Help.

With some distance between them, Naor stopped. He turned around and saw the monster had not followed him. Again, the Nail cried.

Louder, he wailed, "Heoooooppppp—"

There was a plop.

The Nail grunted and dropped to his knees before falling face forward into the grass. Naor saw it sticking through the back of the man's skull: the handle of a combat hammer.

In what he would later remember in flashes, a Hammer appeared through a break in the trail. Hands lifted Naor. Carried him away. He screamed, he begged, his protector only hastened. More Hammers arrived. They surrounded the fallen body. One retrieved the weapon from the stranger's pulpy and lifeless skull. Together, they kicked the corpse while the trees of the courtyard quickened into a mess of dark greens. Blurring, the boy could no longer hear his own screams.

A DOOR SHUT. Footsteps.

Mother's voice suddenly came into focus. "They've gone, Naor. I told them you'd speak to me first. It's time to hear your tale. Come out with it."

Naor wasn't sure what time it was. If it was still the same day. Before him, here at the dining table—yes, he was at home, that's right—a plate of ka cushion had been prepared, now cooled. How long had it been there? Little claws on his leg. The dog looked up at him. Wiglaf wanted for his lap. Closer to the food.

What was the rule?

"Naor! Please! Talk to me! Did it attack you? Let's start there. Just nod or shake your head. Did it hurt you?"

"Did it . . . hurt me?"

"The boy spoke!" He heard Mother exclaim. Father burst into the kitchen, his puffy face bright from tears.

"Son," he said, sitting. "Tell me. Tell me all of it." Ricard held his son's hands.

Naor swallowed. "Are nails . . . people?"

Ricard looked to Eryilia. Eryilia walked to the window.

"The falling nails. Those are . . . people?"

"Those, Naor, are not people," Mother said, her back to him. "They are Nails."

"But . . ." Naor breathed, searching for words, finding only flashes. "Flesh and bone, Mother. I saw—"

Mother stomped over to the table. She grabbed her son by the shoulders, her eyes filled with fury, the smile from yesterday so far away, likely never returning. Eyrillia spoke to her son slowly and sternly. "They are Nails, Naor. I am sorry you had to find out this way. You deserved a proper pilgrimage. The philosophers on the path would have explained everything. It is a cold lesson, but a necessary one. It is the truth of our world. Of Sor's Justice! It's a beautiful thing, Naor. We are Sor's chosen."

"Yes. Yes! Then you return with a full and grateful heart," Father continued. "And you learn your purpose in all this. See, Sor established this dome so we may govern the lower Parallels. It is an awesome and incredible honor."

Naor pulled his hands away from his father. He shook off his mother's grasp from his shoulders. He wiped his tears. "If we govern, then we have the power to change. We can set things right."

"Things are right, Naor," Mother stood tall now, her voice no longer quivering. "This is Sor's Just Society as He designed it. The Nails not only raise Sor's Staircase, but the kingdom itself. Without them, we would have nothing. It is their purpose, son. They live to serve, just like we live to serve. It is the way of things."

"But, certainly, there's been a mistake?"

Hopefully, Naor looked at his parents. Yes. He knew suddenly that something had been misinterpreted. The Scrolls of Sor would never permit such cruel carnage. One thousand ages had passed since Sor reclaimed the mountain from the evil Soulless Kings who forsook His wisdom, His peace. Why would Sor replace evil for evil? There was no sense to it. "The King must know! We can request audience and—"

"That's enough, Naor." Eryilia's scolding broke Naor's momentum. "What you speak of is impossible. I understand you're unraveling. A demented, evil Nail snuck into our peaceful home, our own courtyard, for Sor's sake, and attacked you. Laid filthy hands on you. Your pilgrimage was stolen from you."

"You can still go," Ricard reassured, nodding, his voice more soothing than the other. "Tomorrow, if you please. With the Swelling Moon. See it with your own eyes, outside of the dome. I think, I think it's quite urgent that you go. Don't you? It is important."

"It is disgusting," the boy yelled. Even he was surprised to hear the words come out of his mouth, for he did not mean to say them aloud. Father's eyes widened. Mother slapped him.

"Your other option, Naor, is to become a Nail yourself!"

"Eyrilia."

"Is that what you want?"

"Eyrilia!"

"I can make that happen!"

"Enough!" Father screamed, slamming his fist on the table and standing between mother and son. "Eyrilia, the boy has been through it today. Let us not add to his nightmares."

Eryilia's hand shook from the strike. No more words were said before she left the room. Ricard stayed behind for only a moment. Soon, he too left, chasing his partner.

Alone, Naor sat in the quiet kitchen holding a hand to his face. He remembered Wiglaf, and hoped he would come to him now, but the dog didn't respond to Naor's timid call. Solemnly, he rose and found his room. He fell into bed. It smelled familiar. It smelled comfortable.

Naor closed his eyes.

The Nail's face. His ripped flesh. His dangling eye. His teeth piercing through skin. Gurgling speech. The combat hammer hitting his brain, like slop pouring into Wiglaf's bowl.

Naor rose. He stood. He walked to his window. Evening. How could it be evening? An entire day, lost. He couldn't remember any of it. Not after . . .

Now, the dome of the Court was quiet. The controlled breeze within the dented dome was perfect and soft. Perching, he stretched his neck, looking out the window near Temple Complex, towards the center of the Court. From this angle he could see the edge of Ascension Stairwell, an ornate spiral staircase connecting the Court and Capital Castle. Fiercely guarded, Ascension was the only entrance to the castle tower. Even if Naor could get through, entering Capital Castle without summons was punishable by death.

If only he could speak to the King.

Naor sank to the floor of his room, feeling hopeless and confused and beaten. He succumbed. The boy's tears could have filled a Parallel. He breathed fast, as if chewing on the air; for long stretches, he couldn't breathe at all. He gasped. He calmed. He started up again. It went this way for some time, but eventually the tears dried, and his spirit weakened.

The rug in his room was soft. He felt the wool with his fingers, making within it the shape of a tower, thinking, thinking, thinking.

18

LADY EYRILIA

Little Wiglaf pushed the bowl across the tile floor. Eyrilia leaned against the kitchen counter, staring into nothing and thinking of nothing, careless for the window behind her and the court-yard that so often stole her time.

"Shall I wake him?" she heard her husband ask. Of course Ricard asked her permission.

Look at him, oats and egg bits in his mustache, a simpleton chin, a belly growing wider, a passion for floundering and an absence of purpose.

"Let him sleep," she declared, her hand offering a miserable wave.

"He will feel better today," Ricard said and whatever else followed she ignored. Eyrilia had not slept. After Naor went to his room she marched to Temple Complex and demanded to speak to Elder Hammer Jonn. She berated the feckless maltworm. Jonn profusely apologized and promised an investigation.

"And which part of its brain will you question?" she yelled. "Your Hammers destroyed the Nail before it could tell you anything!"

Oh, she could relive the scene forever. The screaming. The demands. The rage. Jonn was drunk when she found him, infuriating her more. She summoned the high priest, but when he arrived at the Elder Hammer's residence, he had the audacity to question her, as if Eryilia was to blame.

He said—

"Eyrilia!" she heard Ricard yell, and she returned from memory. "He's gone."

"Who?"

"What do you— Naor, our son."

"Gone where?"

Ricard marched in and out of the kitchen wearing panic like a scarf. Eyrilia rolled her eyes and stumbled into her bedroom where she fell into her bed and instantly found sleep.

When she awoke she found her home quiet and empty. Wiglaf laid next to her with his paws in the air. She pushed the dog off the bed, sat up, and yawned. The bells of Temple Complex rang in the distance.

"Oh no."

All at once Eryillia knew she was late. Her committee was to meet today at the first ringing of the bells.

She jumped from bed and haphazardly shed yesterday's dress. She ran to the washroom and powdered her face, her underarms, her chest. She sprayed perfume. She tied her hair with a ribbon.

It was all done in under a minute. The next minute was eaten by the first dress she found and then the wearing of it. She grabbed her shoes and ran from her home, failing to close the front door. Remaining at the threshold, Wiglaf watched her go.

Naor. That little shit.

Eryilia did not run through the courtyard. That would be unbecoming of a proper chairwoman. She did rush, however. Having woken only twenty-five minutes prior, she reached the Great Hall of Temple Complex in respectable time. She entered and sought the committee chambers, quickly finding the familiar corridor leading to the Committee for the 18th Parallel. From behind the closed door that separated them, she could hear the impatient chattering of its members. She would not enter yet. Her breath was too wild and her face likely too flushed. She smoothed her dress with her flustered hands. She stood at the door and continued to listen as her blood cooled and her lungs calmed. She heard the boy's name. They spoke of Naor!

I will cut him and roast him.

Enough waiting. She boldly entered the committee chamber, and the members rose to meet her. They bowed. Spiritlessly, she returned the gesture. Everyone sat.

By order, they would wait for her to speak.

"Forgive me—"

"Is your boy fine?"

"Was he harmed?"

"How did this happen?"

"What did the Elder Hammer say?"

"Please!" She held her hands out as if they could block their questions. "Everyone is healthy. The boy lives. It was just a scare.

Our Elder Hammer has some questions to answer, trust me on that. But our purpose here today will not progress that matter."

Rebuked, the members of the committee fell silent. She looked to Alcon who encouragingly smiled at her without teeth, nodding. She rolled her eyes.

"Let's proceed—"

Lady Eyrilia began as the door to the chamber burst open. Her committee members gasped as Ricard ran into the room breathless. "This is a crime!" she yelled at her husband. "You cannot interrupt whichever meeting you please. Leave and we will discuss whatever you have to say later."

Ricard surveyed the room and saw his mistake. He bowed. "I beg your pardon, Chairwoman. May I please have a moment? It is urgent. About . . . the boy." Eyrilia saw the committee members look at each other. She heard whispers. She bit her lip. The damage had been done.

"One moment," she offered, quietly imagining later strangling her partner in bed.

Together they left the room and closed the door. She pulled Ricard far from it and into the nearest hallway. Frantically, he spoke: "I checked in the courtyard, all throughout. I searched the lesson rooms. I spoke to Shaeron. They confirm that Naor did not begin his pilgrimage early."

"What do you speak of? What is all this?"

Ricard's face changed from glum to surprised. "You don't know? Our boy is missing, Eyrilia. He wasn't in his room this morning. He wasn't anywhere. I told you. You never listen."

Shaking her head, she said, "I will kill him myself."

"Don't you see? What if Naor was taken? What if there are

more Nails sneaking in here? What if he was targeted because of you—our family's position?"

"The boy is sensitive and careless. He is hiding and finding his feelings. Like his father."

"I checked everywhere," Ricard continued, unhearing. "I checked every Lessons chamber, notified the other children's families—"

Eryilia lost her breath, as if she were punched in the stomach. The man did what?

"How could you be so careless? You are threatening everything we have. Everything! The boy is hiding in the courtyard somewhere. The Hammers will find him. That is the last I will hear of it. Go home."

Ricard lowered his face. He looked as if he wanted to say something else, but the words never came. He simply nodded and left.

Lady Eyrilia again smoothed her dress. She took but a second before reentering the committee's chamber. Once again, the committee stood and each member bowed. She returned the gesture with a wave of her hand. "Now," she said, "where were we?"

19

DAELAN

The Hammer slid his fingers along the First Parallel's cavern corridor as he walked. The walls were always wet down here. It was not clear why or from which source the soft trickle originated. This wetness made the corridors feel alive, as if the great mountain had swallowed them all whole and was slowly digesting them.

If so, this Parallel is certainly the mountain's asshole.

He approached the Elder Hammer's cavehome and knocked on the old wooden door. It was heavy, notched and weathered but somehow dry. Doubtless another inexplicable object designed by the kingdom's mysterious wizards.

Sneaky shits.

Daelan had heard whispers of a recent raid. The Swords had rushed the wizard's hall and squashed whatever unauthorized evils they had been devising. But Daelan knew that castle gossip spread like groin fever, and what was heard was not always true. Let a lesser Hammer worry of wizards. Daelan had more pressing concerns.

"Come on already," he heard from the other side of the door. Daelan entered.

Holo's cavehome was the largest in the First Parallel. The dwelling was bright due to a wide window that opened towards the Parallel's northern port. The main entryway split a smoldering brazier from adjoining rooms designed for shitting and sleeping. Daelan approached Holo at his stonetop desk, sitting in a royal chair adorned with cracked golden paint.

Likely something smuggled from the castle.

Holo's desk was cluttered with tankards and decanters, stacked plates buzzing with flies near puddles of dried, melted wax. On the far side of the desk was a glass bowl filled with water; in it swam a prized purple fighter, the fish that feeds on flesh.

Daelan stared at it.

"You've never seen one before," Holo said as he wiped his mouth, catching Daelan in a rare moment of awe.

"Never. I have only heard stories. Children losing toes from swimming in the streams bordering the Treelands and the Northern Arm. That sort of thing," Daelan explained. Distantly, he realized he now knew a little more about Holo. The Elder Hammer must have served in the Northern Arm. "I've also heard of Hammers who led Nails to those streams and pushed them in. For punishment. For show. I never had the pleasure."

"I see you are not afraid to break some rules, after all, eh Hammer Daelan. Eh? Haha!"

Daelan furrowed his brows. "Sir?"

"Last I checked, Hammers were not allowed to speak of the past."

"A Hammer has no past. All that matters is the hand gripping us now."

"Raise your head, Daelan. Even you are allowed a sip of sin."

"Especially when goaded by my own Elder Hammer."

Holo rubbed his chin. His eyes burst wide and a smile grew. He raised his finger to indicate "one moment" and sauntered to his large window overlooking the shore. He hunched and stretched his chubby arm over the ledge, and it returned with a cage full of small white birds. They flapped in frenzy as Holo opened the door and reached inside. Calmly, he coaxed a bird into his meaty hand and clasped it securely. "Delicate little bitches," he said. Holo closed the cage and dropped it back over the window where it dangled. The birds squawked in defiance to his clumsy release. Holo returned to his desk and softly mimicked the bird as it nervously cooed in his hand.

"Gird your loins," he told Daelan. The Elder Hammer had reeled him in with this chintzy production, and Daelan was annoyed at himself for allowing it. Daelan did not want this. He wanted only to yell at and lecture the lazy heretic, but here Daelan was, eyes open wide like a child desperate for a story's end.

Holo plunged his hand into the bowl for only a moment before pulling it out. He counted his wet fingers on his lips. All there. The fish attacked the bird with the fury of Sor's justice. A fierce whirlwind rattled the bowl as if Arou itself was shaking. The bowl's surface splashed with tail and feather. The water swirled into a deep red that obscured the glass entirely, hiding the hunter's final strike.

"Sor's mercy," Daelan managed. Holo cackled. His volume still took Daelan by surprise, how it bounced off the walls of smaller rooms or traveled down the corridors. The sheer audacity of it. Holo was a force; Daelan understood that now. The longer he served underneath the Elder Hammer, the more he would grasp Holo's grip on the Parallel. Daelen understood now why he had remained in power so long here, the foundation of the entire mountain.

"It is something," Holo said, calming, his face redder than usual.

"You are brutal with birds but not with Nails."

The change in Holo's face revealed that he knew the bonding was over. "My friend, you confuse brutality with rule," Holo said. "That cannot be our way."

"You are the Elder Hammer," Daelan said plainly. "A leader, a ruler. Not a friend."

Rolling his eyes, Holo settled back into his chair. "There have been some reports . . . well, many reports."

"I am adjusting."

"Before you know it your time will be up and you'll be on your way to bigger and better things. Or maybe you will stay here. Get fat from the crab like me. Haha!" Holo lifted his tunic, grabbed his belly and shook it.

"Anything else, sir?"

Holo looked Daelan up and down and saw, perhaps, trouble brewing in some shape or way but could not yet define it nor prevent it. Was his Hammer truly cooling? To Holo, Hammer Daelan was written in a language he could not yet read or speak.

"Try to learn a few names, Hammer Daelan. And you will do well here."

"Names?"

"Local customs, son."

Daelan nodded his head as he kept his gaze to the floor. He could no longer look at his Elder Hammer. His hands, he realized, were shaking.

20

LAYALA

Legs dangled over a ledge.

Layala and her brothers watched the water work: the dedication of the current, the collaboration with the wind. Ocean swimming was a dangerous dance, and Layala was uncertain if her brothers were truly ready to learn the unforgiving and hostile lead of the sea.

"How much longer?" Silus asked.

"She already told us." Marin said with an annoyed whine.

"We sit here and we look," Layala explained again. "We watch the tide. We learn its patterns."

"In and out. I think I got it," Silus cracked. Marin chuckled.

Layala rolled her eyes. She sighed. She should have taught her brothers how to swim much earlier, when they were kinder and still thought of their older sister as a magnificent being who should be followed and mimicked. Now, the boys had each seen nine ages. She would battle impatience as well as pliable attitudes. Besides, ever since Hammer Daelan's arrival, slipping out of the Parallel had become trickier. Studying the tides from the cliffside above was the easiest method she found, but it would only progress them so far. Her brothers needed the beach.

It didn't take long for Daelan to overpower Pon's casual management of the port. The crabbers, fishers, and collectors of the sea could now only leave the Parallel with a kingdom pendant. They claimed a pendant when they worked and turned it in when they returned. Hammer Pon, who looked as annoyed as anyone else, administered the pendants and refused to let Layala pass without one, let alone her brothers, this morning when she tried.

"But how will they learn the trade?" Layala had asked Pon.

"You might not know this, Layala of Shit's Bottom, but I do not care."

"I will speak with Holo," Layala warned.

Pon shrugged her shoulders. "Me thinks even Holo's trying to avoid Daelan's bad side."

If it were up to Layala, and it never was, she wouldn't bother teaching her brothers at all. Her dad taught her the trade and that should be enough. Shouldn't it? Hadn't she crabbed better than Thomas? She swam faster and further and had traversed the rockstacks he swore were never worth the risk. She had dropped their traps in unexplored seas and uncovered prosperous pools with larger and bluer crabs. And what was her reward? She got to teach her brothers to replace her, to steal her craft. For what? So she could make babies? Like Vann? Become another mother her children couldn't stand? The caves were too low for Layala. That was the truth of it. The sea was open and infinite, and she spoke the tide's tongue.

"Is it cold? It looks cold." Marin said. The boy was smarter, more inquisitive than his brother, Layala knew, but Silus was the braver of the two. Perhaps bravery conflicted with logic. She mischievously wondered, more frequently than she cared to admit, if they were supposed to be one child, perfect and complete, but were split.

"It's a real steam bath, Marin," Silus deadpanned. "What a dud."

"The sea? Yes, terribly cold," Layala replied. "The more you swim the thicker your skin becomes. It's difficult to explain."

"Or you've just got kelp for brains," Silus teased.

"That is always a possibility," Layala admitted. The wind picked up and she felt her hair pull behind her, as if it were reaching for the warmth of the community fire pit down the trail.

"It's cruel, isn't it?" Marin asked. "Being so close to the water yet unable to swim it."

"With time, with time."

"That's not what I mean," Marin said. "I know you will teach us, Lay. What I mean is, us, sitting right here, so close but unable to reach it." Marin stretched his small arm. Perhaps he was braver than Layala knew. The salt was already in their blood.

"We could jump in," Silus suggested. "We gotta learn somehow."

Layala slapped the back of her brother's wild head. "You have learned nothing. That wave," she said and pointed, "crashes your ugly skull against that rock. Whether you know how to swim or not."

"You're lying."

"Watch it," she said, and they did. "I told you. We can only go in at the shoreline. It's the only way."

Silus looked helplessly at Marin. Marin looked to the horizon. She saw sadness and disappointment in her brothers and shook her head. An older sister was a terrible thing to be. Her brothers endlessly annoyed her. They interrupted every moment, every meal. They threatened the balance of her and her dad. Yet she loved them. Layala would find a way to teach her brothers, and then she would mourn when the sea took one or both, for that was the way of the ocean.

No. The salt is in our blood.

"We're going tonight," she announced.

The boys looked at each other and smiled.

LAYALA RETURNED TO her family's cavehome and found her mother carving a shape out of a block of wood. "My blade," Layala demanded, offended.

"Just borrowing it, dear," Laya replied.

"Stop, you're making it dull. It's not a carving blade. Give it back!" Layala stretched her arm and opened her palm. Laya ignored her daughter and continued carving.

"Please, mother."

Laya patiently set the wood down and looked at her daughter, blinking. "I am just trying to make Swelling gifts for your brothers. You were supposed to keep them out of the home, occupied all day."

Layala tried to snatch the blade, missed it, and then grasped her mother's hand. Fumblingly, she pried her mother's stubborn fingers off the hilt.

"Layala! What has gotten into you?"

"It's my blade! I earned it myself."

And you never make me anything.

Layala decided not to say that aloud.

"Fine," Laya said as she stood, wiping the dust off her knees. "I'll just tell your brothers that their sister was too selfish, because only she was worthy of holding the sacred blade."

Having no sheath, Layala stuffed the small blade in the back of her waistline. "You want to make them something? Jump in the water and find one yourself." She stomped out of the cavehome and hid nearby in a darkened corner of the mountain's corridors, blinking through stinging tears. Layala had earned everything she had. Her brothers had earned nothing.

And her mom? She did the least of them all, actually, following her father like an ungrateful and aimless shadow.

Layala wiped her face. Hateful words filled her brain.

Today was a good day to yell at her mother, she decided.

Layala marched back into their cavehome and, to her disappointed surprise, found her mother back on the floor also crying. Whatever vengeful words simmering in Layala's head dissipated.

"Here," Layala said earnestly. "Take it."

"No, no."

"Take the blade."

"I don't want to bother you."

Layala rolled her eyes. Here it comes, the guilt. "Please, I am sorry. Here.”

Laya made an effort to refuse Layala's sudden kindness, and Layala felt that old heat rise again in her chest, but instead of feeding it, she simply walked over to the abandoned block of wood, which held the nascent shape of a boat, and plunged the blade into it.

“There, it's done.” Layala walked back to the door and moved to leave. “I'll keep them out late. I'm finally teaching them to swim, just so you know.” She hoped that would please her mother. Laya had been nagging her daughter to do just that for eternity.

Instead, her mother asked, “Are you sure? That new Hammer. He's been watching the port closer. It's not worth the risk, dear.”

Layala closed her eyes, sighing.

“They deserve a Swelling gift from their sister, too. I promised them. It's not like you could teach them.”

Layala left before her mother could say another word.

ON THE NIGHT of the Swelling Moon the sun did not sleep in haste. Even after the horizon swallowed the light whole, the sky would not fully darken in those long months. But the darkness, no matter its depth or reach, enabled the errands of the night, and Layala, Silus, and Marin waited for it now.

“Patience is our weapon, time is our shield,” she explained. It was not easy to teach time. Her brothers struggled with the concept. For Marin, patience was a fish in a tide pool; he could reach for it but not yet grasp it. For Silus, he too saw the fish, but he jumped in and squashed it, emptying the water as he did it. Her brothers were simply not ready.

But was she? Memory was kind when the judge was oneself.

What was true was that she had waited too long. Everything had become more difficult. Not long ago, Layala would have just given Hammer Pon some smuggled wine or promised her the largest crab from her next haul, but the loafing Hammer had hardened under Daelan's spell. Layala knew all about shifting tides.

If they were to make it to the beach they simply had to wait for Pon to leave her post.

"This is taking too long," Silus whispered.

"She will leave for supper soon. And shh."

"Are you sure she can't see you?" Marin asked. "You are so tall."

Silus covered his mouth with a giggle as Layala shushed again. Marin's eyes went wide. He did not mean to poke fun at his sister. "That was a serious question," he clarified in a whisper.

"Just shut it," she told them both.

Unexpectedly, Pon did not leave when the sun did. Time was now against them. The tide would reverse within the hour and the beach would disappear until morning, its flooding more dangerous than ever under the influence of the Swelling Moon.

They heard snoring.

"It's alright, Layala," Marin said. He put a hand on her arm. "We can try again tomorrow."

"No, no, no," she said. "There's still time."

"Patience, yes?" It was Silus who said it, and Layala was filled with a love she didn't know she had. The boys looked different, she realized, seeing them with new eyes. They were young men, very young, but soon they would be old enough to fish and fight. They needed to learn the water, she decided fully. She had waited too long. Layala found a small rock in the dirt. She winked at her brothers.

"What are you doing?" Marin pleaded, but it was too late. She threw the rock. It hit Pon's table and scurried off. The Hammer stirred. She looked left, right, down, and up. At last the Hammer shook her head and yawned. Cracking every bone in her neck, she stammered off into the inner Parallel, likely searching for supper and sex in Holo's feast hall.

Layala again leaned into time. She held her hand to show the boys how she wielded patience. She waited long after Pon had disappeared, perhaps too long to make a point, and ensured the passage was clear.

"Come," she commanded, and the boys followed.

They passed the Parallel's port entryway, climbed down the steep ledge to the shoreline, and landed on the beach's sand. A smile broke through one and then the other. Silus ran his hands through the sand, collected a handful and playfully threw it at his brother. Marin absorbed the shock of it. Then he laughed. He quickly built his own arsenal and launched for revenge. They chased each other around in a circle. Layala watched her brothers run around like idiots and thought she had never been happier, at least not since she pulled her first cage out of the water with her father watching, laughing from his joy.

Feeling her cheeks redden, she proudly shushed her brothers and reminded them of the minutes they were losing. They found the shore and halted when the water reached their knees. The sea was warmer than they expected.

"Arou's great trick," she explained. "The water is warmest just when the sun leaves."

She showed them how to float and had them take turns and practice. She taught them about breathing, because breath only existed when one could no longer have it. "Hold it and count five," she told them. She plunged each underneath, their nervous heads under the anchor of her steady hands, and resurfaced them, Silus coughing and Marin spitting. "Now breathe."

After a few rounds of this, the Wavelo Nails stood together holding hands, the sibling's smiles bright in the glow of dusk. The beach would be covered within minutes, so she called it.

"Time. Let's go."

They retreated from the water and hit dry sand, the size of beach increasingly lessening, and progressed back toward the tall ledge they would need to climb to reenter the Parallel.

She felt his presence before seeing him.

"Layala," Marin whispered.

"Layala the Nail," Hammer Daelan pronounced loudly with a devious hint of formality. He stood atop the ledge, looking down. "I was told to learn a few names. What are theirs?"

Layala swallowed panic. She stood in front of her brothers, one arm protecting each. "They have no names. They are but lowly Nails in service of Sor."

"Ah," Daelan said. "How proper. The way Sor intended." Daelan paced slowly. He pulled the combat hammer from his holster and pounded it into his palm as he walked.

"Please," Layala began. "They fell in. I was helping them before the tide—"

"They fell in," Daelan repeated. "They fell in."

She heard a brother whimpering behind her, she was not sure which.

"I can give you what you want," Layala said, and she stepped forward in offering.

The Hammer stopped pacing. He looked at the tall, wet Nail, taking in every inch of her, and he shook his head. He laughed.

"This whole Parallel seems to think it knows what's best for me, what I want. You know what everyone gets wrong? I chose to be here. I earned it. This Parallel is mine."

"Please," Layala pleaded again. "The water is rising. They cannot swim. We will do whatever you ask. Please." The water was now fully at her ankles and rising quickly.

"Only one of you must pay for the sins of the many." Daelan proclaimed his judgment calmly. "Choose one to suffer, and I will let two of you return. Sor's justice."

Layala reached for the blade in her waistline and found nothing. Her eyes closed. She remembered plunging it into a block of wood and in her mind quickly cursed her mother. Desperately, she scanned the ground.

She stepped forward more and fell to her knees, which splashed into the quickening rush of tide that flooded the beach more every second. "Take me," she said. "I'm the one who suffers."

Behind her, her brothers yelled, they cried.

She gripped a passing conch and hurled it. The shell hit the Hammer's chest but did little else. Its purpose was distraction. She charged the ledge and scaled it, her lithe, tall frame nimble on the rock wall, and tackled the Hammer. As she fought him, she yelled at her brothers to climb.

The Hammer and Nail rolled on the ground. She heard the boys screaming for help, remembering now they could not scale the ledge without her, for they were just children, small and trapped in the moon's hungry and rising tide. Hammer Daelan rolled on top of Layala and slammed her head onto the smooth rock below it. He squeezed her neck. Layala gasped for air and slapped the Hammer's arms but it was of no use.

Below her she heard her brothers' fading screams.

She looked to the ledge and saw the water rising beyond it.

The world turned darker than it should have been during the long months of Arou.

21

SALAMOHAN

The shrine was alive. Priestess Salamohan could feel its energy, its breath. She had entered the sacred inner room of the First Parallel's temple only to replace its candles but upon arrival halted and fell to her knees. Salamohan was being called.

Many candles were still lit, about thirty or so, and they flickered together in small waves, growing small then large then small again. The shrine was windless. Built in the exact middle of the mountain, each Parallel's shrine sat directly underneath or above its adjoining Parallel's shrine, allowing for easier passage whenever Sor's souls traveled.

For the priests and priestesses of Sor's faith, meditation was a powerful tool.

Salamohan frequently meditated but rarely communed, for even the priest of the lowly First Parallel was shunned. She was old, as most priests were, but Salamohan was strong. One had to be strong to survive so long in the Kingdom of Kulloh-Sor, priest, Hammer, or Nail. All priests shaved their heads and marked their skin with the sigil of the King, but Salamohan had let her hair grow. She did not fear retribution from the Court anymore, from the high priests, from Sor himself. Where would they send her? There was no lower posting.

She closed her eyes. She counted her breath. She opened her palms.

Disconnecting was easier when called, something she hadn't felt in ages. Today was no exception. Salamohan released her soul, and it swam through the air.

They were taught to look away from their bodies as their souls lifted, as it could jar the disconnection and pull the soul back down. Now, the soul looked; it did not recognize the body.

It will expire soon. Whoever that is.

The soul rose through the great mountain in just seconds, passing Parallels and the evenly spaced rock between them. It saw every temple, every Nail, and every priest. It heard chants and wailing. It smelled the fragrance of fire and the aroma of incense. Higher still—the 28th, the 29th, the Court, Capital Castle. The higher Parallels were smaller, and the soul flew faster, passing empty temples, quiet temples, temples filled with rubbing bodies, squeezing and screaming with passion. The soul soared ever higher still, to the Forbidden Parallel, reaching, stretching, finding water and—

"Sister Salamohan," a solemn voice grabbed her, a high priest of the Court.

The soul remembered. It was attached to a body. Salamohan.

"I'm here," Salamohan replied.

"Praise Sor."

"Praise Sor."

"You were straying. What dealings bring you above the Court?"

As the soul communed with the high priest, the soul also communed with Salamohan. Existence itself was an echo. Her voice came before the words did. "I was lost."

"Careful."

The souls did not appear as bodies, but they did have forms. The soul of the high priest continued: "Expunge him."

"Who?"

"Holo. Daelan shall be anointed in his stead," the soul of the high priest explained. Then its form and the light surrounding it disappeared.

The soul's fall back to its body was harrowing yet succinct. Salamohan stirred. She blinked. She pulled herself up in total darkness, for the candles in the shrine had blown out. She heard the soft trickle of water. Her own breath. She wept. "The blood-shed," she said and covered her mouth. Her head felt heavy, her hair too long.

22

MOURAD

Mourad sat at the viceroy's table, hand over mouth. He sweat from the morning light reflecting off the lake, pouring in through Eda's large windows.

Mourad read the letter again.

> *Listener: I must go to the Rho at once. I*
> *will return in five days. I trust you can*
> *manage the chamber in my absence.*
> *-Viceroy*

Her viceroy stamp was marked in wax. The letter was an impressive forgery for a dullard. It was plain to see it was written by another hand, but the most obvious hint of fabrication was the message itself. Eda would never trust Mourad to manage anything. The woman was as controlling as she was crude. Further, why wouldn't she take Mourad with her? He was her trusted advisor and confidant. Cousins by blood. It was obvious, yes. The viceroy was taken against her will. It was the only explanation.

Mourad first found the letter yesterday morning and thought it a lame attempt at humor. Eda had a way of disappearing after long evenings, especially if lust was in the air, and Mourad did not seek her out for the rest of the day. As evening approached he returned to her inner room, and, when he didn't see her, Mourad began furiously searching throughout the chamber. He repeatedly returned to the balcony and to his frustration found nothing out of the ordinary.

What now? Mourad was a listener with nothing to hear. The letter promised a return, but three days remained. He could not yet raise any alarm. If the chieftain were to discover the viceroy had fled the province without his approval, or indeed had been taken against her will and was missing (or worse), he would nominate and place a temporary ruler. That, certainly, would invite disaster.

"Oh no," he said aloud and clicked his tongue twice.

Was Faziah an agent of the chieftain? It was all so plain and obvious. Yes, the chieftain hired the Rhoian leader—if that even was her—to seduce Eda and draw her away from her chamber. In his frantic mind all events were now colored with suspicion, including the elegant tribal dinner with flavors not seen in Prir since the wasteful days of Viceroy Haasher. Eda did not order the food and neither did he. The clues he missed earlier now smacked him in his uncommonly unshaven face.

"Excuse me, Listener?" Mourad turned and saw a servant girl standing at the doorway.

"What is it?"

"Visitors for the viceroy. And . . . yourself, of course."

Mourad folded the letter and stuffed it into his pouch. "I did not know of any meetings." He stood and looked at the girl. "Regardless, the viceroy remains ill and indisposed. I will fill in. Who is here?"

"A chamber ship from Einn. Our scopes reveal Viceroy Cavl and Viceroy Merl, and their listeners."

"Cavl, Merl? Coming here?" Mourad rushed to the window and craned his neck but failed to see the docks. Instead, he rushed to the balcony and leaned over the ledge. His hands touched something crusty on the balcony railing, and he absently wiped them off on his robe. There he spotted the arriving party. It was as the servant said: the viceroys and their listeners.

Mourad could entertain province saints and district heads for five and, if needed, fifty days, but viceroys were another breed. They would expect to see Eda directly. He suspected this was all part of the chieftain's plan.

Exasperated, Mourad clicked his tongue twice.

"VICEROY CAVL OF Einn and Viceroy Merl of Vier," the servant girl announced. The listener bowed.

"And I believe you know our listeners," Cavl said with a hand extended to the two men behind him.

"Of course," Mourad replied. "Akhil, Saim. A pleasure as always." They all bowed. Mourad led the group to a nearby table where they sat. Another servant entered and poured tea.

"We were told Viceroy Eda has fallen ill," Viceroy Merl said. "That is unfortunate. We have rather pressing issues to discuss."

Mourad nodded with a tight smile. He knew every word he would say, and every word he would not say, was to be scrutinized by their listeners. Akhil and Saim were exceptionally shrewd. Mourad briefly considered running out of the room and jumping over the balcony. He never did learn to swim. How hard could it be?

"It must be pressing to come so urgently without notice. This cannot wait until the next viceroy chamber session in Einn?"

"Correct, Listener," Viceroy Cavl said. "May I ask if the illness is serious? I will inform the priests and begin fervent prayer for Viceroy Eda."

I am sure you will.

Mourad said, "While the Viceroy of Prir may be an outspoken unbeliever, she will appreciate the gesture. I certainly do. It has been an ugly bout of food illness."

"Food," Listener Saim interjected. "I heard she fell ill two nights ago. After the chieftain's great speech."

Akhil continued the thought, "Yes, certainly. Food illnesses last only one day. Are you sure she has not recovered? Unless it is more serious than you are letting on?"

"Ah," Mourad said and restricted his tongue from clicking. Buying time, he stood and walked around the table, putting his hand on each listener's shoulder. "My dear viceroys, I believe you have chosen the best listeners in Arou."

Likely recognizing the stalling tactic, the listeners feigned appreciative bows.

"Viceroy Eda is recovering but is very weak. She had not slept these last two nights and now rests as if spellbound. I beg of you not to make me wake her. There are bears I'd rather tickle."

He chuckled, but his company did not join in laughter. Mourad continued, his throat feeling dry, "I am here as her listener, as you well know, and can take company in her stead. Let us plainly discuss what pressing issue led you to visit Prir's friendly docks."

The viceroys looked at each other. Cavl nodded. It was as he expected, Einn was in charge even here. Any listener worth his weight could see that Merl was but a puppet. The provinces should be equal under the chieftain's rule, as was established by Trisrca's founders, but much had changed since those early, earnest ages.

"The prophecy," Cavl said.

"Ah," Mourad began, "the chieftain's favorite topic at the speech. The man from the stars who will lead us into war and help us retake that glorious and stinky mountain."

"Solin. He Who Climbs the Sun," Listener Akhil said.

"Gentlemen, Prir does not waste its time with such fantasies."

"Call it a fantasy in my province, Listener, and we will have your tongue," Cavl calmly declared. In the heat of even this moment, Mourad recognized a welling of pride, of excitement within him—the burden of leadership. The listener was holding his own even against the viceroys of Einn and Veir.

"Mourad, the time of debate is over. The prophecy is coming true."

"How convenient for the chieftain, having now seen one hundred ages," Mourad suggested.

"This does not come from the chieftain," Saim clarified. "Words from the desert. Visions, signs. Did it not seem odd to you how full the Chieftain's Hall was during his speech?"

"I thought they were there to glimpse the most progressive viceroy in Prir's history."

"Enough!" Cavl stood, his chair kicking back and falling to the floor. "All you need to know, Listener, is that He Who Climbs the Sun is coming. The chieftain will no longer need Prir's support for an invasion. The prophecy supersedes the Founders' Principles."

Mourad raised his hands, finding more courage with every bureaucratic poke and prod. "So, a man from the stars is coming, and you don't need Prir. Why, I beg, are you here?"

The silence in the room revealed a faint unbalancing of power.

The Listener Akhil replied, "The chieftain, in his bountiful grace and fierce wisdom, invites Prir and its leaders to rejoin the faith. All sins forgiven, all slights forgotten."

Mourad sat, leaned back in his chair, and put his hands behind his head. "Let this listener summarize what he has heard. You want to wage a war we cannot win for gods that do not exist because of a prophecy that will never come true and . . . you still need us to do it. You need Prir. Our citizens, our young, our old. And you'll need the tribes too. But to get the tribes, you'll need to show full alignment of the Three Hearts. Has this listener heard everything correctly?"

The room returned to quiet. Only swooping birds from outside the balcony filled the air.

Mourad leaned in, smirking. "Well, what are you offering?"

For the first time since arriving at Prir, Viceroy Cavl smiled.

23

EDA OF PRIR

Eda revived the memory again. The sloppy chugging of wine. The brazen hand on a knee. The quickening desperation of her hungry heart. She was a fool.

"I want, so desperately, Viceroy, to talk to you about the prophecy," Faziah had said.

Guh.

Eda could vomit again just thinking of the scene. Vomit, of course, was what Eda did just moments after Faziah's request. She ran to the balcony's edge and purged over the rail, plopping three courses of waterfare, lubricated in a film of half-digested wine, back into Trisrca's Lake of Life.

"Viceroy, I hope I did not churn your stomach," Faziah had said next. Was that the worst part? The look on Faziah's face? It was all the worst part.

There was more. Another purge. Then the chills struck her as she fell back to the floor. The vomit was not the ugliest thing to come out of her mouth that night.

"You must be joking," she told the leader of Rho.

"Humor is not in my family's blood."

"Neither is intelligence, it would seem," Eda said, wiping her mouth. She wished she could remember the look on Faziah's face and hoped it had been one of patience. For unknown, illogical reasons, Eda continued to speak. "Perhaps I misunderstood who you are, Leader of Rho, believer of child's tales."

"Clarify your point," Faziah had replied in the Trisrca tongue, revealing her first hint of offense, albeit a small one. Eda only shook her head. She remembered now how fast everything swirled, the world out of focus.

Eda's brain found its footing, and she yelled, "You are a minion of the chieftain!"

Faziah's face remained frustratingly patient. Instead of returning Eda's volume, she simply sat next to the viceroy on the floor of the balcony and sighed. Much to Eda's surprise, Faziah grabbed her hand, slimy as it was. "I am a leader of an independent Ornvia people. I do not answer to the chieftain. Unless I am mistaken, that is your job, Viceroy of Prir."

"Funny," Eda told her, and she pulled her hand from Faziah's. Whatever attraction, friendship, or collegial kinship—whatever it was—existed between them had fled. Eda had little patience, and could certainly have no feelings for religious fanatics, even believers as beautiful as Faziah.

"It is as I said, humor is not my blood. As you know, I am a Seer. Your reaction does not surprise me, Eda of Prir. I foresaw all of this."

"Oh gods," Eda said, rubbing her face. "Your visions. You 'Seers of Rho.' Let me guess. You foresaw the fulfillment of the prophecy."

Faziah smiled. Eda remembered her smile like a stab wound. "Solin, yes."

"Solin," Eda repeated in a low voice, nodding and staring at her own feet.

"You must come with me. Tonight."

Eda looked at Faziah and laughed. She pointed and cackled. It was another ugly moment. Eda had never thought less of another person. She wanted everyone in the viceroy's chamber, in all of Prir, to run onto the balcony and point at the crazy tribal woman.

Look and laugh!

"I don't know what you have heard of Prir, Faziah of Rho, but maybe you should hire a listener. I haven't believed in the prophecy since I was a child, if ever. Go to Vier or back to Einn with this horse dung."

"You mistake my intentions, Viceroy. That is exactly why I am here." Faziah stood. "Enough of this," she said before three slow snaps. Eda heard a rustling. She felt the sudden pinprick of a dart land in her foot. As she faded, Eda saw a daunting and terrifying vision of ghosts appearing from nothing, slowly invading like wraiths from a children's tale, the same sizes and shapes as Faziah's sisters. She could not scream because her mouth no longer worked, and for the first time that she could remember, Eda believed in the existence of demons.

THE VICEROY SAT alone in the cabin of a dark, dusty carriage. It was not an opulent wagon, but neither was it spartan. The bench was cushioned. The paneling was painted clay red with silver flecked along the trim. The black curtains were embroidered and silky rich to the touch. Her hands were not bound. A bowl of fruit rested on the floor. She was weak from hunger but refused to eat, not until she knew more. How long had Eda been asleep? The light peering in through the edges of the cabin's curtains told her night was over; that much she did know.

Prir's chamber would be looking for her by now. Mourad would be looking, at least. Oh, her idiot cousin! How could he let this happen? Her Listener of the People could not hear his own farts. And yet, to her own complicated heart, she admitted to wishing he was here by her side. What would Mourad tell her to do? The cabin door was unlocked and easy to jump through.

"A viceroy never opens her own door," Mourad would say. "Remind them who you are."

"An orphan who needs to piss," Eda said aloud to no one.

It was only a few minutes more before the carriage halted. She heard footsteps crunching on gravel. Birds twittered in the distance and, beyond that, the civic rumblings of what sounded to be a small tribal towne.

"I am coming in," a familiar voice declared. The cabin door swung open. Eda shielded her eyes from the punishing light. With her other hand she instinctively reached for her dagger, and to her surprise, found it still on her hip. She pulled the blade and held it in front of her, aiming at the open door. A short, fragile elder came through the opening. He sat across from her and smoothed the wrinkles in his dark trousers, carefully patting the dust off his arms.

"The road is a filthy venture," he said. Familiarity came before recognition. Eda certainly knew this man. It took her too long, but she eventually comprehended the retired viceroy in front of her. She had never seen her predecessor out of his traditional robe, the one Eda never bothered to wear.

"Viceroy Haasher," Eda processed aloud.

"No, no. I served, and now it's your turn. Just Haasher will do. Or Old Man, like the sweet Rho children say."

Eda was hungry, tired, confused, groggy, and frightened in her capture. A Pririan leader she once adored, and later despised for his political embrace of the chieftain, appeared before her. Haasher was her captor? Unless—

"Were you captured as well?"

Haasher smiled and lowered his head, as if both humble and embarrassed or in the least, uncomfortable. It was less than an age since the Chamber Transition Ceremony, and yet Haasher looked as if two decades had passed. The man's frame was thin and feeble, yet his skin had darkened and thickened from the desert sun. His hair had thinned, making his wispy ears look as if they had grown.

"No," Eda answered for him. "You are part of this."

He nodded and returned eye contact. "All will be revealed and you will see you are in good hands," he told her. "Safe."

"Good hands?" she exclaimed. "Your hands are filthy! You were once a great leader. Then you forgot the people you served. Taking bribes, living lavishly, letting the chamber warm to the chieftain's fervor."

Haasher sighed and stood. The peak of the cabin's ceiling

comfortably fit his short height. It was Haasher's carriage, she instinctively concluded.

"From what I understand," Haasher began to say as he exited the cabin, "your dinners are quite lavish as well." He disappeared beyond her sight.

The gall of the man.

It was not her fault!

She wanted to scream but knew it would do no good.

Let the crazy old fool think what he thinks.

"Are you coming?" she heard from far outside the carriage.

She waited, because she knew they were waiting, whoever the others were. Hastily she grabbed the bowl of fruit before entering the dominion of her captors.

BY HORSE, THE Rho dwelled a two-day distance from Prir. Mourad had estimated one hundred members, but Eda saw now that was far too low. A community of four hundred tribal members, maybe more, maybe less, obliquely bustled before her. Towards the west, a vast field of poppies stretched into the hilly distance. Beyond it, Eda could see corn growing, and other crops her limited longsight couldn't identify from so far away. Instinctively she knew there was more than just farming in this towne, but it looked to her that most hands were busy tending to the fields. This was a desert, she had to remind herself. The ground was dry, the sun hot. Eda casually wondered where the water came from to keep such blooming crops so lavish. The settlement was too far from any of Ornvia's major tributaries. She considered the weight of the air: thick and humid. Perhaps they farmed in a storm pocket. She did observe, with fresh realization, that both the farm and its adjoining towne were designed to withstand flooding.

Where she stood now, a single wide road of crushed red rock split about two dozen buildings, some large, some small. At the end of the road on the left rested a lofty but tumbledown grain shed. All of them were old structures, built of wood but reinforced with clay and stone and raised off the flooding ground. She noticed next shuttered windows and doors that swung on posts. Eda mused they were likely of some fashion from five hundred ages before.

The Rhos did not build this towne. At some age, after a battle or a sickness, the Rho had come and claimed it, a common story of the desert tribes and the lands they settled on. Whether the Rho first seeded the poppies or only found them here was a story Eda suspected she would never know.

The Rho worked with stained dust on their legs, their arms and their torsos. Their hair was thick, like Faziah's, and ornately designed. Some had towers of hair, others shot off their head like a branch. Eda saw a Rho with a bird in a nest atop his head. They stopped briefly to look at Eda but overall seemed unimpressed with her presence.

Eda reached Haasher. He stood in the humble shade of a nearby saloon and squatted as he talked to a group of children. They smiled and jumped. He handed each of them a small gift, and they scattered. Eda saw a child clutching a powdered orange rock candy.

"So, this is where you disappeared to. The Rho."

"Welcome, Viceroy Eda. Officially. May your eyes rest and

your heart see."

"Is that what they say?" Eda asked the former viceroy.

"Indeed, indeed. The Rho have seen a great many things, but they are not the only reason you are here. Nor am I, young viceroy. I hope by now you know that you are truly not a prisoner. Some theatrics were required, I am afraid. Eat, please, please. Fruit to ease your stomach from your sickness two eve's ago."

Eda froze. "Two? I've slept for two nights?"

Haasher shrugged his shoulders. "You needed the rest. So your heart may see."

Eda rolled her eyes. Then she attacked the fruit. It was a mindless race between her fingers and her teeth. The bottom of the silver-flecked bowl disappointed her ravenous appetite.

"There will be more," Haasher said and chuckled. "Come and meet my co-conspirators." He began walking up the steps and onto the deck of the saloon.

"Haasher," she said and stopped him. "It's been two days. Where can a nice, friendly non-prisoner like myself find a toilet?"

"Ah, of course. You should freshen up. The Rho have many things, more freedom than you could ever grasp, more happiness in Arou than what truly seems possible, but they do not have toilets. For now, enjoy the tents." He gestured to the tents along the outer edge of the road.

"Tents. Wonderful."

As she walked towards them, Eda yearned for Prir's chamber. Plumbing was a privilege in Trisrca, and even Eda adjusted to having private toilets with drainage ramps, cleaned weekly by her servants. Prir did not have one solution for plumbing, but many solutions depending on the location or the district. Eda campaigned, as much as any candidate could campaign in Prir, on a few central topics, salient of which was centralizing sanitation. Time passed, and it was all too easy to forget the problems of plumbing when hers had been fixed.

She shook her head and took the opportunity, as usual, to curse the name of her cousin.

DID THE FLIES mistake her for shit? She swabbed another one away in the stuffy stench of the tent.

Poetic that the sprawling fancy dinner from her courtly tribal visit found its unceremonial end in a hole in the ground of a makeshift tent in the desert. Eda sat and did her worst. It was a relief greater than sensual climax, sweeter than winning viceroyship, and more fulfilling than slapping the old chieftain in his face, the latter she could only imagine.

They'll move the tent when the hole was filled, and Eda suspected that day was near.

All those potatoes, they make you think you're invincible, that you can keep drinking the wine.

She suspected most of the wine was already out of her body, exorcized the night of the dinner.

The memory returned without mercy. "... So desperately, Viceroy, ... about the prophecy." The balcony edge. The plopping. The confusion and embarrassment and anger.

Gods-be-damned! That prophecy. All Eda had ever tried to do was avoid the distractions of religious fervor and childish prophecies. Let the people pray in their temples, and let the leaders govern with only the wisdom of hunger and thirst. Yet here she was, Viceroy of Prir, taken against her will, deep into the deserts of Ornvia for some sort of . . . conference?

She washed herself with a rag floating in a dirty bucket and pulled up her trousers. She opened the tent flap. In the distance, the Rho still came and went, hauling carts and sacks and tools, busy with their own important tasks. Haasher's secretive party waited inside the frail-looking saloon building at the edge of the old towne's road. No one was watching her, she realized. Eda could just walk straight to the carriage that brought her, untie the horse, and ride it home. She could travel through the rest of the day and into night and onto morning. Find her way back to Prir, to Mourad, to her people.

But would she? Eda felt an annoying curiosity churn within her. Who else was inside that building? Why did they bring her here? What was Haasher up to, really?

Before she knew it, Eda had pushed through the old swinging door, entering freely into the saloon. Whatever happened now she could only blame herself. Perhaps that was Haasher's plan all along. The old politician had a knack for engendering self-manipulative action.

Inside, Eda found a very plain and nearly barren parlor. The floorboards creaked as her weight found them, some protesting louder than others, mewling like a woken baby. She ignored them. Along the main wall were built-in bookcases, mostly empty, though a few meaningless relics from forgotten families survived to collect desert dust. In the middle of the room at a small, circular table sat her captors: Haasher, Faziah, a Border Captain she recognized from the Chieftain's Hall but could not remember his name, and, to her ultimate dismay, Leod, her rival from the Chieftain's High Council who frequently thwarted her reform efforts. No one stood. They all looked upon her in silence with neither smile nor scowl.

"Not who I was expecting, I must admit," Eda said to break the silence.

"Please, sit," Haasher insisted, pointing at the remaining open chair. "Join us."

"And what exactly am I joining?" Eda took the chair and dragged it away from the table to the other side of the room against the wall. She would sit but not rub elbows, especially with Leod, the puss of the chieftain's favorite pimple. He was a short man with long reach, keen and informed. If the chieftain required a Listener of the People, Leod would be his.

Eda sat. She saw for the first time a jug of water on the table alongside a short stack of cups. Awkwardly, Eda stood again, walked back to the table and poured herself a glass of water. She clinked the cup to the water jug. "A'scoullee," she said and then drank. Briefly, she met Faziah's eyes before returning to her seat on the far side of the room.

Haasher spoke first.

"Our founders did not leave the mountain willingly. As long as there has been Trisrca, there has been a desire to abandon it and retake Eccoulous, what the false kingdom calls Sor's Crown."

"Three kings exiled. The prophecy. Solin. Retake the mountain. I have heard it since I was a little girl."

Leod interjected. "Four."

"Four what?" Eda asked, insolent with Leod's minimalist smugness. His face, his natural resting face, was enough to make her punch his bushy eyebrows.

"Four kings. Three to the hills, one to the sea."

Eda shook her head with conviction. "Three kings. It's always been three kings."

Haasher spoke again, "If you are willing, there is much for you to learn."

"There will be time for all that," Leod offered to Haasher. They exchanged a brief look before Haasher agreed and nodded. Leod continued, "But you are correct, Viceroy Eda. There are only three kings that matter to us in this present moment, for Trisrca is our prime concern. As long as there has been Trisrca, there has been a prophecy, and as long as there has been a prophecy, there has been a group. A very selective group tasked with preparing for the prophecy's fulfillment. A representative from each of the Three Hearts, as well as a Seer and a guide. This group was established by the first chieftain of Trisrca, many generations ago, and it lives on today."

"I am not joining your little . . . party," Eda said.

"Please, let us finish," Haasher politely implored. "You've come all this way. You might as well hear what we have to say."

"I have come all this way? Funny way to put it."

The room was silent again. Leod raised a hand to Faziah, offering her the floor. It's a gesture Faziah didn't need, and that too annoyed Eda. She allowed herself to fully look at the leader of the Rho, to process her presence. The woman was still beautiful and commanded an air of elegance, but she was less mysterious in the sweaty daylight of a barren parlor. Eda released the embarrassment she had been holding from their last encounter. That was done now. Eda was a viceroy of Trisrca, and though she was still learning how to wield the title, she knew that explanations were due her, and if they did not satisfy, she would use the power of her chamber to snuff out whatever foolishness this was.

Faziah spoke. "Ages passed, chieftains came and went. This group, the group that was to prepare for the prophecy, was forgotten, but not by all. It became something else. We are something else."

"Zeit-be-damned," the Border Captain exclaimed. When he stood to push in his chair Eda noticed the arbalest draped behind his back—the weapon of a border captain. He approached Eda and extended his hand. "Call me Yorke. You politicians love to talk. Chatty chat chat. Let's just cut to the bone."

"Wonderful," Eda said. She liked Yorke already, though impatience could be dangerous. She recalled Mourad telling her that, one of her cousin's many unrequested pieces of advice.

Yorke said, "We are the Bound Accord. We're here to kill the prophecy. No one here wants an invasion. Trisrca is what we have, and it's all we need. Fazzy here saw He Who Climbs the Sun in her dreams, so—"

"Visions, Yorke, not dreams. Dreams are just wild brush strokes of the soul."

"Right, visions."

Eda was trying to keep up, but she was briefly hooked on Yorke calling Faziah "Fazzy." Eda asked, "Why do you need me? I am not a guide."

"You are correct that you are not a guide," Leod said with a smile.

"Viceroy of Prir," Haasher continued. "We need your ears and your influence. Leod as you know is from Einn, Yorke is a senior border captain from Vier. Faziah is our Seer. I am now just an old man, guiding us all together.”

"The Bound Accord, huh?" Eda stated plainly. She thought for a moment and then added: “I do not believe in prophecies, but the thing about prophecies I do understand is that, if true, you cannot keep them from happening. That’s what makes them a prophecy. If Solin is real, there’s nothing we can do.”

Yorke laughed. “Darlin’,” he said. “This won’t be the first man from the stars we’ve killed.”

24

JAH'RI

"Rejoice! I have given you Nails. Oh! I have given you Hammers. Build for generations, for millennia, however long it takes. My staircase will serve as my Temple and my Promise. When I judge it honorable and finished, I will rejoin this realm, my kingdom, and walk down its sacred steps. Let the Nails worship through their sacrifice. Let the Hammers praise with their fists."

—The Scrolls of Sor (rumored)

All Nails were told of the great mountain's past, which Sor first shaped in the Era of the Gods, later revoking it from the men who managed it, and returning the territory to be ruled by the true line of Sor. When Sor left this realm He gave his world-born son, Joeth-Sor, scrolls of wisdom and instruction, the excerpts of which were proclaimed widely and loudly with every plucking.

Jah'ri learned another word from his time in the King's Court, religion: the belief in and practice of Sor's scrolls. This word revealed to Jah'ri a new reality, for he was unaware that belief could be a choice and that even many of the kingdom's own priests mocked the faith. Other kingdoms had other religions, he was told, and there was some private debate of Sor's legitimacy within the castle's own walls. "A lesson you would do well to not repeat."

Whenever Nails were plucked for Sor's Staircase, there were small squabbles—nothing like the haunting memory from Jah'ri's youth, the vulgar, targeted death of his mother that required the rare swinging of a King's Sword. Normally, the instructions were simple and the Nails complied. Gather and pluck. There were, of course, Nails that ran and cried and fought, but in truth, most of the plucked Nails did not know what horrors awaited them. Many had never seen a falling body. Most thought they would simply serve in a higher, holier Parallel.

"Do you not see?" a priest told Jah'ri as he pushed the Hammer out of his private chambers. The priest stood at the door, out of breath and suddenly suspicious, aware of the danger in his words, in their rendezvous. He lowered his voice: "It is not religion that creates this madness, but power without end. Religion is just a distraction. The Nails fall. The Hammers pluck. The Court gets fat. The King reigns. On and on it goes. Busy, busy, busy."

"And what of your faith? Is nothing real?" Jah'ri did not know why he asked it.

"Real . . ." The priest mumbled, growing impatient. "Listen, Hammer. Write down all your very important questions. Seal them inside a scroll. Roll them. Bind them. Stand on the mountain's edge and cast them into the sea. Another generation, another age will find your queries. Let them answer. Our salient task is to live. Breathe, breathe, breathe."

"I am no coward, priest. I am here for answers."

The priest chuckled and swiftly slammed the door. Jah'ri stood alone in the candle-lit hallway, holding his uniform. "On and on it goes," he repeated to himself.

OF ALL THE memories that swam through his head at the sight of Shyloc, it was the priest and his foul, sobering message that flashed in his mind's eye.

On and on it goes.

Within Jah'ri was an urgent and desperate need for reasoning, but there was none to be had.

Reason had abandoned Arou long ago.

The Nails walked the steps. The Hammers swam to Shyloc. Distractions, the movements of kingdom life. The false shape of purpose. Endless busyness. All eyes on strife and none on the King.

On and on it goes.

Jah'ri swam towards the Isle of Brecca and its eternal protector.

LEGENDS SURVIVED ONLY when their stories were told. Shyloc came from a forgotten time, when Arou was young and its many mountains remained unshaped and evolving. There were more tales than truths. Some believed Shyloc came from the ancient Grenden, an ocean species that warred against the dragons for dominion of early Arou. The Grenden and their followers trapped the dragons and by doing so, formed the great mountains as their dungeons. The Grenden won the war and ruled the planet, but it was short-lived and ill-fated. Those who fought for the dragons sought revenge and cast spells on the Grenden, trapping them through the spirits that haunted the Elder Fire. Eons passed and the Grenden diminished and disappeared.

But Shyloc remained.

Jah'ri was closer and the beast was clearer. Shyloc was shaped like a snake with a long narrow snout. Its body was black but sheened purple in the moonlight with lightning crackling off its skin like sand carried through the wind. The ancient sea serpent rested tall and surveyed its domain. Like an arcane guardian awoken from its slumber, Shyloc lunged with a righteous and terrible fury, capturing a trespasser whole. Jah'ri heard the demented crunching of muted screams but swam through it, reaching and pulling, reaching and pulling.

Jah'ri was too close to another Hammer, he realized, so he swam away as was instructed. "Do not wade within the ripples of another's hand," their commander warned them. "Spread and survive. Approach from every angle. Swim as the beast feeds."

It was true: the ancient one was dedicated to its meal, distracted even. Shyloc chomped with its head raised in the air as if taunting the moon itself. The beast chewed for only a few more moments, and then it plunged underneath and disappeared. Water exploded, but as the violent splash settled, the ocean's surface returned to a maddening state of serenity, a pool with an omnipotent and unseen pursuer.

"SWIM!" Jah'ri heard a Hammer yell.

The warm waters surrounding Brecca came alive as the remaining Hammers' hands and arms hopelessly spun into action whilst their feet kicked splashing trails, their hearts beating frantically as if trying to flee from their own condemned cages.

Only a few seconds passed before their misery returned.

A Hammer was clutched and raised in the air.

Jah'ri emptied his mind and swam faster and harder, finding new strength where he thought none was left. Shyloc again dove, creating another explosion of water; this time it did not disappear but returned rather suddenly, its predacious eyes blinking just above the surface. Its skin began to glow. Lightning pulsed brighter and faster off the beast's body, generating power that peaked and released as a shockwave that stunned the three Hammers closest to it. A giant mouth captured one stunned swimmer and pulled him below. Again, the water's surface returned to calm. The other two Hammers, stunned and stiff, called for help as they floated anxiously. They screamed. They cried. This was the best thing that could have happened to Jah'ri and the other Hammers who remained knew it as well. He could make the isle if only he kept his pace. Brecca stood triumphantly before him, another fifty strides or so. Jah'ri heard another stunned swimmer get captured, her gargling scream muted as she was pulled down. He heard the voice of the remaining stunned Hammer, trapped and awaiting his death.

It's not Saz, it's not Saz.

But of course it was. Saz was crying, his large voice hoarse from the screaming. Saz screamed Jah'ri's name, and that was what ultimately stopped him. Jah'ri paused for a moment. Brecca was closer than ever, the water feverishly hot from the river of Elder Fire feeding back into it. He closed his eyes and cursed.

"I'm here," Jah'ri told him as he arrived. He grabbed Saz's leg. "I have you. Come on." He pulled the floating Hammer towards the isle.

"Jah'ri? What are you doing?"

"Can you move?"

"What are—are you insane? Get out of here!"

"You were just screaming my name!"

"I would never have come for you. You idiot!"

The water strengthened, and Jah'ri felt a pull underneath. "He's coming," Jah'ri said. "Can you move yet?"

"Yes," Saz said. "I'm just remaining perfectly still on purpose. I'm having a great time!"

Jah'ri swam faster. The water underneath pulled harder. They were getting nowhere. The beast was coming, and the isle was still too far away. Thirty paces. Maybe twenty-five. Jah'ri smelled the breccel mineral. The air tasted sweet and slightly sour, like winter fruit from the groves in the Southern Arm. His mind hungrily drank the memories. The water exploded, and Jah'ri returned to now. All at once he had never been so present, so tuned to his world and the creature threatening it.

Shyloc stretched its colossal neck, reaching otherworldly heights, and prepared to strike. Jah'ri realized Vaera was just ahead of him. She turned around and smiled, for she was nearest to Brecca.

"TERROR!" she yelled to Jah'ri before she was yanked into the air screaming.

Shyloc chomped. No time to watch, no time for fear. The distraction would be enough.

"Saz, I need your help. Saz? Saz? I need your help, Hammer." There was no answer. There was no time to look. Jah'ri held him still.

The water was ferociously hot near the rocky shore of Brecca, which stood only ten strides away. Jah'ri knew he was running out of time. He could sense the eyes of the beast on his back. He could feel the shift of the current push against him. He could hear the crackling hum of electricity charge.

The ancient one lunged towards Jah'ri. He pushed Saz away and dove underwater where the head of a giant, all teeth and tongue, submerged and followed him. Jah'ri pushed against the beast's slimy snout with his hands and feet, feeling its electric chaos and the hint of something else: a wave of a message, a memory spoken not through voice or image but pulse, as if the water itself was coded.

Some sort of trick to distract him, Jah'ri thought. He shook the haunted, hypnotic vision from his head and then, underwater still, saw something true.

A miracle.

Jah'ri briefly forgot to keep moving. Remembering Shyloc would stun the waters any moment, Jah'ri breached the surface and once again grabbed Saz. He had only seconds to reach the miracle he saw: a shore platform, just ahead under a thin layer of water.

The isle was even closer than he knew. Shyloc's hum reached its breaking point. Jah'ri pushed Saz onto the ledge. An explosion of light and sound erupted, and for one caustic, confused moment night turned to day.

Jah'ri latched onto the shore platform's edge and jumped into the air as the surge reached him. He was hit and flung far forward, landing with a splash on hard rock.

He rolled inland until his body halted, stunned and paralyzed. Jah'ri could breathe and did it quickly as the shock poured through the valves of his heart and involuntarily chattered his teeth.

He was thankful, at least, as much as any warrior could be thankful in the throes of battle and the bowels of the mission field, that he was stunned right side up. The primeval tide pools of Brecca would not drown him today, so close to finishing his mission. Jah'ri watched the stars, the true and the false, the quincunx constellation, as he listened to a chorus of chaos behind him.

Terror.

Rage.

Hammer

Pain.

His breathing calmed. His eyes closed.

For the first time in his life, Jah'ri dreamt of nothing.

25

———————

COMMANDER PRIME

//Processing//

What can be and cannot be finds cohabitation resulting in the unfamiliar processing of an impending error or possible unforeseen result, commonly referred to as . . . a feeling.

The machinarch thought, if thinking was really possible for a machine, it thought more of this feeling. It thought and it felt. It did not breathe.

Strange, to feel one's own order slipping away.

The machinarch sat inside the skyship as it hovered far above the Isle of Brecca, monitoring the progress of the Hammers, counting the casualties and calculating new averages.

Counting—

//Processing//

The kingdom had three flying ships. Most believed these

ships flew to distant worlds, even to the Heavens themselves, where the Godly Grandson took counsel from the Celestial Father.

//Processing//

One ship was allocated to monitor the continual advancement of Sor's Staircase, though it had been inoperational for 324 Arouan ages. Another ship transported the King to his quarters in the Southern Arm where he feasted and mated and slept. The final ship, Commander Prime's, monitored and guided the Hammers on their annual quest to Brecca.

It was not known where the skyships came from. The kingdom had removed that data from its records—

//Processing//

The skyships were foreign, engraved with exotic and unremembered symbols. Logic would dictate they were captured long ago from another race, another time. The spoils of war. Like all machines, one day they too would shut down. The wizards—

//Processing//

Commander Prime's life utility, much like the Hammers, had almost been used to its completion. This was not a feeling. This was a simple calculation. Its replacement was—

//Processing//

Commanders failed because they were imperfect machines built by imperfect creatures. Machinarchs had a lifespan of six point eight ages. They were recycled, rebuilt and reprogrammed by the wizards who tested and tinkered in the halls of the 35th Parallel. Soon, this Commander would expire too. It sensed the sickness within it, a failing of parts and a slowing of processing—

//Processing//

The view from the sky was—

//Processing//

The view from the sky was one of power.

//Processing//

The ancient slave attacked. It shocked and stunned its prey. It consumed. Commander Prime had monitored this ritual for many ages. Likely, many of its machinarch parts had witnessed this ritual before in a different machine with a weaker processing unit.

Commander Prime's eyes focused.

What was and what was not—

//Processing//

Blunt instruments were not designed to think. Only the hand holding the tool could change its course. A Hammer rescued another. This was forbidden. Foolish. This was the feeling.

//Processing//

Both Hammers were dead.

Commander Prime reclined and rested its eyes though they were not eyes and they did not strain. A machine should not so easily tire, but this one required a divergence of power to its central processing unit to complete a new calculation.

//Processing//

"Hammer Jah'ri," the machinarch concluded.

//Processing//

"Louder," the Replacement Commander demanded.

"Hammer Ja-Jah-Jah'ri," Commander Prime repeated, its mechanical voice starting to slip as its life utility came to an end. "Defied orders. There." It pointed.

"The Hammer who carries the blood of the revolutionary?"

"The re-reb-rebel Nail, yes."

"Louder."

"Disregard," Commander Prime replied.

"Did the Hammer expire?"

Both Hammers, the rescued and rescuer, remained lifeless.

"Un-un-uncertain-n-n."

Commander Prime proceeded with its analysis and scanned the waters for remaining Hammers, continuing its greater calculations.

What can be and what cannot be—

//Processing//

The machinarch had it again. The feeling.

26

JAH'RI

None of it mattered. The missions. The kingdom. The Hammers. Shyloc.

Jah'ri awoke desperately tired, sick from the exhaustion. It was still night. He heard the serpent patrol the shore, but it must have been no longer hunting, for the screams had ceased.

He could let himself fall back asleep. It would be so easy. Maybe he wouldn't wake up. Perhaps that was alright. Fall asleep forever. Let Brecca's strange purple crabs feed. Let the river of Elder Fire consume him. Rest. He had earned the deepest of sleeps. A crab pinched his cheek, and Jah'ri smashed it with his hand.

This was how he learned he could move again.

He clumsily readjusted his limbs until he found himself standing. The crabs scattered and disappeared into pocked holes.

Jah'ri oriented himself: the water, the cone, the distance. He would finish his quest, but first he stumbled back towards the water's edge to retrieve Saz. The body was easily found. Jah'ri dragged him inland until the shore platform fully turned to land.

"You made it," he told the corpse. Jah'ri sat down next to it. He saw the body was missing an arm. "Most of you." It was a sour joke, but he knew Saz would have appreciated the humor. Saz was never a friend, not really. The Hammer would have killed Jah'ri if he knew his hidden mission. And Saz would have made the worst kind of Sword: entitled, empowered, relentlessly cruel. Jah'ri was thankful, then, that Saz's death would never come from his hands.

"You want to know what I'm up to?"

The corpse did not respond.

Jah'ri had a story, and he told it. It all came out, freely and with tears, a release he never knew he would feel. To say it out loud. He laughed through the tale, he cried as he conversed with the dead. He knew it was madness, but he no longer cared. Jah'ri continued, "I'm going to take my reward. Infiltrate the Swords. I'm going to kill them all, Saz. The Swords. The King. I will tear down that castle tower. That was the plan, at least. Another mission I was given. I'm not so sure . . ."

Jah'ri realized he had been holding Saz's remaining hand and dropped it.

"In truth," he continued, "I can no longer see my mother's face, only her eyes. Perhaps because they are my eyes. I do not even remember my love for her. Only the sudden absence of that love. She is but a mist and shadow in my mind. Saz, Saz, do you hear me? Revenge is more of a curse than a mission. I wasn't sure if I would see it through until I saw the fat bald godman and his orange fingers, and I knew he had to die. That I would be the one to kill him."

The corpse was dumbfounded.

"I know," Jah'ri said. "I know. Something worse will replace him, perhaps a greater evil or a fatter king, but it won't matter. That will be someone else's fight. On and on it will go, because that is the way of Arou, a dungeon planet. Where the jailers are jailed."

Crabs approached again to test the corpse and begin to pinch and pull its flesh. Jah'ri looked behind and above him. The cone rumbled. He processed, for the first time, its brazen heat. Brecca was not an isle designed for rest. They would both burn soon.

Jah'ri rose and looked out to the sea. He saw the back of the beast rising and falling in the distance. There had been a message, hadn't there? Like a false wall suddenly moved, Shyloc, in the midst of its plunging terror, spoke when Jah'ri touched its skin.

Destroy.

He raised his head to the isle's cone.

Destroy.

"Yes," Hammer Jah'ri announced. "I can do that."

First, he squatted and reached forward in a whisper. "I need something from you, Brother Saz, and you're not gonna like it."

JAH'RI ABANDONED THE body and walked inland with an extra arm. It hadn't been easy. The muscles and bones in Saz's shoulder proved difficult to pry. Jah'ri pulled Saz's ankle blade and plunged it into the socket, kicking and stomping until the limb popped. Jah'ri sliced the remaining sinew and skin and apologized to the crabs who now munched on a lesser meal.

Now, Saz's fingers dragged through the soil as Jah'ri marched past the base of Brecca's cone and began to climb. The river of Elder Fire spilled over the opposite side, but the heat was as punishing as ever. The ground was hard, the incline steep. Jah'ri took a small break and looked behind him to see another Hammer, what looked like Hammer Rannold, scooping the breccel into his vial. Rannold paused when he felt Jah'ri's eyes watching him from above. Jah'ri could only imagine what Rannold saw when he looked. The moment was only temporary as Rannold collected his reward and dove back into the water.

He must think I'm insane.

He looked down at Saz's arm.

Perhaps that is not too far from the truth.

Patiently, Jah'ri watched the swimming Hammer leave the isle, attempting to avoid the beast a second time and return to Sor's kingdom a hero, a Sword. Indeed, the swim back would be a new test for Rannold, another journey.

"Some other time," Jah'ri said to himself and laughed.

Were they the only two Hammers to make it to the isle, him and Rannold? Chunks of Hammers floated in all directions, reminding Jah'ri of pieces of bread that children threw into the courtyard's ponds that fed the fowls. There, even the birds' stomachs filled. He remembered ignoring every instinct within him to dive after the bread and consume every uneaten grain. The presence of fowls themselves, visiting from the ponds of the nearby Treelands, were enough to tempt his inner Nail, and he regularly shook off visions of breaking their necks and running away from other desperate, hungry eyes seeking to steal his prize.

It was pure instinct, controlled but never dormant.

His thoughts returned to Brecca. Jah'ri restored his full attention to the cone before him. He surmised it was about an hour's climb to the top, and he became thankful. The peak was the only favorable distance of this entire mission.

Saz's arm draped upon his shoulder, he climbed. The heat was overwhelming and became more unbearable with every step, but he pushed further. Jah'ri casually wondered if his skin would even be able to withstand the peak's furnace. Maybe he was not the first Hammer to attempt this. There could have been others whose stories were never told because they quickly melted in the fiendish and infernal blaze of Brecca. Jah'ri grunted. He yelled through the heat. Each step was its own small mission. Jah'ri slipped and started to fall but pulled his own blade and stabbed it into the ground for purchase. Saz's arm slipped away from him, but he grabbed it by the hand and secured it. He climbed again.

After what felt like eons, the peak was now just steps away. The world had never been so red, so hot, so powerful. He turned away from it and faced the ocean. He was thankful for the cold air of the breeze that slapped him now. He could see Shyloc. From above, he measured its full scale from head to tail and could only shake his head. It swam without hunting and seemed to sniff the floating bodies.

Jah'ri realized this was his best and only chance, that it had to be now. He stuck Saz's arm into the caldera of the cone. Willingly, the limb became a torch.

"Come here you ancient piece of shit." Jah'ri waved Saz's arm wide and slow. He screamed. "I'm here! I'm here!"

Shyloc did not look towards Jah'ri. Instead, it lowered into the depths and disappeared, as if uninterested and tired. Jah'ri continued frantically waving Saz's arm. The torch steadily burned but rapidly shrank, skin dripping like hot wax, flesh scalding flesh. He waved faster. He screamed louder. The ocean rested quieter. The night became still. Jah'ri fell to his knees and threw away what was left of the limb. It rolled and disappeared. Jah'ri breathed and breathed and breathed. The serpent must have filled its filthy and wretched stomach with the brains and bones and spleens of the 38th Parallel, the bravest Hammers of the Kingdom of Kulloh-Sor, the King's Hammers, and Jah'ri feared that the ancient sea beast had finished its meal.

Perhaps there was no message. Only timeless evil and cold hunger.

Destroy.

A new mountain grew before him. The wave crested, and Shyloc's head emerged, lightning crackling off its skin. The beast had returned. Shyloc stretched its neck and raised its head to full height, and it was as Jah'ri hoped: the serpent's head stood tall at the same height of the volcano's peak. Its eyes stared at Jah'ri, and they saw each other plainly. The beast's eyes were not soulless or vengeful. They were old and wise.

They were haunted.

They were chained.

Jah'ri suddenly felt reverence and, unexpectedly, something close to kinship. He could study the serpent's eyes for hours had it not opened its mouth. Shyloc's largest fangs were each the size of a Hammer. The two warriors, Shyloc and Jah'ri, were separated by a league of water, but it would not matter. Shyloc could likely reach greater distances if it charged.

Hammer Jah'ri stood his ground and waved his own arms.

"Destroy!" he yelled. "Destroy!"

Shylock lunged. Jah'ri jumped. The peak of Brecca exploded behind him as Shyloc slammed into its cone. Jah'ri fell and rolled down its side. He slammed into the ground hard and cursed. An angry river of Elder Fire began to spew and pour down all sides of the isle's cone. He jumped to avoid the stream and the chunks that fell closest to him. Shyloc screeched. He saw the beast lift its head from the rubble. Jah'ri ran toward it, up what was left of the cone.

"Destroy!" he yelled again, louder.

Quicker this time, Shyloc shot forward and again Jah'ri jumped. Another screech turned into a scream as Jah'ri saw fire on the beast's face, smoke rising from it. Shyloc became erratic, its body wild, lightning shooting in every direction. Its body smashed into what was left of the cone and then crashed into the water, causing a wake so large it covered the isle completely.

The beast was gone, and the cone was destroyed.

After the water retreated, Jah'ri found himself alone on the shallow shore platform of Brecca. A pool of Elder Fire that bubbled out of a small bowl, slowly spilling and covering what was left of the ground around it. Jah'ri pulled the vial from his pouch on his shoulder and captured the last of the isle's mineral before the water and the fire conspired to hide breccel from the kingdom forever, or until whenever time built Brecca anew.

27

COMMANDER PRIME

The Replacement Commander watched the destruction of Brecca from the sky and nervously tapped on buttons that enlarged images from below and projected them onto their viewing window.

"I have checked the logs from our Sacred Archive. This has never happened."

"I could ha-ha-have-ve told you that," Commander Prime replied. "This is . . ."

The words did not come. Only feelings.

Jealousy.

Rage.

Joy.

Commander Prime was . . . not itself. This was what shutting down was like, Commander Prime realized. It did not know if it should have expected a sudden stop or a gradual death. It seemed to be both. The machinarch's circuits grew hot as spasms jerked its neck and shoulders. Echoes of voices, tunes and tones, sounds of all sorts overlapped within its mind, that is, whatever part of its imperfect build included the mind.

"Continue," the Replacement Commander demanded.

"Continue w-w-what?"

"It appears you are failing. You speak without order or purpose. You should not be here."

"Yes."

"Take us down."

"Yes."

Commander Prime hummed a distant tune it heard within the inner machinations of its skull as it pushed the controls.

The ship descended.

28

JAH'RI

*Y**ou won't come back. Understand? You can go anywhere else. Why would you go there?*

The voice of the Elder Hammer of the 37th Parallel returned to Jah'ri.

"It's all I've ever wanted," Jah'ri told him then and told him again now.

Death decides it.

You and your little throbbing hammer.

And Jah'ri, it had your eyes.

With wings, my darling.

Jah'ri stood in the middle of time itself as the Sea of Cashmu, endless and vast, spread in every direction. No Shyloc. No Hammers. No kingdom. Only a traitor alone with his thoughts. Tremors shook what remained of Brecca's shore platform, and

Jah'ri almost lost his balance as another piece of land slid away and fell into Arou's abyss.

You won't come back. Understand?

There was little left in him. Whatever reserves Jah'ri had were now gone with the isle he helped destroy. He knew if he swam he would drown. Death was not a new consideration for Jah'ri, nor was it unusual practice from a kingdom that celebrated utilization. Inevitability was a tool's only choice.

Jah'ri's hand blocked the rising sun, soon to be covered by clouds rolling in from lands unknown. He turned away from its blinding presence. The warming light had cooled him or, at least, reminded Jah'ri of coldness, and for the first time since he scaled Brecca, he shivered.

Jah'ri smacked his lips, envisioning a slurp of slop.

Give him the fattiest chunks in the pot, the thickest and gummiest, undercooked the better, burnt was fine. He would take anything. He would eat it raw and drink the blood.

His tongue watered at the memory of his last bowl in the Holster, eating with the dead, telling his dream to Saz, to a room filled with Hammers listening and snickering. The fish and the bird.

Shake them both with salt and throw them in the pot.

He would eat them too.

In front of Jah'ri, the color of the water changed. It danced red and blue and green. Strange his brain would do that, because those were not the colors of slop.

Above him the skyship descended.

Jah'ri saw it now, the false star, Commander Prime's ship. Its lights were bright even at dawn. It hovered just above and in front of him.

Jah'ri raised his hand. "One," he yelled. "One bowl of meat slop."

Another tremor struck, this one more violently, and Jah'ri fell face forward into the shallow water. He pulled himself up to his knees and grunted.

"Two, make it two," he yelled louder, coughing, his voice now hoarse and thin, breaking like the shifting rock he stood upon. He used what little strength was left in him to stand.

Jah'ri could not see the machines inside the skyship, but he knew they watched him. All was revealed now. No more hiding. No more deceit. The kingdom would know who Hammer Jah'ri was and what he had done. They stared at one another: a man standing firm on a disappearing isle and a machinarch dying slowly on a flying ship—and yes, another, a replacement machinarch, stronger and faster. The top and bottom of the skyship spun as the hull hovered steady. A blue light began to pulse at the ship's edges.

A door opened.

PART THREE

AFLOAT IN THE CLOUDS

They are free. That's your first reaction. The clouds are limitless and free. Their forms are never final, for they breathe and bend and break. They disappear and then someday reappear, a new form and yet the same. The clouds are one thing, and yet they are nothing. The power of the clouds, you finally decide, comes not from any one kingdom's inability to capture or control them, but because they persist above power altogether.

It is a view you cherish, your first act of true worship.

You feel hope for this free and graspless realm. The pace of the skyship reminds you of sailing in the Southern Arm. You only ventured once, and there, too, you flirted with joy. Now, you wish you could fall through the skyship's clear floor and feel the wind brush your hair and the clouds wash your filthy hands, but you suspect it is bolted shut with purpose.

You are bleeding.
Touch your stomach and remember.

29

JAH'RI

Balance was tricky whilst the isle reckoned with its fate, but Jah'ri stood tall nonetheless, powered, it would seem, by exhaustion and madness. Above him, the skyship hovered, its lights twirling on his skin. Atop the skyship's ramp he saw the outline of a figure, what looked like Commander Prime, but as the figure approached, Jah'ri saw it clearly and remembered: the Replacement Commander. The machinarch was the same height and build as the old commander, but when this machine jumped off the end of the skyship's ramp and landed in the shallow waters of Brecca's failing shore platform with an authoritarian splash, its power became clear. This machinarch was faster and stronger. Prouder.

"Hammer Jah'ri," the upgraded machine began, "you have been busy. You assisted a broken Hammer. You incited the slave beast to destroy the isle it protects."

"Shyloc is no longer one of your Nails."

The Replacement Commander stopped as it reached Jah'ri. "You admit your crimes?"

Jah'ri reached for his combat hammer and was surprised to find it still on his hip. He raised the weapon into a fighting stance.

"I pronounce you guilty of treason in the name of King Kulloh-Sor. Death would be a gift, one I shall not easily grant. I shall make you feel the King's wrath, slowly, terribly."

"Proclaim it clearly, machine, once and for all. Is there slop or . . . ?" Jah'ri could only smile at the thing.

He was devastatingly tired. His body was Brecca—every muscle strained, pulled, or pulsing. He was certain that parts of his skin had permanently burned from the caldera's heat. His lungs had taken in both water and sulfur, and he breathed like a fading Nail lost in the salt mines of Mount Muloh-Sor. Cuts covered his body from the slamming and rolling and falling. Shyloc's electricity still swam through his blood, and his hand could not hold its weapon still from its rush. Jah'ri would not win this fight. He knew that. But he would die as he so recently learned how to live: standing in open defiance against a kingdom that thieved hope and butchered will.

Come here.

Jah'ri did not even see it strike. He simply felt something hit his stomach and looked to find the hilt of a blade protruding from his body.

"Oh," Jah'ri said and fell to his knees.

He felt a kick to his chest and clumsily landed backwards, splashing into the shallow water. Jah'ri spat blood.

The Replacement Commander stood above him, its silicone scowling. "From Nail to Hammer and back to Nail again. Treasonous like the rotten womb that bore it. Fitting, your infected bloodline ends in the sea."

"Why . . . why is it fitting?"

Beyond skin, its eyes spun. "Strange human need. Your hunger for the past."

Jah'ri laughed.

The machinarch tilted its head in confusion. Laughter must not have been an expected response. It was not Jah'ri's intention to distract, for Jah'ri was a lunatic and impatient for death, but his instincts remained. He reclaimed his fallen combat hammer, and swung it one last time. The weapon found a steel leg and landed with a dull and pointless thud.

The Replacement Commander pried the weapon from Jah'ri and held it high. "First, I shall shatter your hands, one by one, then your arms, then your shoulders, then your sternum, then your knees, and finally your feet. I will leave you to watch from my skyship as you swallow this vile water, and I will count the seconds until you expire."

Jah'ri's combat hammer fell, accompanying the horrid impact of crunching.

Dizzying, the sound of it.

And the bitter smell of sparks.

After a brief seizure, the Replacement Commander dropped.

Jah'ri felt nauseous. He squinted at the slouching metal figure. "Commander?"

"How d-dr-dr-dramatic!" Commander Prime said. "Goo-good news-s-s! My central processing unit is m-mi-mis-misfiring as my life un-uni-unit con-continues to drain."

Jah'ri felt more like a toy than a tool, and whatever game this was exhausted him even more. "End this trick, machinarch, and kill me now. I am ready."

"Pish-ish pish," it said, eyes pulsating with new dizzying patterns that rotated and blended colors. Having shed most of its synthetic exoskin, Commander Prime extended an entirely metal hand. Not so long ago, that same hand gripped Jah'ri's neck and held him off the ground, but now, it reached out in friendship.

Jah'ri did not grab it. Regardless of the hand's owner, Jah'ri was not sure he wanted to rise. Standing would coax vomit, he was sure of it, and in truth, Jah'ri was afraid to see blood purge from his stomach.

Brecca cared not. Sonorously, the ground rumbled and continued to fall into the sea. Elder fire erupted from the small remaining caldera, just above the water's surface not far from them. A glob landed on Commander Prime's metal arm and melted through a piece of its frame. "L-lo-look at that," it said casually.

"Leave me," Jah'ri ordered. "Go back. Tell the King I destroyed Brecca. That it was Jah'ri of the 5th Parallel. The son of a Warrior. That with time the Swords at his side will fall. And—"

Commander Prime lifted Jah'ri into the air, cradling him like a sleeping child. The Hammer screamed. Consciousness swam with cold steel, and life became an elusive idea.

"What a da-day," he heard Commander Prime say as his own body convulsed. Drifting in and out of consciousness, Jah'ri heard something else, something playful, like the sound of a child whistling. He felt himself floating towards the deepest and darkest of voids.

THE RELIGION OF Sor promised life after death, but this offer extended only to the royal family, for they were Sor's direct descendants. But with hearts came beliefs, and each generation of Nails birthed new denominations of the faith. Parallels squabbled over conflicting sects. All branches of the faith were forbidden, of course, so the quieter they worshiped, the longer their roots took hold. The Hearers of the Sor-Song was the only denomination to emerge, expand, and escape from one singular Parallel. The Hearers believed the scrolls were initially misinterpreted after a priest's private writings were recovered many ages ago. It was not a staircase that should be built, but a song that should be sung. Every Nail would sing, and every Hammer would dance. The Hearers believed in a nameless realm where all members of the kingdom, the high and the low, would sync with the vast and endless song of Sor.

Jah'ri did not hear a song.

He did not hear the voices of the ethereal chorus soothing and guiding his soul to the hereafter. The void was muted, if not anechoic. The Sor-Song, it turned out, was utter gullshit.

Jah'ri was surprised, if surprise was something his soul was still capable of, assuming his soul was what currently was being, that his consciousness had survived and all was not black. This realm was endless though it was not empty. His eyes, if he had eyes, had adjusted to the darkness, and he found tranquil shades of color embedded into the terminal dark, the coldest of blacks and the warmest of grays. Thin lines separated these planes, and between them were echoes of limitlessness, the hopeful promise of yellows and blues and greens and reds. He had to swim towards this plane, if swim was the right word, and fit through the limitless lines to find whatever eternal realm awaited him next, if it truly was him that swam. There was no existence without breath, and yet breathing was not required here. Why swim further? This was the peace he sought, the rest he desired. He could stay here for eternity, if eternity had not already passed, and disappear into the wonderful nothingness of the muted realm.

Someone else.

Could others occur here? A form without form, a templeless usher, limbs from wisps of nothing, growing and reaching, a hand swiped clear a map of dirt—

Mother?

Then light.

Breaking free his hearing, the growing canals of his ears heard something like a hiss. The Formless retreated.

Loss.

He felt, yes, yes, he felt loss.

The thin line of color between the planes magnified into an explosion that would soon consume him, like a tidal wave of existence. The choice had been made for him.

Jah'ri was swallowed by life.

"HI-I-I-I-I," COMMANDER PRIME sang. "Welcome b-b-back, Hammer Jah'ri. How was death?"

Everything blurred but, slowly, Arou came back into view.

Jah'ri's brain struggled. Some version of Commander Prime stood above him. For a moment, he thought he was back at the Holster. Had Pond Scum just swallowed him whole?

No, no. That was a different time.

What cruel fate it would be to survive the swim only to go back and live through the Holster again. No, something else had swallowed him. What was that?

It was all too much for his mind.

He rolled onto his side, scanned his environment. He saw clouds through the glass floor that held him. It further troubled his brain. Hadn't he just been swimming in an endless sky?

Slower than he's ever moved, Jah'ri pushed his body upwards into a sitting position. It took some time, and he grunted through most of it.

"Was I dead?" he asked.

"Quite de-dead," the machine responded and then started humming as it turned away from Jah'ri, sitting back at the ship's control panel.

"Why did you bring me back? I was . . ." He tried to remember, but the memory faded like blood draining from a wound. There was darkness, a stolen finality. Every second of life that returned took Jah'ri further from his death, for the two could not coexist.

"Where are we?" he asked instead.

Commander Prime stuttered to Jah'ri with a spilling cup of what looked like hot tea. Jah'ri took the mug and stared at the steam rising from it. "Tea on a machinarch's skyship," he said. "I must be dreaming, if not still dead."

"The skyships were m-ma-made for living b-be-bein-beings with mouths and stomachs. I do not know which. Isn't that s-s-silly-illy? I know every-th-everything about the k-kingdom, yet that information is concealed from me-e-me, as if it were erased from the kingdom's a-a-a-a-arc-archives."

"You speak as if . . ." Jah'ri's brain was still foggy. He wanted to ask but could not form the words.

"Yes, yes, Hammer-er-er. Whoever created the skyships-ps-ps left them be-behind. Those ornery wizards are involved some-how. Drink up! Up! Drink! Ornery!"

Jah'ri blew into the cup and finally took it to his lips. He drank. It was not the slop he was craving, but after an overflowing bowl of blood, despair, and death, nothing had ever tasted so true. He drank again. In truth, food would be another matter. He likely would not be able to eat for quite some time. He braved to touch his stomach and found the bleeding had stopped. The wound was stitched.

"You patched me up. And . . ." He closed his eyes to catch the words. "You shocked my heart into beating again?"

"Isn't that n-neat?" Commander Prime returned again to his control panel. "What a day."

"Sor-be-damned. I was not supposed to live, Commander. I . . ." The words fled him again. He finished his tea and set the cup on the glass floor. He felt dizzy from the effort of sitting and laid back down. That was enough sitting up for today. He watched the clouds for a few more minutes; occasionally they broke, and he saw the ocean below it.

"We're still over the sea? How long was I gone?"

"Your b-b-br-brush with the infinite abyss-ss lasted an entire thirty-two point three seconds. We have only been f-fl-flying for eight point eight minutes."

"That can't be right. I feel . . . as if I were gone a lifetime." That old mortal pastime, the lassoing of the logic of time, was much too heavy a burden, and instead, Jah'ri attempted to clear his mind by following the shape of the broken clouds.

"You and I b-both, fr-friend."

The skinless machine whistled a tune that jumped in and out of key, as if struggling to keep power. It looked at Jah'ri and raised a metal hand with its thumb up.

"What is wrong with you, Commander Prime?"

It nodded. "Welp, I m-me-men-mentioned-d-d-d the wizards. You know, those slithery green-skinned practitioners of s-sci-science? They form the machinarchs. They belong to another race from another world. Don't ask me which or where or who. What do I know? It doesn't matter. What matters-ers-ers is I believe they d-de-designed me to malfunction spectacularly. And wowza, did it work."

"Do you serve them, then? The wizards."

"I cannot answer that." Commander Prime asymmetrically rested its eyes and returned again to the controls, pushing a few buttons. After a moment, it continued: "Not because I don't w-wa-wan-want to. I am just a tool, much like you are-are-are-are. Or were. Motive is a privilege I am excluded from."

"You avoided my question, Commander. Where are we going?"

"Tell m-me-me what you see. Look below-low-low."

Jah'ri looked again through the floor and saw just a glimpse of the blue below the clouds. Waves broke in an odd language, a pattern that splintered the tide, as if a river swam through the sea.

"Shyloc," Jah'ri said. "Are we following Shyloc?"

"I am afraid-d the ancient one f-fo-follows us."

"Revenge?"

"L-lo-logic would suggest it-it-it-it-it-it-it-it-it needs a new m-mas-master. You fr-freed Shyloc. Now the creature serves you."

"But the beast is free! It does not need a master."

"It ch-chose-ose you, Jah'ri. That's the th-thing-ing about free wi-will."

"Choice. Decisions. Free will." The words rolled in Jah'ri's mouth like ice, refreshing and foreign but elusive to grasp. "It is my decision then. Where we go?"

Commander Prime stood to clap its hands. "If I may, I-I-I-I suggest we, I suggest we ram this sh-sh-sh-ship into Sor's Staircase and take it down, m-m-m-mu-much like you did Brecca's cone. You seem quite keen on d-dy-dying. I have little time left. What do you say? Do you say? What do you say?" The lights of the machinarch's eyes twirled with hope.

Jah'ri thought on it. Choice was a strange burden. He wondered if a warrior could ever really be free. Was it ever even his choice to carry revenge in his heart, or to tear down Brecca? Was Fate the mistress of Free Will, or did he have that backwards?

Jah'ri abandoned whatever trail of logic his mind wandered through. He returned his gaze to Shyloc swimming below the ship. Perhaps this creature, the ancient one, could only taste freedom if Jah'ri crashed their skyship into Sor's Staircase. Then Shyloc would be free to roam forever unfettered from the maw of debt and subservience.

"Take us down and hover," he told Commander Prime.

"Oki-e-e-e, d-dokie."

As Jah'ri tried to stand for the first time since dying and living again, he wondered how much blood he had lost and how long it would take for his body to replenish it. Jah'ri laughed at his own weakness. Commander Prime joined him in laughter, not knowing why. His blood swirling with sweat, Jah'ri's began working in earnest on his greatest and most courageous task, the act of standing. He cursed every god, Hammer, and Nail he could think of.

Per his instructions, Commander Prime lowered the skyship to just above the water's surface. He opened the door and extended the ramp. Jah'ri reached for the railing along the ramp and began. He felt a metal hand grab his shoulder.

"H-Ha-Hamm-Hammer Jah'ri, are you sure-re-sure are you?"

"What do you mean?" Jah'ri asked Commander Prime.

"It may destroy us. That would-uld ruin my d-da-day."

"I thought you said Shyloc served me now. That it was bonded to me. 'Logic,' you said, 'logic would suggest'—"

"I was just r-r-riffing," Commander Prime said before abruptly turning away and returning to the skyship's control panel, whistling.

"Sor-be-damned," Jah'ri exclaimed. He had died once. Why not do it again?

Leaning all of his weight onto the railing, he stumbled down the ramp faster than he meant to. The wind hit his face. He shivered terribly. Jah'ri realized, rather sourly, that he was not yet ready to feel, smell, and taste the open ocean air again. He stood over a calm surface and waited for the beast. He knew it would arrive. Finally, it joined him. In what felt like an immobilized nightmare, the surface quaked, and with the slow dread of primeval horror, Shyloc's colossal head breached the wind-capped waves before him and the two were, once more, face to face in the

Sea of Cashmu.

Shyloc did not destroy him. Plainly, they stared at each other in the light of the day. He studied Shyloc's skin, which was scarred and pock marked amidst nature's mystical patterns that were likely laid an eon ago. New, fresher wounds were plump and seared.

"You are a warrior," he told the ancient one. "Or perhaps you were a ruler. I suspect the passage of time has taken your memories, much like it has taken mine. I was tied to a mountain, much like you were tied to an isle."

Shyloc listened.

Jah'ri continued: "Me and you, we have some decisions to make. I am new at this."

He looked to the west and, for the first time since leaving the Cove of Kullan-Sor, saw the boundary of the Kingdom of Kulloh-Sor, the faint misty base of the great mountain. "We must decide to live or to die. What do you say?"

Shyloc said nothing. Jah'ri was not sure what he expected. He scoffed at himself, his own foolishness, but the ancient one finally did speak. The beast raised its head to the sky and roared the deepest and loudest roars Arou had ever heard, a call-to-arms that shook and rattled the ramp of Commander Prime's skyship. Jah'ri reaffirmed his grasp on the railing and winced at the pain in his ears, the only thing left on his body that hadn't been hurting. Shyloc finished and lowered its head, as if bowing.

"I b-b-believe you have-have-ve your an-answer," Commander Prime said. Jah'ri looked and saw the machine at the top of the ramp. "If only we knew what it m-me-means-eans."

"I know what it means," Jah'ri said.

30

A LETTER

My friend, I have escaped!

Oh Dffai, the Treelands are alive with freedom. I cannot foresee if this letter will reach you. I plead to Arsia, our goddess and true founder of Arou, that it will. As you read this, you will see I have ciphered these bold and urgent words with our ancient script.

I do not yet feel the effects of this system's effulgent star, its rays unfiltered on my skin. The tree canopy is thick and protective. Perhaps beautiful. I feel as if I have left all of Arou behind entirely. How long were we trapped in that tower? How many centuries?

Eccoulous, the true and rightful name of our mountain (I speak aloud as I write, can you imagine being so free?) is still too close. I can see part of the thief's staircase when the canopy allows me a view, but I will not linger long. Doubtless, the watchers of the castle will soon hunt this roving wizard.

I let a boy from the Court inside the castle. It was foolish, I know.

It happened like this. The Hammers standing guard fell asleep as I strolled through the threshold passage and opened the gate. The efficacy of my sleeping mist pleased me as did the device which delivered it (three seconds to disperse, four seconds for suppressing the pineal glands).

Copiously, I recorded all my notes just now before beginning this letter. Science must remain our priority, my oldest and most exasperated friend. This boy was sneaking into the castle. I do not know his reasons. His mouth dropped at the sight of me (the sheltered child had never seen a 'wizard' before, so he studied the greenish hue of my skin as if it were some riddle).

I had no time and little patience to deal with such ignorance. He entered as I fled. The castle is large and empty, yes. He may wander through it the rest of his short, miserable mortal life, but we cannot risk it. Find him before he is captured and questioned. Do what you must.

I travel now to the Holster and from there will report my findings. I expect success. If the machinarchs respond as designed (remind me of our wager?), I will continue to the Southern Arm where . . . Well, I dare not yet write it, not even in ciphered script.

Stay patient, Dffai. I saw the device you designed and while its mechanics are lovely, its timing is . . . ill-fated. I pray to Arsia that you remain steadfast in your reluctant stubbornness.

The line of Sor reigns thoughtlessly. I still see the carnage the Swords wrought on our order, the last of the true line, killed in our own hall. Ah, as do you, as do you. We will reach Arsia soon enough. We will tell Her, and She will return to speak this reign out of existence.

My bird will not linger long. Reply in haste once you've found the boy. Avoid using Arsian Hand if it delays your words. There is little time.

We shall revive in Her blessed shadow!

—Rfael, the Order of Arsia

31

RICARD

The Nails in the 29th Parallel felt it when they woke: the quiet hum of expectant dread, almost undetectable but present, like ripples in the air from the flutter of wings. A plucking. The priests would soon arrive, and the Hammers would pluck. Here, just below the plateau, the plucking of Nails led to the falling of friends and the cleansing of splatter. Those that learned to feel it refined their sensors with every age that passed. The signs were present; the morning air was heavy and tasted of salt and cabbage; the portcullis creaked with anticipation. But there was more. Something else. Today's air was different. This new dread unknown.

With the eyes of the Court just above, Nails of the 29th were plucked here more than other Parallels and not just for the staircase. Servants were needed in the Court, Capital Castle, or shipped farther to the Northern and Southern Arms. The Nails would never return home, because a Nail did not have a home; a Nail was merely an instrument of the King.

It was here where the Children of the Court embarked on their pilgrimages, where they learned the truth of the world: Sor's Just Society. When the ascendant scions walked the 29th's smooth pathways, guided by their philosopher, they witnessed a high-functioning community that was well-fed, respectful, and grateful. Patches of grass were allowed to grow wherever the sun could reach and even sunflowers bloomed. Berries sprouted from the overgrown vines interwoven along walls and over passage-ways. Nails of the 29th were not granted electricity's magic, but they often benefited from its proximity, for the food was fresher in the 29th Parallel, the tools sharper.

The Nails were the correct level of filthy. Less but not hope-less. Near to provisions, yet forever hungry. The lesson was that Nails could only be fulfilled by the kingdom's usage.

"Sor created Nails for His mighty purposes, and the Ham-mers to guide them. Look around, and see Arou as Sor intend-ed." The philosophers taught as they walked. The children of the Court learned with their eyes and ears, and their hands did not touch.

RICARD IMPATIENTLY WATCHED the dome's portcullis rise. He stood just ahead of a small troop of Hammers, who he would lead down into the 29th.

Just an hour prior, the Elder Hammer approved Ricard's re-quest to search the 29th under the pretense of Naor having been stolen by Nails—only after Ricard burst into the Elder Hammer's private chamber as he slept and demanded action. Ricard did not consult Eyrilia, but he would deal with his wife later. She thought him careless, a fool. She could call him what she liked. Ricard was a man of action.

Inside the great mountain, cavern corridors led to iron gates separating Parallels, but these corridors were dark and labyrinthian, treacherous for unfamiliar feet. It was not uncommon for philosophers and priests to stumble upon slouching skeletons, clothed and clutching weathered maps that once promised daylight.

Outside, pulley carriages transported plucked Nails to the plateau with the wizard's cable, which was finicky and required much upkeep, not to mention planning; the Court's committees aligned their usage with one another before issuing orders, as the pulley carriages were incommodious and slow. Propped ladders stretched off each Parallel's cliff side and reached high to the passing carriage cab, which only paused briefly for onboarding passengers.

Exterior switchback trails provided the most direct route between Parallels but were rarely used, often overgrown, and particularly dangerous when the wind was strong and the moss was moist. Terrain altered depending on the Parallel's position upon the mountain and whichever weather haunted it. These trails were eventually blocked by a Parallel threshold gate, a portcullis guarded by Hammers, and thus, only the privileged used them.

Ricard did not wait as instructed for the portcullis to clear but hastily ducked underneath its iron teeth to pursue the exterior path of the 29th, uncaring for the Hammers who followed him. Dead zones separated every Parallel. At the plateau, the wild mountain slopes were steepest and required surefooting from the philosophers and children who frequented it. Ricard refused to slow. He pushed past the cliff's edge and jumped down its side, steadfast into the rocky and wet winding trail without regard for his own lackluster, golden-strapped sandals. He ventured off the zigzagging path to save more time, and when confronted by an ancient and immovable boulder, hopped over the thing, found his footing, and began again. It went this way for some time until the portcullis for the 29th Parallel came into his view.

"Incoming, citizen of the Court," he yelled. A sitting Hammer stood and straightened her back. Ricard reached her and pointed to the five Hammers straggling behind him far up the trail. "We're here to search. Have you seen a boy from the Court? On his own?"

"A pilgrimage?"

"On his own, I said. Likely stolen."

The Hammer's eyes widened. Instinctively, she looked around. "No, I am afraid I have not. I have only seen young Nails, sir."

"Show me," Ricard ordered.

The portcullis of the 29th lifted, and thus the nightmare began. The local Hammers were briefed, and along with Ricard's Hammers, they threw every Nail they found to the ground, ransacking their rooms, holes, and cavehomes. Distant Nails ran and hid into the shadows of the mountain's corridors, but the Hammers followed and flushed them out too. Eventually, all Nails were brought forward, propped onto their knees, their hands behind their backs.

"Naor!" his father screamed.

Ricard feared he had taken too long. The boy had been destroyed or worse, assimilated. How similar Naor sounded to Nail when screamed. Would he recognize his own son if he wore the Nail's garb and a holy layer of dirt? Like all children of the Court, Ricard was taught on his own pilgrimage to avoid looking into their eyes, but now he must. He must.

Ricard saw a Hammer standing over a young Nail, punching and clutching its tunic. Was it Naor? The hair held a similar shade and thickness. He ran over, pushed the Hammer aside. He grasped the bloody Nail by its collar and looked closely, deep into its eyes, and found color—his own!—and dropped the Nail back to the ground.

"Naor!" Ricard screamed again. "Naor!"

In relief, the Nails exhaled.

32

NAOR

The white of his bone. A dangling eye.
"I... Nail..."
Choking. The grunt.
The squish of his brainy pulp.

Naor woke to the echoing of his own screams. Frightened, he hurriedly searched his face for dangling eyes, and to his great relief found only sweaty cheeks. His echoes reverberated in the exposed joists of the abandoned drawing room, blending now into the gloomy howl of wind that pushed through the castle's putlog holes, rising and falling in key, as if it were whistling some primeval tune.

When the clamor finally ceased, Naor felt weak, teetering in the awkward incantations that bridge waking and sleeping, trying desperately to separate dream from memory from reality. Waking on a cushioned bench in an unfamiliar room did not help. He rubbed the crick in his neck. He stared at foreign walls. He brushed his fingers through his hair and casually wondered what Mother would have said at the sight of his unkempt head in such a public place.

Mother . . .

A grim understanding of his situation arrived.

Naor felt his ears redden with embarrassment. Whatever righteous insanity possessed Naor to sneak into the castle was now clouded by the reality of what he had done, the magnitude of it. Citizens of the Court only ascended when called. Trespassing into a higher Parallel, let alone Capital Castle, was an offense punishable by death.

And Mother, would her chair be taken from her? Would she ever forgive her son? Naor swallowed, thinking. No. Probably not. Naor was simply in so much trouble. Had any other boy of eleven ages broken so many rules in one day?

He thought back to the reckless, impulsive footsteps that brought him here.

To appeal to the King.

Naor's plan had been a simple one: to throw himself at the feet of the Hammers who guarded the threshold passage at the base of Ascension Stairwell between the Court and Capital Castle and request an audience with King Kulloh-Sor. He was certain it would work, that the King would grant his request; it was this certainty that pushed Naor through his panicked fright, walking a path he had only heard tales of. He saw torch posts lighting a quiet open-air stone corridor, which snaked and disoriented him. It was otherwise still dark, and the solitude began to disturb him. Frequently, he scanned the menacing darkness behind him as he heard his own footsteps echoing like rhythm bones.

Thinking back on it now, Naor remembered spinning as he tried to regain his bearings. That was when he bumped into the green man. He didn't scream, but if Naor was honest with himself, his trousers briefly wetted.

The green-skinned man wore a black robe (and were his eyes really yellow?). He was bald. In the torchlight his face was unreadable, but his shoulders held the timeless confidence of an acolyte. They looked upon each other for a quiet moment. The green man eventually gestured at the threshold passage Naor had obviously been searching for. Naor was simply too dumbstruck to be grateful he had arrived, for, adding to his dismay, dead Hammers scattered around the ground of the dark tunnel mouth.

The green man raised a solemn finger to his fleshy lips. Relieved, Naor understood the Hammers were merely sleeping. His eyes darted back to the stranger. Was he escaping? After a curt bow, the green man quickly disappeared into the snaky corridor, deeper into the Court.

Naor looked back to the open gate, at the sleeping guards, and behind them both into the open path leading to Capital Castle. Any and all logic deserted Naor as he ran through the threshold passage. Before he could stop himself, he was already climbing the winding stairs of Ascension for what felt like ages. The stairwell evened and he entered a long, opulent grand hallway with arched high ceilings and scattered alcoves. Here too, the guarding Hammers slept, their bodies lazily sprawled across a wine red rug. The green man did this, Naor surmised. He did not know why or how, nor did he wish to find out. He jumped into the first hallway off the main path he found, leaving behind the castle's sleeping Hammers.

The realization hit him rather suddenly. Naor was no longer home. He stood in the 31st Parallel, the first level of the castle, looming above the Court.

If only Piers could see me now.

He peeked into closets. He explored a library. He passed through private quarters. His eyes widened at the discovery of a kitchen. It was all empty. Other than the sleeping Hammers at the Parallel's entrance, it became obvious that these rooms were continually vacant, left to the spiders and their webs.

"Where is everyone?" he had said aloud to himself.

Satisfied he wouldn't be discovered, Naor foraged every dusty cupboard and drawer in the kitchen, finding only one salted fish tail and a dried bovine heart, left behind from Sor-knew-when. Even the Hammers who guarded the entrance apparently wouldn't touch this food, but for once, Naor couldn't be picky.

He imagined telling his father what he ate, that he did it without crying. It took him some time to chew the dried bovine heart and a Sword's bravery to swallow it, but the hard, flakey food succumbed and was enough to settle his bellowing stomach. Not long after, the full weight of his exhaustion pressed upon his eyelids. He had not slept the night before, and though time passed strangely in these windowless walls of the castle, he was certain he had already lived an entire day. He soon stumbled into a circular drawing room with tapestries on the walls.

How odd.

He found a cushioned bench.

Rugs on the walls but not the floor.

Sleep took him only seconds later.

Now, in the broken light of the following day, there was only one direction left for Naor: to the highest Parallel, the throne room of King Kulloh-Sor. He planned to explain everything, what he saw, who he met, why he ran. He practiced the scene in his head as he searched for the next passage threshold that would lead him higher, onto the next Parallel, the 32nd.

"My King! Holy Kulloh-Sor," Naor would say as he threw himself to the floor.

"Speak, my child," the King would offer, standing tall with his muscular body and long white flowing hair, confusion pressing upon his worried brow. "Rise. What urgent matter could incite such a bold and fearless citizen to approach these hallowed and holy chambers?"

"I'm here to speak for the Nails, my King. How they're treated, how they fall off the Staircase. You probably don't even know. How could you, a King as busy as you."

Naor would make sure and say that last part lest the King be offended.

The godly King would grow increasingly concerned and step down off his sacred podium. He would approach Naor and take his hands. "You came a long way. Tell me, tell me everything."

Perhaps it wouldn't go as smoothly as that, but if Naor could just get in front of the King, he could petition. Naor imagined returning home, knocking on his own door. His parents would open it, and as Mother raised her hand to strike her son, she would see King Kulloh-Sor and gasp. Then she would remember to bow.

King Kulloh-Sor would say, "You have a good boy here, Eyrilia. Take it easy on him, will ya?" And his mother would cry and father would hug him and the King—

A voice.

And another. Naor froze in the middle of a long hallway. He heard two Hammers standing guard in the distance. He dropped to his knees and hid behind a nearby dresser. He peeked. The Hammers stood at the base of a wide staircase, a golden arch over their heads.

"No gate," Naor whispered to himself, smiling.

The passage to the next Parallel is only a simple stairwell.

"The strangest feeling," one Hammer told the other. "And the most haunting dreams."

"I don't remember a thing. One minute awake, the next I'm drooling on the floor."

"You don't remember your dreams?"

"Never. I don't believe in 'em. Not really."

"You mean you don't have dreams?"

"I mean, what, is there even such a thing? When we wake, our brains slap memories onto our eyes. I think it . . . it helps us return from whatever land of death we visit every night. It prepares us for that, maybe."

"Philosopher over here."

"Stay in this empty tower long enough, you'll see. Your mind wanders. The creaking, the cobwebs. All I'm saying is what if dreams don't really happen? It's just our brain coming back from the dead. Sleep is a form of surrender."

"I think I fell asleep while you were talking." The Hammers

laughed.

"Yeah, yeah. Come on. Let's do our round."

To Naor's horror, the Hammers left their post and began a slow patrol towards his direction. Naor kept low and scattered backwards. Around a slight bend, he was grateful to find a wardrobe and trembled as he quietly closed the door just as the Hammers reached him. He tasted thick dust and gagged to stop a cough.

The Hammers halted. Naor held his breath.

"What is it?"

"Thought I heard something."

"Rats. Probably fighting a tower spider. They're common in this Parallel."

"Tower spiders? Those are real?"

"I've seen 'em. Size of your fist, a little bigger. Terribly evil."

Naor heard something scatter in the wardrobe.

"And it's the strangest thing."

"What's that?"

"Huh, you see them lying around here and there. When they die, they shrivel up and look like dried bovine hearts."

Naor covered his mouth. His stomach churned. Would this nightmare ever end? Suddenly everything was alive and crawling in the wardrobe with him. He was too afraid to look.

Please leave, please leave, please leave.

He did feel something on his shoe, but it was too dark to see. It now crawled up his leg.

Please leave, please leave.

Something crawled onto his shoulder, the weight of an armless hand, slowly tapping. The other phantoms he may have invented, but this creature was real. An appendage tested his neck. He shivered as it crawled into his hair.

Hope returned to Arou as the Hammers relented and abandoned the hallway. Naor waited as long as he could. As the critter crawled across his face, he burst through the wardrobe's door and re-emerged back into the castle hallway's dreary light. Whatever was on him screeched and scattered back into the unholy darkness of the wardrobe. Naor twisted and shook the goosebumps off his body, rubbing his hands everywhere.

Nothing more was on him, no creature or critter he could find.

His stomach grumbled but not from hunger. The boy had eaten a dead tower spider. He had chosen to ignore its crunchier, skeletal texture, assuming it was age and dust and—oh! He felt it coming but did not know where to put it. The dresser? He ran down the hallway and found the dusty furniture. He pulled a drawer and emptied within it the sins of his stomach, retching wildly. Neatly, he closed the drawer.

Footsteps.

Naor knew he had made too much noise. He ran to the end of the hallway and found the next passage threshold. Thankfully, the passage to the 32nd Parallel remained unguarded. There was no time to pause, look, or pray.

All he could do was climb. Never once did he look behind him.

For a short eternity, Naor climbed another grand, curving stairwell, carpeted and immaculate, minus the dust. The distance between each step seemed to grow, but Naor knew he was only tired. Upon reaching the 32nd Parallel, a solemn, soulless place,

Naor found the first empty room he could and collapsed on the ground, and slept.

CHOKING. THE GRUNT.

The squish of his brainy pulp.

"I . . . Nail . . ."

Naor awoke.

There was little exploration to be had here, for the 32nd was emptier than the 31st. He passed through the entire Parallel without concern of being seen—not even guards stood at the entrance or exit, so when he reached the passage threshold, he incautiously entered.

The 33rd Parallel was shuttered.

Doors busted, windows covered. Loose, decaying debris scattered across the floor. It looked to Naor as if centuries earlier a monster broke loose and damaged the entire level and no one had ever gotten around to cleaning it up. The cobwebs were thicker there, and he shivered anew at the thought of more tower spiders lurking.

It had already been a long day of traversing, hiding, and climbing. He did not know if night had actually come, for the castle seemed perpetually nocturnal, but nevertheless his weary body again craved sleep. He felt the familiar pangs of hunger (he had been ignoring it all day) but could still not imagine eating, not really. Perhaps if he could just sleep it off he could beat the hunger and solve it tomorrow.

He decided to climb one more Parallel, for he knew he could not sleep in the 33rd. It didn't matter if he wasn't being brave.

There was something sinister about this Parallel. He couldn't quite figure it out. It wasn't just the cobwebs either. There was a cold, lurking feeling of eyes, from every shadow and every dark corner, following him and waiting.

He found the next passage threshold, predictably unguarded, and left in haste.

By the time Naor reached the 34th Parallel, he felt weak from hunger, and because of the exhaustion, caution fled him. He did not pause to even check for Hammers at the Parallel entrance, nor did he recognize the sounds of life brimming just above the stairwell's final few steps.

"You!"

Naor heard an angry voice and his terrified eyes followed the sound. A Hammer pointed directly at him. "Nail, what are you doing? Back to your station."

Naor looked down at himself and realized how dirty he was. Though his clothes were from the Court, they were stained and torn. The skin on his hands were layered with dust. Sor only knew what his hair looked like. And his eyes ... had hunger turned them desperate?

When Naor looked past the Hammer, he was surprised to find a bustling and crowded Parallel. Nails. The servants of the castle lived here. They were dressed, surprisingly, in similar garb as Naor. They carried brooms and dusters and toolboxes and trays.

"Well? Come on!" The Hammer grabbed Naor by the collar and hurried him to the servant's quarters. "And don't let me catch you wandering off again."

He flung Naor away.

Naor stepped into a room of cots. Those that noticed him couldn't care. It seemed every Nail of the castle lived at their own pace and had much to do. He followed the smell of food to another nearby room. It looked similar to what he fed Wiglaf, but it wasn't a tower spider, so Naor ate every bite and licked the bowl, pausing only to smile at the memory of his dog.

Later, he found an open cot and laid there, propped up, counting the Nails in the room, reaching seventy-seven when his brain told him it had had enough, and he slept.

HIS DREAMS DID not let him rest. There was far too much for his mind to unravel and process. The stairs, the windows, the cobwebs, the closets, the food. And at the center of it all was a green-skinned man with yellow eyes in a dark robe. In the dream the green man did not flee from the castle. He stood over Naor and watched him sleep. He slowly placed a cold green hand over Naor's mouth. The man said, "Shhhhhh."

33

PON

Hammer Pon searched for life but found none.

After waking in the middle of the night, she forced herself out of bed, for she had sought sleep without dinner, a rarity but a necessity from her pounding head.

When she reached Holo's Feast Hall she found no monstrous fish on the table. No boiled sea eggs. No grilled lizard tails. In fact, the room was entirely empty, unusual for this time of night when the First Parallel was merry and the drinks were many.

Odd.

She limped away, her stomach singing for supper.

Her leg was a bitch tonight. Earlier today, she had sat for too long at the Parallel's port entry, her lazy ass (truth be told, she fell asleep again), forgetting to take walks and stretch like she was told to do. It was the only advice she ever received about her leg, which swelled at the foot and stung at the knee. The First Parallel's only philosopher, Vua, was a know-nothing joke. Even the philosophers of the Shield found soothing salves to rub and cool the skin. They had access to the wizard's tinctures and pouches of ground seeds. Philosopher Vua might as well have slapped Pon on the back and wished her good luck.

She returned to the Outer District. All of the First Parallel, it would seem, was gone. Even the community fire pit was cold. "Hello?" she yelled. The echoes of her voice were the only response.

Eerie.

Pon shivered.

She continued her quest for food by turning inward into the mountain, cursing the sensitive swelling of her foot.

Pon considered that she could be dreaming. What had she eaten today? Anything adventurous? Certainly no crab. Since Daelan's arrival, crabbers were finding little success. Sad, how quickly things can change. How fast— Oh! Pon remembered now—what she had eaten. Holo had given her a bag of salted fish offal. She worked on it until her teeth hurt.

Holo had been preoccupied this morning, hadn't he? What had Holo said to her? He went on and on about it. Pon had been preoccupied too, looking away from the boisterous oaf as he ponderously thrusted into her.

Now she wished she had listened. Perhaps she should have stayed awake at her post, too.

Where the hell was everyone?

Dread suddenly filled her as she forgot her hunger, the swelling of her foot, and the pain in her forehead. When she reached

Holo's cavehome, she found the door ajar and the room behind it dark and quiet. The familiar sounds of communal lovemaking or pooled snoring were gone. Neither was there the retching of vomit or frisky laughter.

All she could hear was a soft and steady splash.

When Pon finally found the courage to enter the room, she screamed. To her horror, the Elder Hammer lifelessly jiggled in his chair, his face plunged into a large glass bowl.

His fish happily fed.

34

LAYALA

When she awoke the morning after her confrontation with Hammer Daelan, the first thing she realized was how sore her throat felt. She vaguely remembered a fight, hands squeezing her neck. Layala tried to clear her throat, but it did not help. She then tried to speak and found she couldn't. The only sound that came out of her mouth was a hoarse whisper and even that hurt.

Next, she noticed she was in a foreign room, spacious and refined, a Hammer's quarters though not as large as Holo's. Her leg was shackled. She tried to pry off the chain clasp, but it wouldn't budge. There was nothing for her to use within reach, no tools or sticks. Layala stood, and as she did the rest of her body ached. She now discovered a bruise on the back of her head. She reached for it slowly and felt a layer of flaky dried blood that was mixed into her hair and underneath it, a sensitive scab. Touching it made her wince.

Rather terribly, her memories returned.

The swimming lesson, the incident with Daelan, and . . . her brothers. Where were Silus and Marin? She had left them in the quickening tide below the wall and desperate for her help. In her heart she knew they survived. Daelan was deranged, but he was not stupid. He would not waste two young Nails from a crabbing family.

Would he?

Layala was not stupid either. Her worst fears began to take hold. Daelan had declared one would pay the price for the others' sins. She sat in uncertainty for a while longer, hoping it was her, that she was paying the price. It was a miserable thing, not knowing. Had her brothers lived or died, and if so, which one? She suspected this was part of her punishment: chained to a foreign floor, voiceless and drowning in the anxieties of ignorance, every passing minute tortuous.

An hour passed before the door creaked open. A Hammer walked through. It was not Daelan, nor was it Pon, but a new face. She tried to speak and remembered she couldn't. The Hammer approached with an air of annoyance and released the chain from the floor loop.

The rest unfolded like a terrible, inescapable dream. She was escorted out of the Hammer's quarters, led to the outer district where she found, much to her surprise, a crowd gathered in front of Hammer Daelan, who spoke behind a rostrum. She was taken to the stage. Priestess Salamohan stood next to Daelan. Layala did not recognize her immediately, for her head was bald.

And where was Holo?

"Sor's Just Society has returned to the First Parallel," Daelan shouted. He spoke of kings and gods and staircases, but Layala's head hurt too much to follow and comprehend the tirade. She scanned the nervous crowd. She found Vann who stared directly at her. There was so much sadness in her friend's eyes.

"Hi," Layala managed to mouth. Vann lowered her head as if a weight were pressed upon it. Layala searched further and found a familiar group, something that resembled her family even though the count was incorrect.

She dropped to her knees.

The air abandoned her lungs. The very blood in her body halted. Silus stood in between her mother and her father. His eyes red and heavy, his face bruised.

Marin was gone.

Taken with the tide and lost to sea.

Layala was only on her knees for a few seconds before the Hammers behind Daelan lifted her back to her feet. Flashes of Marin ran through her mind: playing and fighting with Silus, trying to snap and whistle, laughing at father's stories, screaming from nightmares in his bed, throwing sand at his brother on the beach, crying in the shadow of Daelan.

They forced Layala to stand, but she refused to lift her head. She could not find the courage to look at her family again; her mother's eyes would be too much, and for once, Layala agreed with them. Daelan had let Marin die, but it was Layala who killed him.

THE PULLEY CARRIAGE ascended the great mountain Parallel by Parallel.

The cab was not yet cramped, but with every stop it gained more Nails, anywhere from three to seven each time. There were no chairs or benches. The cab was windowless, but the roof was open. She sat in a corner and leaned against its grubby walls. When she craned her neck she could see a cable attached to a rail and beyond that, an open sky.

Layala had been the first Nail of the day to climb the long ladder and reach the inside of the carriage, which hung rather delicately from cables propped along the mountain's northern cliffside. She onboarded with a small group at the 3rd Parallel where the pulley carriage ended its descension route.

Time was strange in the Shine of the Swelling Moon, whose face floated full and bright in the daylight and stretched walking hours. She now remembered little of the walking path to the 3rd Parallel, nor did she know how long she had been in the cab. She was exhausted, dehydrated, and lethargic. The only measurement her brain could currently track was the shrinking of cab space and perhaps the increasing heat.

Distracting herself, she searched her memories. Did she really see nothing from her walk through the Parallels? Her head had been lowered, though not by order of the Hammers that guided her. Some walkways were wider and others narrower, some paths rocky and others dusty. From what little she could recall, Layala caught glimpses of the same pattern: downtrodden people (Nails, they are Nails) and Hammers—one group always ruling over the other. The Nails were hungry, or perhaps she attributed hunger to them. It added to her guilt and kept her head low. When smuggling, why did she ever ask for anything in return from these poor people? There was enough fish and crabs in the sea for everyone. She should have smuggled everything out and given it away for free. These Nails had less than nothing. A sickening thought swam through her and she wondered, briefly, if it were Hammers at the other end of her smuggling rope. If that were the case, she didn't charge them enough.

Along the way to the 3rd Parallel, the walking group halted at junctions or Parallel thresholds. Nails would approach each other to whisper when the Hammers weren't looking.

Where are you from?

We can make it, we can escape.

I won't go, I won't go.

There are more of us than them.

Layala ignored them all, and they learned to whisper somewhere else.

There were more wending, windy trails, including an open path of crushed gray rock surrounded by green spike-weed that was sticky to the touch and harbored hunted insects, a Parallel within a Parallel, Layala remembered thinking, and then it was done. The walking Nails had reached the station. They watched the cable shake and heard distant gears trundling. A stern realization seemed to settle upon the coalition. Nails began to scream and cry and push against one another. Layala remained still, loathe for the fear that gripped them.

The Station Hammer eased their spirits when the pulley carriage arrived. He explained how to carefully climb the ladder and enter the cab safely, lest they fall to their deaths. Layala did not wait for him to finish talking.

"Exactly . . . just like that," the Station Hammer agreed.

OCCASIONALLY A GULL passed overhead. The sky remained blue with spotted thin clouds, weakened by a mountainside that pulled in weather only to destroy it. The sun settled directly overhead and cooked the cab with force. The hot, sticky smell of sweat, breath, body odor, and lost liquids sizzled in the sunlight. Somewhere else in the cab a Nail contributed to the sweltering stench with vomit. Layala wanted to cry but found she couldn't. Whether it was from lack of liquid or loss of spirit, she couldn't say. Layala remained on the ground in the pressing corner of the cab, wrapping her tired legs in her arms, and buried herself.

THE SUN RELENTED, and the cab dropped in temperature as the pulley carriage continued its ascension. Layala allowed herself a smirk. It took her too long to realize.

Now I am the one in the cage pulled to the surface by a long rope. What a haul.

SHE WOKE TO the feeling of a stranger's head on her shoulder. It was the old woman who had entered from the 6th Parallel, bone-thin and layered with ages of dust. Layala looked at her own skin and realized she was the cleanest Nail in the cab, a result of having had consistent access to the sea, swimming freely in the morning glow of the sunrise. She was lucky to live like she did as long as she could. She placed her hand on top of the old woman's and held it. Layala fell back asleep.

A VIOLENT SHAKE startled the Nails in the cab. They soon began screaming after realizing they had arrived. Layala hated that even though she had accepted the reality of her own death she was frightened when the moment arrived. The cab door swung open, and Nails were pulled one by one. There was no ladder at the plateau, for the pulley carriage settled on the same level as the ground into a station house where the Nails were gathered and prepared. They screamed.

The old woman was pulled from Layala's arms. Layala was the last to leave, as she was the first to enter. Her body shook, and her stomach felt as if it were folding. She was surprised by the extent of her own fear. She realized she was not moving nor responding to the distant voices yelling at her. A Hammer came for her.

"I 'ear you're all the way from Shit's Bottem," he said as he clutched her kicking legs.

The crabs, she realized, were never fighting her. They were just afraid.

AS THE STATION Hammer led the Nails down a dirt-based pathway inside the station house, Layala touched a thin, rickety wall. She could have burst through it if she wanted to. Her last look at the sky from the cab revealed the emergence of the evening stars, and she hoped that, if there was any goodness left in all of Arou, she would be allowed to stretch her body and sleep properly, one last time, before the kingdom claimed her for whatever death they designed.

They were taken to a simple room.

Sheets were spread on the floor. Off to the side, a waste hole had been dug in the ground. Some took their turn in the hole, others had nothing left to give. Layala found a sheet and used it as a pillow. She was asleep within seconds, avoiding, thankfully, the communal weeping that lasted throughout much of the night.

THE NEXT MORNING, all the plucked Nails stood together in the darkness and gazed at the morning light peeking through the slats of the station house. Water was given to them from the smallest cups. They were handed something that felt like bread, but tasted of soil, as if the wheat was mixed with Arou itself.

"Strength for your journey," the Hammer told them. Or was it a philosopher? She could not see. The stranger spoke softer and clearer. He explained what would occur, and from those words she determined he was a priest.

His voice was loud and joyful. He paced proudly as he spoke.

"Rejoice! You are about to serve King Kulloh-Sor, his Greatness, anointed by the gods, who is himself a god in the form of a king, who will be watching the progress of your worship from atop Capitol Castle in the 38th Parallel. You will each carry a sacred stone and a pouch of glue. Carry it to the top and place your stone. Return and, praise Sor, you will fetch another. Each stone you take and place builds Sor's Staircase higher and prepares us one step closer for the return of Sor, the Great Mountain Builder. Rejoice! Rejoice! Rejoice! Your life has meaning and your death, should it come, serves the highest purpose."

A long door rolled open, and light poured into the station house. The Nails could hear the wind but not yet feel it. Curious, Layala's eyes adjusted, and she lowered her hand. She could feel her resolve return. It was time. Whatever death trap this was, it mattered little to her. Again, she pushed forward first, leaving the station house without order. The wind kicked her hair, and she breathed a thinner and warmer air. A weathered hand clutched her shoulder. When she looked she found a priest, a short man with long gray hair that blended into his beard.

"The stone," he said, pointing to a messy stack of gray cubes. Layala nodded, and the priest smiled, revealing rotten teeth. "Ah, a true believer," he said.

Layala was confident she was the least informed Nail in the bunch. The First Parallel was uniquely out of touch with the rest of Kulloh-Sor's kingdom. She had heard rumors, of course, of stairs atop the mountain but assumed they were naturally built into a slope or cliffside. Seeing it now, she could have never imagined something so lofty and gauche, out of place like a desperate barnacle, with Hammer guards posted at the bottom and on platforms along the way up.

What was important now was that none of it mattered. Marin's body floated in the Sea of Cashmu, bloated and soft, feeding the fish from their incessant little bites. Or perhaps something larger had already come and swallowed Marin whole. The boy no longer existed in any form; his blood stirred into the water and dissipated like salt in bone broth.

Layala climbed.

AS SHE GAINED height on Sor's Staircase, she succumbed to her curiosity, nearly dormant as it was, and gazed at the windy world atop the plateau. A perplexing domed city rested on the earth beneath, its center crowned by the rising spires of the castle towers, which appeared to grow from the dome itself. She could see neither the whole of the tower nor the whole of the stairs, but she noticed, now and then, the winding stars brushed close enough to the tower walls to feel connected.

A route for escape.

But then she remembered there was no escape for the guilty. Whatever happened was what she would deserve.

Something cracked in the distance. She turned around for the first time and saw a clear view of the sea. From here, at this height, the water looked foreign to her, hard and serene, too blue, missing its force. The ocean remained nonetheless astonishingly beautiful to her. She next noticed a storm brewing in the distance, something fierce.

At this height, in this world, it is not the tide you watch, but the horizon.

When the storm reached her, she would be high enough to jump and fly and disappear into it forever. Then she would join Marin, and the sea would take them both.

She continued. The day was long, but she was nearing the end of it. She passed the final Hammer guard long ago, and when the rail ended, she sat her stone down and rested. She watched gulls float overhead and wondered what this world looked like to them. If they understood it. If she did. Layala studied the incoming storm to pass the time. It had moved inland and already looked weaker, though as she expected, the wind picked up. The heart of the storm would reach her within the hour. Would it be strong enough to rip her off?

She pulled herself up again but abandoned the stone. Enough of that. Layala was ignorant of much of the trials of the kingdom but knew one thing for certain: no one was building anything here.

She climbed.

LAYALA AWOKE ON the precipice of the staircase, unsure of when she fell asleep. The storm expeditiously arrived and with it, night. Was that a blast of lightning that woke her? Something loud and terrible. The wind was getting as strong as she suspected it would. It blew in a steady stream of dark, thick clouds that obscured her view. Last she could see clearly, she was still well below the castle tower's top. Overtaking the tower had become a meaningless and silly goal, but it continued to drive her up the stairs—an absurd promise to herself to rise higher than the King. Then she would find a way to die.

There had been close calls: slips on wet stones, wild whips of wind. Each time she learned she was not yet ready to die.

Layala felt a small rock underneath her callused foot. She stooped to pick it up and closed her hand over it. She could not see the castle, but she knew it was within striking distance. She threw the rock and heard it hit an uncaring wall. Layala screamed without sound, ravaging what was left of her throat. In her dismay, she grabbed her head and pulled her wet hair. Her body was drenched from the deathly drizzle of the storm's clouds. Perhaps she was ready after all.

Layala stepped forward, her toes weightless over the edge

of the staircase. She could not see anything above or below in this storm. She supposed that was for the best. She closed her eyes and saw the faces of her laughing brothers; her mother, as she best remembered her—younger and smiling; and her father, holding the rope and showing her how to pull. Layala spread her arms. All she had to do was lean forward.

The memories swarmed her and forged out of the mystic wind into something real.

She could hear him.

She could hear Marin crying: the sensitive brother, the one always so easily hurt, the dead one floating and feeding the fish. It was not a memory. The sound came from just above her. What madness was this? She followed the sound up the stairs.

"Marin!" her hoarse voice yelled.

She ran, as fast as she could handle, slipping every few steps. She stood again and climbed further, faster. He cried louder. She was sure it was Marin. She knew that cry. Just up ahead, she saw him. The boy was sitting on a step with his face in his hands, sobbing, cold and alone. She approached the ghost.

Only a few steps from him, she reached with an outstretched hand.

"Marin," she whispered again.

She touched his hand.

The ghost lifted its head and screamed.

35

NAOR

Naor watched a green-skinned man hover through a dark hallway. Was Naor floating as well? It felt to him like he was being carried.

No, that can't be right.

Naor rubbed his eyes and righted his brain.

The green man was only walking, that was all. Naor followed just behind him.

It was still the middle of the night, but Naor suspected, like most of the castle, this hall was always dark. This area was foreign to him. He had seen more of the castle than he ever dreamed he would, more than he could possibly remember, but he knew with certainty he was somewhere new, possibly in a new Parallel. Unlike the stone-built walls in the Parallels below, these floor's walls were wooden. The long boards looked wet and warped, reminding Naor of a boat, or at least, what he thought a sea-faring hull from those old stories would look like.

"Hello?" he asked the green man, who halted and turned his bald head.

"We are almost there." The green man's voice was low. He spoke with a choppy cadence and guttural accent Naor had never heard.

"Where are we? Who are you?"

The green man turned around fully. "My boy, were you sleepwalking?" He crouched. "Don't you remember?"

Now there was a green man and a red boy, for embarrassment colored Naor's face and heated his ears. The boy did not trust this stranger. Naor shook his head, confused.

"You did not hear a thing I told you. This is good."

"Good?"

"I hypnotized you. I was worried I had lost my touch, and in some ways . . . well, you pulled yourself out of your slumber, so I will need to revisit my methods."

"Hypno . . ."

"The truth is we must hurry. These halls have many eyes and ears and . . . well, sharp claws. Make haste."

The green man stood and disappeared around a corner. Naor hurriedly followed and found him just before he turned again. Naor rushed to catch up as another turn took him down yet another hallway and then through a flurry of doors.

"Ah," the green man whispered, as if he was not sure where he had been leading. They turned their final corner and entered an anteroom with a large stone door and above it, an apse with painted symbols that blended astronomy, math, and machinery.

The green man fiddled with the latches on the door. Naor looked behind him to mark which entrance he came from. He was surprised to see many doors.

This is the center of a maze.

The green man grunted as he pushed against the large door. "Help me," he implored. "I am older than I look." Naor pressed his weak weight against the ponderous door, and it budged, croaking like a disturbed courtyard toad and opening wide enough for them both to enter. The green man crossed the threshold. As if waking from yet another dream, Naor felt treachery in the dusty air. He looked behind him and before he could make the choice, a green hand grabbed his shoulder, pulled him inside, and quickly slammed the door shut. Naor's screams were swiftly muted, leaving behind mere echoes that aged and died in the wizard's anteroom.

"WELL, LOOK," THE green man said as he let Naor go. He showed Naor his light green palms. Naor knew the move and was dubious. He stepped away until his back pressed flat against the door.

"Are you going to kill me?"

The green man lowered his hands. His face, however, remained plain. He didn't speak. It seemed to Naor that he was deeply weighing the question. Thoughtfully, he replied, "If I wanted to kill you, or hurt you in any way, you could do nothing about it."

Naor thought through the answer, decided he didn't understand it, and moved onto a new question. "What is this place?

Where am I?"

Though the boy was still frightened, curiosity beckoned his attention, and he began to scan the room. It looked to Naor like a messy and very old workshop. He saw a dozen or so workstations positioned every few steps from each other. There were tables with jugs, jars, and decanters. Other stations held interlocking mechanisms and strange machinery. Some stations were cluttered with papers, books, scrolls, ink pens, old food, and tinkering tools. On the middle of every table, a dim bulb of light pulsated.

To his horror, Naor saw something else: broken body parts piled into a basket. Legs and arms. Hands. Feet.

The green man followed the boy's eyes and said, "Ah, do not worry. Machinarchs."

Naor's face must have shown confusion.

"Machines," the green man clarified. "More tools for your King."

He pulled a nearby stool and pushed it to Naor. He found another for himself and sat. "You have many questions. I admit, I do as well. You query. I query. That is how this will work."

Naor nodded.

"Well, where are you? This is what you asked me. You are in the Science Hall of the 35th Parallel."

"The Wizards of Science," Naor said to himself, unbelieving. Louder, Naor said, "You harness magic for the entire kingdom."

"That is what they call us, yes. Wizards. But there is no magic in our hall. We harness the natural world. What you can see and what you can not see. Science. Its power is everywhere."

"What does that mean?"

"My turn," the green man said. "Tell me your name, and how did you get into this castle?"

"That's two questions."

"Your name then."

Naor felt himself growing more comfortable with the stranger, but he occasionally glanced at the workstation with the thin tinkering tools. "My name is Naor. And you already know how I got into the castle. You left the gate open for me. Don't be so tricky!"

Naor saw, maybe, the smallest hint of an emotional response within the evasive lines of the green man's face. He paused before he asked, "It wasn't you, was it?"

"Is that your question?"

"No." They sat together in a moment of silence. "What is your name?"

"Dffai of the Order of Arsia. Are you from the Court?"

Naor nodded.

"Your turn," Dffai reminded.

Naor noticed for the first time an unusual window in the far end of the room. It was half filled with bricks, as if boarded up to keep something out or, perhaps, to trap someone inside. The top layer of bricks were pasted white from what looked like bird droppings. Below the window, broken bricks were scattered on the floor.

"How many of you are there?" Naor asked.

"There is only one of me."

"That's not what I meant."

"You want to know how many wizards there are? Well, you have seen the other one, Rfael, and now you have met me. We are all that's left. Why are you here, Naor of the Court?"

Naor considered the question and felt aimlessness in his answer, matched only by a sense of hopelessness that hovered over him like a dome. He did not have an answer. Not really. He buried his face in his hands.

"What am I doing here? Sneaking and running, spiders and wizards! I am not exactly the brave one." Naor felt that familiar tingle of tears. He blurted, "Father just tries to get me through the day without crying. Mother says I'm too sensitive. Says I'm weak. The truth is I'm the last person who should be here. Send Piers. Send Shaeron. Send Frenklin for all I care. He's the one cut out for adventure. I just like to read about it."

"Frenklin."

"A boy from my lesson hall." Naor wiped his eyes. "Piers. Preferably Piers."

Dffai nodded his head. "Naor, you have not answered my question."

"Oh. Right." Naor straightened his back. Wiped his eyes again. He realized he lost himself for a moment and embarrassment colored him again. "I ran away from . . . my life. There was a Nail—a man. In the courtyard. He fell from the sky. Snuck into the Court. He was barely a man when I found him. They put a . . . a hammer into his . . . his head. King Kulloh-Sor should know about it. He can stop it, can't he? All the Nails? All the falling?"

Dffai listened without reaction or emotion and responded only in summarization. "A boy from the Court wishes to appeal to the King on behalf of the Nails. Amazing."

Naor nodded. "You don't look so sure."

"Is that your next query?"

Naor shook his head. "Your skin is green. Why is your skin green?"

"This is how we look on the planet where we come from. To me, you are the strange skinned one, Naor of the Court."

"You are from another planet. So it's true. There are other worlds."

"You have spoken both untruths and truths. You are wise to assume I come from another planet, but in fact I was born on Arou many ages ago. Far back, even before Sor ruled the great mountain, which the ancients called Eccoulous. My maker, and our goddess, Arsia, settled here and claimed Eccoulous as her prize. This is where the word 'Arou' comes from, Naor of the Court. Arsia's Prize. Over time, the word lost its meaning and gained a greater scope. Arsia's homeworld—the one with all the green-skinned people like me—is much more advanced. She left us here and tasked us with progressing it. I am boring you."

Naor stopped yawning. "I'm sorry. So Sorry." Naor stood from the stool and wandered throughout the room. "Are you sure? Philosopher Shaeron never mentioned any of this."

Dffai jumped into a stance, the quickness of it startling Naor. The wizard's eyes sharpened. "Do not be dull, boy. Your philosophers are but mice sniffing moldy crumbs."

Dffai must have seen the boy grow tense and added, "Forgive me, Naor of the Court. It is not your fault you have been misled. You are a seeker of truth, for you ask the right questions. Ask me another. Please." Dffai turned and fiddled with some papers. Naor swiped a tinkering tool, a long thin metal stick with a flat end, and slipped it into the waist of his trousers.

"It is your turn, Dffai. To query."

"Yes. Yes, I suppose it is. What do you plan on doing with that sliver?"

Naor's heart sank. The wizard saw him take the tool after all. "You answered every question of mine, Dffai. Except for the first one."

He turned to face Naor. "Am I going to kill you?"

Naor grabbed the handle of the sliver tool in preparation for whatever came next. Even in this moment, tense and terrible, the boy was pleased with his own confidence. He had eaten a tower spider, after all.

Dffai stood and approached slowly.

He halted and crossed his arms. "No. I am going to help you, Naor the Brave. I am going to help you find the King. And you will do something for me. Won't you? Yes. Yes, it is a fair exchange. You will deliver a message to the King from the last wizard."

DFFAI TINKERED AT his workbench as he told the tale.

"When Sor conquered the great mountain from the Soulless Kings, as you have learned to call them, he also captured the Order of Arsia, who had peacefully coexisted with the mountain's rulers as their distinguished guests, helping them progress each of their regions through science and technology."

"That was you, right? Order of Arsah?"

"Arsia, yes. Sor trapped our peaceful kind in a makeshift dungeon underneath the Court. Ironically, it was what later became the crypt for Sor and his line of rulers. He left us there for decades until he realized our true value as engineers, healers, crafters, and inventors. Sor released us as slaves. We were ordered to help him design and build this castle. And, of course, to teach him how to power and fly our skyships. During these awful ages we gained the title of Wizard, but I couldn't exactly tell you why or when."

Naor didn't believe that. "I have a feeling you know exactly who first called you wizards. And when."

Dffai's head turned toward Naor, his yellow eyes blinking. "May I finish my tale or not?'

Naor sat on the ground, cross-legged.

Dffai continued. Naor learned that wizards were mortal but aged slowly; even they had never solved the mystery of their own lifespans. Being all male, they could not breed without Arsia, and over time, their order diminished: some by their own hand, others from the brutality of whichever king or queen ruled. The wizards were susceptible to viruses and other illnesses, but historically they had engineered solutions, which were subsequently diluted and passed throughout the castle and, occasionally, down to the Parallels for the benefit of others. In fact, by command, Naor had learned, the wizards were responsible for the development and structure of the Parallels themselves, the pulley carriage transportation system, the plumbing structure, the lights that powered the Court and the castle, and even the skyships left behind after Arsia's departure, among other advancements.

Ages passed and the Order of Arsia was forgotten. The Wizards of Science replaced them, subject to the desires of each sitting ruler. Never fully assimilating, the wizards earned a reputation for distrust and trickery, for it was commonly suspected the wizards were trying to contact Arsia and to beckon her glorious, vengeful return.

Occasionally, the wizards were accused of manipulation and subterfuge whenever their work led to death or sickness or destruction. The King's Swords would respond by visiting, reminding the wizards who they served and also who had abandoned them. These visits often ended in bloodshed, so the wizards, forever mechanical, steadily turned the 35th Parallel into a maze designed to obviate these grievous visits. Unhurried but deliberately, the maze became more advanced over time and succeeded in its mission. That was, until recently, when the King's Swords finally emerged victorious into the wizard's anteroom and charged into their hallowed hall, bloodthirsty and desperate to serve the King's vengeance.

Three wizards lost their lives.

Dffai pointed to a stain on the floor.

"It was down to just me and Rfael. Then he left on his fool's errand."

"Were they right? Were you trying to contact Arsia?" Naor realized how accusatory that sounded and rephrased. "I mean . . . they weren't right to do what they did. I'm just asking—"

"Did we do what they accused us of doing? Always. The power that lights your Court serves a dual purpose, as does the staircase built to memorialize Sor. It is an antenna. We send and receive signals into the stars, hoping we will someday reach Arsia's homeworld."

"All this time, and you've never reached them?"

"Space is infinite, Naor the Brave. Without a map, one is perpetually lost. And though I wish I could tell you our technology is perfected, it is unfortunately limited and slow. Any message we send can take one thousand ages to reach its destination, and by the time it does, we may all be gone."

The day was spent in conversation much like this as the wizard worked on a small device. It took a few hours for Naor to feel comfortable, but it was not until Dffai showed him how to open the door and even left it cracked open that he fully let his guard down. He gave Naor some food and water and went back to work. Naor fell asleep and woke up later to eat more.

"There," Dffai announced in his usual low and solemn voice. He leaned back from the workstation and stretched his shoulders. Cracked his neck. "Come see."

Naor jumped off the floor and jogged over to the table. He saw what looked like a silver ball with a stripe of gold down its middle, small enough for Naor's hands to hold yet heavy. "This is your message?"

"It is a gift to the King."

Naor backed away. "It's dangerous, isn't it? You want to kill him. You want me . . ."

Dffai picked up the ball, threw it just above his head, and caught it. "Extremely dangerous, but you must first twist the top and bottom ends in the opposite direction. Then you roll it to his feet. Then you run."

"I can't. I won't kill the King, Dffai. I'm . . . I'm . . . That's not what I came here to do."

Dffai set the ball back on the table, and turned to face Naor fully. "I suppose if Frenklin were here, he'd do it, would he? Or . . . who was the other one, Piers?"

"No, Dffai. I don't think so. We are children of the Court. We serve King Kulloh-Sor."

"Naor, Naor. It is not Frenklin or Piers I need. It is you. Earlier, you said you shouldn't be here. I disagree. You are the only one who could be here. Your strength comes from your sensitivity, your ability to observe the natural world and feel what is out of place. It is difficult to stay in harmony when the world around you is so out of tune."

Naor grabbed the device off the table.

"Remember," Dffai continued, "This is the deal: I'll get you to the Kulloh-Sor's throne room, but you have to take this with you." He plucked the ball from Naor's hand and put it into a belt bag. He draped the belt around Naor's waist and tightened it. He stood back and looked at the armed boy. "I cannot control how you will use the device. That is fully up to you. I trust that when the time is right, you will know what to do."

Naor felt the weight of it on him.

THE DAY CONTINUED how it began with Naor following Dffai through long, twisty corridors. The green man moved swiftly for someone who had seen so many ages. In fact, if what Dffai said was true (and Naor was not sure how much of anything he had learned was true), Dffai was older than these passages. The wizard stopped suddenly and pushed a camouflaged piece of stone within the wall, which promptly unlocked a concealed door with a satisfying pop.

"Whoa," Naor said. Dffai shushed him as they entered.

It was another steep staircase, but this area was unlike the previous steps that connected the Parallels within the castle. Instead of ornate arches and winding halls with carpeted steps, this tunnel was low and carved.

Like climbing through the inside of a stone snake.

The wizard was tall but somehow seemed to shrink his large frame and moved easily through the climbing tunnel. Naor occasionally brushed his belt bag along the wall, and every time it startled him. The device weighed heavily on his side, for he was not yet used to carrying it.

Dffai halted. Naor looked ahead and saw that this corridor was near its end. "The 36th Parallel," he whispered, and he waited. If Naor had learned anything, it was to be quiet. Dffai was satisfied with whatever he was waiting for and then pressed into another stone on the wall and opened a new hidden door with which they exited the secret staircase.

They successfully navigated through the 36th without being spotted, though it was a busy floor, and it took many hours. "The royal line lives on this Parallel and the one above," Dffai whispered to Naor. He whispered other phrases like "a cesspool of privilege" but Naor could not hear him clearly as he moved, and he was not sure if Dffai was even talking to him.

As they approached the next hidden staircase, Naor looked through an open window along the opposite wall and saw another day turn dark with storm clouds rapidly coming in. Naor felt exposed in the hallway as Dffai searched for the hidden stone that would open the next secret tunnel. He wanted to tell the wizard to hurry but decided he had no choice but to trust and wait. Dffai, however, became increasingly befuddled and uncertain as his hands pressed into immovable stones.

"Oh no," he whispered.

"What is it?"

"They found it. Our passage. And they blocked it."

Naor looked around nervously. "What does that mean? Is there another way?"

Dffai abandoned the wall and calmly turned around. "The time for questions is over. I'm afraid you are caught."

"Caught?"

Dffai raised his hands and looked beyond Naor. Naor turned and saw only shadows, but from the shadows, a tall man emerged. His shoulders were broad, his chest proud. He held a massive blade. Naor gulped, both frightened and starstruck. A King's Sword.

"A wizard and a trespasser. An odd sight," the Sword said.

Naor the Brave stepped forward. "I come to appeal to King Kulloh-Sor. As a member of the Court, I request an audience."

The Sword looked down and tilted his head. "The Court, huh?" He smirked. "He is as you described, Dffai."

Naor's eyes widened and his stomach dropped. His legs felt weak. "Dffai?"

"Let the King know I reported the trespasser immediately," Dffai told the Sword. "I brought him directly to you at the time you requested."

"You are an unending source of information, Dffai." The Sword looked down at Naor and said to him: "Even when it comes to his own rotten line. Though Rfael got away, suspiciously, before the information reached my ears."

"You were unreachable. Let this make us even."

"Enough!" the Sword yelled. His echo bounced and traveled down the eerie hallway. He returned his attention to Naor. "So, this little man wants to kill the King, huh?"

"What!" Naor yelled, incredulous. A torrent of emotions poured through him.

"Look in his bag. You'll find a device. Some conspiracy from the Court, I'm afraid."

Naor could not believe what he was hearing. He should've never trusted the wizard. Had their sordid, perfidy reputation turned true? He wanted so badly to see goodness in those yellow eyes. Mother had once scolded Naor upon finding him in tears, and he remembered her wisdom now: "You earn your reputation. Always." That memory fled him as the Sword pointed his battle blade at Naor's throat. Naor gulped and raised his hands in the air. The Sword retrieved the metal ball out of Naor's belt bag and held it high.

"Strange device," he said.

"It's not mine. It's his! He made it. He gave it to me!"

Dffai said, "Never lie to a Sword, Naor. Their minds are as sharp as their blades."

"How could you?" Naor screamed. "She's not coming back, Dffai. Arsia's gone! You're alone! And I know what that's like . . ." His voice trailed off. "I was your friend."

Dffai stood expressionless.

The Sword now rested his battle blade in front of him, its tip piercing the ground. "I'll take it from here, Wizard. Make sure you aren't seen. Your skin spoils appetites."

"Of course," Dffai said and bowed. Naor found no more words to say and already regretted the ones he had just yelled. He watched Dffai's black robe fade into the shadows of the 36th Parallel.

Naor continued to stare into the empty darkness for a little while longer until he heard the Sword speak.

"So . . . we have much to discuss. Don't we, Naor of the Court? Let's start with—"

As the Sword lowered his hand, the ball pulled down with an unusual force. He let go, but the ball stuck to the top of his battle blade and remained there, as if glued. "What evil is this? Tell me, child!"

Naor could not speak because he did not know. He watched in terror as the Sword furiously tried to pull the ball off his blade. The top and bottom of the device began to twist as he pulled it. Naor felt his skin tighten as he realized. "Oh geez," he said simply and looked up and into the bewildered eyes of the Sword. "I'm sorry!" Naor ran. The Sword heard a series of clicks and watched as the device began to twist by itself.

"Get back here!" the Sword yelled desperately at Naor. Something louder overtook his screams. Naor ducked. The explosion was quick but deafening, leaving the Sword in pieces and bursting open the wall behind him. The storm spilled into the castle hallway.

Naor's ears were ringing. To his surprise, when he shook his head, dust and debris formed a small cloud in front of his face. His clothes and skin were covered in similar white. He was dizzy. The hallway appeared to him at the wrong angle, as if Father were holding his feet and spinning him upside down, like they used to do. He attempted to stand but managed only to raise one knee. In the distance, Hammers ran toward him. He glanced behind and saw more of the same. Naor stumbled and crawled over to the cracked opening on the wall where the Sword had recently exploded.

Looking through the hole, he saw an arch just below him. It connected the castle to Sor's Staircase. When he jumped, the drop was farther than he realized, and he landed with a painful thud. He winced and gritted his teeth, unsure if he had actually screamed, for he could not hear his own voice. He looked up and saw the Hammers pointing to him from above, but they did not follow. Naor picked himself up and limped along the arch towards Sor's Staircase. The sky was dark and the wind was fierce, but the walkway was wide enough.

Unknown minutes passed before he reached the staircase. Slowly, he climbed over the lip and laid his back against the angled steps.

His body writhed. His ears whined. His mind twisted.

The only thing the boy could do was cry. Naor cried loud and long, and when his lungs started to give out, he buried his face in his hands and wept.

Something. Did he sense the presence of another? Ghoulish eyes watched him. Something evil on the edge of the world, born from the storm, reaching with claws.

A hand touched his, and he screamed.

36

JAH'RI

"Closer," Jah'ri ordered Commander Prime. Steadily, the skyship approached the great mountain from the Sea of Cashmu. "And climb. I want to see Sor's Staircase from the sky."

"A-an-and then? Then? And?" The failing machinarch's stuttering had worsened, its voice now incapable of voluble pauses, its pace infrequent.

Jah'ri thought for a moment. Possibilities battled in his tired brain, every decision and its consequence, the true costs he would likely never know. He settled on an answer. "We'll fly to the Southern Arm where the King grows fat. But we shall live. All of us."

"Speak-k for yourself-lf-lf," Commander Prime said as it whistled an airy tune. "I am malfunctioning-ing-ing-ing more every m-mi-minute," it sang.

"All of us, I said. We will find a way. I owe you my life, so you must have yours."

"You and-d that-at-at g-gi-giant sea ser-ser-serpent will live on-n-n-n f-fo-forever. I will be melted-ted-ted for w-weap-ons-pons. Do not f-fr-fret-et-et, Hammer Jah'ri. I ca-can-cannot f-fe-fear death, because I have never re-real-really lived. I-I-I-I h-ha-haven't even t-ta-tasted slop. Melted! Gi-giant! Live-live-ve-ve-ve." Commander Prime slowed the ship and, just a short distance before reaching the mountain, pulled the control knob towards its body. Jah'ri stood next to the control panel. Together, man and machine viewed their slow ascension of Sor's Crown through the ship's observation screen, which was wide and clear through a thick glass that tinted when deactivated.

The day was still early in the Kingdom of Kulloh-Sor. With the sun rising behind them, the commander's skyship cast a large shape over the Parallels as they ascended. Shadowed eyes looked skyward, the fragmented tools and instruments of Sor's Just So-ciety.

Jah'ri saw the First Parallel only briefly, and it looked as mis-erable as he had imagined. The Nails there walked with what looked like the weight of the entire mountain on their shoulders. In the market square of their outer district, a Hammer paused his whipping. A pregnant Nail cried on her knees, her back bloody and bare. The Hammer looked to the ship, raised his hand in a simple wave, and then continued the whipping.

When the skyship reached the 5th Parallel, Jah'ri considered asking Commander Prime to halt but decided against it. Jah'ri had avoided sentimentality thus far in his life; there was little reason for starting now. From his brief glance through his limited view from above, the Parallel looked much the same.

Dry and flat.

A mesa upon a world, below a world. The shanties were still there, of course, growing like an organism that was vigorous yet diseased. His old shanty was hidden somewhere in the middle; it could not be seen from the air. He then craned his neck to catch a glimpse of the market square where he once challenged Hammer Atan. A new Hammer stood guard now, but he did not recognize the young man. Jah'ri counted his breath to calm his nerves as his home Parallel passed out of view.

All Hammers who saw the shadow of their ship paused to wave or salute. Jah'ri wondered if these Hammers were indeed new, or if he had once served with them and purposely avoided their eyes, having chosen to avoid any connection. He conversed only with his Elder Hammers. They showed him where to stand, who to strike, and how hard. It wasn't until he reached the Holster that Jah'ri began to look his fellow Hammers in the eyes, commiserate in the battlefield, and share their dreams. Saz, Sindhi, and Rannold. Even Vaera. He knew now that they were indeed his friends, a word with power. He felt their deaths like little daggers scraping his heart.

The skyship continued to rise, and seeing the Parallels in quick succession astonished him. As he rose, everything improved. The buildings were stronger, the paths cleaner, the clothes warmer, the markets fuller.

It did not take long for the shine to fade. Death besieged progress in the dead zone between the 9th and 10th Parallels.

Jah'ri had heard rumors of the Bucket but had never seen it. He had never been sure it really existed. Conveniently, the Bucket was excluded from the Holster's painting of the great mountain. It was a wide rocky ridge that curled up at its edge. Due to how the width of the great mountain shrank from this point onward, the Bucket acted like a platform, or a trap, for catching falling Nails. At first, all Jah'ri could see were the gulls, stirring like one giant entity in atmospheric patterns, a sea of feathers and beaks eating and picking. When the skyship passed, the gulls were spooked, and they exploded into the sky, scattering into a storm that for a moment obscured the ship's observation screen. When the frenzy cleared, Jah'ri saw the bodies: piles of plucked and discarded Nails, their sun-bleached bones picked of flesh.

"Poor bastards," Jah'ri said to himself. He knew his father's bones laid somewhere in that wasteland. The ship ascended past the Bucket, and he was relieved to abandon it.

The King will answer for that too.

He surprised himself with vengeful thoughts for his father, a man who was but a swirling mist within an already thin memory.

After the skyship flew through the 11th and 12th Parallels, Jah'ri grew tired and limped over to the chair in the center of the ship, above the floor glass. He thought of Shyloc. The ancient one, too, did not know how to live without a warrior's yoke. When he touched its snout, Jah'ri received what he could only explain as a projection of feelings and intentions. Jah'ri did his best to interpret and then returned his own message, projecting a vision of the Southern Arm.

Shyloc descended below the surface and disappeared.

Now, he hoped the ancient one would ignore him. Let it taste and swallow freedom, ride it like the crest of a wild wave from another world, another time, and truly vanish.

THE SKYSHIP RATTLED. Startled, Jah'ri realized he dozed off. Though his body still ached he found the sleep had treated him well, so he stood and stretched as carefully as he could before returning to the control deck and its observation screen.

"Where are we—" he began to ask Commander Prime, but then he knew. The skyship had reached the plateau. He saw the wide dome of the Court and Capital Castle with all its competing towers and spires. Jah'ri would never understand the equipoise that kept this massive, loathsome structure standing. Alongside both, the base of Sor's Staircase shone white, recently cleaned from the previous storm's onslaught. Hammers guarded the bottom of the stairs. Even now, Nails feebly approached in a single-file line, carrying their accursed, obstinate stones. Many, but not all, turned to look as Commander Prime's skyship's shadow briefly blanketed them.

"Strange," Jah'ri said, as the ship pulled higher.

From this angle, Sor's Staircase looked neither powerful nor menacing but a solemn and costly blunder. It was a godless temple built from the bones of unbelievers, feeling awkward and aimless in the sobering light of cooled fervor. Occasionally he saw Nails climbing, turning this way and that. Some were sitting. Some were sleeping. One Nail slipped and fell off the side.

"Poor fools," Jah'ri muttered, not knowing what else to say.

Higher the skyship flew.

"Look!" Jah'ri pointed to the uppermost spire of Capital Castle. The stairs kept going, but Sor's tower had finally reached its peak. "Slow down. I said slow!"

Commander Prime did not respond. Jah'ri shook the machinarch's shoulders, but the skyship continued to rise, and the castle tower quickly disappeared from their view. He swatted its metal skull. The machinarch was stubbornly lifeless, its eyes dark and circuits cold. In his dismay, Jah'ri failed to see the top of Sor's Staircase—the sheer cliff that abruptly ended and hadn't been expanded in ages—as the skyship rose ever higher. Panicked, Jah'ri tried to pry Commander Prime's hands off of the control sticks, but they were latched tight. A thick, decorated knob on top of each stick obstructed Jah'ri from sliding Commander Prime's hands up and off. Next, he pushed the machinarch's defunct body forward but nothing would budge.

The skyship's interior lights stuttered as the hull began to shake. Jah'ri, too, felt the growing pressure on his ears and worried his eyes would soon burst. Outside, blue rapidly faded to black. "Space," he said aloud to no one. The observation screen splintered. To the side of the viewing pane, a panel emerged that was formerly camouflaged into the skyship's hull, some dormant feature awoken by the elements. Zapping emitted from this panel, long and steady like a wave that never quite crested, but growing, and surged. A garish, pulsating green exploded from the panel and slathered every surface and corner, wrapping Jah'ri's palms, his fingertips. The color seeped through the hull and transformed the skyship into a glowing orb, a heavenly and hopeless celestial mystery seen briefly from Sor's Kingdom to Ornvia, from the trading ports of Moh to the telescopes of sea gypsies. Then, the green radiance launched into the ether above Arou and far beyond it, leaving behind a bent, dull metal ship.

This was no time for mysteries.

Jah'ri searched for his combat hammer and found it on the skyship's floor. He promptly returned to Commander Prime and swung at the machinarch's suspended hands. Furiously, Jah'ri hammered on the left hand until something shifted. The skyship spun uncontrollably, and Jah'ri was suddenly flung to the floor. To his horror, the control stick had popped off completely, along with Commander Prime's left hand. The look on the machinarch's face remained the same: nothing.

Hastily, Jah'ri regained his balance and swung again, this time with a better angle on the machine's wrist. The commander relinquished its grip, and the ship stopped climbing. He dropped his combat hammer, falling to the floor soon after in exhaustion. He looked through the cracked observation screen finding blackness and below it, a hint of blue. Jah'ri floated between two worlds, it seemed, and a memory returned to him. Something from his time in the muted realm. There had been just a touch of color. Hadn't there?

Crunching. That was the only word for it. The skyship sounded like it was crunching. The glass on the observation screen cracked deeper. The glass on the floor in the center of the skyship did the same. Commander Prime's right hand still grasped the control stick, but it was loose enough for Jah'ri's fingers to slip through and push it forward.

The crunching, cracking ship wobbled but managed to slowly descend. It wasn't fast enough. Every attempt to push the control stick any further failed, so, against his better judgment, he lifted his combat hammer and swung it again. This time he hammered the machinarch's elbow. It budged forward, just enough to increase the angle. Jah'ri struck the machinarch one last time and found success. He fell forward with a haunting crack into the increasingly splintering observation screen. The skyship now plunged at greater speed.

As the skyship abandoned Arou's final boundary and fell back towards the planet's surface, the pressure in Jah'ri's ears lessened, though his stomach lurched and rolled. The skyship was falling too fast. Outside the window he saw flames. It had become a fireball. Its glass no longer cracked but sizzled. Jah'ri found the seat in the center of the skyship and wrapped himself with the rope that dangled from it. The observation screen finally broke through and fire swarmed the control console, fully covering Commander Prime.

The flames retreated as quickly as they came, but now hostile wind filled the ship and attacked him worse than any foe or beast ever had. The skyship passed through a cloud layer, clearing his view of the world below.

Sor's Staircase.

Sor's Kingdom.

Beyond that, an immensely brown land with disparate patches of trees and boulders. Perhaps the Shield or the Battlelands, it did not matter.

Rapidly, it grew.

Jah'ri tightened his grip on the seat's rope. He closed his eyes. He did not know the word for irony, so instead he just said, "Funny."

For the first time in his adult life, Jah'ri yearned to live.

37

SINDHI

If Hammer Sindhi swam straight, she would eventually hit the Northern Arm. Back to her father. To the halls she knew intimately, made of stacked iron ore turned purple by time. To the winds that blew from the snow-capped peaks of the Endless Range. Wind that, in memory, didn't seem so cold. Not now. When Sindhi made it to shore—and she would make it to shore—she was certain she would never be cold again. Out here, in the Sea of Cashmu, west of Shyloc's fierce and fiery temple, the cold gripped Sindhi's skin and leached its remaining warmth. Brecca was warm, she remembered. A gift and a curse. She thawed there on the shore, watching in awe as the beast preyed on the Hammers of the 38th Parallel. One by one. Three, maybe four minutes passed until she shook off the trance, remembering her mission was only half complete. Victory meant swimming past Shyloc twice. She knew she had to leave while the cursed sea serpent was still distracted.

Vial in her hands, she collected the breccel with a modest and unceremonial scoop.

Sindhi waded into the sea, remembering more.

But what was left to remember? Only screams, flashes, bursts. Tears. The gritting of teeth. Arms reaching and pulling, reaching and pulling, reaching and pulling. Every stroke a gift. Away from the hell of Brecca, its glorious and bewitching warmth, and back to the frigid depths of the Sea of Cashmu—the return swim to Sor's Crown.

Now, her eyes found only salty mist whispering secrets above the sea's surface as it passed, like lost kin estranged by progress, but she knew her homeland was out there, somewhere. Straight ahead probably. Yes, the Northern Arm. Sindhi must first bring with her a battle blade—the weapon of a Sword.

Eyes upon the enemy, hand upon the hilt, feet upon the wind.

Sindhi would be the first Sword from the Northern Arm.

Would she also be the last Sword? Something had happened. The isle had . . . burst. Had it been a waking dream? An aftereffect of the Holster playing with her mind for so long?

Dreams, she knew, could not be trusted. What was real and what was imagined was of no concern to her. All that mattered was returning to the castle.

Forge her battle blade. Pledge to the King.

Sindhi could not wade for long or her body would cease. She had to keep swimming. It was the only way to mute the pain, the exhaustion, the longing for sleep, no matter the cost. She drank through the filtered straw in her uniform and began again. Long desperate strokes. Sor's grace, this time passing waves pushed her towards the mountain. She was thankful for that generous gift, to be no longer swimming against the mountain's pull. Some waves did crest, even out here in the middle of the sea, and those she rode if she caught them right, her body propped like a flat dinghy.

Careful.

Silent waves preyed upon the distracted.

It happened now.

Sindhi turned. She dove. It was too late. Something upon her. She struggled, her arms tangled. The net was thick and tightening. In her panic water found lungs, and she coughed and spat and gagged. Spinning, the sea's surface rolled around her, revolving like the moon and now she was dragged. Her head plunged and breached, plunged and breached, each visit to the surface bringing with it the sound of men cheering.

A MOUTH ON hers. Then rising. The gushing. Sindhi awoke coughing and confused. She cleared all the water she could out of her lungs, her throat, her mouth. Her shaking hands touched a wooden platform; her whole body rested upon this solid base. A middle-aged man sat next to her and laughed at her bewilderment, her predicament.

"The kiss of life," he said and laughed some more. "Was it good for you?" The man turned, and the others cheered. The others . . . How many were there? Where was she?

Sindhi realized she was on the bow of a rather large ship, larger than anything she had seen in the King's Fleet. A tattered flag proudly waved, five stars making a quincunx. Her eyes followed ropes to hinges to sails to boxes to doors. Layers and levels of sea-soaked rooms, stacked. People, so many bodies, alive and looking at her. It was like a Parallel upon a deck.

Sea gypsies.

"I am a Hammer of the 38th Parallel of the Kingdom of Kulloh-Sor," Sindhi announced as she attempted to stand, her body weary and empty of its strength. The man sitting near her whistled. A spear was thrown. He caught it and pointed the tip at Sindhi's throat.

"It's a little Hammer, ain't it?" he said. Some from the gathering crowd chuckled.

"Lower your spear. You are in kingdom waters."

"Oh," the gypsy said, his smile revealing golden teeth, others missing. "You hear that captain? Says we're in kingdom waters. We better shit off the side then, eh?" More laughed.

Sindhi quickly and nervously scanned the crowd. Who was their captain? The men and women on this vessel did not wear standardized uniforms, but an array of linen tunics, short pants, stockings, and pantaloons, clothing in every color, tight and loose and repurposed. Some sunburned men wore only breechclouts. Despite this, Sindhi could sense there was order. They were waiting for command.

It came. "Find out what she knows or throw her overboard," a deep voice from the crowd announced. She still could not find where it came from. The frustration gritted her teeth.

The man with the spear grabbed her arm and lifted her. He signaled to a nearby woman who joined. She grabbed Sindhi's other arm. Sindhi was led back to the net that captured her, which now was tied to a high pillar and stretched tall. When they backed her into the net, she leaned her body against it. The man's spear now angled at her heart.

"We know all about your little swim. We've been fishin' for Hammers."

The woman spoke next. "How many made it? How many Hammers?"

Sindhi shook her head. She felt the tip of the spear pressing. "I . . . I don't know."

"Then she's useless," the woman said. "Drain 'er blood and keep 'er for chum."

"If you know about our swim, then . . ." Sindhi tried to find the words that would keep her alive, but, dizzyingly, she still would not reveal more than absolutely necessary. Sindhi was a Hammer of the King and soon to be his Sword.

"Then what?"

Sindhi gritted her teeth, summoning whatever courage was left. "Then you know we swim alone. We come back alone. As far as I know, I'm the only one."

The man with the spear kept it steady while freeing a hand to scratch his head.

"Felton," the gypsy woman said. Sindhi almost didn't recognize the word, it was so out of place. "Did you see a Hammer named Felton?" The look on Sindhi's face must have been humorous, for the woman chuckled.

"Hammer Felton?" Sindhi repeated to the sound of whistles. "How do you . . . ?" Her brain attempted connecting missing dots, but nothing out here made sense. Sindhi briefly considered this all to be an elaborate hallucination, a death dream on the water, but the pressure of the spear pressed further, and she felt its sharp tip penetrate her uniform and scratch the skin of her breast.

"When did you last see Hammer Felton?"

Sindhi shook her head.

That deep voice from the crowd spoke again. "Break her vial."

"No!" Sindhi screamed and tried to move but more hands came to restrain her. Below her, the gypsy's vessel carved through choppy waters.

"When did you last see him? Answer!"

Squirming did no good. There were too many hands, too many arms. Somehow, incredibly, the spear knew exactly where to look as it moved to the pouch on her shoulder and pressed hard against the hidden vial within it.

She breathed, closing her eyes. She spoke. "Felton didn't swim. He was injured. His hand . . ."

Sindhi lowered her head, unbelieving how quickly she had caved. All to save herself, her vial, her future. It was disgusting. In the least, she should've better bartered. These were sea gypsies after all. Trading was their business. She could have swapped false information for a dinghy, but her spirit had been too weak, her mind too fragile.

"Shit," the man said as he pulled the spear away.

The woman's eyes did not stray from Sindhi's. "She's a liar," she announced to the surrounding crowd, to the captain.

"Release me and I'll tell you everything."

A pause. Sindhi heard the creak of the mast. The crest of the waves. The caw of the gulls, circling and following the ship from nowhere to nowhere.

"Break the vial," the deep voice declared.

"No!" Sindhi screamed.

"I want to do it," the gypsy woman said. The man threw his spear to her. She spun it and rammed the blunt end of his weapon into her shoulder, crushing the vial inside her vest pocket. Sindhi screamed until her voice cracked.

She sobbed with no sound, for nothing was left. She had been so close and now only misery remained. Crestfallen, Sindhi felt her own spirit dropping to the deck. They let her go, and she rolled onto its slick wooden boards, slamming into it with a dismal finality.

The gypsy woman squatted and whispered: "Now you barter for your life." She stood and placed her foot on Sindhi's head, pressing. More of the same followed: yelling, ordering, information, information, information.

She heard another familiar word, the name of their captain, and it unlocked something Sindhi did not know she had within her—madness. It was Sindhi's turn to laugh, the only thing left after a life of serving, proving, killing, an age of training, days of swimming, long strokes through bloody, kinetic shores, escaping . . .

The woman released her foot from Sindhi's cackling head and backed away. The Hammer laughed and laughed and laughed and laughed. They said it again, the captain's name. Too much. It was all too much.

He revealed himself by standing before her, their old captain. Long, thick white hair. A darkened gray beard. A tall and proud man. Skin thicker than the sails. The captain's eyes confirmed it and, finally, Sindhi knew Hammer Jah'ri's tale.

She reckoned she knew more than he did.

"She's moon mad. Be done with it," the captain ordered. He turned to leave.

Unknown arms lifted Sindhi and pushed her back to the ship's edge. "Your name," Sindhi yelled between laughs of lunacy. "I know your name! Your name!"

Captain Jah'ri halted. The old man turned his head, raised his hand, signifying that Sor's Hammer had earned a few more seconds of life. "Impossible," he refuted. "Jah'ri is a Denan name. Not a word mountain whores know. Tell another lie and I will open your throat with a fish hook."

Sindhi's laughter had subsided. She was winded. Boldly, she shrugged off the arms holding her and approached the captain. Blades appeared, as if out of the mist, and surrounded her. She spoke through them. "I know not the name Denan. I only know Jah'ri. He is a Hammer. Do you hear me? A Hammer! A man with your own eyes. Your face. Swimming in these very waters."

The old man returned his full attention to the small Hammer. Sindhi suspected he was not only weighing her words, but auditing her eyes, her posture. She felt naked. As if he could see through her tattered uniform, as if he could peel back her skin. Some gypsy trick.

Sindhi understood her limited leverage. Like a child playing Scraps, she made the only move she had left. "Your son …" The way the captain's eyes evaded her own told her she had found the truth of it. "Your son named him. Spare me and I will tell you what I know, for there is more. Much, much more."

Captain Jah'ri seemed to think through her offer, running

calloused fingers through his dark beard. Finally, he shook his head and looked to his waist. A pouch on his belt. A string. The man was distracted. He fished out a large hook, the size of his palm, its steel grimy from use. Sindhi's eyes widened with terror, and she stepped back. The sea gypsies cooed with reverence.

"It was my daughter who named him," he replied, closing the pouch and stepping toward her, the hook protruding through the middle of his fist like a claw. "You gave me hope today. In return I will give you rest. Quick but painful. That is the way of the sea."

"I can tell you more!" she screamed. "Felton, Jah'ri. There's more to know!"

The old man raised his hook.

38

———————————

LADY EYRILIA

Lady Eyrilia laid awake. How long had it been? Today marked four. Four days since she struck Naor, since she threatened him, since the boy disappeared. Three days since Ricard burst into her committee, blaring like a sad horn and pronouncing all their troubles to the world. Two days since Ricard marched into the Elder Hammer's quarters, against her very specific wishes, and demanded a troop of Hammers escort him to the 29th Parallel.

One day since she lost her chairship and was voted out of her own committee.

Eyrilia knew what would happen before she even opened the committee's door. What else could happen with so many rumors flying? When she saw them there, all meeting without her, the consequences of her family's selfish mistakes and poor judgment (at the cost of her lifetime of sound judgment), stung Eyrilia. The Lady of the Court became enraged.

"What is the meaning of this?" She wanted them to state it plainly, to see which traitor would be the one to take her place. Alcon, her deputy chair, slowly raised.

"Lady Eyrilia, the committee of the 18th Parallel has chosen to remove your chair."

"My chair?" she scoffed, feigning surprise.

"In light of recent events, of course." Sweaty, pale, eyes downcast, how weak Alcon looked in his intrepid moment of bravery.

"An opening and you took it."

"My lady."

"My son is missing! Likely stolen from the Nails plotting Sor knows what—"

"My lady!" Alcon raised his voice, giving Eyrilia what she wanted. "Your son has been implicated as a co-conspirator. You are welcome to appeal to the high priest and the Elder Hammer."

True surprise colored her face. A co-conspirator? Her child? The one who ate only Ka Cushion and cried every time the wind blew? "Lunacy," she said. "You should all be ashamed. Look at me. Look at me, I said!" Her screams echoed throughout the chamber.

Making a scene was not part of her plan. She merely wanted to hear the pronouncement of excommunication and watch them vote, one by one, noting who stayed loyal, and then leave with a proud dignity that said little but wished them well. She would apply to a higher committee as a regular member before working her way back to chair. She would later host each traitor for supper and watch them beg and grovel for a spot in her new, better committee. She would laugh, and all would be right again in Arou. But when all the members of the 18th committee raised their heads and stared at her in disgust, in reaction to her unplanned screams, it was the first time since Eyrilia was a little girl that she felt lost and unwelcome, as if she had stumbled into her father's study and interrupted his important work.

"Fuck you," she told them and abruptly left, suddenly careless to stay for their vapid vote.

Now, she lifted from bed and slowly paced down the hallway, rubbing her eyes, her neck, casually unsure of how much longer her family would be granted this home.

Her family. She found Ricard sleeping in Naor's room. He must have returned in the night. Her last conversation with Ricard was unkind. She had a habit of that, she knew. Eyrilia called him a fool, told him he was weak, that his anxiety was as fruitless and feckless as he was. She told him the boy had run away because his father had taught him how to be weak.

"Striking a scared child does not make one strong, Eyrilia," Ricard said before leaving. She screamed wordless rage as he slammed the door.

Now, Wiglaf raised his head from within Ricard's arms. The dog yawned and pushed his little body up, hopping to the floor. Ricard didn't wake. She left him to his anxious dreams and led Wiglaf into the kitchen. She found a match and struck it. She threw it into the stove where the wood and kindling caught; as always, it was prepared the night before by the servant Nail who cleaned their home and delivered their food. Eyrilia found the kettle, put it over the fire. She rummaged through their cluttered and busy pantry, her mind hazy like the morning dew obscuring the dome.

"No jars of slop," she warned the dog. All she could find was a piece of dried bovine. "Here," she offered, and threw it to the other side of the kitchen. Wiglaf briefly examined with sniffs before taking it to the corner where he would begin the great task of his day.

Eyrilia found some dried leaves and petals in a drawer and chopped them finely. She slowly scraped the neat pile into a ball infuser. As she waited for the water to heat, she returned to her window and soaked in the morning view of the courtyard. There, she felt within her a distant welling.

Eyrilia did strike her son. There was no running from that. She threatened him. Did her father not show her the same form of love? From it she was strengthened. It was a cruel thing when a mother could not wield her own parent's love.

What else could a parent give her child?

Noar was never strong in the same ways she was. The boy took after Ricard, his false father. After everything she did to bring Naor into the world: secretly taking the Hammer's seed, carrying the child in her womb, birthing and raising, teaching and scolding, hitting and threatening.

Her kettle began to whine.

Eyrilia had worn anger like a shield her entire life, and it suited her well.

But now everything felt heavy and distorted, a size too big. Sor-be-damned, her kettle wouldn't shut up. Blindly, she reached for it and burned her hand, yelling every profane word she knew as Wiglaf ran and hid. She picked up the kettle by the handle and threw it. Ricard ran into the room. She didn't see the look of shock on her husband's tired face; avoiding that common trigger was likely for the best.

Either way, it mattered not. Eyrilia was too busy crying in front of her shattered kitchen window, wiping her eyes like a scolded child.

39

DAELAN

There, he saw it. The tide changed. Sor's grace, there were patterns in the water. A system. How it pushed against the mountain and flooded its shorelines. How it retreated and exposed rock stacks, revealing absconding sea life that was once safe and now doomed from the changing of the tides and the roving, hunting shadows of gulls. The system worked because it had to. Because order begot efficiency. Life demanded it.

Elder Hammer Daelan was pleased with his progress.

There was still much to learn. The First Parallel had the largest assemblage of interior passageways, cavehomes, and personal quarters. It was far too easy to lose one's steps or disappear from the sight of command, but progress had been made. More torch light, better markings. Daelan blocked various passageways entirely until he could better learn where they led. Those who complained were whipped. What concern were they to him? Nails could always find a new hole.

The route to the temple was the clearest and cleanest path, the only corridor that mattered, and now, every day, grateful Nails filled the temple in fervent worship of their god: Sor, the one true lord of Arou. Nails were but parasites scratching the base of Sor's Crown, but even parasites could labor. Forcefully they worshiped, and when they returned, they scrubbed the gull shit from stone steps or harvested molluscs from the underside of rocks or scrubbed the scales from the heaves of netted fish or carved new quarters for the expanding brigade of Hammers, more arriving everyday.

The Nails were to be strengthened, and Sor's kingdom again made whole.

Daelan's Hammers ransacked their quarters and removed any and all personal items, which were now forbidden and punishable. Many cavehomes were closed. The Nails combined their pits. They were only tools of the kingdom. Nails did not have belongings because they did not belong. Sor's Just Society. It was right, and it was good. A system. Order.

Last night, Daelan lit a large fire in the community pit. Their sinful personal items and hidden, unnecessary food was thrown into it. Daelan proudly watched it all burn. He saw the looks on their faces, Nails watching whatever false grasps of humanity they had left burn and blow away with the smoke, and he was satisfied. Then he ordered the retrieval of a faceless carcass. It took many hands, for Holo was still heavy, and they flung him into the fire.

Proudly, Daelan announced, "If you are hungry, your sinful

and blasphemous former leader will be done soon. You all deserve nothing, but from my grace and the King's love, you will soon be fed. Eat, for you will receive nothing until Holo's bones are picked clean."

REESTABLISHING POWER, SERVING his King. This was why Daelan came to the First Parallel. It was his calling. What he was meant to do. Who he was meant to be. This morning, a kingdom skyship visited him. A great honor. They gazed upon Daelan's progress firsthand. The whip was even in his hand, striking the young Nail bitch. Daelan was not above doing the work himself. Not like all the other lazy Elder Hammers who ruled from the comforts of their couches. The kingdom had now witnessed his leadership, and Daelan would be known far and wide. Soon, he would be invited to the 38th Parallel to bow in front of his King.

Something was in the water. A whale? A shark?

Daelan looked with keener eyes. He could not find it again. Just before he turned away, a small wave crested, and he saw a splash. Choppy waters. No, someone swimming! With interest he watched the stranger progress towards shore as he casually nibbled on some bread. Was it a Nail trying to escape? Most did not know how to swim. No, no. The stranger moved with a quickness and efficiency that suggested the training of a Hammer, maybe even a Sword.

Daelan did not know Hammer Rannold, nor was he familiar with his secret mission. He did not know how long the Hammer had been swimming, or that Rannold saw a mysterious isle explode as he swam away. Daelan did not know that Rannold gave up hope on the return swim, that he was haunted by visions, that he saw the Ancient Evil, the beast Shyloc, in the waters far away from Brecca, as if it were following him and hunting Rannold, or how he saw Commander Prime's own skyship come down to the shore and speak with the beast directly. Daelan did not know that when the fog cleared, Rannold saw the mountain and realized he was almost home, and it was this new hope that filled his empty heart and lifted him inland.

Daelan did know that the helpless Hammer swam into a small whirlpool. He desperately paddled and kicked but another wave came and sent him into a rock stack that looked, as the locals suggested, like the tip of a fish tail, where his panicked screams ceased in crescendo.

"Fish Tail. Swirl bait. There it is."

The strange things you see in the First Parallel.

He took another bite of bread and threw the heel into the water before returning back to work.

40

LAYALA AND NAOR

Monsters in the dark.

Naor jumped to his feet and rushed the stairs. Layala jerked backwards, in her own fright, and lost her balance. Her feet tangled on wet stone. Naor turned to see the tall stranger clumsily wobbling her arms. He saw something else: real fear in her face. He realized quickly this was no monster or ghost, not a Hammer or a wizard. His instincts told him to reach. The stranger grabbed Naor's hand and pulled, finding purchase in the dark chaos at the dizzying edge of death. He leaned his full weight against the stairs and fell backwards, pulling her forward. Their foreheads clashed as she landed on top of him. Naor yelled. The stranger jumped away from his small body and fled further up the stairs, disappearing just up ahead into the thick violence of the raging storm.

Naor was not sure who or what he just saved. He considered that she may have indeed been a spirit, wandering Sor's Staircase whenever the sea's storms blew.

A spirit would not be so afraid to fall.

This had been a person. He had felt her skin. She butted his head, for Sor's sake. It still hurt, he realized.

"Come back!" he yelled. "I'm sorry!"

LAYALA REACHED THE next small platform and stopped climbing. In the distance, she heard what sounded like yelling, but most of it was lost in the wind. Not Marin. Layala had been a fool. A delirious fool. She was not the only Nail on this staircase, of course not. Others were as doomed as she was.

Nothing had changed, she knew.

Do what you were about to do.

Layala stared into the empty, howling wind.

She couldn't.

Instead of jumping, Layala simply collapsed onto the floor.

NAOR FOUND THE stranger on the platform's ground, sobbing in silence.

"I'm sorry . . ." he told her.

She raised her head and scooted backwards.

Naor lifted his hands. "It's alright. I'm sorry I scared you," he said, yelling every word.

Her fingers over infinity, Layala stopped scooting after reaching the edge. She fought to speak but touched her throat and shook her head.

Naor pointed to his ears and said very loudly, "That's fine. I can't hear a thing anyways." He smiled widely. "Just a terrible ringing," he clarified as he tapped his ears. "There was a... uh..." Naor looked at the castle tower and made a playful sound. "BOOM!" He laughed and shook his head. "I don't understand it."

Layala could see only the faint outline of the castle tower in the distance, but as the wind blew away the storm's busy clouds, hints of the boy's troubles were revealed: what looked like a small fire blowing through a clunky, odd-shaped window. She returned her gaze to the boy and saw him plainly. His clothes were ragged and dusty, but underneath the grime she found signs of privilege in the weaving of his tunic, the trimming of his messy hair, and the confidence and comfortability of approaching a stranger.

"Are you alright?" he yelled as he asked.

What a question.

She wanted to be cruel and push the boy away, but she remembered the kindness of his outstretched hand as she tottered over the abyss. She mouthed the words: "Your name?"

"Naor," he announced, adding, "the Brave." He smiled warmly. "I guess?" The boy was sweet, and it sickened her. Did she now have to be responsible for another innocent child who would soon meet his demise? Cruel, too, that fate would pair her with a child so close in size and demeanor to Marin. She did not have time or energy to process or even properly feel the disappointment.

Naor sensed her mind astray and waved gently to recapture her attention. "Your name?" he bellowed the question.

Layala returned to her feet, grunting through her throat and feeling every muscle ache. She mouthed slowly: "Lay-ah-lah."

"Latathala?"

"Lay. Ah. Lah."

"Lallalla"?

She shook her head, waving off a faint smile. An idea came to her. She pantomimed sleep with her hands under her head. "Lay," she mouthed.

"Lay," Naor repeated aloud. She nodded.

"Ah," she pantomimed with a big open mouth.

"Lay-ah."

She nodded and then mouthed, "Lah."

"Lay-ah-lah," Naor said. "Layala. Nice to meet you!" Naor extended his hand for her to shake. She looked at it, unsure of its meaning, and extended her own hand in the air without touching his. Naor started laughing, and then Layala felt the strange sensation of her shoulders bouncing. She was laughing too, she realized. How long had it been? For both of them, laughter felt like a gift that was stolen, one neither thought would ever return.

Naor grabbed her hand as she flinched; he squeezed gently as he shook her hand up and down briefly before letting go.

"Are you a . . . Nail?" he asked her. Layala took her time with the question and thought it through. She nodded her head.

"You?" Layala mouthed, likely already knowing the answer.

"Me? No, I am a . . . friend to Nails."

She pointed to the castle and shrugged her shoulders. Naor struggled to connect her question but eventually saw it. "No. I'm from the Court," he replied. Confusion found her face, so he clarified. "The . . . uh . . ." He made a half sphere with his hands.

"The dome." Layala remembered seeing a city on top of the mountain's plateau surrounded by a strange glass. She nodded. Naor said, "I haven't seen a friendly face in a long time."

Layala looked away from the boy. Aimlessly, her eyes searched the dark clouds. Whatever or whoever brought Naor to the stairs, his fate hadn't changed. They were both still doomed. Not to mention, guilt weighed heavily upon her head, as did the sobriety of certain death.

"What do we do now?" she heard Naor ask her.

Nothing.

She wanted to tell him, but could not say that.

Almost aimlessly, she pointed, surprised to find her finger in the direction of up.

THEY CLIMBED TOGETHER throughout the night, Layala ahead and Naor just behind. The thickness of the storm began to pass, but it was still difficult to see much beyond a dozen of their own steps. She occasionally looked back to make sure the boy was keeping up. His eyes were down as he climbed. He mumbled to himself. Layala recognized the look from her own brothers: the boy was playing games in his mind, imagining life on some other world, in some other time. She admitted she was intrigued to know more of the boy's story (if anything, to help pass the time), but her throat would simply not allow her questions, so they continued on in silence.

Time was difficult to measure on Sor's Staircase. Layala suspected they had already climbed for many hours. When they reached another small platform, she stopped and pointed to the ground before sitting. Naor abided without issue.

They looked out at the sea as the view to the west cleared.

"Look!" Naor said and pointed. She saw it too. Far away, to the north in the Sea of Casmu, lightning surged without a storm. They sat and watched the show. Something burst. Layala and Naor looked at each other. It was too far to see or understand.

"What was that?" he asked her.

She shrugged her shoulders. Other flashes came but it all died down rather quickly and the view returned to nothing but moonlight shimmering black water. Beyond it, the horizon teased the first colors of a sunrise. Layala found its light in the boy's eyes.

He is not Marin.

And who was she, Layala wondered? What was she? A crabber? Swimmer? Smuggler? Sister? A Nail?

She tapped Naor on his shoulder and spoke in the clearest voice her crushed throat would allow. "I . . . not a Nail." Her voice was still hoarse. It hurt her to say the words, but she was glad she did.

It was Naor's turn to get lost in his own thoughts, but eventually he emerged with a soft, sad smile and nodded.

"Sleep," she whispered.

"Can you . . . uh . . ." The boy was embarrassed to ask. Layala understood and nodded. He laid on the stone platform, arms under his head, as Layala kept the pressure of an unsteady hand on his shoulder, securing him safely.

SHE DREAMT SHE was falling and screamed as she woke, one hand on the edge, the other still on the boy. He stirred. "You okay?" The sleepy features of his face swam in the fading memory of a cold dream.

Layala wiped her eyes, nodded. "We should go," she whispered.

They climbed, rising with the sun.

THEY REACHED THE top of a wide spiral section of chipped, blocky stone. They turned a corner and, for the first time in countless hours, faced the south.

Layala saw nothing.

Layala saw everything.

Arou, improbably untouched and unreasonably serene. Forests, deserts, rivers—words she didn't know, lands she had never dreamed—blankets of minor mountains cooed by storms, flat land cities, and sweet rippling coastlines, generously infinite and free. She didn't see the castle. Sor's Staircase continued behind them, rising seemingly without end, but just below their feet was their prize, and Layala peeked over the ledge to see.

It was just below them, Capital Castle. They had overtaken it.

Two seconds of falling. Perhaps three.

It was a considerable drop straight down to the tower's peak, but not impossible. The wind could take you in that time, Layala knew, especially up here where gusts attacked like cove sharks. The wind reminded her of Wavelo's tide; she spent many steps over the last few hours considering their relation. One of many games her mind played to pass the time and distract from her own weakness.

When her eyes focused she found another problem and what little warmth remained inside her froze. She tried to hide her tears and the shudder of her jaw from Naor, but Layala was simply devastated and could no longer don the shawl of bravery, courage, or even simple purpose.

Her plan had been simple: Climb higher than the castle's top and then jump down to its topmost spire. They would find a way inside the tower, and she would show Naor how to escape. Now, all they had done was use what little strength they had left to needlessly climb a staircase of death.

The very top of the Forbidden Parallel was indeed a spire, or cone, reaching out of the tower's top. On it, hundreds of black spikes protruded from its wooden roof. There were leftovers of Nails, but not many, just a few bones twisted between the spikes. Most Nails likely didn't make it this far, Layala concluded. The few that did all had the same idea, but the promise of impalement was all they had found here. Certain death at the top of the world.

Layala cleared her throat and tried her best to project her voice. "Naor," she managed.

"Hey," he said, "I can hear that." He tapped his ears. "The ringing isn't so loud."

"That's good," Layala said with a grimace. Her throat still writhed, but what didn't? She would use her voice with whatever time she had left, though how could she tell a boy he would die? Was this her real penance?

Layala sat for a final time, and Naor, again, followed her lead.

"I'm so hungry," he said.

"Me too."

She looked at the boy. Had he always been that thin? No, she suspected not. And his hands moved with tremors. He was withering away and almost gone. Much like her, she imagined.

"I am from the First Parallel," she told him, finding more confidence in her ravaged voice. He looked at her in disbelief. She already knew what would come next.

"Poop's Bottom?"

Her eyes widened and her brows lifted.

"I mean . . . I'm sorry. That was . . . rude."

"It's okay." She touched her throat. If Layala weren't about to die, her voice would need a break, for her throat felt as if she had swallowed and crunched an entire crab shell, claws and all. Instead, she pushed. "There are many names for my home. We call it 'Wavelo.' The more I see of Arou, the more I know. Wavelo was the happiest and freelest land in the entire kingdom."

"Was?"

"Was." The word barely came. She nodded her head as she massaged her throat.

"The Court wasn't so bad," Naor explained. "It can be a happy place. As long as you know where to look. And where to . . . not look. I miss my dog."

Layala shook her head in confusion.

"Dog? Like, woof woof?" He stuck his tongue out and breathed fast and heavy. She shook her head again, but Naor was satisfied, having pulled a fresh smile from her depths. "I guess you don't have those down there. Dogs are great. I'll get you one."

She nodded, and they sat in silence for a little while, the

wind steady and melancholic.

"We were going to jump onto the roof, weren't we? But we can't. Because of the spikes."

Layala didn't respond. She just stared at nothing in particular.

Naor continued. "Let's go back down. We'll find a way off. There's got to be a way."

She stood as still and lifeless as a temple. There was nothing left in her. She had to tell the boy they had reached their end. Even if Layala could speak clearly and without pain, she was not sure she could ever find the words. Instead, she pointed. "What is that? Anything to eat in there?"

Naor looked at his belt bag. "Oh," he said. "I forgot I was wearing it. A friend . . . um, not really a friend. See, it was holding a weapon."

"Weapon?"

He opened the wizard's bag and searched through it. "Wait," he said and then pulled out a small piece of folded paper. Naor unfolded it and read aloud two scribbled words:

My message.

"My message?" he said again, distressed. The wind ripped the paper from his hand, and they watched it twirl and fly away. Naor looked at Layala. In return she saw, perhaps, the first real hint of anger in the boy. "My message!" he screamed. He stood and began to clumsily yet furiously free himself from the belt bag, his shaky hands fumbling with the knot. "I hate him! I hate this castle. I hate this kingdom!" The wizard's belt bag freed from Naor's waist with a click. He pulled it off and bundled it into a ball. The angry son of the Court threw the bag into the wind.

Standing aside each other, they watched the bag fall onto the tower's roof and hook onto a spike. It spun around and slid to the base where it defiantly rested.

Layala held his hand. He turned to her and hugged her, disappearing into her thin embrace. Layala remained tall and stiff, unsure if she wanted to allow herself to feel, to melt. She did not deserve his warmth nor his trust. Yet her hand found the top of his head, and she brushed his dusty hair. She returned the hug without reserve, telling the boy it would be alright.

When Naor finally raised his eyes, he was surprised to see Layala's head tilted. It reminded him of when Wiglaf was confused or curious. Despite Naor's sorrow, he laughed.

"Look!" Layala pointed to the sky.

Naor's head tilted when he saw it too.

41

JAH'RI

Plummeting at the speed of a falling star, Jah'ri was surprised it was taking so long to crash. It gave him too much time to consider his death, to think about the impact, how quick it would happen, how much he would feel. He wasn't quite at ease enough to meditate, but he leaned on that mental muscle to control his breathing.

Every blink brought him closer to Arou's surface. In between the crispy crushing of his eyelids, which were nearly frozen from the atmospheric elements, Jah'ri thought of the Southern Arm and hoped he would crash there, directly into a citrus grove. It was the only patrol he ever relished.

He remembered Shyloc, touching the beast's electric skin and yearned again to speak its strange language. How he wished he could tell it goodbye. How he wished it'd finally be free. He blinked again and saw his mother, her hand swiping the dirt map.

With one hand he clutched to the chair's belt, which wrapped tightly around his torso. His other hand stretched out towards the open viewing window as Arou came ever closer.

Jah'ri swiped the map.

The world did not clear.

He smiled. It was worth a shot.

Instead, Jah'ri would settle for another dream. As the skyship hurled closer towards Sor's Staircase, Jah'ri raised a finger to block it.

"Neat," he said.

Jah'ri tightened his grip on the seat's rope.

The skyship shook as it nicked the top of Sor's Staircase, wobbling and slowing slightly, but plummeting all the same. It hit and crashed through another layer. Stones burst through the skyship's window. Jah'ri squinted. Coming up quick, higher than he ever would have expected, were two Nails on the stairs, just above the uppermost spire of the castle.

He screamed, "Move, you idiots!"

42

———————

LAYALA AND NAOR

t was the sound of the world ending, as if every creature who ever existed on Arou roared all at once, like the summoning of the Unknown Infinite for the destruction of Meaning.

But what Naor would always remember was seeing the crash before hearing it.

The tiniest little delay between motion and sound.

Layala and Naor cowered as the plummeting skyship burst through an entire flight of stairs, just above them. The stones burst. Each with their own story, they cried again.

It all happened in only seconds.

Layala screamed. Naor jumped away just before broken steps from the staircase fell upon him. Everything shook. The skyship blared, crushing through staircase landing after staircase landing, before finally pivoting away from all the careless destruction it had caused and disappearing into the eastern horizon.

There was not enough time to process the fact that Sor's Staircase would soon be falling. The sections of the stairs above them had already started falling, most of it directly onto the castle.

Desperately, Naor looked back to the roof of the castle tower, where his belt bag still lay among the wretched spikes. He searched for escape, for hope, for anything.

There must be a way down.

Then, from above, something unfathomably large and terrible blocked his vision. A chunk of Sor's Staircase—an entire flight of stairs—falling directly into the castle.

The peak of the tower exploded. Part of its conical roof slid away while wood and stone and iron erupted upwards, slamming into Sor's Staircase before breaking apart into endless pieces and tumbling toward the dome below.

The staircase buckled under their feet.

Naor couldn't tell if it had come from the blast or if the mountain itself had begun to shake.

Smoke began to billow out of the castle tower and covered them both, forming a thick, obscuring fog.

"Layala?"

Hadn't she just been standing next to him? Naor's hands waved through the fog.

"Layala?"

His feet found the edge of the wobbly stairs, and his body tipped over.

Layala grabbed his hand just before he succumbed to the precipice. The smoke blew away in a lofty gust of wind, and he saw her clearly. There was a smirk on her face, some demented side of her he had not yet seen.

Hoarsely, she yelled, "Swim between FishTail and CrabClaw and you avoid SwirlBait."

"Layala!"

"FishTail and CrabClaw!"

"I don't like this!" His eyes widened as she let him go.

LAYALA WATCHED THE boy fall into a ring of smoke, into the castle below.

He looks like a bird.

Naor disappeared and landed, one way or another, into the Forbidden Parallel where life and death fought for air amidst the raging flames.

Only one thing for her to do, and she did it.

Time slows when reality fails. Light shines translucently, as if it were illustrated by the hands of Meaning, before being ripped and tossed, a casual throw that aims for infinity. The air itself loses its breath. The memory of motion echoes until it shatters.

The world falls.

Through the wind and the smoke, blue into white into gray, Layala jumped.

She sucked in breath.

She swam through the air.

Layala dove above all of Arou, holy chunks of Sor's Staircase plummeting with her, into the center of a treacherous and sinister circle. The opened spire of Capital Castle swallowed her, as it had Naor. She couldn't help a panicky breath as the smoke stung her eyes. It moved through her body, to her lungs, stabbing her there, overwhelming her, all of this in only two seconds. Gravity pulled her further, and when Layala landed she was punched by a surface so heavy, so flat, so familiar, what she had briefly seen through a break in the smoke, yet it now surrounded and attacked her.

Water, atop the world.

It's a cruel thing when a swimmer drowns.

Layala coughed while she spun, inhaling water. Her hysterical hands tangled into her own hair. If she were inverted she wouldn't have known. It wouldn't have mattered. Panic seized her. Death, that familiar predator, pounced, pressing into Layala's limbs like a blood-soaked blanket, like a bed, like a crib, like a grave, like a cage, like a combat hammer smashing squirming legs. And was that Marin she saw in the water with her? His reaching hand?

NAOR PLUNGED HIS hand into the King's fiery pool. He laid on the edge, having survived the fall and escaped the pool, and he reached. Layala splashed like a fish breaching the surface. He cried and screamed each time he lost his grasp. Finally, and regrettably, Naor seized a chunk of her hair and pulled hard, hearing a rip. It was enough to get her to the edge. Naor grabbed under her arms and pulled her atop the stone base next to the pool.

He rolled her over.

"Please, oh, please!" Naor pleaded.

Not knowing what to do, he screamed, "Hurry!" The castle

roared, and the smoke billowed. Fire encroached on all sides. He pounded her chest, and that was what woke her.

43

EDA OF PRIR

The sky was empty of prophecies. Eda sat on a low ridge, her boots feeling heavy. She watched the clouds offer shade to every hillside but hers and swallowed piss-warm water from her canteen. Nothing here. Nothing to see. All the people in all the world, and they recruited Eda to stare at the sky in the heat of the desert. It had been a few minutes since her last impatient outburst, and even she was starting to annoy herself with her own complaints.

These people, the Bound Accord, were certainly patient. Insane, but patient.

"Tell me about the fourth king," she asked no one in particular, hoping the distraction would eat enough time.

Leod, who stood nearby, replied, "He was—"

"Not you," Eda said without looking.

He scoffed. "Viceroy, you must see I am not the man you think I am."

"A spineless tool of the chieftain, as bound as a boil. The scent is the same."

She heard Leod angrily mutter as he walked away.

Replacing Leod was Haasher, his old eyes expectant with the burden of an oncoming lesson. "We all have roles to play, Eda."

"Killing Prir's reform amendments is a role then? Makes it worse, doesn't it? No, no. Leod is a snake that serves only himself. I am trying to help my people. Our people, Haasher. Prir. Those living in the here and now. These prophecies . . ." She gestured to the empty sky. "They distract from progress. Come back to Prir with me. Abandon this fantasy and help me lobby for real change. The chieftain's chamber will listen if we are united."

Haasher nodded at his replacement, the lines in his old face revealing little. She remembered now how Haasher, through many political ages, trained his face to become a mirror, how aptly he reflected the desires of those who appealed to him.

She could not trust him any more than she could trust Leod.

"You must understand, Eda, the importance of all this. The chieftain will do anything for his holy war against Sor's Kingdom, and Prir will fall because of it." Haasher brushed the dust off his hands for effect. "Prir will be emptied, because our peaceful people, your peaceful people, will all be slaughtered. Sure, some may come back. But it won't be the same. Prir will never be the same. Trisrca itself may never recover."

Eda began to speak, but Haasher continued, artfully adjusting his tone.

"Now, you asked about the fourth king. You know Prir, Veir,

and Einn, the expelled kings and founders of Trisrca. They left together because they were aligned, believe it or not." Haasher chuckled at his own joke. "It's true, it's true. A rare time where our provinces coexisted. You must realize, Eccoulous did not have the transportation it does now—the pulley carriages. There was an earlier version that connected a few territories, but, back then, no one king could rightfully manage an entire mountain. They coexisted out of necessity. The fourth king, Denan, ruled the first five realms, what Sor's Kingdom now calls the first five Parallels.

"Legend has it that King Denan was unfriendly to his fellow kings. A bit of an isolationist. He distrusted them and often rebuked any attempt at coexistence, assuming their intent for conquest of his land.

"Sor, back then, was a sniveling, puerile leader of a roving sea kingdom. It was he who approached Denan and got a foothold in his land. Sor was but a mercenary looking for labor. He rested his fleet at the mountain's base. Certainly, Sor had desires of his own, but Denan couldn't see them. He was blinded by his own distrust of his neighbors, who wanted nothing from him. By the time Denan understood Sor's ambitions, it was too late; Denan had opened his ports and his land to the mercenaries, and they were overrun by Sor's pirates. Denan himself escaped, as did many of his chiefs and children, taking Sor's ships as they left. 'A fair trade,' it is rumored Sor had said, jolly from the loss of his fleet, for he had gained the mountain's foothold and grew his army tenfold. It was not long before he waged war further up the mountain, absorbing each unsuspecting kingdom as he went."

"Did the line of Denan survive? Do they live today?"

Haasher smiled with closed lips and shrugged his shoulders.

"Some say they were cursed to the sea and will sail for eternity. Others claim they settled into old ruins in the far west jungles. Then there are those of us who believe that, even today, the line of Denan plots to recapture their stolen land, one thousand ages later. You look surprised, Viceroy, but believe me: Sor's Kingdom is home to many spies."

"The chieftain believes that, doesn't he?"

"Insiders, like our mutual friend Leod, give us this information at great personal risk. You would do well to remember that next time you so easily push him away. And yes, the chieftain, he believes a storm is coming to Arou, that the mountain will soon be at war from all sides. He wishes to gain his footing first."

Haasher grunted as he stood.

Eda shook her head. "Haasher . . . if this turns out to be real, whoever this guy is—"

"Solin."

"Sure. Look, I can't kill him. I won't. Never again will I take a life. You know this about me, yet you recruit me to a group of prophecy killers. I have become adept at learning to read through your intentions, but this . . . I'm at a loss."

Haasher nodded. He kneeled again, wincing through weak joints. His voice lowered. "Eda, the prophecy is only fulfilled if He Who Climbs the Sun is taken to the chieftain. It is not enough for a fireball to streak across the sky. Solin must stand beside the chieftain as he declares war."

"I don't care," she urged. "You could have recruited anyone."

"I recruited you and your pacifism." Haasher lowered his voice to a hoarse whisper. "Your shiny idealism might blind you to the fact that you're not the only one here conflicted about murdering a stranger. If anyone can think of a way to avoid both murder and war, Viceroy Eda, it will be you. It will be you."

He patted her on the shoulder. She smirked.

Unbelievable. How good was Haasher at making people like him?

Haasher added, "Watch the skies, Viceroy."

44

JAH'RI

Jah'ri screamed through the whole ordeal.

When he crashed into Sor's Staircase, the ship changed trajectory suddenly, turning irrationally, with a preternatural feeling of limitlessness that could only be described as time bouncing, a sensation that flipped his brain and nearly knocked him out cold.

For most, Sor's Staircase was a death sentence, but for Jah'ri it was his salvation.

The skyship crashed through enough layers to slow it down, then, after hitting the largest landing, altered its deep descent towards a more favorable angle.

Jah'ri would still crash, likely soon, but now his skyship would slide, instead of landing face forward.

He hoped.

But now, adding to his confusion, the skyship flew upside down. He could see the Treelands through the viewing window, technically above him.

The Treelands would have been a good place to land, but the skyship never slowed, and soon, the trees thinned and were replaced by an immensely brown land with disparate patches of boulders and valleys. Perhaps the Shield or the Battlelands, it did not matter.

The skyship curved closer towards Arou, dipping.

And that seemed to do it.

THE HAMMER NEVER lost consciousness.

Though technically awake for the skyship's impact, his brain simply paused, for it had seen too much already. It was too bright to see and too loud to really understand much of anything anyways.

The forward most tip of the skyship, technically its top half, leaned into the stubborn ground; this was what shattered it into pieces. Jah'ri was then flung into the open air with the seat he had tied himself to. The chair landed with the back of its iron frame in the sandy ground and dragged for a terrible time, stopping only after hitting a boulder, which was abrupt and maddening. The rope unraveled and momentum hurled Jah'ri further into the red dirt.

On instinct and adrenaline, Jah'ri jumped to his feet and began to walk.

He stumbled around aimlessly for a little while, nodding at the bits and pieces of skyship all around him.

The wreckage burned. He stopped to stare at the flames curling in the wind like waves in the sea. The water and the flames were one. The bird and the fish. The Hammer and the Nail. The screams of his mother. A faceless cleanser. Sour water. Hard bread.

HOW LONG HAD Jah'ri been staring at the flame? He was not sure. He stumbled around some more, kicking burnt pieces of the skyship's hull. There was not much of it here. He looked to the west and saw a long stretch of wreckage, larger pieces much further away. He still didn't feel the damage to his body: the hits to his skull, the rope burns on his skin, whatever bruises laid underneath. There would be time for all that.

First, he would search for the metal shape of a friend.

45

EDA OF PRIR

"There!"

Eda heard the sound of yelling. She looked everywhere but the sky, unused to this new duty she'd been assigned.

Watch the skies indeed.

The cry came again. "There! There!"

Faziah pointed.

It was an incredible sight. Everything Faziah said it would be. It began as a simple fireball in the sky, hovering patiently just above Arou. No one spoke as it glowed green and exploded. For a solemn moment, the group remained quiet before the fireball returned with righteous and determined speed, this time streaking across the midday desert sky.

The Bound were not far from the impact, and when the star collided with Arou, Eda felt the ground shake. A diabolic plume of dust erupted. Solin. He Who Climbs the Sun.

"I cannot believe it," she said.

"Your unbelief has made you strong, Viceroy, but now you must reconcile a new world with many weaving strands." Faziah was smiling, almost laughing.

"In other words," Yorke said, standing just behind them on the ridge, "Fazzy was right."

"Yes," Eda said, briefly glancing at Faziah as she grinned. "Fazzy was right."

"We should go," Haasher announced. Him and Leod were standing together on a nearby peak. "The impact will attract other desert tribes. That streak was likely seen all the way to the Southern Arm, for those that were looking."

"We know that Faziah was not the only Seer with the vision," Leod reminded the group. Eda was so in awe she forgot to scowl at the chieftain's sycophant.

They found their horses at the bottom of the ridge, spooked but tied securely. Eda watched each Bound member soothe their frightened horse and calm it. "You fine?" she asked the horse in a lame attempt. It did not reply. "Good. I'm a viceroy, you know. You'll be okay."

"Call it by its name," Yorke suggested. He had already mounted and was ready to leave.

"I . . . don't know its name."

"Then give it one. Hy'ah!" The Border Captain and his horse charged toward the plume.

It did not surprise Eda that she was the weakest rider. In Tris-rca, aristocrats went to Vier to learn to ride horses in the wide-open fields and meadows behind the province.

Eda was never an aristocrat. She was an unlucky child with a Border Captain for a father who disappeared along the border and a mother who died a few ages later from a fever. Eda was twelve. Not that she thought about it all that much. Nothing came easy, nothing came free. Her Uncle Steul had a little money and an extra room. Steul took her in, but it was her older cousin Mourad who made her feel human again. Not because he was kind, but because he was cruel to her when others were only kind. In fact, Mourad made an extra effort to remind Eda that she was not special, that Arou was indifferent to her pain. Somehow, she later suspected, Mourad's insensitive truth saved her. She grew strong and sharp and one day, her wit matched his. She caught him in the butt of a joke with a group of friends and watched him suffer like a dog chasing fish underwater. Mourad never told her he was proud of her, but from then on he followed her lead, and that was enough to establish the strange relationship that led them to Prir's Viceroy's chamber.

Now, she wondered, as usual, what Mourad would think: Eda on a horse, fearlessly riding towards wreckage from the stars, she and her intrepid group of prophecy killers.

Could she kill again? Would she?

Eda remembered the Hammer in her lap, bloody hands grasping hers. He was only a boy. In battle, there was no such thing as murder. A soldier only performed their duty. That's what Yorke and Leod and Faziah would tell her now. That there was always a reason to kill.

She spoke to her horse. "Kill one so others may live. Does all that make sense to you, Reformer?" The horse scoffed. "Well, it's a better name than my first idea: AssHurter."

The horse ignored her.

She looked at the lessening dust plume that blended into billowing smoke and urged Reformer faster.

With an impact so great, Eda was unsure He Who Climbs the Sun would live long enough to be killed. Faziah's vision ended with steps in the desert, and even Faziah admitted a Seer's visions were unreliable. "Visions hide lies within truths and truths within lies," she had said. Eda nodded and pretended she didn't have any more questions.

Yorke was the first to reach the wreckage. He dismounted and frantically began his search. Haasher, Faziah, and Leod arrived next. Eda was a few minutes behind and by the time she arrived, Yorke pointed to the eastern stretch of the wreckage. "Search there," he yelled.

Eda nodded and hid her disappointment, craving a break from Reformer, the horse made of rock. Approaching the wreckage, she rode to the east a few minutes more and dismounted. The Bound Accored had prepared her for what she would see, but the scale briefly overwhelmed her.

A scattered ship from another world.

What was a skeptic supposed to do on a planet full of prophecies and spaceships? She squatted and half-heartedly kicked large pieces of metal debris.

A pair of eyes. She jumped! "What in the shit hole?" she yelled. Eda covered her heart from the fright. It was not any ship wreckage she was looking at, but a metal head. Decapitated. Staring into nothing.

She crawled towards it. "Are you Solin?" she whispered to the metal head. "Are you He Who Climbs the Sun?"

A shadow.

"Excuse me," she heard from behind. Eda screamed, scattering away, wildly kicking the dirt. An alien man reached down and plucked the metal head from the desert.

Eda squinted. Was it an alien? Or just a terrible looking man? What little remained of the traveler's clothes were charred. His skin was terribly burned. Fresh wounds blended with scars on his arms, legs, and torso. What marks were new and what were old she could not say. The man did not look at Eda. He cradled the metal head in the crook of his arm and walked away.

Solin. It's Solin.

"Hey," she said. "Hey!" The man didn't respond. He didn't turn around. Eda stood. "Ah, shit," she said, exhaling.

With a mix of revulsion and regret, Eda pulled her blade from its sheath.

46

—————

THE FORBIDDEN PARALLEL

"**C**aptain, look!" And he did.

Before he could plunge his metal hook into the Hammer's brain, Captain Jah'ri stared at the sky, where everyone was pointing. A streak of fire in the distance plummeted through the clouds. The Denan Acolytes had a word for this curious wonder, but it escaped him now. With his free hand, he rubbed his forehead, searching. It finally came to him, as bright as the fire in the sky.

Comet.

He said the word aloud.

"I don't think so, Captain," a deckhand replied and handed him a spyglass.

Shivering, Sindhi repeated the same words over and over, unknowing, uncaring. "There's more to know. There's more to know. There's more to know."

Captain Jah'ri turned to the soggy Hammer and said, "Indeed."

THE HAMMERS IN the Shield gasped in horror. Beyond the Kingdom of Kulloh-Sor, even in hazy daylight, the soldiers of Trisrca along the border stopped to look. Deep in the Treelands surrounding the castle, a wayward wizard stood atop a great boulder and watched silently in awe, his yellow eyes reflecting the faraway, vengeful streak that shot across the sky.

IN TRISRCA, ON the chieftain's holy platform in Einn, the old leader stared at the sky in amazement. The chieftain watched as a fireball from another world tore across the sky.

Solin. He Who Climbs the Sun.

We must fetch him to fulfill the prophecy.

War has come to Arou.

IN THE SOUTHERN Arm another leader watched the sky. He lay on a bed in a room open to the world as a young Nail fed him morsels of fruit. Thin clouds covered an otherwise empty view, offering the endless gift of light shade, as if the world itself had sworn allegiance to the line of Sor.

"My King," he heard a timid voice. "My King?"

"Not now. Can't you see I'm busy?" He threw a chalice in the direction of Kolm, who should have known better than to interrupt. He did not care if it hit the pest, as long as the bug flew away.

"King, I implore you. The castle. It burns!"

King Kulloh-Sor pushed away the Nail. He sat up. "My castle?"

Near his panicked assistant Rhial, a Sword twice the height of Kolm, entered. At Rhial's feet, the King's chalice lay cracked like the skull of a Nail.

"It's true," the Sword told his King. "We are under attack."

IN THE COURT, Eyrilia sat in the courtyard where Naor had met his wayward Nail. She felt the grass. She stared at the rocks along the footpath splattered with dried blood.

How speedily life moves, the cold immediacy of change.

Is this what mourning looked like? She wondered if she would come here every day for the rest of her life, seeking signs and listening.

Arou shook. A sudden boom atop the dome almost burst her ears. Something had indeed slammed into the glass protecting her city, the Parallel she has known her whole life. Pieces fell again and again, not Nails this time—what looked like large chunks of stone banging and cracking the dome itself. She heard citizens within the courtyard screaming and fleeing to nowhere, for there was nowhere to go. Eyrilia knew with quiet reserve that the castle was falling, and something else: strange, the connection between a mother and her son.

"Naor," she cried. "What have you done?" The dome shattered, and the Parallels fell.

THE LIGHT, A signal.

Incoming.

A green finger pressed a button and muted an alarm. Yellow eyes read the transmission. They blinked. They read it again.

"Inform the council," the scientist ordered.

"Repeat. Confirm."

"A message has reached us."

HAMMER FELTON BOUNCED a small ball off the walls of the rec hall of the Holster, his hand still bandaged from Saz's devious blade. Felton could have swam. He would have made it too. He had been ready, but the impulsive idiot wounded him. Miscreants like Saz were allergic to order, to reason, to honor. Cursing Saz had become something like an addiction, his name bittersweet Rho Dust; the loaf had no idea how many plans he had ruined.

He imagined Saz swimming, Felton finding him in the water and—

Spinning, he looked.

"Commander-Sergeant?" Felton asked, bewildered. Behind him, a machinarch paced in a small circle. Felton slowly approached it. "Are you . . . ?"

Felton heard a similar noise and followed it into the Holster's main corridor. Another machinarch was there, laying on its back, legs twitching in the air as if trying to walk. Felton confusedly and cautiously walked past it, continuing into the Feed Hall towards the sound of steady pounding, at once both haunting and rapturous. Felton's brain sought logic but found none. The last remaining machine faced the giant painting of Sor's Crown. The machine repeatedly plunged its head into the painting's center, puncturing the canvas and striking the stone wall behind it.

"Sor's mercy," Felton said. The machine halted. Its neck twisted. The head, slowly turning, revealed colorless eyes. Felton fled. The machinarch followed.

IN THE FORBIDDEN Parallel, Naor and Layala rested atop a crumbling castle tower. There was no king. There were no Swords. There were no answers. Chaos consumed emptiness.

Startled, Layala blinked through blurry vision and found Naor's incredulous smile above her. His streaky cheeks puffed with misery, and he wiped them. She didn't hear whatever he was saying. Her head felt as if it were still swimming. Then she began to cough. Water spilled from her mouth and bile followed it. There was nothing to do but get it out. When the coughing subsided, Layala realized there were bigger problems. In moments, it seemed, the floor underneath them would collapse. There was also the issue of encroaching flames. In which order those deathly scenarios happened was unclear. She looked back at Naor.

"I can't believe you dropped me," Naor yelled at her, still smiling. "Who does that?"

"It worked," she managed to say as she struggled to her feet. Instinctively, her hand found her head and soothed its soreness.

"What now?" Naor asked.

Again the boy looked to her for answers, and again she had none. Despite the overwhelming smoke, the room around her came into focus. The King's Parallel had been a ruse. There was no throne for ruling, nor was there a shrine for communion with the gods. This was a circular oasis designed for relaxation. For a view. For nothing. It must have looked beautiful before the clamor and the chaos. Now, massive chunks of the ceiling's painted scenery scattered across the floor, denting the stone or bursting through it entirely. In every direction the surrounding walls had been fashioned with glass. Their melting terrified her, as if the windows themselves were sobbing like a wailing prophet, a forerunner for the tower's impending doom. Worse, Layala feared the window's burden. The remaining layers of the roof yearned to fold.

Only briefly could she look upon the King's Pool. Shallow, she realized, her body still shaking from the frantic gasping of near-death. Even in the pool's deepest pit, where she had flung wildly, the water was not a particularly profound depth. She could have stood. Later, she would have to remember to be embarrassed, but now there was simply no time.

Now, the Parallel was failing.

"Layala!" the boy screamed again. "What do we do?"

Shrugging off the disorienting blanket of death, and ignoring the terror that stalked her now, Layala grabbed Naor's hand and replied, "We run."

IN THE DESERT, a broken Hammer held a metal head. He stumbled into a foreign land while the world behind him split and shook and crashed. A stranger followed his shadow. He saw her and paid her little mind. Jah'ri reached for the compass on his uniform but found only charred skin. He lost the compass long ago, somewhere in the water, the sky, the fire, or the dirt. No matter. Jah'ri sighted the sun and turned southward.

He had a king to kill and a friend to wake.

The voice . . . he didn't hear it anymore. Maybe it had never been there at all. Perhaps, like the compass, it too was left in the sky or burned away in the skyship's wreckage, sizzling with Jah'ri's dreams and nightmares, his haunted memories. The fish had swam, and the bird had flown. From here, whatever steps Jah'ri made were his to take.

Infinity extended before him.

First, the free man would search for a fresh bowl of slop.

THE SPEAKER OF THE
SPIRIT-SHARE

Y ou don't hear it anymore either, do you? The voice. From here, Jah'ri's journey is his own.

Yours as well, I am afraid, for this is where we must break. I am not as young as I look, you know? Find me tomorrow. I will be here. We will speak and share-spirit more of Arou and its many warriors. You will again feel the mist of Shyloc breaching the surface. You will hear the chants of the Nails tasting freedom, those that can be freed.

We will learn and we will remember: Power is a disease.

It spreads across the cold universe in search of warmth, embedding deepest into mortals, where insatiate lust blooms in the name of meaningless self-sabotage. It attacks itself and thus grows larger, feeding on strife, satisfied only from its own death, for that is how it grows in the body of another. Power then cements itself into our foundations, societal and structural, and from there it cannot be separated from the living. Like air, mortals evolve and learn to live with power at the cost of their own destruction, rarely even knowing it's there.

The lie takes hold: that power is necessary.

Our dreams speak to us in riddles of warnings. Then we wake and we forget. The cycle continues, and we march, we march, we march.

We will learn and we will remember.

Oh, enough of politics! I am desperate for sleep.

THE END

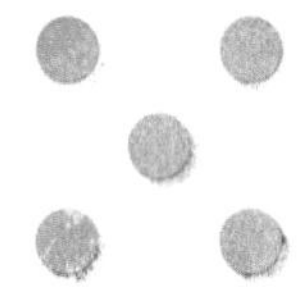

THE STORY ISN'T OVER.

THE FALLEN PARALLEL

IS COMING.

SCRAPS

THE GAME OF SCARCITY AND SURVIVAL

OBJECTIVE

BE THE FIRST player to collect exactly 38 points using a combination of tokens known as Grubs, Gems, and Rocks.

- **Grub:** 3 points each
- **Gems:** 2 points each
- **Rocks:** 1 point each

Exceeding 38 points results in penalties.

SETUP

1. **Gather the tokens into a pouch:**

   Place all available tokens (Grub, Gems, and Rocks) in a pouch. Players use whatever tokens they have on hand—shards of metal, beads, stones, actual gems, real food, etc.

2. **Distribute the first tokens:**

   Each player begins with 5 random tokens drawn blindly from the Scraps pouch.

3. **Determine the first player:**

   - Most commonly, whoever draws the best tokens goes first, with turns proceeding clockwise.

   - Different Parallels may use other methods such as drawing the worst tokens, the youngest age, a knowledge of secrets, or a show of talents or strengths

GAMEPLAY

On their turn, players choose one action:

1. **Draw:**

   Take 1 token from the Scraps pouch.

2. **Trade:**

   Exchange up to 3 tokens (total) with another player or the Scraps pouch (e.g., trade one Grub for two Gems).

3. **Declare Lucky Scraps:**

Turn one Gem token into a Lucky Scraps token:

- Declare one Gem token Lucky Scraps by turning it face down or marking it (such as scratching it).

- This declaration is public so that all players know which token is Lucky Scraps.

- Relinquish an additional token of their choice back to the Scraps pouch.

Lucky Scraps tokens are "wild" and can substitute for Grub, Gem, or Rock during trades or scoring.

Each player can only have one Lucky Scraps token at a time.

4. **Challenge:**

Depending on the Parallel, players may challenge another player in a competition. Examples include:

- A dice roll or other luck-based challenge in resource-poor areas.

- In the Court, players are often quizzed on the history of the reigning lineage of Sor or other high-culture topics.

- The winner of the challenge claims one token of their choice from the loser.

5. **Pass:**

Skip the turn to strategize or avoid penalties.

When it is not their turn, players are encouraged to engage each other in side bartering or challenges.

SCORING AND WINNING

- Players aim to collect tokens to reach exactly 38 points.

- If a player's total exceeds 38 points:

  - They must immediately discard 3 tokens of their choice back to the Scraps Pile.

  - Their turn ends.

- The first player to reach exactly 38 points and shout "Scraps!" wins the game.

- The player must shout "Scraps!" in order to win.

LUCKY SCRAPS
(WILD TOKENS)

LUCKY SCRAPS ARE whispered to carry "favor from Sor's Swords." In order to carry this favor, the player must give up something valuable, hence the requirement to sacrifice a token to get Lucky Scraps.

In a world without formal tools, players might creatively mark their Lucky Scraps using what's available:

- Smearing dirt on it.

- Chipping or denting the token with a rock.

- Balancing it differently in their pile to signal its uniqueness.

ACKNOWLEDGMENTS

Before I had published a novel, I would read authors' Acknowledgements and wonder how on earth it could take so many people to publish a single book. Now I know. It takes a village. A Parallel, if you will.

First and foremost, thank you, dear reader. You risked your time and money on a debut author which says a lot about you. We need more people like you. You should run for office.

To my wife, Megan, for having the patience to read every iteration of this story and the courage to put up with me as I pursued it. This book doesn't happen without you.

To Provender Press, especially Angela Grace. You embody the root words of your first and second names. Thanks for taking a chance on me.

I'd like to recognize my beta readers, particularly authors C.J. Switzer, Leonard Carpenter, and Timothy McGregor. Additional thanks to Peter Bretton, Milan Lostica, Graham Stream, and the entire Morrison family, chiefly Suzy, Tyler, and Jimmy.

Shout out to Scott Stanley for his help on the game of Scraps.

I borrowed many names from real-life heroes: Eda, Naor, Mourad, and some others. Thanks for being gracious with your names and, dare I say, quite adventurous.

There's a soundtrack that goes along with this novel featuring music that was written alongside the story. The novel and album are strange bedfellows, but one can simply not exist without the other. Thanks to Robbie Frazer, John Miller, Annie Johnson, and Aaron Boyd.

A final and special thank you to my boys, Coen, Nolan, Michael, and Hunter. And Hudson, of course. We can never forget Hudson.

ABOUT THE AUTHOR

Kevin Carver's storytelling is deeply inspired by his obsession with old vinyl records, too much coffee, and the stern timelessness of John Steinbeck and Ray Bradbury. After graduating from the University of Rochester's creative writing program and Gonzaga University's communications and leadership graduate program, Carver has enjoyed an erratic career of writing, music, and marketing.

When he's not revising manuscripts or producing soundtracks to accompany his writing, you can find him chasing the sunset with his family on the California coast.

COLOPHON

This book was typeset in EB Garamond using
Adobe InDesign. Published by Provender Press in
McMinnville, Oregon, with peanut butter, chocolate
chips, and frequent gardening breaks.